Sister Teresa

Sister Teresa

THE WOMAN WHO BECAME SAINT TERESA OF ÁVILA

BÁRBARA MUJICA

THE OVERLOOK PRESS
Woodstock & New York

For Mauro,
and for my children and grandchildren
with love

This edition first published in paperback in the United States in 2008 by
Overlook Duckworth, Peter Mayer Publishers, Inc.
New York, Woodstock, and London

WOODSTOCK:
One Overlook Drive
Woodstock, NY 12498
www.overlookpress.com
[for individual orders, bulk and special sales, contact our Woodstock office]

NEW YORK:
141 Wooster Street
New York, NY 10012

LONDON:
90-93 Cowcross Street
London EC1M 6BF
inquiries@duckworth-publishers.co.uk
www.ducknet.co.uk

Library of Congress Cataloging-in-Publication Data

Mujica, Bárbara Louise.
Sister Teresa : the woman who became Saint Teresa of Avila / Bárbara Mujica.
p. cm.
1. Teresa, of Avila, Saint, 1515-1582—Fiction. 2. Nuns—Spain—Fiction.
I. Title.
PS3563.U386S57 2007   813'.54—dc22   2006047136

Book design and type formatting by Bernard Schleifer
Manufactured in the United States of America
US ISBN 978-1-59020-025-4
UK ISBN 978-07156-3790-6
10 9 8 7 6 5 4 3 2 1

About the Translation

I FOUND THIS MANUSCRIPT IN DIJON, IN A TINY ANTIQUARIAN'S SHOP ON THE Rue Sainte Anne, near the old Carmelite convent. It was a pile of yellowed, crumbling papers tied with a ribbon, colorless and frayed from age. I skimmed the first paragraphs. The document appeared to be a *testimonio personal*, a type of spiritual chronicle people used to keep, often at the request of a confessor, but not always. I read the opening sentence: "All I wanted was to get away from Seville." I ran my eyes over the next few sheets, and my hands began to tremble. This appeared to be a text written by someone who actually knew Saint Teresa of Ávila.

I bought the manuscript for practically nothing. A superficial examination convinced me it would be easily decipherable. Once I started translating, though, I faced some real problems. Should I try to maintain the antique feel of Sister Angélica's writing or render it into modern English? Should I translate names? Should I divide her unbroken text into paragraphs and chapters? Sister Angélica wrote as she spoke, in a colloquial Spanish that would have been easily accessible to readers of her time. I opted to preserve her informal, clear style by translating her words into modern, conversational English. However, in order to conserve something of the early Spanish flavor, I left names in the original, for example *Juan de la Cruz* instead of John of the Cross. For the sake of readability, I divided the text into paragraphs, applied modern punctuation, and added chapter titles.

Most of the information in Angélica's *testimonio* is correct and verifiable. Sometimes her quotes are very similar to passages in Saint Teresa's own writing. All of the poetry she attributes to Teresa was, in fact, written by her. As Angélica foresaw, Teresa was beatified in 1614 and canonized in 1622. Immediately afterward, the Archbishop Pérez de la Serna named her patron saint of Mexico City.

I have found historical information about nearly all the people mentioned in this *testimonio* except for the author herself, Angélica del Sagrado Corazón (Pancracia Soto), and her lover, Braulio. However, I plan to continue my investigations.

The Foundations of Saint Teresa

Prologue

We'd just escaped from Seville and were heading north through the mountains. Torrential rains made the roads nearly impassable. Still, the lurching of the rickety cart was preferable to Seville.

Teresa was dozing fitfully. I tried to concentrate on her erratic breathing, but images of Seville crowded out her wheezes. In my head I could see them, lined up in their black robes: the inquisitor, the secretary, and the notary. The inquisitor spat out questions, while the secretary took meticulous notes, occasionally motioning for me to repeat slowly, so he could get it all down. I couldn't hear them. It was a silent image, but sometimes silence can be deafening.

It wasn't a formal trial, they said, just an interrogation. One by one they brought us into a murky, musty room lit by flickering candles placed at regular intervals along a table. A torch in the corner of the room cast an eerie light on the faces of the black-robed men, transforming them into ghouls. They asked questions about . . . well, I don't know what they asked the others, but they asked me about my parents, when my father had died, whether or not there were books in our home. Fortunately, we had no books. If you had books, you might be Jewish. Jewish people are known to like to read, so books in the home are incriminating. There's no sense in lying to the inquisitors. They have ways of finding out what they want to know.

They asked me how many times we'd moved when I was little, but I didn't remember ever having moved. After my father died, my mother and I went to live with my aunt, but I was too young to recall. Anyhow, we only moved from one side of the street to the other. We didn't come to Ávila from a distant city. That was lucky, too, because if you shuttled around a lot, especially if you traveled into or away from areas with a large *converso* population, you were suspect. That was logical, of course. The inquisitors were always very logical. If you lived among heretics, you could be contaminated. If you moved into a place with *conversos,* it might be to join your Judaizing relatives, and if you moved away from such a place, it might be to avoid the authorities. *Conversos* were Christians of Jewish background, and some of them practiced their old religion in secret. That's what the inquisitors were trying to find out: whether you were really a good Catholic. When they asked me if my mother swept the walk on Friday, I said she cleaned on Wednesdays and Saturdays. Jews clean on Friday in preparation for their Sabbath.

Not long before, a woman named Isabel de la Cruz had been condemned for heresy. She'd been a sister, just like us. The inquisitors warned us to take care to tell the truth so we wouldn't wind up like her. Isabel had visions of Our Lady, only the inquisitors said they didn't come from God, but from fasting for days at a time. Spurious visions, they called them. Self-induced visions, the product of food deprivation and pride. Pride because she wanted to be known as a holy woman. At the bottom of it all was her desire to cover up her filthy Jewish ancestry, they said. What tipped them off was that she never ate pork, not even at Christmastime. One of the sisters in her convent turned her in.

I wonder what it would be like to be bound to a post, to see the torch approach in their hands, to feel the flames lick your toes, sear your ankles, scorch your knees. You can pass your finger quickly through the flame of a candle and not feel a thing, but if you hold it there, the pain becomes unbearable. How long could you stand it? Would you smell your own flesh burning? How fast would you die? Would you be unconscious by the time the fire reached your torso? Would one explosive conflagration put you out of your misery? Poor Isabel de la Cruz. They all said she had it coming. But I pray she repented before she died so she won't burn in Hell forever.

I squeezed my eyes shut in order to block out the terrible images, but in my head I could still see the inquisitor. His inaudible questions reverberated in my skull. I must be going mad, I thought. Or perhaps I'm already mad. The ordeal in Seville was enough to unhinge a saint.

He told me to recite the first prayers I'd learned from my mother. I said the Hail Mary and the Our Father. He wanted more. I uttered the Credo. It was important to deliver it smoothly, without hesitating. Of course, I know my prayers perfectly, but under pressure you can stumble. If you do, they think you didn't learn those prayers as a child, that you learned them later, and that now it's difficult for you to recall them. And that can be dangerous.

Why am I here? I kept asking myself. I could be home with a nice husband. I would have married Basilio if it hadn't been for Teresa. I'm here because of her. I became a nun because of her, because there was nothing else for me to do but to follow her. No, I became a nun because I love God. Or . . . was it because of what happened with Basilio? To be honest, I'm really not sure.

Finally, they let me go. They let us all go. I wondered about Teresa, what they'd asked her and how she'd answered their questions. Underneath that controlled façade, she must have felt terror because everyone knows her family is . . . No, better not write it.

We were traveling slowly, creeping along at a snail's pace in a creaky covered cart that shuddered when the wind pounded its sides. I wrapped my shawl more tightly around my shoulders and tucked my sandaled feet under my body for warmth. The icy gales of a mountain storm can chill you to the quick, even in early summer.

We'd started out in good spirits, accompanied by Fray Julián and Teresa's brother Lorenzo, who'd made money in Quito and insisted on hiring a smart coach with elegant horses. Teresa fussed a bit—she hated ostentation—but at last gave in. "Why should we complain about Lorenzo's generosity?" she whispered to me. "*Cuando viene el bien, mételo en tu casa.* When luck comes calling, invite her in." She was feeling better than usual. Her headaches had subsided and for a change she was holding her food. Before we left Seville I'd ground some charcoal and made a pastille to settle her stomach.

Seville had been oppressively hot, but as we traveled north, the temperature became more bearable. Lorenzo arranged for us to stay at a comfortable inn, where the beds were clean and not flea-ridden. A hunter gave us some pheasants and a couple of rabbits for a good price, and an *hortelano* sold us some fruits and vegetables. We asked the innkeeper's wife to prepare a meal with what we'd bought, for, like most inns, this one provided only lodgings, not food. We ate out in the garden—a delicious feast of pheasant, rabbit, and greens, with oranges, figs, and cherries for dessert. Teresa devoured her meat with relish.

"For such a devout woman," teased Lorenzo, "you eat like a tiger!"

"Brother," she growled, hardly looking up, "when I pray, I pray, and when I eat, I eat."

You'd never guess she was just interrogated by the Inquisition, I thought. What a gift she has for letting go of her worries and enjoying the moment.

After dinner we chatted in the shade. "Do you know what happened to the Jesuit who went hunting?" began Teresa. Tiny wrinkles formed at the corners of her eyes. She was trying hard to keep a straight face. "He was hoping to bring home a few rabbits for dinner. All of a sudden, in the middle of the woods, he came across an enormous, snarling bear! The Jesuit took off as fast as he could, with the bear bounding after him. But then he came to a cliff. There was no way to escape. He fell to his knees and prayed, 'Dear God, please put religion into this wild beast's soul.' To his amazement, the bear stopped in its tracks and fell to its knees. 'Oh, thank you, God,' cried the Jesuit. 'Thank you! Thank you!' Of course, he couldn't hear the words of the bear, who was saying, 'Dear Lord, for this meal I am about to receive, I am truly grateful.'"

We all burst out laughing. Lorenzo adored Teresa. We all did, but I loved her more than anyone because I was the one who knew her best. I was the one who accompanied her day and night. I was her constant companion. I'd taken care of her from the time she was practically a child. Even though I was five years her junior, it was as though I were an older sister. That afternoon of mirth and clear skies offered a lovely respite, but we couldn't relax for long. Memories of Seville were still close and threatening. We had to get away. We had to keep moving.

Lorenzo left us at Malagón, where he had business, and we continued on with Fray Julián. Since women can't travel alone, Fray Julián always accompanies us. I don't mind. He's so gentle and unobtrusive, like a loyal hound who sits at your feet by the fire, always happy to do your bidding. We left the luxurious coach Lorenzo had hired and climbed into the wobbly, mule-driven vehicle provided by Julián. The storm hit just as night began to fall.

Gusts of wind battered the slats of the cart, whose wheels screeched in agony as they inched through the muck. Fray Julián rode up beside the canvas-covered window.

"Mother Teresa!" he called. He was right next to us, but his voice was barely audible.

"She's dozing!" I called back.

"What?"

"She's dozing!"

"I am not," Teresa stated resolutely. Her eyes were wide open. "I'm awake. Dozing is for ninnies and old women."

I looked at her, smirking. "Of course. And you're a chick with feathers still damp from the egg."

"Sixty-one isn't so old! What is it, Julián?" she called through the window.

"We have to stop! We can't go on!"

"Stop? I don't want to stop. I want to reach Toledo by morning."

"There's no chance at all we can get to Toledo by morning. We may not even get there by evening. We have to stop, Mother. The driver and the horses are exhausted. Anyhow, we're hardly moving. The roads are treacherous. We have to find a place to hole up for the night. At least, for you to hole up. An inn or something. The driver and I can sleep in the cart."

She was silent a moment. I thought she was going to insist. I thought she was thinking up reasons why we simply had to push ahead. She could be like that. Stubborn, I mean.

Instead, she said, "All right, Julián. How far are we from San Miguel de Pinares?"

"Not too far. A quarter of an hour under normal circumstances."

"And under present circumstances?"

"I don't know. An hour, maybe. Maybe more, if we can get there at all. Why?"

"There's a tiny convent in San Miguel, and I know the prioress. We were together at the Augustinian sisters when we were young. There's also a men's convent down the road. I'm sure they'll let you and Carlos spend the night."

Fray Julián must have ridden his mule up alongside the driver, but you couldn't hear a thing because the wind was so fierce it smothered the sound of the animal's hooves. A moment later we caught his muffled call through the canvas.

"Carlos thinks we can make it, but it will be slow going."

I don't remember what Teresa answered. Perhaps I nodded off or perhaps my mind wandered back to the inquisitors. The next thing I recall is Teresa banging on the door of a convent no bigger than a cottage. It was surely way past the nuns' bedtime, and I expected the extern to respond, but instead, Mother Paula herself came to the door.

"Whoever is banging on my door at this time of night better have a damn good reason!" she howled from inside. *"Salve María purísima."*

"Sin pecado concebida. We're freezing and starving and can't go on," Teresa howled back, "and that's a pretty damn good reason! Besides, we're old friends."

The door opened slowly and a bleary-eyed nun with the face of a plump, yellow raisin peered through the crack. "Teresa de Ahumada! Is that you?"

"Yes, it is. And this is Sister Angélica," she said, nodding towards me.

"I remember Angélica," she said. "Only her name was Pancracia then.

That was decades ago. You were a plain little thing in those days," she said, looking me up and down.

Bony and thin-lipped, I was used to being called plain. It didn't bother me.

"We're on our way to Toledo," said Teresa, "but we got caught in the storm."

"Well, don't just stand there, woman. Come in and warm yourself. I'll light a fire."

"At this hour? No, Paula, please don't bother. All we want is a place to sleep and maybe a bit of bread. We'll be gone before Lauds."

But we weren't. Dawn found us reciting Lauds with Mother Paula and her seven spiritual daughters, the only inhabitants of the rustic convent. The downpour had continued all night, and the roads were blocked. We waited for a messenger to come with news of Carlos and Fray Julián. Mother Paula thought they'd probably found lodgings with the tiny community of Benedictines a stone's throw from her convent.

"What needs to be done?" inquired Teresa. "Need your floors scrubbed? Your pots washed? Might as well make ourselves useful while we're here."

"Sit down, Teresa. Rest."

Teresa only obeyed the first half of the command. Resting was not something she tolerated in herself or in anyone else. Instead, she squatted on a cushion by the window ledge and readied her writing utensils, glad for the opportunity to catch up on her correspondence. She's a zealous letter writer, not because she enjoys composing missives—in fact, she calls it a form of martyr-dom—but because her work demands it. Since she began founding convents, she writes constantly. There are licenses to apply for, appeals to be made, protests to be lodged, thank-you notes to be written to anxious mothers who send quince preserves in hopes she'll accept their daughters as novices. Often she writes late into the night, or even all night. "You know what Hell is like, Angélica?" she once said to me. "It's one endless letter the flames never consume."

"I'll see if I can help in the kitchen," I said. But she didn't answer. She was already lost in her writing.

I stood there watching her. The rain had stopped and a gentle sunlight washed into the room through the window, bathing Teresa in its glow. She was lovely in spite of her sixty-one years, frequent illnesses, incessant trav-els, and coarse brown habit. Her skin, subtly rosy, was still smooth and taut. Her round face looked rounder encased in a wimple, but it had lost none of its juice. Her enormous eyes, deep brown, almost black, sparkled like those of a girl. Her small nose, slightly hooked at the tip, sat proudly on her face, which was bejeweled with three tiny moles—one beneath the nostrils and two over the mouth to the left. In our youth these had been considered natural adornments, marks of beauty coveted by plain women, like me. Her hands, once reputed to be the loveliest in Ávila, fluttered with the grace of doves. I looked down at my own hands, chapped and raw from pounding bark, mixing compounds, and washing apothecary jars. There was nothing "angelical" about me but my name. I turned to leave, heading for the kitchen. In a convent there's always work to do—lentils to pick the stones from, peas to shell, pots to scour, fires to tend, and, of course, spinning and sewing. Work that befits an orphan like me, lowly and homely. Suddenly, inexplicably, I started to cry.

That afternoon Mother Paula received us in her cell during the *recreo*, the hour of leisure we would have spent under a tree chatting and embroidering if the ground had been dry.

"So . . ." she began cautiously. "What's the news from Seville?"

She must have known something was going on. Teresa was a celebrity, and people were interested in her. News travels slowly, but it travels.

"Too many priests." Teresa looked directly at her friend, as though hurling a dare.

Mother Paula glowered. "Too many priests?" she said finally. "We're lucky if we can get a scrawny Benedictine to come around once in a while to hear our confessions."

"Priests are like manure," Teresa said unflinchingly. "You have to spread them around in order for them to do any good. Put too many together, and they begin to stink."

Mother Paula stood staring at her, then suddenly let out a snort and began to heave with laughter. "Isn't that the truth," she said, wiping her eyes on the sleeve of her habit. "Ah, Teresa, Teresita . . . still the hellion. You haven't changed a bit. You must be exhausted from your travels. There's a bit of orgeat I save for special occasions."

"Orgeat?" She sat there pondering the offer. "Is there water?"

"The well water here is contaminated," answered Mother Paula, "but Sister Mercedes collected some buckets of rainwater this morning."

"Bring us rainwater, then," said Teresa, a little too imperiously.

Mother Paula pretended not to hear. "Never mind," she said. "I have something better."

She disappeared, then came back a moment later with a small pouch, which she opened onto the table. Dark, almond-shaped grains rolled over the rough wood. Mother Paula caught them with her fingertips and eased them into a little pile. She touched them gently, lovingly, as though they were precious gems. It was clear she held them to be things of great value, but to me they just looked like some kind of bean.

"What is it?" asked Teresa.

"Chocolate!"

"Chocolate . . . I've heard of it."

"My brother sent it to me from Mexico. He's over there exporting chocolate and getting rich. The French can't get enough of it."

I could see how that could be true. Ever since Cortés had brought cacao beans back from Mexico at the end of the 1520s, chocolate had been fashionable among rich ladies. I'd heard about it when we went to visit Teresa's aristocratic friends, but I'd never actually seen it.

"I thought . . ." I whispered.

"Yes, Angélica?" said Teresa. "Speak up!"

"I thought you drank it." I couldn't imagine how you could turn the beans into liquid. Did you boil them in water and drink the juice?

"Yes," said Mother Paula. "You do drink it. But first you have to grind the beans. You see? I'll show you."

She was busy mashing up the beans into a mortar with a pestle. "Look," she was saying, "that creamy substance is cocoa butter. The mixture of ground beans and butter makes a chocolate liquor that you can let solidify into blocks to use later. Look, I'm going to put this aside to harden. Here are some tablets I made the other day, all ready to brew. You'll see, I'm going to prepare a delicious drink. It will take awhile."

I was fascinated. The chocolate emitted a pungent aroma like nothing I'd ever smelled before. It was intoxicating. What did it remind me of? Cinnamon? Cloves? Orange blossoms?

"I don't know," said Teresa. "I can't say I care much about the potions of the rich. As I said, clear, clean water is good enough for me."

"Then go outside and drink up the puddles," growled Mother Paula. "Come on, Teresa. Don't tell me you're not curious."

"I hear the church fathers want this concoction banned. They say it has diabolical qualities. It makes you think unholy thoughts."

"Not these cacao beans," said Mother Paula confidently. "These cacao beans were processed by monks in New Spain."

"Well," said Teresa, "I suppose it can't hurt to try. It hasn't been banned yet. Anyhow, with Lutherans overrunning half the world, God has more to worry about than what three silly old nuns are sipping during their *recreo*."

When the chocolate was ready, Mother Paula poured it into small wooden bowls. We crouched on cushions, the bowls cupped in our hands. Mother Paula stretched out her legs in front of her, then leaned back on a wall and closed her eyes. "I feel very naughty," she said dreamily. She was a woman in her late sixties, squishy and white, with a forehead as crinkled as a wadded up handkerchief.

"Do you think we're committing a sin, Mother?" I asked anxiously.

"Certainly not, child," said Mother Paula. "I'm sure Heaven is awash in chocolate. In fact, it's perfectly possible that instead of ether, Heaven is made of chocolate."

It was absurd that Mother Paula called me "child." I was a woman of fifty-six.

"And if they ban it?"

"Then we won't drink it anymore," chortled Teresa. "What's the point of worrying about it now, Angélica? It's like wiping yourself before you shit."

She sipped slowly, deliberately. "I'll never let them drink chocolate in *my* convents," she murmured. She inhaled deeply, savoring the aroma, then closed her eyes, like when she fell into rapture—only she didn't seem to be in communion with God at that moment. "Wait," she said abruptly. "I have brothers in the colonies, too. Lorenzo is back from Ecuador, and he brought me something. You're not the only one with contraband under your pillow, Paula."

Now it was Teresa's turn to disappear. She returned with a small cloth packet containing something tangy-smelling. "I bet you've never seen *this* before!" She opened the packet.

"It looks like a torn-up brown leaf. Do you eat it?" Paula asked.

"Not even the Duke of Alba knows about this," said Teresa, "but my brother Lorenzo says the Indians take great pleasure in it."

She extracted some of the brown stuff and rolled it into a straw-like tube. She put one end in her mouth and lit the other with a taper. Then she breathed deeply. For a moment she looked superbly serene, then impossibly impish. A rich, sharp odor filled the room.

"What is it?" I asked.

"It's called tobacco. Lorenzo says it has medicinal properties. The Indians use it to dress wounds and to treat headaches. They roll it up into a reed, like this, to smoke during celebrations. Lorenzo says that in the New World the saintly fathers of Our Holy Mother Church are quite fond of it. They put it in pipes and smoke it."

"And the saintly mothers?" I asked.

"And now they've started to grow it all over Christendom," Teresa went on. "Even here. There's a doctor, Nicolás Monardes, who claims this weed cures a slew of diseases. Lorenzo thought it might be good for my migraines." She rolled thin reeds of tobacco for Mother Paula and me, and the three of us sat there in a kind of delirium, sipping chocolate and puffing on the strange tan-colored sticks.

The brew was bitter and the smoke burned my throat, but it was the first time I felt peaceful—relatively peaceful—since we'd left Seville. I closed my eyes and tried to think of God, of Christ's sacrifice on the Cross. But my mind kept wandering back to my own sacrifices. Why am I here, in this out-of-the-way convent? Why did I have to face the inquisitors in Seville? It's *her* fault I left Ávila, I thought. Why did I follow her? Why? As if I had ever had a choice.

It was Vespers. We gathered in the minuscule chapel—Mother Paula, her seven spiritual daughters, Teresa, and I. Our voices floated upward to God through the roof of the convent. Upward like angels, fluttering, translucent, through the crisp, rain-washed, evening air. Soon glimmering stars would materialize, circling the earth, transforming the night sky into jeweled lace on velvet. *Magnificat anima mea Dominum, et exultavit spiritus meus in Deo salvatore meo . . .*

The tiny cloister was quiet now, so quiet you could hear insects creeping along the window ledge. The sisters had retired, exhausted from clearing out the debris—odd branches, uprooted shrubbery, even a smashed bird feeder—the storm had dumped in their garden. Many of their plantings had washed away and the entrance to the house had been muddied. The clearing and cleaning, when combined with the daily spinning, mending, picking, peeling, cooking, and tending to the elderly among them, had made the day especially wearisome. And then they had to pray for the Pope, the cardinals, the bishops, the inquisitors, the provincials, the holy fathers, their sisters in religion, their families, their patrons, unconverted Indians and those rascally Lutherans who were setting the world on its head. Only Teresa was awake. And I.

Teresa lit a candle and made her way noiselessly down the corridor toward the chapel. I followed and, hiding in the shadows, watched her kneel before the crucifix. Jesus's face was illuminated by a shaft of moonlight, eerie, otherworldly, and indescribably beautiful. In the dark Teresa's rough brown habit lost its coarseness and her upturned face, lit by the glow of her candle, looked almost iridescent. Her eyes were fixed on the image of Our Lord, which seemed to quiver with an awareness of her presence. Engrossed in prayer, she didn't hear me cough gently. She appeared engulfed in serenity, transported to another dimension. "My God," I said to myself. "How I love her!" She remained there for a long time—I don't know how long. In ecstasy. Motionless. Radiant. I held my breath. I felt as though I were in the presence of the Virgin.

"She's a saint," I whispered. "She really is what people say she is. A saint."

I tiptoed back to my room and knelt by my cot. "Father," I breathed, "tell me what to do with this blessing."

That's when I realized I would have to help keep her memory alive after she was gone. I was the one who loved her best. I was the one who knew her best. But I couldn't trust my memory because memory is fickle. She would surely be beatified, then canonized. I would be called upon to testify. I had to write it all down—everything I remembered about her, everything that happened to her. I had to write a *testimonio personal.* And what if I died before I could bear witness? It didn't matter. My *testimonio* would speak for me.

I'm not a learned person. I don't know Latin. I'm a plain woman, the daughter of a seamstress, and I write the way I talk. But I have known Teresa Sánchez de Cepeda y Ahumada all my life, and I'll tell her story as I know it.

Sister Angélica del Sagrado Corazón

15 June 1576

PART I
The Belle of Ávila

CHAPTER 1

October Roses

IT MUST HAVE BEEN OCTOBER, BECAUSE I REMEMBER THE AIR WAS CHILLED and crisp, the way it is before the snows begin. The winds were just beginning to whoosh over the sierra. Some of the peaks of the Guadarrama were already dusted with white. Still, my aunt resisted lighting the brazier. Coal was expensive, and she was thrifty by nature.

"It's winter already!" urged my mother. "Light the fire!"

You know what they say about Ávila: *Nueve meses de invierno y tres de infierno.* Nine months of winter and three of hell. By that reckoning, it was certainly time to haul in some coal.

"What will we do in December if we light the brazier in October?" protested Tía Cati.

I was only eleven, and I didn't see the logic of her argument. I was peeking out behind the burlap my mother had hung on the windows to keep out the nip. An icy sun hung low in the sky. Shadows crept along the road like prowlers, hugging the houses. Dusk came earlier every day. The mountains loomed enormous against the darkening heavens.

It was getting too dim to sew, but my mother and Tía Cati were still sitting on their cushions and drawing their needles in and out of fabric. They were edging the muffs—decorated sleeves—of the dress that Teresa de Ahumada would wear to the palace of the Count of Mollén.

"Get away from the window, Pancracia," snapped my mother. "Come finish your work."

I had learned to embroider as soon as I could hold a needle. The child and niece of seamstresses, I knew the difference between satin and taffeta, baize and flannel, frieze and cotton. I loved the feel of gossamer on my fingertips. I dreamed of grosgrain ribbons. I had stitched side by side with grown women practically since babyhood. Now I was supposed to be detailing the *jubón*, or camisole, Teresa would wear under her gown.

"Pancracia!" my mother called again. "This outfit has to be ready by tomorrow!"

I remained motionless, mesmerized by the scene unfolding before me. A girl, lithe and quick, had darted out from an alley. She wore a dark-colored dress, burgundy or russet, trimmed in lace and partially concealed by a cape. Her steps were so dainty that she seemed to glide over the dirt road, like the statue of Our Lady that flies along on wheels during the Holy Week procession. Her face was invisible behind a *mantilla*, but there was something about the movement of her hands, about her quick, nervous gestures . . . Her delicate fingers quivered like the feathers of a dove. "Doña Teresa!" I whispered.

I wondered what she was doing in our part of town. The Cepeda Ahumada family had a mansion in the affluent old Jewish neighborhood. Now my mother and aunt were standing behind me. "Pancracia, come away from the window!"

I tugged on the burlap. It came flapping down to the floor. I turned to look at my mother and tensed. Clumsily, I struggled to lift the cloth and reposition it on the window.

"Pancracia, sit down this instant!" barked my mother. She raised her hand to smack me, but Tía Cati quieted her with just a touch on the shoulder.

A male figure appeared from behind the chandler's shop, his cape flapping loosely on his shoulders. His long, tapered, gloved hands showed that he was a person of position. Aside from his white gloves and the stiff, fluted ruff at his throat, he was dressed all in black. The rules of fashion allowed young men to wear colors, but in Ávila, that most conservative of towns, most wore black. His tight, padded doublet tapered into an elegant squeezed waist, then flared out into a skirt over trunk hose and stylish boots.

Teresa flew to him. It happened many years ago, but as I recreate the scene in my mind, I can see her shoulders quivering with emotion. For a moment they stood face to face, she looking up at him, he lightly touching her arm. Then he leaned forward and it seems to me, although I can't be sure, that he kissed her.

He took her hand and they vanished into a passageway. I felt my heart flutter. What had I just witnessed? What was he going to do to her now? Would he touch her bodice? Would he press her against him? I caught my breath. We all knew who he was: her cousin Javier. The whole town knew they loved each other, but to meet in the open like that, to kiss in the street . . . Even as a child, I knew that Teresa was flirting with danger.

Teresa Sánchez de Cepeda y Ahumada was a heartbreaker. When she walked to church, head covered modestly but eyes flashing, armies of young men appeared out of nowhere and formed brigades on either side of the path. Those who caught her dart-like glance swooned and fell to the ground, some never to recover. People said Teresa caused more fatalities than the king's militia.

"Too pretty for her own good," said the women who gathered in my aunt's *estrado*. In hushed voices they would talk of the scandalous way in which Teresa flirted at the fair or the bullfights, which she attended with her cousins.

The *estrado* was the most important room in my aunt's house, the room where I lived my childhood, lost in dreams of blue-eyed dukes on white horses. At one side, in an alcove hidden by a heavy curtain, was my aunt's bed, which she had shared with Tío Celso when he was alive. The *estrado* was a sort of ladies' haven where we gathered to embroider, spin, or sew. It was the place we received guests, other women from the neighborhood, most of them as poor as we but from respectable families that had once had a bit of money. Widows of successful artisans—weavers or beer makers—who tried to carry on the family business, but barely made ends meet.

On chilly mornings we'd gather around the brazier to work and gossip and warm ourselves. My aunt, Catalina Fuentes de Rojas, had carpeted the cork platform where the coal-filled receptacle sat in order to protect it from the flames. Each of us had her own cushion. Mine was covered in a faded green remnant Teresa's father had given me. My mother, Inés Fuentes de Soto—she of the sad eyes and sharp tongue—sat on a cushion the color of withered red geraniums. Tía Cati's was the most elegant, far too elegant for a woman of her station. It was deep blue velvet with bits of tinted glass sewn into the fabric. Tío Celso, a successful tailor, had designed suits for titled gentlemen, and one delighted customer had rewarded him with a remnant of velvet large enough to make a cushion for his wife. Other cushions were strewn over the platform, none of them remarkable. These were meant for my aunt's friends, women who came to gab and embroider. Needlework is always more pleasant when done in the company of others.

My aunt regretted only that her own daughters weren't among us. The two eldest, Catalina and Irene, lived in Madrid with their husbands, a gilder and a musician. Bernarda had sailed for the Americas on one of those ships that take poor Spanish women to soldiers and colonists in need of wives. Doña Cati's two sons, Celso and Felipe, had themselves gone to the Americas and picked out brides from among the white-skinned virgins considerately supplied by the Spanish crown. Well, to be honest, not all of them were virgins. Some had agreed to the hazardous voyage precisely because they weren't. For those damaged flowers, it was either the high seas or the convent. There was no other choice. Anyway, both boys died abroad, Celso of fevers and Felipe in a skirmish with Indians. Tío Celso, heartbroken beyond recovery, joined them in heaven within a year of Felipe's death. God keep them all in His boundless embrace.

Around the platform Tía Cati had placed short-legged chairs and stools, where my grandmother, also named Catalina, and her sister Beatriz had sat sewing when they were alive. Now these stools were often occupied by neighbor women, sometimes as many as eight or ten of them. Since Tío Celso had died with no male heirs, my aunt was allowed to keep the house and its furnishings, including a chest, a wall tapestry, and a large, mahogany-framed mirror. Her father—my grandfather—was dead, and she had no brothers. Otherwise, she would have had to go to live with a male relative like other widows, but as it was, she was free to live with just my mother and me, the two women eking out a living as seamstresses. My aunt didn't consider herself poor. She had a house, furniture, and a few luxury items. The house, she knew, was a bit too grand, but it was hers and that was that. She didn't complain. Why should she? My mother, on the other hand, had nothing. All the material goods she enjoyed belonged to Tía Cati. She named me after Saint Pancracio, patron of job-seekers, because she was terrified of being without work.

"She runs wild since her mother died. Don Alonso should see to her marriage," growled my mother, who had had caught a glimpse of Teresa though the window. "She and her cousin Javier played together as children, but it's unseemly that . . ." And she and Tía Cati lowered their voices so that I wouldn't hear gossip that might contaminate my purity.

Although I was just eleven, I would soon be taking an interest in men, and all the moralists said that if you plant the seeds of licentiousness in a little girl's mind, by the time she's a *señorita*, they'll have grown into gargantuan weeds.

"Don Alonso should have kept them apart from the beginning," murmured my mother. "Father Evaristo always says you have to separate little girls from little boys. If you don't, they begin to think it's natural to keep company with the opposite sex."

I only remember snippets of conversation: "lover . . . cousin . . . honor . . . murder . . ."

Murder? What could it all mean? I was too young to understand the law of honor, which dictated that any indiscretion by a woman was punishable by death. According to Father Evaristo, the neighbors, and everyone else, women were weak, terribly weak, and that's what made them easy prey for Satan. Women yielded easily to temptation. Like Eve.

"Daughters of the First Sinner!" thundered Father Evaristo from the pulpit. "Thanks to her, mankind fell from grace, redeemed only through the sacrifice of Our Lord Jesus Christ!"

"Lord Jesus, keep us free from sin!" pleaded the congregation.

Because women were likely to go astray, men had to rein them in, watch them like hawks. According to the laws of honor, if a woman transgressed—or was even suspected of transgressing—the men responsible for her had the right, the duty even, to take vengeance. That meant murder. A dishonored husband, father, or brother was expected to kill not only the seducer who had sullied the family's reputation, but also the errant woman. And if she was innocent? No matter. Suspicion alone was enough to justify a bloodbath. After all, if gossips were dragging a family's name through the mud, it was incumbent on the males of the household to cleanse it. Only blood could remove the stains from a man's honor.

"If your right hand offends you, cut it off!" roared Father Evaristo.

Plenty of men took his words to heart, but Teresa's father was different from most men. Everybody knew it, and everybody knew why.

Alonso Cepeda had been born in Toledo, a city throbbing with *conversos,* many of which had made fortunes as moneylenders. People turned up their noses at the New Christians, but those same people ran to Moisés the *usurero* or Solomón the *prestamista* when they needed a loan. Even the king of Spain wasn't above taking cash from a former Jew to finance his wars.

Teresa's grandfather, Juan Sánchez of Toledo, had obtained a letter of nobility in 1500. I know the date because it was the same year my aunt Cati was married, and she always said that the Sánchez family had become titled the same year she was "yoked." Tía Cati liked the Sánchez family, and she understood why Juan needed those documents. A letter of nobility was supposed to prove that you had *sangre limpia,* "clean blood," that is, that you were an Old Christian, with no taint of Jewish or Moorish ancestry. Of course, everyone knew such papers could be had for money, even if your ancestors were rabbis.

Nobody was really sure why Don Juan had come to Ávila, but people tried to guess. Some brushed aside the obvious, insisting it was because there were business opportunities for an ambitious young man in our city. The laws of primogeniture stipulated that only the eldest son could inherit, and Don Juan, not being his father's first-born male child, had to make his own way. At the time, Ávila was growing rapidly, with people flooding through our gates every day. Woolens and silks were big business, and an industrious younger son could make a go of it.

Others spoke openly of the Sánchezes' Jewish origins. My mother was one of them.

"He's as Jewish as Herod," she once said.

"Or as Jesus," retorted Tía Cati.

"What a sacrilege! Jesus wasn't Jewish!"

"He most certainly was," insisted my aunt.

But my mother stood firm, sure that such an idea would send us all straight to Hell. To protect me from the curse she thought my aunt had unleashed, she made me say fifty times a day for a week, "Jesus wasn't Jewish. Jesus wasn't Jewish."

Things had gotten bad for Jews in Toledo toward the end of the last century, and many of them sought refuge in Ávila, where Jews, Christians, and Muslims lived in relative harmony. But then, things got bad even here. Harsh new laws forbade Jews to wear ornaments of gold or silver and clothing of silk, brocade, or velvet. Worse yet, they couldn't lend money for interest, which turned out to be bad not only for the Jews, but for everyone. We were at war with Portugal at the time, and how were we going to fund battles without the Jewish moneylenders? The nobility complained, and the legislators changed the law. Then they ordered the Jews to cough up the necessary *maravedís* to beat the Portuguese. When the time came to repay these loans, though, the authorities suddenly remembered the decrees against usury and defaulted.

All this happened before I was born, but sewing by the brazier in my aunt's *estrado,* the women of our household talked about these things endlessly, always in hushed voices.

I was a child then. I didn't understand things. But I did grasp this:

Teresa's family was still in danger. The authorities were ever on the lookout for *converso* backsliders.

The Santo Niño de la Guardia brought it all to a head. This was a famous case that people are still talking about, even now, eighty years later: Toledan Jews were accused of kidnapping a child from the village of La Guardia and crucifying him, then using his heart in demonic rituals. They were guilty, of course. They confessed under torture. If you're innocent, you don't confess, no matter how horrible the pain, because God gives you strength. If you're really innocent, you can bear anything . . . I suppose.

They were burned at the stake in the Mercado Grande, outside the city walls, and that sent the crowds into a frenzy. Suddenly, people who had Jewish friends, bought cloth from Jewish merchants, or sold candles to Jewish households had an abrupt change of heart. The incident unleashed an anti-Jewish rampage. If you owed a Jew money and he was badgering you for it, now was the time to run him through with a knife and set his house on fire. If you were mad at a Jew because he'd snubbed you in the street, you could knock him senseless with a plank and leave him to bleed to death. If you had your eye on a pretty Jewish girl, you could rape her with impunity. And if you were nursing a grudge against a Christian neighbor, you could claim he was really a Jew and throw him down a well. Carnage erupted in every part of Ávila. Thugs roamed the streets from the cathedral to the shrine of San Esteban bashing in the workshops of Jewish artisans, setting fire to their stables, peeing on their cadavers, and stealing their goods.

Well, I understand the Jews killed Our Lord Jesus, but still, I don't see how setting fire to a cottage and murdering innocent children—potential Catholics, after all—is doing the will of God. It doesn't make sense. Of course, I'm just an ignorant woman. But I guess those ruffians knew what they were doing because our holy Catholic monarchs, King Ferdinand and Queen Isabella, validated their acts by passing an important law: Jews would either have to convert or leave the kingdoms of Castile and Aragón.

In Ávila, most Jews converted. They became *conversos*. But the question was this: Could you trust them? Were their conversions sincere, or were they secretly practicing their old religion? Every person known to be a *converso* was suspect. For New Christians like Don Juan Sánchez and his sons, the safest road was assimilation. They had to wipe out their Jewish past. They had to prove they had no tainted blood. That's why they needed patents of nobility.

Well, the facts are the facts, and you can't change them. And the fact is that Ávila was full of *conversos*. They controlled the textile trade and they stuck together, one helping the other. So maybe, as some folks said, that's the real reason Don Juan came to Ávila. He had contacts here. He had a chance to make money. He could start a new life, hiding behind his patent of nobility. Who would know what he had been in Toledo?

My grandmother Catalina knew. She had been in Toledo on June 22, 1485, the day of the penitential procession, and in the years before she died, I heard her describe that horrible event more than once. "The penitential procession." When she said those words, she closed her eyes and her features became pinched, as though she were squeezing some terrible memory out of her mind. She took deep, uneven breaths. Her voice became scratchy, like rusty hinges. I was very young, but I remember.

"It was an exquisite day," she told us one afternoon as we patched and stitched. "One of those days when you think nothing bad can happen. The sky was as translucent as an aquamarine. Cloudless, perfect. One of those days when you're sure God is smiling.

"They divided them into two groups. They clothed those in the first group in *sambenitos* and those in the second group in *sambenitillos*."

She didn't have to explain what these were. We all knew. Even I, a child. The *sambenito* was a full-length, yellow cloak decorated with flames and bright red devils. The *sambenitillo* was a shorter version, knee-length and decorated with black crosses. The term "San Benito" was a corruption of *saco bendito*, holy sack, the name of the costume penitents wore.

"Juan Sánchez and two of his sons, twelve-year-old Álvaro and ten-year-old Alonso, were told to put on *sambenitillos*."

"Dear Jesus," whispered my aunt, but my mother hushed her.

"Along the road," continued my grandmother, "stood neighbors. Decent people. Shoemakers, carpenters, blacksmiths, cartwrights, fletchers, washerwomen, weavers . . . all kinds of people, each with a pocket or an apron full of stones. Children carried stones in their fists. They were all there to show their support for the Catholic Church. They went as an act of faith.

"Juan Sánchez and his sons, along with the others dressed in short, yellow cloaks, were to parade down the road, stopping at every church in Toledo and finishing at the cathedral. They were to carry out the same ritual on seven successive Fridays, always wearing the *sambenitillo*. This was the first day of a seven-week torment.

"The inquisitors lined up the penitents in single file. Juan and his sons did not walk together. The holy fathers placed the boys at the end of the line, out of kindness. By the time the children moved into the street, most pockets would be empty.

"When the inquisitor in charge gave the signal, the procession began. As the first penitent moved forward, the neighbors began to spew curses: 'Jewish pig!' 'Son of a Jewish whore!' 'Christ-killer!' 'Devil! Fiend! Beast!' Then came the rain of spit and stones.

"A pebble hit Juan on the upper cheek, almost knocking out his eye. A rotting mass of deep red—a beet, maybe—splattered on Alonso's head. He struggled not to cry. All of them were dripping with spittle."

My grandmother's eyes were watery and she looked as though she were going to gag.

"Oh God," I whispered. I closed my eyes and imagined the beautiful Doña Teresa wearing a *sambenitillo*, spittle oozing from her ear. These things were still going on.

No one asked what was going to happen to those wearing the long, yellow cloak that was a parody of a monk's robe. That group was going to make a different pilgrimage. Those poor souls would be marched to the stakes, their lines interspersed with rotting corpses of exhumed heretics and effigies of fugitives, all clad in *sambenitos* and mock bishop's miters. The living, the dead, and the hideous figurines, all dressed alike. When they reached their destination, they would be mounted on posts. Then, a distinguished guest would light the torch.

My grandmother Catalina had lived in Toledo with her first husband, and she had sewn for Doña Leonor, the wife of the cloth merchant Juan Sánchez. He was a wealthy man who had married into a prestigious family, that of the financier Simón de Fonseca Pina.

"They lived like princes," my grandmother said. "But they weren't haughty. Don Juan always had a kind word for everyone, and Doña Leonor never sent me away without a bit of mutton or a pail of tripe for my children."

In the beginning it seemed to my grandmother that the stars were smiling on Sánchez. He had everything, and everyone loved him. But the stars are treacherous. After the birth of their second child, Doña Leonor died, and Juan Sánchez took a second wife. Inés López was from a less distinguished family, but her father, a merchant from Tordesillas, was a respectable man.

Around this time the municipal authorities called the city's rabbis to a secret meeting outside the gates of Ávila. They promised them immunity from persecution if they would reveal which of their people were still practicing Jewish rites. Then they leaked this information, making sure everyone in the Jewish community knew the rabbis were spying for the church. Finally, heralds circulated among the most affluent neighborhoods, announcing that any Jew who confessed his false faith and repented publicly would receive light punishment.

I guess Juan Sánchez weighed his options. He was a businessman, a practical man. He must have thought it would be better to give himself up than to be turned in by an underhanded rabbi and dragged to the picket. I'm sure he had no desire to wear the long, yellow cloak, and even less desire to see it on his three boys. According to the law, any male child older than ten—the age at which boys started learning Hebrew—was obligated either to repent or suffer the consequences. As it turned out, only the younger two, Álvaro and Alonso, marched in the procession. Don Juan's oldest son, Hernando, took off for Salamanca, where he became a Christian and changed his name.

"I'm not sure Don Juan took his conversion all that seriously," whispered my grandmother. "It was just something that had to be done. The same with Hernando." My grandmother pursed her lips. Her eyes were sad. I felt the air turn suddenly heavy.

"That's sinful!" gasped my mother. "That's wicked!"

But neither Tía Cati nor my grandmother opened their mouths to condemn Juan Sánchez. A thought started to gnaw at me: Doña Teresa, the most beautiful young woman in Ávila, was from a *converso* family. Was she really a clandestine Jew? For a long while, no one spoke.

The brazier crackled and warmed our fingers. How could such things as penitential processions and public executions exist in a world where women gathered to stitch and gossip in the pleasant glow of the fire? It didn't make sense to me as a child, and now, after all these years, it still doesn't make sense.

"And Don Juan?" asked Tía Cati finally. "Is that when he came to Ávila?"

"Not right away," said my grandmother. "He left the two younger boys with his sister and took off with his wife for Ciudad Real. The inquisitors had been there before Toledo, so he figured they wouldn't return for a while. The first thing he did was change his name to Cepeda."

"Why Cepeda?" asked Tía Cati.

"His wife had Cepedas in her family, and it was a fine Old Christian name. Soon he had made enough money selling cloth to bring Álvaro and Alonso to Cuidad Real. But he was still vulnerable, so he took the bull by the horns. He figured out a way to secure his position and at the same time make a pile of money. He became a tax collector."

"A tax collector?" echoed Tía Cati.

"Of course. In order to be a tax collector, you have to have a patent of nobility, and with his connections, he bought one. Now he could prove he was an Old Christian."

"But he wasn't."

"No, of course he wasn't. But he was rich, and his sons became rich as well, especially Alonso, Teresa's father. When they were old enough, the boys bought their own patents of nobility. Now, everyone calls them *Don*, as though they were aristocrats."

"Well," said my aunt, "Don Alonso has always been good to us. Whatever Juan Sánchez was, his son has always shown us kindness."

"Everyone loved Doña Beatriz," added my mother. "Beggars never came away from her door wanting."

She was referring to Beatriz de Ahumada, Don Alonso's second wife. She had been an Old Christian, of course. New Christian men always took Old Christian brides. That's the way they cleansed their lineage. Their children would be only half *converso* and *their* children would be only one quarter *converso* and so on. Don Alonso's first wife, Doña Catalina del Peso y Henao, also an Old Christian, had brought him a very nice dowry—about one hundred thousand *maravedís*, according to my aunt, who always knew everybody's business—but she had died young. His second bride was a lovely girl of about fourteen, who, like her predecessor, brought substantial wealth. Before the year was out, she bore a son, Fernando. Then came another, Rodrigo. On March 28, 1515, Teresa was born. She was baptized on April 4, with two neighbors standing for her as godparents, in the thirteenth-century Church of San Juan, by the Mercado Chico. After Teresa was born God sent Doña Beatriz six more children—Lorenzo, Antonio, Pedro, Jerónimo, Agustín, and Juana—after which He in his infinite mercy saw fit to take her from this world. She died in childbed with Juana.

As is the custom here, some of Don Alonso's eleven children took their father's surname, while others took their mother's. Teresa took Doña Beatriz's, so that even though her full name was Teresa Sánchez de Cepeda y Ahumada, she went by Teresa de Ahumada. It was a fitting choice. She was, like Doña Beatriz, beautiful and fun-loving, curious and tough. Besides, they were both avid readers, especially of books of chivalry, those sumptuous tales of handsome knights who risked their lives for beauteous ladies—novels preachers like Father Evaristo said should be kept away from women lest they fill our fragile brains with naughty ideas.

As a little girl, what I knew about Teresa was that she was beautiful, mischievous, and headed for trouble. The neighbor women were obsessed with her. They all had an opinion.

"She runs around with those scatterbrained cousins of hers, Ana and Inés. Those two have the Devil in their farthingales."

"She's a lonely little thing. That's why she seeks company."

"What kind of company is that? Don Alonso had better open his eyes before it's too late. The girl's a flirt—¡Una coqueta!—giddy and vain. She cares for her hands as though they were pampered pets, always massaging them with almond paste or bacon fat."

"Ever since her mother died, he can't do a thing with her. The whole town knows she and Javier are lovers."

"María tries to keep a tight reign on her, but an older sister is not a mother. Besides, María will be married herself before long."

"Why doesn't Javier just ask Don Alonso for Teresa's hand?"

"Don Alonso has to get María married first. One thing at a time, Cati."

The evening I saw Teresa and Javier meet in the shadows, my mother, aunt, and I were alone in the *estrado*. The neighbors had gone home, but we still had hours of work ahead of us. Mother and Tía Cati stitched and sewed, slaving away at a deep blue-green party dress for the very girl they were gossiping about. My mother's needle moved in and out, her fingers quivering like butterflies as she tacked the lace trim along the hem of the overskirt.

The next afternoon we hurried down a crowded street in the old Jewish quarter, the dress carefully wrapped in clean straw. A maid showed us into the pantry. Teresa had gone out with her cousins and their *dueña*. As soon as we heard them trot up, I ran outside. All three ladies rode fine, sturdy mules. Teresa was an excellent mount, and she rode a dapple as pert as its rider. Her laughter rose above that of the others, high-pitched and sharp, like shattering crystal. The ladies came inside and threw off their capes, which the *dueña* gathered over her arm. "The dressmaker is here, *señora*," said the maid.

In Teresa's *estrado* we unpacked the dress. I stood there gaping at the town beauty. Suddenly, she looked down at me and winked. "Little Pancracia," she said. "How lovely you are."

I wasn't lovely at all, and I couldn't imagine what made her say such a thing. I looked down at my shabby sandals.

Teresa let out a prickly little squeal when she saw the dress. "It's wonderful! Did you help sew it too, Pancracita?"

Teresa shared spacious quarters consisting of a sleeping alcove, a dressing area, and an *estrado* with her sisters María and Juana, the latter just three years old. Mother helped her put on the dress so that Tía Cati could make last-minute adjustments. "It's beautiful! It's flawless!" she breathed. My mother and Tía Cati turned to leave.

"Leave Pancracita here with me!" begged Teresa. "She can help me get ready!"

My mother looked stern. The Ahumada girl used cosmetics and reputedly bathed in lavender water. My mother had no desire that such upper-class depravity rub off on me. After all, it was going to be hard enough to marry off a child like me, an ugly orphan with no dowry.

"Let her stay," commanded my aunt unexpectedly.

My mother's face turned the color of grenadine. Tía Cati gave her a knowing look and asked Teresa to excuse them a moment. Dragging me in tow, the two women ducked into a storage alcove. "It's an opportunity for her!" whispered by aunt. "If the Cepedas like her, maybe they'll take her into their service!"

I expected my mother to say, "And what then? How will I ever get her married to a cobbler's son after she lives a while with the likes of Doña Teresita?" I imagined her saying "Doña Teresita" as though she were spitting. But that's not what she said. What she did say was this: "How can you even think of such a thing! They're Jews!"

That should have been the end of it. After all, how could you rebut such an argument? But that wasn't the end of it.

"Don Alonso is as pious as a monk," countered Tía Cati.

"That's not saying much." My mother crossed her arms resolutely. "The point is, I don't want trouble with the authorities. They see you coming to a house like this a few times, they think you're one of them." She glanced around to make sure there was no one within earshot. "I'm afraid for Pancracita," she said. "I'm afraid for us all."

My aunt thought about it awhile. My mother added, "She paints her lips and darkens her eyes!" She had reverted to her old arguments. It was a sign the battle was over.

"It's expected of girls of her class," snapped Tía Cati. She went back to the *estrado* to thank Teresa and accept her invitation.

It was true that Teresa bathed in lavender. I bathed her myself. While I rubbed her hair with olive oil, she chewed anise seeds to sweeten her breath. Then the *dueña* perfumed her with more lavender water, holding it in her mouth and spewing it onto her chemise-covered body. Afterward, the maid did her hair in a knot and bound it in a silk hairnet. I applied powder to her neck and shoulders, while her cousin Inés swathed her face in a foundation of *solimán*. Finally, her cousin Ana applied pink to her cheeks, vermillion to her mouth, and charcoal to her eyes. At last she was ready to don her *jubón*, her corset, her *ropa baxa*, her horsehair farthingale, and her lovely new dress, over which she slipped the gold-embroidered taffeta girdle that had belonged to her mother. The *dueña* brought in a pair of gold chains, an emerald ring, three gold bracelets, and jeweled earrings also inherited from her mother. Teresa smiled and kissed my cheek.

"Thank you, Pancracia," she said. She slipped me a bit of lace. I looked at it, trying to decide whether I would sew it to my cushion or hide it in my tunic.

That night, as I lay next to my mother, I thought of Teresa at her party. Was Javier caressing those dove-like hands? Was he covering her delicate lips, as crimson as carnations, with his own, or nibbling those earlobes, pink as rosebuds and studded with gold and jewels?

The next day we returned to Don Alonso's house to collect payment, and once again Teresa asked my mother to allow me to stay awhile with her. "Please, Pancracita is such a sweet little friend! I love having her with me."

Friend! She had called me friend! The prettiest, most popular girl in Ávila had called me friend! My mother was holding several gold coins in her hand. Now was not the time to argue. I accompanied Teresa, Ana, and Inés to Teresa's quarters, where they picked up their needlework. I hadn't brought my embroidery, but I made myself useful teaching the young ladies new stitches. I was younger than they, but much handier with a needle. Soon they were gossiping and giggling, their sewing forgotten. All of a sudden, a small dog ran into the room, all fluffy and clean. I'd never seen such an animal. He looked like a wad of starched organdy.

"You silly creature!" laughed Teresa. "What are you doing here?"

I laughed nervously when he came near me. The only dogs I had seen were large, wolf-like farm dogs, with alert ears and sharp eyes to guard against predators.

"Mus! Mus! Take him to Silvia," said Teresa, looking at me and signaling toward the other room, where I assumed the maid was dusting or sweeping.

"Pick him up?"

"Yes, pick him up before he soils something."

I picked him up by the middle and went to look for Silvia. She was gathering *ropa blanca* for the laundress. When she saw me, she put down her basket, took the animal and disappeared.

Don Alonso was in his library talking to another man whose voice I didn't recognize and whose face I couldn't see. The door was only partially open, but I could see Don Alonso's jaw tighten as he looked down at his fingernails, then up at his interlocutor. I didn't mean to overhear them, I swear I didn't, but they were talking about Teresa, my new friend. I guessed from the exchange that the man I didn't know was one of Don Alonso's brothers or maybe a cousin.

"You have to do something about this, Alonso," he was saying. "The whole town is talking. Either marry her to Javier or put her in a convent! You can't take care of her—a man alone with a passel of kids! She's too much for you."

"Teresa doesn't want to get married yet. I asked her."

"You asked her? What's the matter with you, Alonso? Decide what you want her to do, and make her do it."

"A girl should have something to say about who she marries."

"A girl should have nothing to say about anything! Get her married before she covers us all with shame."

Don Alonso was silent. I saw him bite his lip and cross his arms, not the way children do when they're showing defiance, but the way a beggar in the plaza might to keep himself warm.

"The family honor cannot be dragged through the mud! Do something, or else I will."

"What do you expect me to do? Put a knife to her throat like those barbarians who show a daughter less compassion than a suckling pig?"

"You can't let this go on. People already look at us as though we had horns." He lowered his voice. "'The Jews,' they'll say. 'Of course they care nothing about losing their honor! They have no honor to lose!' Put her in a convent, Alonso!"

"No! I will not bury my Teresita in a convent!"

"*Hombre*, be reasonable! It will only be for a while! Just until this gossip about her and Javier blows over. In the meantime, she can be serving Our Lord Jesus Christ."

"To Hell with Our Lord Jesus Christ!"

Suddenly Don Alonso turned. He was staring right at me. He knew I had heard him. I felt my quivering limbs stiffen. Our eyes locked. I wanted to run, but I couldn't. What would he do to keep me quiet? I had his life in my hands. I could accuse him of heresy, but before I got the chance he could slit my throat and throw me down a well. He could say he had caught me stealing and that I was so ashamed I ran to the well and hurled myself in. I imagined them hauling up my body. I was just a seamstress's daughter. What would it matter to anybody if I died?

Don Alonso stood staring at me, his eyes like dead ashes. I looked down at the floor, then up again, right into his eyes. I didn't see anger or fear. What I did see was a terrible weariness. He knew, I think, that I wouldn't tell. Without speaking, we had reached a kind of agreement.

But then, in a few days, when Don Alonso sent for my mother and me, the fear came back. I started to cry. "No!" I whimpered. "I won't go!"

"What's the matter with you, child?" snapped my mother. She grabbed me by the arm and squeezed hard.

"Please don't make me go back there!" I pleaded. "I don't want to go back there!"

She looked at my aunt. "It was your idea to let her stay with that vixen! They must have done something to her!"

I just stood there and howled. "No! No! I won't go back to that house."

"Don't be silly." Tía Cati was a kind woman, but, like the other women who gathered in the *estrado,* she had no use for moody children. For them, children were like pieces of furniture. You put them down where they'd be most useful and didn't think about them again. She took me firmly by the hand and pulled me whimpering toward the door. I strained to get away.

Before I knew it we were standing in Don Alonso's study. To one side was the library, to the other, a chapel with an image of Our Lady in a blue robe, a small gold crown on her head and the infant Jesus in her arms. I shuddered. Don Alonso, in black from head to toe except for a small white ruff, stood looking at me. His eyes were kind, but I thought it was a trick. I was cowering behind my aunt, trembling.

"*Buenos días, Catalina,*" he said. Teresa came in. She curtsied and kissed his hand.

"*Señor,*" she whispered. She looked very different from the day we had brought her the new, forest green gown. She wore no cosmetics and her eyes were puffy and red. Her drab, grey-black dress made her skin look sallow.

Don Alonso got right to the point. "Doña Teresa is going into the convent," he said. "It's a temporary arrangement." I peeked out at Teresa from
behind Tía Cati's skirts. She looked miserable. "She will need a servant and
has asked that Pancracia accompany her."

For a moment, no one said anything. I stepped away from Tía Cati and
almost swooned. Teresa smiled at me. Even with those sad eyes, she looked
beautiful.

"Doña Teresa is very fond of the child," he said. "She enjoys her company." He took a little pouch out of a drawer in his writing table. He opened
it and poured out a thick silver chain, then put it back into the pouch and
handed it to my aunt.

"Please!" begged Teresa. "I'll be able to bear it better if I can hear
Pancracita's sweet laughter every day."

Don Alonso looked at me beseechingly. I was overwhelmed by the
thought that Doña Teresa and her father actually seemed to need me. The
decision, however, was not mine to make. The idea of accompanying Teresa
to the convent for a few months was attractive. The beautiful Teresa! I'd be
in charge of taking care of her—bringing her food, perfuming her bathwater
with rose petals . . . emptying her bedpan! Could a creature as lovely as Teresa
shit?

"For how long would it be?" asked Tía Cati.

"I don't know," said Don Alonso. "Five or six months. It will be worth
your while," he added, looking at the pouch. "We can work out an arrangement advantageous to us both."

"I'll have to ask her mother."

"Ask her."

I wondered if Don Alonso was just trying to get his hands on me in order
to slit me open and tear out my heart for one of his Jewish rituals? "It won't
be so bad if I can hear Pancracia's sweet laughter every day," Teresa had said.
Did she mean it, or was this just part of her father's evil scheme?

I don't know what Tía Cati told my mother, but she must have mentioned the chain. Well, I thought, at least I'm saleable. Anyway, before the
week was up, Teresa and I were climbing into the carriage that would take us
to Nuestra Señora de la Gracia, the Augustinian convent where Teresa was to
be a boarder and I was to be her maid.

Teresa, in a subdued, brown dress and cape, lifted her dainty foot onto the stepladder that was used to get in and out of the carriage. As she did so, she exposed an ankle discreetly sheathed in a black, woolen stocking. A young cavalier blew her a kiss from the street.

"All the roses in the garden are flush with jealousy, for they can never compare with the exquisite Teresa," he said, bowing and tipping his hat with a flourish.

"Well, take a good look," she called back merrily, "because I'm going into the convent and you may never see me again." "Shht!" scolded María. "Don't make a scene." Teresa's sister was going to accompany us to the Augustinian sisters to settle Teresa in.

Once we were inside the carriage, Teresa's mood changed. Her face became pinched and her lips quivered. A teardrop clung to her thick, fringe-like eyelashes. She stared blankly at the curtained window, then sighed, bit her lip, and squinted as though trying to shut out the light.

I was too young to concern myself with what she was feeling. All I felt was excitement. I thought: We're going, we're really going. This isn't part of some diabolical scheme concocted by Don Alonso to kidnap me! This is an adventure! We're going to Nuestra Señora de la Gracia, and I shall have Doña Teresita all to myself!

But Teresa just sat there, her eyes unseeing, her face wan.

The carriage—an elegant, metal-framed covered wagon—slid along the street. María adjusted the curtain so that no one could see inside. It was strange. It was October, but in the fresh, cold morning air I could smell roses. Ever since, I've associated that fragrance with Teresa.

Sister Angélica del Sagrado Corazón
Toledo, 16 June 1576

CHAPTER 2

To Love and Serve the Lord

ARROGANCIA IS PRIDE, CHARACTER, SENSE OF SELF. IN SPAIN *ARROGANCIA* IS A virtue, and Ávila is an arrogant city, a wellspring of fearless *caballeros* who in bygone days served God and sovereign. Tucked among the mountains of the Central Plateau, Ávila is the highest city in Spain and watchtower of the kingdom. It basks in its *alteza*, its "highness," its "haughtiness." It lords over the Valle de Amblés, flaunting its gorgeous palaces, *casas nobles*, and ancient churches in the *románico* style. But more than anything, Ávila takes pride in its massive wall, the immense medieval fortification that encircles the inner city. I thought I'd spend my life in the embrace of that wall. And I might have, if it hadn't been for Teresa de Ahumada.

The carriage made its way out the city gate and snaked its way up a hill to the south. Once we were beyond the walls of Ávila, I pulled back the curtain. As day broke, a breathtaking patchwork of greens unfolded before me. We arrived at the gates of the convent of Nuestra Señora de la Gracia just after daybreak. The tiled-roof, two-storey building adjoined a sturdy church with an imposing entrance. The coachman brought the horses to a slow halt, then jumped down and opened the carriage door. Teresa sat immobile, her feet as leaden as the double-locked trunk painted with roses and baby's breath. "Come, Teresa," said María. "We're here."

Teresa let out a sharp, short breath, as though someone had thumped her on the back.

"Come, Doña Teresa," I urged, echoing her sister. But Teresa seemed oblivious.

A convent servant helped the coachman carry the trunk inside. Teresa's maid Silvia had stuffed it with heavy blankets, silken sheets, flannel mantles, and fluffy coverlets—the finest Don Alonso could supply. In addition, Teresa had brought two chemises, warm underskirts, woolen stockings, her porcelain dishes, silver goblets, a jeweled cross her mother had left her, vials of lavender, chamomile, and mint for her bath, oil for her hair, a pretty doll dressed in satin and white lace, and her favorite novels. The two men staggered under the weight of the chest.

At last, Teresa climbed down the ladder, gripping the sides firmly, ignoring María's outstretched hand. I didn't offer my own.

Doña María de Briceño y Contreras was waiting for us in the parlor. She was a plump woman with a strong gaze, a deep voice, and a no-nonsense demeanor. She reminded me of my aunt's best hen—meaty, voluble, and self-assured.

"Come in, dear," she said to Teresa. "Sit here. Let's chat a while."

Teresa smiled as though she had clay in her mouth. She curtsied as she'd been taught, then sat in the chair Doña María indicated. Teresa was to be a *doncella de piso,* a boarder—one of the girls whose parents sent them to the convent to be educated. She had no intention of professing. She lifted her chin and pursed her lips.

"Sister Clemencia and Sister Sepultura can carry your trunk inside. They're peasant women, young and as strong as men. You don't need to unpack right away."

Teresa nodded. The Briceño woman got right to the point. "I am the novice mistress and head of the convent school," she said. "I sleep with our boarders in their dormitory, eat with them in the refectory, and accompany them to chapel. If anything is troubling you, come to me."

Teresa's jaw tightened at the word "dormitory." We had both assumed she'd have a private cell—perhaps a large, airy suite with plenty of room for an ample, feather bed for her and a small, box-type bed for me. We'd talked about it while she was packing. "It's an elegant convent, Pancracita. The best families send their daughters there. I'm sure we'll have a nice room. You'll be more like my little sister than my maid. You'll sleep in my room and we'll share all our secrets!" I'd lapped it up. After all, what more could I want? A big room with my own bed and a sister who was the prettiest girl in Ávila. Me! The daughter of a seamstress!

As it turned out, the sisters of Nuestra Señora de la Gracia were more concerned with reciting the Office and spinning than with making things comfortable for their boarders. Doña María—or Sister María, as she told us to call her, even though she was a noblewoman from the powerful

Briceño family—made it clear from the beginning that austerity was the rule. Our jobs were to pray and to work, Teresa at her studies and I at my domestic duties. Although the nuns had their own cells, Teresa, she explained, was going to have to sleep with other *doncellas de piso*. She would store her elaborate cross and her gorgeous doll with the Mother Superior. No ruby rosary beads. No perfumed hair oil. No books of chivalry. Teresa listened, her face frozen in a scowl, like a convict listening to a judge pronounce his sentence.

"Your father told me you weren't anxious to join us here at Nuestra Señora de la Gracia."

Teresa wasn't going to give Sister María the satisfaction of a reply. I looked from one to another, wondering who was going to back down first. Suddenly the novice mistress noticed me. I'd been standing awkwardly by Teresa's side, feeling like a chicken in the wrong coop.

"Sit down, child," she said. "What's your name? Speak up, tell me your name."

"Pancracia," I whispered.

"Ah! A daughter of Saint Pancracio! How fortunate. You'll never be without work."

I opened my mouth to say something, but she'd already forgotten me and turned back to Teresa. "Lots of our young ladies aren't anxious to join us in the beginning. But they get used to us. And then, when it's time for them to leave, they don't want to. But they can't stay. Someone has to procreate, after all. The nobility must produce offspring."

Teresa's lips remained glued. Her jaw tightened, almost imperceptibly.

Sister María described the routine. The daily Hours, or prayer periods: Vigils, Matins, Lauds, Prime, Terce, Sext, None, Vespers, and Compline, each with its own psalms and orations. There would also be lessons—religion, grammar, penmanship, arithmetic, music, needlepoint. No Latin, of course. Girls were not supposed to learn Latin. And no Scripture. Scripture was only for learned men. Only poor, misguided Protestants thought that everyone should read the Bible. Her voice droned on and on. I began to doze.

"Pancracia!" she snapped suddenly. I opened my eyes. "Go with Doña Teresa. Sister Casimira will show you to the dormitory." Sister Casimira had materialized out of nowhere. When had she come in?

Teresa got up and ran her hand over her skirt, as if to flatten out the wrinkles. Another nun came in, one who wore a white veil instead of a black one. She waited for Sister María to acknowledge her presence, and then asked permission to speak.

"What is it, Sister Milagros?"

"I have a message for you from the *Madre*," whispered the nun. "Concerning the girl." She looked toward Teresa, a little resentfully it seemed to me.

The two of them stepped outside. When Sister María returned, her face was a bit ashen, but she was perfectly composed. "It seems your father has arranged for you to have a private cell, Doña Teresa." An unmistakable flash of insolence tinged Teresa's smile. "I assume you'll be taking your meals there," said Sister María. Her air was detached.

"Yes, ma'am."

"Yes, *Sister*," the nun corrected her.

"Yes, Sister."

"Good. Pancracia will bring them up to you."

So, we were going to have a cell after all. But of course. Don Alonso was not going to let his darling Teresa be treated like a nobody.

Teresa's room was not the luxurious cell I had imagined, but a small, serviceable space with an undersized bed and a wash basin. I was to sleep on a mat on the floor. Two habits were folded neatly on the bed. The sisters wore a white tunic and surplice with a black girdle, a white gimp and yoke, and a black veil and cowl. Sister María provided Teresa with a plain, white habit, similar to the ones the novices wore. I was to wear a grey one with a white veil, like the other servants. Our guardian had taken on her hen-like demeanor once again, clucking and scurrying as she explained to Teresa what was expected of her. Teresa looked around the room indifferently, pretending not to pay attention, but Sister María kept on talking. She was explaining about the choir when she remembered, once again, that I was there, too. "Go to the kitchen, child," she said. "The cook will give you instructions. Make yourself useful." She didn't sound unkind, just businesslike. Anyhow, I was used to taking orders. To be honest, I glad to have something to do besides linger in Teresa's shadow, feeling worthless.

There were other girls my age in the convent and several who were younger. Some were orphans of noble lineage whose relatives gave them to the nuns to educate. Some were the younger daughters of large families with elegant surnames but insufficient means to provide marriage dowries. A few were the bastard daughters of dukes or counts, girls who commanded respect because of their noble blood, but who could not be allowed to reproduce. There were also schoolgirls, widows, women whose husbands were off at war. Most of the commoners were maids, girls like me who served boarders or did manual labor.

The kitchen nun put me to work peeling carrots, washing cups, sweeping floors, carrying water. Between one task and another we stopped to pray. Now and then I caught the eye of another servant girl, but we worked in silence, speaking only when absolutely necessary. I thought of my mother and aunt back in the *estrado*, sewing and gossiping or bickering half-heartedly. I imagined the neighbor women coming by to share stories. Suddenly, I regretted the day I'd ever laid eyes on Teresa de Ahumada. Hadn't she said we were sisters? Then why was I shelling peas while she said her prayers serenely in her cell?

Around two o'clock I brought her up her dinner. I found her in the cell sobbing. Her face was crimson, her eyes swollen, her nose snotty. The town beauty! She looked like a decaying vegetable, all spongy and runny. I didn't feel sorry for her. I just stood there, annoyed. What did she have to cry about, this spoiled little rich girl? I was the one who had spent the morning cutting my fingers with a pairing knife.

In a while her weeping grew softer. She gasped and swallowed, trying to control her breathing. "I hate her!" she blurted out finally. "She's a witch!" I couldn't imagine who she was talking about. She drew a pretty lace handkerchief from her sleeve and wiped her nose. I was surprised they had allowed her to keep the bit of fancywork. "A witch and a bully!"

"My mother?" I said finally. I knew she wasn't talking about my mother, but I couldn't think of anything else to say.

"Of course not, you ninny," snapped Teresa. "What does your mother have to do with any of this? Sister María, of course! The troll!"

I put down the tray with Teresa's dinner on a small table. "What happened?" I asked. She glowered, then squeezed her lips into a pout. "Well?" I said. I wasn't in the mood to listen to her complain. I was exhausted.

"She told me how lucky I was to be here. She said my father was a very wise man to put me in the convent. Soon I'd forget all about my pretty dresses and my fine jewelry, she said, and then I'd be ready to devote myself entirely to God. Soon I'd learn the convent routine—getting up at three in the morning for prayers, eating onions and turnips and a bit of bland chicken once a week. She said the private room and meals alone were okay in the beginning, but that eventually I'd be expected to conform. 'I want to keep my own cell,' I told her. 'Well, Doña Teresa,' she said to me. 'If you want to keep your own cell, you'll have to become a nun.' The hag! I don't want to become a nun! I won't become a nun! I'd rather spend eternity in Purgatory!"

What she was saying was sinful, but I didn't contradict her. She might throw something at me or refuse to give me dinner. I waited a minute before responding. "Well," I said, "you could always get married."

She sat there, immobile. "Your cousin . . . he loves you," I ventured. "Everyone says so."

She stared straight ahead. The tears had stopped, but her eyes were still puffy and red.

"I don't want to get married."

"You don't? Why not? Everyone says . . ."

"I know what everyone says," she cut me off.

I was stunned. Don Javier was considered one of the most desirable bachelors in Ávila. Even kitchen maids knew that. He was self-assured and detached in a way that became a gentleman. He held his head high, and when he walked, his gait was so even that the wispy feather in his hat hardly bobbed up and down, but instead, floated through the air as if borne by the breeze. People said he was quick-witted and droll—a polished conversationalist, urbane and gallant with ladies. And he was handsome, so handsome that he reminded me of those fairy-tale princes in the ballads the minstrels sing in the square. He was of *converso* background, of course, but his father held enormous tracts of land to the north of town, which Javier, as the eldest son, stood to inherit—a detail that could make a noblewoman forget his Jewish blood. And Teresa was turning her back on all this? How could she not want to get married?

"But why, Doña Teresa?" I knew it was the wrong question to ask, but I couldn't believe what she was telling me. How many times had I fallen asleep at night, not with images of the death and resurrection of Our Lord Jesus Christ in my head, but with the memory of that dazzling young man darting out from behind the chandler's shop? The impeccable hands gloved in kid, the tight-fitting doublet that hugged his body like a lover, the fine, narrow waist, the muscular legs, the black cape floating loosely about his shoulders, caressing his arms . . . In my dreams I saw him removing his jasmine-scented gloves, slowly, one finger at a time. I saw him gazing into Teresa's eyes, touching her arm, running his knuckles slowly over her bodice. I saw him leaning toward her, kissing her mouth. And then it wasn't Teresa in his arms, it was me. Older, prettier, elegant and ladylike, even though I was . . . I am . . . the daughter of a seamstress.

"I don't want to marry! Not him, not anybody!"

I bit my lip. I felt guilty . . . also angry. Her words offended, somehow, my awakening senses. How could she not want him? *I* wanted him. How could she discard so cavalierly what I desired so intensely?

I should throw away these pages. Certain things shouldn't be committed to paper. On the other hand, by the time anyone finds this, I'll be old or dead, so it doesn't matter. That's what I like about writing. You can put down anything that comes into your mind, as long as you don't show it to anybody. Just putting quill to paper makes you feel better. Like a good confession. Only better than a confession, because the sour, old priests make you feel like garbage after you've told them your secrets. They pry them out of you ("Don't be afraid, child. God is merciful.") and then they scowl at you with their knit brows and their frigid eyes. Better just to write it down. Let the paper absorb your evil thoughts. Of course, confession is one of the sacraments of our Holy Mother Church. Confession is essential. I'm just saying that writing is good, too.

I didn't know what to say to Teresa. "Why?" was the only thing I could think of. "Why don't you want to get married?

She took a deep breath and blotted her eyes, even though they were dry now.

"I'm afraid," she said. Her voice was barely audible.

"Of what? Of what men do to women?" I'd listened to them whisper in the *estrado*. I'd seen dogs mating in the streets. I'd seen rams and ewes. I knew about such things, in spite of my mother's efforts to keep me innocent.

"Of dying," whispered Teresa. "I don't want to die, not now, not so young."

I thought about it a minute. Dying? What could she mean by that? But then I knew. I'd heard other women talk about it before. Getting married meant getting pregnant. Getting pregnant meant being pampered and getting to sleep late, even if you were just a seamstress, but it also meant danger. Pregnancy brought the possibility of dying in childbirth. Hadn't Teresa's mother gone to the grave after giving birth to Juana?

I wasn't angry any more. I understood Teresa's dilemma. What was worse? To immure yourself in a convent for the rest of your life or to marry and risk death?

"Well, then, you'll have to stay in the convent," I whispered. What choice did she have? Women like my mother and Tía Cati could live by themselves and sew, but a rich merchant's daughter had no options. She either had to marry or devote her life to Christ.

I expected her to start in again about how she'd rather suffer forever in Purgatory, but instead, she said, "I can't do that, either."

I looked at her. "But Doña Teresa, if you don't marry, you'll have to take the veil."

"They'll never take me here. . . . I've sinned."

"We've all sinned. Father Evaristo says it's the curse of Eve. But Jesus takes away the stain on our souls so we can go to Heaven and be with God after we die."

"This sin is too great." She began to weep again softly.

I ached with curiosity. Even though I knew I shouldn't, I ventured, "What did you do?"

"Something very bad."

What could it be? I wondered. Yes, Teresa was reputedly wild, but could she have committed a sin so grave it would prevent her from entering a convent? Suddenly, I thought of her father. I remembered the words I'd heard him say: "To Hell with Our Lord Jesus Christ!" Terrible words! So terrible, I thought he'd murder me for having heard them. It was true, then, I thought. They were *marranos*, pigs, Judaizing *conversos*. And Teresa was one of them!

I must have appeared mortified because Teresa looked at me with sad, tender eyes and reached out to squeeze my hand. Instinctively, I drew back. However, in a moment I recovered my wits. I slid off the bed and busied myself ordering the utensils for her dinner.

"I won't tell anyone," I said tersely.

She thought I was asking her to reveal her secret. "I'm sorry, Pancracita," she said. "I can't tell you. You wouldn't understand. You're too young."

"What's to understand? That you practice blood rituals on Friday nights? I already know all about it!"

"What? Who ever put such a horrible idea in your head?"

"Your father."

She burst out laughing. "You silly child! My father's a saint. What can you be thinking? It has nothing to do with my father. It has to do with my cousin."

Her cousin! I felt myself redden. What sin had she committed with her cousin? The cousin she didn't want to marry! The cousin *I loved!* There! I'd thought it. I'd articulated the word, *love,* if only in my head. Had they . . . ? I pushed the idea out of my mind. And it's only now, after all these years, that I can give a name to what I felt at that moment: *jealousy.*

Suddenly, I felt hungry. I couldn't have dinner until Teresa had eaten, so I nudged her toward the table.

"Eat! You wanted to have your meals in your room, so stop fussing and eat," I said a little too abruptly. After all, who was I to talk to her like that? I expected her to lift her hand, as my mother would have done. Instead, she got up dutifully, sat down at the table, thanked God for her food, and ate. I wondered if she would leave anything for me.

When she was done, she knelt on her prie-dieu and prayed until Sister María de Briseño called us for chapel. By that time, I had eaten, too.

Once I got used to it, I didn't mind the convent a bit. Teresa spent her days studying and attending to her religious duties, but I was too busy to pay much attention. Within a few days I was no longer bringing her meals to the cell. She was eating in the refectory with the other boarders. I still had to clean her chamber, take care of her clothing, empty her bedpan, bathe her and brush her hair, but most of the time I was occupied with kitchen duties or tending the garden.

One day Sister Milagros was mending the mantel of the Virgin that stood in the vestibule. Her thread kept knotting. I could see she was pulling it too tight.

"Here, Sister," I said. "I can help you with that." I spoke without thinking. I was so familiar with needlework that I reached for the fabric instinctively.

She was taken aback. I had broken the silence. I, a mere servant, had addressed her without being spoken to first. I didn't wait for her to respond. I took the mantel and squatted on the floor. I broke her thread and pulled it out. Then I redid her work, taking tiny, perfect stitches. When I was done, I handed the cloth back to her and went about my chores.

The rest of the morning I felt fleeting pangs of guilt. I'd broken a convent rule, and Sister Milagros was sure to tell the prioress. The sister clearly wasn't fond of Teresa. Much to everyone's surprise, Teresa was getting thick with Sister María, the same Sister María she'd called a witch! Resentment was growing among the boarders and even the nuns. Getting me in trouble would be one way to get back at her. But then I thought no, Sister Milagros had no reason to complain about me. She could easily take credit for my fine mending, never telling anyone who had really done it. In the future, I thought, I could help her out again. She would certainly appreciate it, and maybe she would even save a bit of squab for me from Thursday's dinner. Thursday was the day we ate meat.

It was late in the afternoon when Sister Agnes, who was in charge of the servant girls, told me that Mother Superior wanted to see me. "In the parlor immediately," she said.

The parlor? My fingers froze around the carrot I was peeling. My first instinct was to run to Teresa and beg her to go with me. She would explain that I didn't mean to be discourteous or disrespectful to Sister Milagros. But instead, I trudged after Sister Agnes to the parlor.

Madre Gisela de San Agustín was a wiry woman with crinkly skin that looked as though it would hold the imprint of your fingers if you pinched it. She was in her seventies, but moved with the agility of an eighteen-year-old. She had bushy, grey eyebrows, a narrow nose, and thin lips. Her smile was easy and warm, but she was reputed to be a tough disciplinarian. Her charges said she never slept, rarely ate, and prayed only the required number of hours, but intensely. Most of her time was devoted to administrative duties: the admission of novices, negotiation of dowries, commissioning of art for the chapel. The cellaress oversaw the purchase of groceries, but Madre Gisela oversaw the cellaress. And discipline. Madre Gisela was very much in charge of discipline. Rigorous, but fair, is what the nuns said about her.

I stepped into the parlor. Madre Gisela was sitting at her writing desk, pouring over what appeared to be an account book. She seemed in no hurry to deal with me. I held my breath.

Finally, she looked up. "God be with you, child," she said.

"And also with you," I said mechanically.

"You are Pancracia Soto, Doña Teresa's maid?"

"Yes, sister," I said. "I mean . . . I'm sorry . . . Yes, Mother." My hands were trembling. I thought of my own mother and suddenly wanted to go home.

"Sister Milagros told me what happened this morning," she said, wasting no time. I looked down at the floor. "She showed me your work. You have a very dainty stitch, indeed. Many of our ladies of noble birth cannot ply a needle with the dexterity that you do."

"Excuse me, Mother?"

"Your talents are wasted in the kitchen, Pancracia. There's a great deal of sewing to be done in the convent. We provide chasubles for Augustinian priests. Did you know that?"

"No, Mother."

"Tomorrow, instead of reporting to the kitchen, I want you to go to Sister Cecilia de la Concepción. She's in charge of needlecraft."

"Thank you, Mother!"

"Another thing, Pancracia. Sister María wants you to come to her tomorrow morning in the schoolroom. She is going to teach you to read. Doña Teresa herself requested it. You may leave now, child. Go with God."

To read? I was going to learn to read? I, the seamstress's daughter? I couldn't believe it. Neither my mother nor my aunt knew how to read, although both were good at counting money. This was the beginning of a new life, I thought, because knowing how to read would make me a different person. As far as I knew, only ladies learned to read. I imagined myself reading those books of chivalry that Teresa loved so much. I imagined myself sitting in the *estrado* entertaining the women with *Amadís de Gaula* or *Flores y Blanca Flor.* My mother would see how smart I was. She would see she had done the right thing my allowing me to accompany Teresa to the convent. She would never thump me on the skull again because she would respect me. I would be a lady—well, not a lady, but just like a lady. And Teresa had requested it! Maybe she really did think of me as a little sister.

Sister María de Briseño was a patient and firm teacher, but I can't give her all the credit. I was a quick student. "*A* is for the Annunciation. *B* is for Bethlehem. *C* is for Christ, our loving king." Day in and day out, until I learned the alphabet. And then, one day, I realized I was reading, reading with ease, and writing too.

Nuestra Señora de la Gracia was new then. The interior walls were smooth and white, and the stone exteriors were solid and sturdy. A local lady, Doña Mencía López, had founded the convent at the beginning of the century. When noblewomen want to flaunt their wealth and independence, how do they do it? By founding religious houses, of course. If you finance a convent, your name will be etched in the portal forever, and your portrait hangs in the parlor. Doña Mencía had a special interest in displaying her fat fortune because, although she was the daughter of aristocrats, she married a silversmith named Jorge de Nájera. It was a scandal, a noblewoman marrying an artisan, but husbands were hard to find. So many men were at war in Italy or subduing savages in the colonies that ladies sometimes had to marry beneath their stations.

When Jorge left Doña Mencía a wealthy widow around 1504, she was anxious to show off her treasure. It was as though she wanted to say to her detractors, "Alright, he didn't get to use *Don* before his name, but he made buckets of *maravedíes*. Let's see who eats better when the drought comes— you with your titles or me with my cash!" I don't remember Doña Mencía myself, but in the *estrado* she was a favorite subject.

When Teresa and I arrived at the convent in 1531, Doña Mencía hadn't been dead for very long. Almost everyone still remembered her. She'd been the convent's first abbess and had ruled her roost with an iron claw. I thought: even if you marry a man without a title, you can become princess of your own principality if you've got enough money. I thought: I'm just the daughter of a seamstress, but if I know how to read and write and do fine needlepoint, maybe I can marry rich. Maybe I can even marry a gentleman like Don Javier. Even though I'd still be my mother's daughter, I'd be an educated girl. I wouldn't have to settle for a laborer with rancid breath. Hadn't Doña Mencía beaten the odds? Hadn't her husband's money made up for his lack of title? Well, maybe *my* husband's title would make up for *my* lack of money.

While I was dreaming of marriage, Teresa was beginning to dream of not getting married at all. "You know, Pancracia," she said to me one day as I was washing clothes with serviceable, brown soap, the kind we used in the convent, "I'm thinking of staying here."

"Staying here? Taking the veil?"

"Maybe. Sister María says I should at least consider it. All my friends are novices already, and they're excited about it. What better occupation can a girl have than to love and serve the Lord? If I did stay, Pancracia, would you stay with me?"

The soap slid out of my hand and landed on the floor. "I'm sorry," I said.

"Sorry you made a mess? Or sorry, but you don't want to stay with me?"

"I didn't say I didn't want to stay with you."

"But you don't. Never mind. I can't take the veil anyhow . . . because of what I told you."

"About your sin? Why don't you just confess and get rid of it?"

"I don't know. It would be hard to talk about . . . with a man . . . with a priest."

"That's what priests are for," I said dryly. But I knew what she meant. I took a breath. "Did you tell Doña María?"

"Oh, God, I couldn't. She thinks I'm an angel. She doesn't know how wicked I am."

Wicked? I thought. She's making herself too important. She's assigning magnitude to her little sins. But then I thought: What if she does take the veil? What then? I was happy in the convent, but the idea of staying there forever, that was more than I'd bargained for. Three or four years, until it was time for me to get married, yes. But forever?

There was a strict hierarchy in the convent, just as there was in town. The nuns and boarders from highborn families received their due. White-veiled nuns—the ones who did manual labor, the scullery maids, gardeners, laundresses, carpenters and painters—those women knew their places. Nobody forgot who was who. Still, thanks to my fine stitch, they all tolerated me with a smile, even the ones with titles as long as the River Tajo. When anyone had trouble with her sewing, she came to me. The other thing is, I was a good reader, which the nuns respected. When other girls had problems with their lessons, I helped them. Sometimes I even felt, well, almost important. But then, Sister María de Briseño reminded me that we were all there to serve God with the gifts He had given us. That meant that no one could take credit for anything.

Of course, even without Sister María's sermons, I knew better than to put on airs. I went out of my way to be modest, to show deference. By bowing my head and bending my knee, I got to sit in the sewing room with the well-bred nuns who ate partridge on porcelain on Thursdays and who received gifts of suckets or pastry on holidays. They didn't share their treasures with me, yet in the convent I lived better than in my aunt's house. As long as I behaved, no one hit me. I had enough to eat. I had freedom to stroll through the garden during the *recreo,* and I was reading and writing as well as any girl my age. Best of all, I had Teresa. Someday I'd leave and get married, of course, but not for years.

At Nuestra Señora de la Gracia nuns received their guests at the grille, while boarders met theirs in the parlors. When Don Alonso or Doña María de Guzmán—Teresa's sister, now a respectable married lady—visited, I accompanied my mistress to greet them and, as was proper, sat on a footstool by her side. I looked forward to those calls. Visitors always brought treats, and I was happy for an occasional break from my regular duties.

One day, Sister Casimira came to get us after prayers. She handed Teresa a note, squinting at her as though she were her confessor. Teresa glanced at the paper and raised her eyebrows.

"A visitor!" she said. "This is strange. I wasn't expecting *Papá* today." Sister Casimira smirked, then looked down, as though avoiding Teresa's eyes. "It is *Papá*, isn't it?" Teresa asked, appearing suddenly alarmed. Sister Casimira didn't answer. She turned and left, her black veil fluttering slightly with the brusqueness of the movement.

I caught my breath. The gentleman waiting for us in the parlor wasn't Don Alonso. He seemed an apparition. He was clothed all black, except for a snowy ruff and cuffs, cream-colored gloves, and a quivering silver hat feather. He bowed respectfully. "Doña Teresa," he whispered.

"Don Javier! What a delightful surprise!" But in spite of her words, she looked shaken.

She turned to me. "Leave us alone, please, Pancracia," she said curtly.

Her words stung like a slap. What did she think she was doing? I always accompanied her when she received visitors. That was my job. I was her maid.

My bewilderment—and my hurt—must have shown on my face. "Doña Teresa," I stammered, "I can't leave my mistress alone with a gentleman in the parlor. It would be unseemly."

"Go! Ask Sister María de Briseño to come," she commanded. "She will accompany me."

I did as I was told.

What happened in that room? I expected her to tell me. After all, I was her maid and confidante. But when I came in that evening to get her ready for bed, she was buried in a book—Saint Augustine's *Confessions,* I think— and hardly looked up. I could see she'd been crying.

"Doña Teresa," I murmured.

She stood up without saying a word. I undressed her down to her shift. She sat on the bed, and I brushed her hair. I don't think more than three or four words passed between us. I assumed she was angry and giving me the cold shoulder. And yet, nothing in her demeanor conveyed anger. She was . . . I don't know how to say it . . . She seemed pensive.

For days after that she floated around like a specter, speaking rarely and always in a hushed voice. What's going on? I wondered. What's going to happen?

And then, one day during the recreation, she came running across the garden to meet me on the path. I was on my way to the sewing room. "Pancracita!" she cried. "Pancracita!" She grabbed me and hugged me and kissed me on both cheeks.

I hadn't expected to see her. I didn't know what to say.

"I took your advice," she exclaimed excitedly. "I talked to Sister María."

"About what?" I had an altar cover to finish for the monsignor. I didn't have time to chat.

"About . . . you know."

I put down my sewing basket and looked at her. "No, I don't know," I snapped. We were still mistress and servant, but I was in no mood to kowtow to her after the way she'd treated me in the parlor. Anyhow, I had responsibilities now. I was more than just her maid.

"About my sin."

"Your sin? Oh, that." I looked her right in the eye. "Something to do with Don Javier."

Javier. Just saying his name made me feel as though someone were tickling my back. I wanted to get away from her. I didn't want to hear about her and Javier. And yet, I did. I was queasy with curiosity. What terrible sin had they committed? What had happened in the parlor? I wanted to know everything, all the details. But about the details, she was tight-lipped. "Sister María told me I should talk to my confessor, and I did, Pancracia. And you know what he told me?" She was beaming now. "He told me that what I did wasn't a mortal sin!"

I shrugged and started to walk away, but she grabbed me by the shoulders.

"Isn't that wonderful, Pancracia!" She pulled me to her and hugged me more tightly than before, then began kissing my face—my cheeks, my forehead. "That means we'll be able to stay here forever, Pancracia! Forever and ever!" She was giddy, like a girl who has sampled spiced wine for the first time. She kept repeating, "Forever and ever! Forever and ever!"

I don't know how to explain what happened next. My temples were searing, yet I shivered. It was as though an oppressive, sweltering summer gripped my head, while at the same time winter ran her fingers, all frosty and prickly, down my neck. I felt squeamish. The pewter-colored sky, the naked trees, the impassive, stone convent walls all seemed to run together into a monochromatic smear. I put my hands on Teresa's chest, right above her breasts. I saw her open her mouth in amazement and heard a shriek that seemed to come from somewhere else. I pushed as hard as I could. The power of my thrust astonished me. I saw Teresa wobble and fall backward like a blurred image seen through glass, but I didn't stop to help her. I turned and ran.

I ran into the convent and down the hall to the sewing room. Sister Cecilia and two other nuns were embroidering in silence. I took my place on the smallest bench and bent over my work. I didn't look at any of them. I took tiny, deliberate stitches. In the whiteness of the immaculate altar piece I could see, as though reflected in a mirror, Teresa's white habit stained with mud. I closed my eyes. In the blackness I saw the palms of her hands, raw and bloody.

I've had a lifetime to think about Teresa's words. And still, I don't understand. Not really. "What I did wasn't a mortal sin." What did she mean? That nothing happened between her and Javier? No, I saw her kiss him. At least, I think I did. Or that she never gave herself to him completely, carnally? Or did she mean something completely different? It's possible she did give him her virginity, but that her confessor thought it wasn't a mortal sin. After all, they were supposed to get married. Or maybe the confessor was one of those randy priests who have a gaggle of bastards tucked away in some hut in the country, poor little mongrels who pass themselves off as the sons of a shepherd or a farmer. As they say, everyone calls the priest "father" except his own children, who call him "uncle." If Teresa's confessor was one of those, maybe he didn't think a young girl's loving her cousin was such an outrage.

I didn't see Teresa the rest of the day. I stayed away from her. I hid in the sewing room. During Vespers I stood in the back of the chapel. She was up front, with her friend Paula—the one who would become the Mother Superior of the convent in San Miguel, where we passed a stormy night or two not long ago, after hightailing it out of Seville. Teresa had changed clothes, and there was no trace of bruises on her face or hands. Her skin was luminous and her habit impeccable. She looked like an angel, all spotless, radiant and good. I wondered if she would tell Paula what I had done. "*¡Perra!*" I muttered under my breath. "Bitch!"

I couldn't avoid her forever. I dallied at supper rather than rushing to the cell to help her undress. She'll claw my eyes out, I thought. She'll show me the hyena all rich girls can be. I lingered by the door before knocking.

"Is that you, Pancracita?" she called before I had even raised my knuckles to the wood. Her voice sounded eerily calm.

"*Sí, Doña Teresita.*" I stepped inside, eyes glued to the floor. I busied myself getting out her hairbrush. I was waiting for her to make her move. I was sure she was going to blow up and throw me out. Certainly, she would complain to her father. The scene in Don Alonso's library flickered in my mind. Don Alonso could still arrange to have me slaughtered. Perhaps I should apologize, I thought. But how could a maid apologize for shoving her mistress into the dirt?

She was sitting on the bed. "Come, Pancracia," she said. "Sit next to me. I want to tell you something." Her voice was buttery. I was confused. I knelt to take off her shoes.

"No," she said, pulling her feet to the side. "Come sit by me."

I reached to undo her wimple so I could brush her hair, but she took me by the wrist and pulled me gently toward her.

"I'm going to become a nun, little sister," she said serenely.

I looked at her, waiting for an explanation. What about Javier? I wondered. What about her Jewish background? *What about the fact that I'd pushed her into the muck?* Weren't we going to talk about *that*? But she seemed to have forgotten all about those things. "I'm going to become a nun," she repeated. There was no trace of anger in her eyes.

She began keeping company with the serious girls, the novices who spent their days on their knees or reading books with names like *The Imitation of Christ*. I would see them during the *recreo* gathered in a circle, discussing their souls and their lessons.

One day, when I entered the sewing room, the nuns were all abuzz. We were supposed to work in silence, but the excitement was so electric that Sister Cecilia was unable to quell it.

"Didn't you hear?" tittered Sister Milagros. "While we were at choir, a star appeared. Right there in the chapel! It hovered . . . you won't believe where, Pancracia! Right above Teresa de Ahumada's head!"

I must have looked at her as though she'd sprouted antlers. Of course, I knew it was possible. After all, God can do anything. But still, it didn't seem likely.

"Really! It hovered above her head, then floated all around the choir. Finally, it floated over to Sister María de Briceño and vanished right into her heart! We all saw it!"

I imagined a sliver of sunlight traversing the stained glass window and resting on the chair back, just above Teresa's wimple. That's all it was, I thought. A sliver of sunlight. But I didn't say anything because I couldn't be sure. Maybe it really was a star or an angel.

The others started to treat Teresa with reverence after that. They spoke to her in muted tones, as though she were a sage. And she played the part.

She adopted a saintly demeanor, bowing slightly in a gesture of humility when anyone addressed her and looking tenderly at the flowers in the chapel, at the inkwells in the schoolroom, at the porridge bowl in the refectory. She spoke to everyone in a creamy voice, as though she were blessing them in the name of the Father, the Son, and the Holy Ghost even though she was just asking them to pass the soup.

I didn't care. I had my own friends and work to do. All the priests wanted me to embroider their vestments. I had the most elegant stitch in the convent. I was happy. Someday I would leave and get married, but for now, this was a good life. Time passed sweetly. I was still Teresa's maid, but her days were filled with prayer and study now. She hardly needed me. In the fall and spring, while she spent the *recreo* absorbed in conversation with her holy companions, I was out kicking a ball around the patio with the serving girls. In the winter a fire blazed in the sewing room, and no one ever mentioned the price of coal. I no longer missed my aunt's *estrado*.

We'd been in the convent about a year and a half when one morning, as I sat next to Sister Cecilia sewing, Sister Casimira appeared and signaled for me to follow her. "Come!" she whispered. "Something has happened!" I raised my eyebrows. She signaled me to be still, not to ask questions. I followed her down the corridor toward Teresa's cell.

Teresa was lying in bed, her hair clumped around a clammy brow. Sister Ignacia, the convent nurse, stood over her. She was a heavyset woman built like a bull, with balls to match.

"Doña Teresa!" I exclaimed. "What's the matter?"

She turned away from me, and then suddenly retched. I thought she was going to throw up, but she clutched the side of the bed and tensed her body, holding it in.

"She looked alright when I dressed her this morning," I stammered. I thought they were going to blame me.

"It came on her suddenly," said Sister Ignacia. "She's been like this for a couple of hours. She can't hold a thing down." The nurse's voice reminded me of fulling irons whacking cloth.

Teresa's eyes, usually bright as tapers, were squinty and moist, and her lips were wan and parched. She seemed to struggle for breath. Then, suddenly, her body convulsed. Sister Ignacia shoved a basin under her chin. Teresa heaved up a greenish fluid, lumpy and malodorous. She moaned, and tears spilled down her cheeks. Her shift was soaked with sweat and vomit.

Sister Ignacia handed me the basin to empty and clean.

"This is what you called me for?" I blurted. "To clean up her puke?" What had gotten into me? How did I dare speak like that to Sister Ignacia? It was as though the Devil had slipped into my brain. Seeing Teresa like that . . . it unsettled me. I was frightened and confused. "I'm sorry, Sister," I stammered. I took the basin in both hands and was instantly overcome with a fit of nausea. I began to tremble and tried to hand the receptacle back to the nurse.

"Go throw it out!" she commanded. "And then wash the basin."

But I couldn't stand the stink. I was shaking violently. "Please!" I cried. "Take it!" Then my wrists went limp and I dropped it on the floor.

"Stupid!" snarled Sister Ignacia. With the base of her hand she cuffed me on the ear so hard I felt my skull throb. I whimpered and put my hand to my head. I lost my balance and fell. Slop drenched my skirt and sandals.

Sister Ignacia threw a rag at me. "Clean it up," she hissed. "Then wash that damned basin and get back here. You have to take care of her."

I did as I was told, holding my breath in order not to gag. I had washed my spare habit that morning, and it was still drying. One of the other servant girls lent me hers. I put it on and ran back to Teresa.

Sister Eugenia was holding up Teresa's gown while Ignacia stuck another basin under her bottom. "She has diarrhea," Sister Ignacia said curtly. "Stay out of the way until she's done. Sister Eugenia will wash the chamber pot, and then you can clean her up."

"Yes, Sister." I turned away. Again, the stench. I felt as though I had an anvil in my stomach.

She looked at me with disgust. "How come you're so squeamish, dimwit? Since when are you such a fancy lady?"

They tried all kinds of remedies. Ground charcoal, saffron water, chamomile. At last, they called a surgeon to bleed her. Nothing helped. She was feeble from vomiting. Days went by. She grew scrawnier. Finally, they called for Don Alonso.

"I'm sorry," Sister María de Briseño told him. "You'll have to take her home. We can't keep her here. She requires too much attention." And me? I thought selfishly. What about me? But I knew the answer. I was there to serve Doña Teresa. I may have been the most valuable embroiderer in Nuestra Señora de la Gracia, but I was not there to sew. Don Alonso wasn't paying my board so I could adorn chasubles for priests. If Teresa left, I left, too.

That very day the same coach that brought us to Nuestra Señora de la Gracia took us back to town. As soon as the carriage arrived at the Cepeda Ahumada house, Don Alonso carried Teresa up to her room and put her to bed. The maid scurried around drawing curtains. Neither she nor Don Alonso seemed to notice I was there, so I gathered up my satchel and headed home.

I knocked at my aunt's door. After a few minutes my mother answered. "Hello, *Mamá*," I said. My mother stood looking at me as if she couldn't quite remember who I was. I had expected her to show some sign of pleasure. Not to squeal and throw her arms around me—that's not the Castilian way of doing things—but at least to smile and kiss my cheeks. I expected her to hustle me into the house and call out to my aunt, "Cati! Look who's here!" Instead, she stood there, staring. "It's me, *Mamá*!" I said.

"I see it's you," she said, finally. "Did you do something wrong? Did they send you away?" She signaled for me to go inside.

"Pancracia!" I heard Tía Cati's voice coming from the *estrado*. "¡*Dichosos los ojos!* How good to see you!" She hurried down the stairs. "Come, child, are you hungry? What are you doing back home?"

"Another mouth to feed," said my mother dryly. "And we're hardly getting by as it is."

Tía Cati signaled her to be quiet. "It's been slow," she said softly. She took my satchel and carried it into the room I shared with my mother.

I looked around. The house looked shabbier than I remembered it. Several pieces of furniture were missing—a stool, a hassock. My mother noticed me staring at the empty space where they had been. "We sold them," she said curtly. "We needed the money."

"It's the tailors' *gremio*," explained Tía Cati, trying not to grimace. "They're cracking down on the independent seamstresses. We used to sew a doublet or a cape for a gentleman every once in a while, but now the brotherhood not only won't let us join, they won't even let us sew men's clothing. If we break the rule, they send the constable after us."

"We're going to starve," said my mother. "We haven't had a new order for months."

"Stop it, Inés," said Tía Cati. "We can still sew ladies' garments. Anyhow, before long Doña Juana will be old enough to start her trousseau, and Don Alonso has promised the embroidery of the linens to us."

"Teresa's sister? She's just a little girl."

"She's four or five, but Don Alonso likes to think ahead. There'll be tablecloths and . . ."

Maybe not," I interrupted. "Doña Teresa wants to become a nun. If she does, her trousseau will go to Doña Juana."

It didn't take me long to see the effects of the *gremio*'s move against the seamstresses. Instead of a slice of mutton, the midday meal now consisted of eggplant and barley bread. It occurred to me to ask Don Alonso for help. He may be a Jew, I thought, but when you're hungry, what difference does it make where the food comes from? But how would I manage to see him? *Mamá* would never give me permission to go out alone.

"I think we should go visit Doña Teresa," I said to Tía Cati one day while we were spinning. "I haven't seen her in days, and I'm worried. She was very ill when we left the convent."

"Don't worry about her," said my mother. "She's rich. Rich people don't stay sick."

"I don't see how we could pay a visit to Don Alonso's house," said Tía Cati. "No one has called for us. A poor seamstress and her niece can't just go knocking on rich folks' doors."

"I could embroider a sachet for her and take it over there as a gift."

Neither one of them thought this was a good idea, but I worked all day stitching flowers on a scrap of silk, and by the late afternoon I was ready. Reluctantly, Tía Cati agreed to accompany me to Teresa's house. I felt as though ants were scurrying up and down my back. I didn't think Don Alonso's manservant would slam the door in our noses, but . . . I didn't know what to think. I prepared a speech as I tramped over the dusty paths next to my aunt. "I'm sorry to disturb you, but if you could just tell the *señorita* I've made a little something for her. Just a trifle."

I needn't have bothered. Silvia answered the door, and even though we had knocked at the servants' entrance, she greeted us as though we were friends of the family. "Doña Teresa will be so happy to see Pancracia!" she said breathlessly. "She's been asking for her."

"She has?"

"Oh, yes. She would have sent for you days ago, but Don Alonso thought it was too early for her to have guests." Guests? Me, a guest? I thought, I'm a maid, not a guest.

Teresa was sitting up in bed, large feather pillows with ruffled cases arranged around her, embroidered sheets tucked demurely under her chin.

She looked like one of the pale princesses from the chivalric novels she loved to read.

"Pancracia!" Her voice was still weak, but her joy was apparent. She turned to the maid. "Silvia," she said, "could you please bring us some cakes?" I watched greedily as Silvia brought in a tray of sweets and placed it on a table near Teresa's bed. I raised my hand to take one, but Tía Cati signaled me to wait until they were offered.

"Have you been reading?" Teresa asked eagerly.

Tía Cati raised her eyebrows, then dropped them into an expression of . . . I'm not sure what. Displeasure? Confusion? I hadn't told my mother and aunt I'd learned to read. For now, they had other things on their minds. Besides, what was the point? We had no books. Books were luxury items.

"No," I said. I thought a moment about what I should say next. "I have nothing to read. In fact, we almost have nothing to eat."

"Pancracia!" blurted out Tía Cati. "Have you no pride? Doña Teresa will think we've come here to beg."

I looked down at my hands. Tears were welling up in my eyes. Tía Cati got up and left the room, perhaps to join the servant women in the kitchen.

For a moment Teresa seemed disconcerted, but then she smiled. She said in a conspiratorial tone, "Well, I've been keeping secrets, too. I haven't told my father about my plan to become a nun. But there's no hurry. He's sending me to my sister's house in Castellanos de la Cañada to rest awhile and then begin treatment for my illness. He thinks the country air will do me good." She paused and took a breath. "The thing is," she said quietly. "It will break his heart. I'm his favorite, and he wants me to stay here, close to him."

I didn't know what to say.

"I have an idea," she said suddenly. The old twinkle was struggling to work its way back to her eyes. "When I go to Castellanos de la Cañada, you could go with me."

She'd caught me by surprise. I'd been away a long time, and I wasn't sure whether or not I wanted to go off again and wait on Teresa. The situation at home was awful, and *Mamá* was crosser than ever, but still, home is home.

She sent us back laden with gifts—a hefty lamb shank, bread, cheese, almond cake, and *yemas*, a candy of sugar and egg yolks that's typical of Ávila. She also stuffed a book into my hands, not a spiritual meditation by Saint Somebody-or-Other, but a chivalric novel, with princes and quests and all those things! It was *Flores y Blanca Flor*! Even now that I'm an old lady and a nun, I still love reading romances. Sometimes I wish I could just lie on the grass and read!

March winds lashed the sierra that night, and it was freezing in the *estrado*. Tía Cati refused to light the chimney, so I sunk down under my blankets and tried to sleep. "Look, *Mamá*, I have a surprise for you!" I wanted to say to my mother, "I can read you a story! Maybe there's not much to sew, but at least I can entertain you with my book!" But I was afraid to tell her.

It was Tía Cati who gave away my secret. Tía Cati was a great lover of stories. In the *estrado* all the women were storytellers. They told about crazy Juana, the daughter of Queen Isabella and King Fernando, who'd gone mad because her French husband wore frilly undergarments, and about Santa Clara de Asís, who threw away all her riches and ran off to form a convent with San Francisco, friend of birds. They talked about them exactly the way they talked about Miguela, the butcher's wife, who'd had an affair with the confectioner. The news that I could read filled Tía Cati's head with images of afternoons in the *estrado* listening to delicious tales of knights and ladies or of feisty saints like Lucía and Ágata—stories full of lustful men and the women who outsmarted them. "Our little Pancracia can read!" she told my mother. "She learned in the convent. Imagine how she'll entertain us!"

Mamá looked at me in disgust. "What a curse," she grumbled. "A girl who reads." But she couldn't resist the allure of *Flores y Blanca Flor.* I opened the book and began, "Your lordship should know I was raised with a young lady in the palace of my father, the king. She was the daughter of a Christian captive who was born the same day as I, and I love her more than anything in the world . . ." *Mamá* tried not to listen, but within minutes she was mesmerized.

A few days later Don Alonso commissioned two new traveling dresses for Teresa. She would be taking a short journey, he said, and would need some muslin frocks and petticoats. He said nothing about my going with her. Instead of making me return the book, *Mamá* and Tía Cati invited their friends over to hear the story, and while they sewed in the *estrado,* I charmed them with the king's intrigues and the lovers' schemes to escape and marry.

We were at Teresa's house for a fitting when Don Alonso broached the subject of my going to Castellano de la Cañada.

"Teresa is going to spend some time in the country with her sister María," he said. "She wants very much for you to accompany her. Would you like to?" I was taken aback. Girls my age didn't make decisions for themselves, so why was he asking me? I thought it must be because Teresa didn't have a mother. She was used to having her own opinions. When she grows up, I thought, she's going to be one of those clever women who know how to get whatever they want.

"Have you talked to my mother and my aunt?" I stammered.

"I want to know what you think," he said. He was standing in the shadows of a dimly lit corridor. He kept slipping in and out of focus, like a page illuminated by a flickering candle.

"Yes," I said, finally. "I'd like to go with Doña Teresa." I thought my tone sounded rather too assertive. "As her servant," I added.

"I'd glad," he said. Don Alonso's voice was soft and kindly. Reserved and outwardly serene, he reminded me of an elegant, old cat reconnoitering familiar territory.

A blasphemous thought came into my head: so what if these people practice strange rituals. As long as they don't hurt Christians, why should anyone care? Anyhow, even though I'd heard him take Jesus's name in vain, I had no proof he was a *judaizante*. I'd heard other men swear, even the parish priest. No one accused *them* of being Judaizers.

When my mother heard about the trip, she asked for an interview with Don Alonso. I was furious. I was sure she was going to wreck everything, refusing to let me travel until he coughed up some exorbitant sum of money. When she came home from their meeting, she picked up her sewing without saying a word. I supposed they had come to some sort of agreement.

On April 2, the morning we were to leave, I helped Silvia pack a locker with food for the trip. Teresa was in high spirits in spite of her stomach ailment. "I feel fine now," she kept saying. "I'm ready for an adventure!"

Don Alonso seemed glum. "He's worried about my brother Fernando," Teresa explained. Fernando had recently left for Colombia, and everyone knew that was dangerous territory.

Just as we were climbing into the carriage, Don Alonso turned to me. "I'm sorry, Pancracia," he said. "You won't be going with us."

I looked at him. "What are you talking about, *Papá*?" cried Teresa. She was obviously as astonished as I was. "We've been planning this trip for weeks!" Don Alonso shook his head sadly and climbed into the carriage next to his daughter. He, Teresa, and Silvia drove away, leaving me standing in the street. I felt as though the earth had shriveled under my feet. I trudged back home. My mouth felt salty and my head hurt.

"They didn't take me with them!" I blurted out when I entered the *estrado*.

"I know," said my mother. "I didn't give my consent."

"What are you talking about?" I screamed. "This trip was all arranged!"

My mother lifted her hand and sent it crashing against my cheek. I felt a burning sensation, as though someone had rubbed sandpaper over my face. A tear trickled from the corner of my eye down my jaw. "Not by me," she snapped. "It wasn't arranged by me."

After a pause she added, "You're to be married."

"Married?" I was the right age, nearly fourteen, and I had been menstruating for more than a year, but the news was so sudden, I just couldn't absorb it.

"But who's going to marry me?" I stammered. "I don't have a dowry."

"Don Alonso has provided the dowry."

"Don Alonso?"

"Yes," she said. "What are you? Some kind of an exotic bird that repeats everything it hears? Don Alonso is a kind man. He's grateful to you for serving Doña Teresa in the convent. He's going to provide a dowry."

Had she called him a kind man? My mother, who was forever harping on his *converso* blood? "And who . . ." I ventured.

"Oh," she said. "We haven't found the boy yet, but with a dowry, there won't be any problem. You're no beauty, that's for sure, but as long as there's money, who looks at a girl's face? Anyhow, there's no hurry. No hurry at all."

I stood there staring at her, my cheek smarting from the blow. "No!" I screamed. "You can hit me all you want! I won't get married! I'll run away to Castellanos de la Cañanda to be with Teresa!" I started to hiccough. Deep in my heart, I wanted to stop hurling threats because, to tell the truth, I yearned to be a bride. A bride with a new dress and flowers in my hair. For one day, a princess. Then I could go live somewhere with my husband, somewhere far away—or at least, somewhere other than the house I'd grown up in. But the underhanded way my mother had dismantled my trip and accepted Don Alonso's dowry money without even telling me—all that left me dizzy with rage. I was a child still and not yet in control of myself. My anger wouldn't let me stop shrieking.

"No!" I screamed over and over. "No! No! No!"

Again, my mother raised her hand, but I ducked before it smashed into my jaw.

Angélica del Sagrado Corazón, Carmelite
Toledo, 28 June 1576

CHAPTER 3

Passages

WHITE AS THE CREAMY WINTER SUN. WHITE AS THE FROSTED MEADOW. I remember the date: November 2, 1537. All Souls Day. The blinding snows of winter hadn't started yet, but the fields were already icy and brittle and the paths slippery with rime. The pasture crackled under our feet as my mother, my aunt, and I made our way to the Carmelite convent of the Encarnación. Four years had passed. I was seventeen years old. Teresa was twenty-two.

We found seats in the women's section of the chapel and sat down. *Caballeros* and *damas,* sumptuously attired, filled the pews. The men wore their hair short, cropped close to the head, according to the latest fashion. Their beards were abundant and perfumed. The ladies' tresses were twisted into braids and adorned with ribbons in intricate designs. You could see the fancy coifs under their sheer, lace *mantillas.* The guests chattered and twittered. Some cried. After all, it was a wedding. Tía Cati coughed softly, then swallowed, as if to prevent herself from coughing again. She'd been doing that all week. "Shhh!" my mother whispered. Don Alonso and his brother Pedro sat together off to the side looking severe and uncomfortable in their nearly identical black suits. I could see them at an angle, but they couldn't see me without turning around. They stared straight ahead. Neither spoke.

And then, there she was, pale as a lily, dressed in a bridal gown. A bride of Christ, clothed in shimmering white satin. White as the creamy winter sun. White as the frosted meadow.

Teresa moved forward between two rows of nuns chanting, "*Veni Creator Spiritus.*" She stopped before the altar. Slowly, deliberately, she lifted her chin and recited the psalm. Her voice was clear and bell-like, "*Quemadmodum desiderat cervus ad fonts acquaum ita desiderat anima mea ad te Deus.*" As the stag yearns for the fountains of water, so my soul longs for Thee, O God.

Don Alonso bit his lip almost imperceptibly and sighed, perhaps in resignation. I wondered what he was thinking. Was he remembering Teresa as a little girl, naughtily filching her mother's pearls? Or was he thinking about the day she and her brother Rodrigo snuck out of Ávila with hopes of being martyred by infidels? (They didn't get very far, but the prank had people chattering and laughing for months.) What images flashed through Don Alonso's mind as his daughter stood before him, dressed in bridal garments and reciting a psalm that told of her yearning for Christ? If Don Alonso really was a *judaizante*, Teresa's spiritual marriage to Jesus must be horribly painful for him. I knew I shouldn't be feeling sorry for a man who might be a traitor to the faith, but I couldn't help it. He had been so kind to me.

He looked around and suddenly locked eyes with another man. It was Don Javier, Teresa's handsome cousin. He sat crumpled in his pew, staring at the father of the woman he still clearly loved, his demeanor that of a prisoner condemned to the gallows. I'd never had the chance to examine him so intensely before, at least, not at close range. His eyes were like dark, moist pools of caramelized sugar. His jaw was tight above his ruff, and the tiny crevices by the corner of his eye deepened almost imperceptibly. The sight of Teresa in a bridal gown must have pierced him like a dagger. Don Javier released Don Alfonso's gaze, then knelt and buried his face in his hands. His body quivered. Was he crying? Was he remembering carefree *paseos* with his cousins—Teresa in rich brocade and a fashionable plumed hat, giggling and gossiping and flirting mercilessly? Was he praying for forgiveness for the sin— what sin?—that had almost prevented her from taking the veil? Or was he praying for her to suddenly change her mind and run toward him with her arms outstretched, smiling and breathless?

My throat tightened. Don Javier! She would never marry him, and I would never marry him, either. I'd abandoned long ago my girlhood dream of somehow winding up with the elegant prince of the Sánchez family. What pained me now was losing Teresa, my friend, my sister. She was going into a convent. What if I never saw her again? I fought back the tears.

The clothing ceremony consisted of two processions. First, the postulant advanced from the main altar of the exterior church to the convent gate, where she met her parents and friends. Don Alonso rose and forced himself to stand straight. He seemed much older than when I'd first met him. He went to Teresa and stood beside her without saying a word. With his two other daughters, Juana and María, and all of his sons except Fernando, who was fighting Indians in the New World, he accompanied her to the entrance door of the convent. There he turned her over to the Prioress, Doña Francisca del Águila, and the other nuns. Teresa then proceeded through the interior church, reserved for the sisters, to the window near the main altar, which connected the cloister with the public area. She was leaving the world and entering God's domain.

She returned to the altar with the prioress. Then, a brittle old priest, also dressed all in white, asked the ritual questions in a crackly voice: "What do you desire?"

"To be one with the Lord."

"Do you take these vows of your own free will?"

"Of my own free will I will sacrifice myself to the Lord."

Again I saw Don Alonso bite his lip, this time more deliberately. "I sacrifice myself to the Lord," she had said. But *he* was making the sacrifice. He was forfeiting the joy of seeing his favorite daughter married to a young man who would have been another son for him. He was forfeiting the grandchildren she would have born. His jaw was taut, his eyes glazed. He looked uncomprehending and horrified, as though he were witnessing his own daughter's crucifixion.

After the conclusion of the questioning, the prioress handed Teresa the black habit of the Carmelite order of the mitigated rule. Teresa stepped away from the altar and, with two nuns, entered into the interior of the convent. A moment later, she emerged wearing the habit.

"Her father gave the swansdown for that garment," whispered my mother. "It's as soft as velvet." She paused. "Of course, that's to be expected of a man like Don Alonso."

My aunt coughed again, and my mother squinted at her, annoyed.

The prioress handed Teresa a girdle, a sign of chastity. Would Teresa be chaste forevermore? I had no doubt of it. Had she had a chaste relationship with Javier? Who could be sure? She said she had sinned, and her sin involved Javier. What had they done? I longed to know. I looked around to see how Javier was holding up, but he wasn't there. When had he left? I hadn't seen him exit. Why had he vanished? Was he jealous of God?

The old priest began his supplications. "May the Lord bless His servant and keep her holy. May the Lord keep her eyes turned toward the Cross."

Now it was time for the tonsure. Teresa's beautiful dark hair lay on her back like a luxurious, silk curtain. The prioress stepped forward, knife in hand, and took a lock between her fingers. I winced as she raised the blade and drew it mercilessly over the tresses. How many heads had turned to admire that exquisite mane? How many men had lost their hearts to those ringlets? One by one, the other nuns followed the prioress's lead, each cutting a lock. Hair fell to the ground like precious remnants. The floor of the *estrado* after my aunt had cut a piece of expensive cloth came to mind.

"Bless this servant who discards her hair out of love for Thee, Oh Lord. Bless her sacrifice," intoned the priest.

When at last they were done, Teresa stood looking like a newborn sparrow, the downy feathers on its crown sticking out in all directions.

Now the prioress placed a white veil on her head, fastening it with a prayer that ended with the words "modesty, sobriety, and continence." The veil symbolized her widowhood. She was a bride of the crucified Christ. The clothing ceremony was complete, and we got up to leave. A group of wellwishers gathered around Don Alonso.

"*Felicitaciones,*" they said. "Congratulations."

Poor Don Alonso. To be honest, I didn't blame him for not wanting Teresa to take the veil. He couldn't have forgotten how he'd been forced to parade around Toledo in a *sambenito* as a child. God forgive me for writing this, but I can understand how someone like Don Alonso wouldn't have much use for the Church. Still, I think the real reason he opposed Teresa's entering the convent was that he loved her so much. He wanted her near. He didn't want to lose her.

"*¡Enhorabuena!*" people kept saying to Don Alonso. "*¡Felicitaciones!*" He accepted their congratulations graciously, but looked away when they said things like, "How happy you must be! How proud you must feel!"

"I'm sorry, really sorry," I felt like saying to him. "I know how hard this must be for you." But, of course, I said nothing of the sort. I didn't even approach him. I kept my distance. After all, I was a seamstress. I was out of place at this event, where *converso* women and their rich husbands put both their faith and their wealth on display.

I imagined Don Alonso saying to himself, hoping against hope, "Maybe she won't go through with it. There's still time for her to change her mind." The profession—the ceremony in which a nun actually takes her vows—wouldn't be for one more day.

By the time we left the convent, the morning chill had lifted and the fields were thawed. It was a long walk from Encarnación to town. My aunt rode a gentle little mule named Caramelo, while my mother and I trudged along beside her.

"Come, Inés," Tía Cati said after a while. "You look tired. Change places with me." Then my mother climbed on Caramelo and my aunt and I walked. I was young and strong. I didn't need to ride. But every once in a while my aunt would cough—an explosion from deep in her chest—and I said to myself, "Tía Cati is the one who's tired. She should ride and my mother should walk."

As I plodded along, I relived the ceremony in my mind. "Modesty, sobriety, and continence." I was glad it wasn't I who was going into the convent. I would much rather marry Basilio, the strong, young apprentice cartwright my aunt had picked out for me. My mother and Tía Cati hadn't been in a rush to find a match. A girl with a dowry can afford to be a little choosy. Not too choosy, of course. Young men were at a premium, since so many had gone to the wars or the colonies. There was a lot of competition. Still, I had an advantage. I not only had a plump marriage endowment, I had skills. If we should ever be in need, I could take in sewing.

We couldn't marry right away, because Basilio's mother had died the year before, and we had to respect the requisite mourning period. "There's no rush," Tía Cati kept saying. "You're young. You have a dowry. There's time." "Money's a strong tether," my mother chimed in. "If the bride has money, the groom won't run off." But you never know what fate will bring.

I had seen Basilio at church and at the festival of San Juan, when everyone is out in the street, dancing and carrying pussy willows. I had seen him at the Corpus Christi celebration, when the nobles and guilds present colorful pageants and real actors perform religious plays in the town square, and on Fat Tuesday, when beggars pretend to be kings and men dress up as women. Of course I'd never spoken with him. We didn't have a cart, so I had no reason to address either the cartwright Anselmo or his son. Still, I found subtle ways to flirt. When he stood at the back of the church with his cousins and friends, I'd turn to flash him a smile. And if I caught sight of him in the street as I walked next to my aunt, my eyes down and my face covered with a shawl, I might giggle softly just to let him know I was there.

Nobody asked me if I liked him or if I had my eye on someone else, but it didn't matter. I didn't know many young men, so to me one was pretty much the same as another. This one was nice to look at and seemed civil enough, so what was there to object to? As I had begun to fill out, my mother took care to keep me indoors. By then I was an excellent seamstress with my own commissions. There was little need for me to step outside, except to go to Mass or, occasionally, to deliver orders. I usually went to church at the crack of dawn, veiled and accompanied by my mother or Tía Cati, so I had little chance to flirt. But once in a while, once in a while . . .

"Modesty," my mother repeated over and over. "Modesty and decorum. Otherwise, no one will want you."

I knew my mother's friends were not nearly so strict with their daughters, but I was different. I was worth something. I had a nice dowry. It was important to keep such valuable merchandise as I was unsoiled. I dreamt of my mother dreaming of me in the cartwright's house, plump and comfortable, rocking an infant while she fed a toddler. The content grandmother living with her daughter and helping care for the children. She would be the queen of the henhouse, surrounded by chicks. She wouldn't have to sew. Finally, she would be able to rest her weary eyes. She would have a comfortable old age because Basilio and I would take of her. She'd be proud of me. She'd never hit me. I understood Teresa's fear of marriage and childbearing, but I preferred to take my chances at having babies to being shut up in a convent the rest of my life.

We returned to Encarnación the following day for Teresa's profession. November 3. A day like any other, and yet, like no other. Why? Not only because that was the day Teresa de Ahumada became a nun, but also because . . . Well, like I said, you never know what fate has in store for you. In the first blush of morning, who knows what dusk will bring?

Again the sisters intoned "*Veni Creator Spiritus.*" Teresa, dressed in her Carmelite habit, glided toward them. In her hand she carried a scapular, a veil, a girdle, and a piece of paper with the *Pater Noster,* symbol of a life of prayer. At a signal from the prioress, she prostrated herself in front of the open grille. The prioress covered her with a black veil. Stretched out with her forehead touching the floor, she reminded me of a large enshrouded swan. I trembled.

The old priest, his hands darting about like small, autonomous animals, stepped forward and said, "Arise, daughter, and light your lamp. Your Spouse is coming. Prepare to meet Him."

The nuns removed the black shroud, and Teresa got up gracefully. "Here I come to You, my sweetest Lord," she responded.

This ritual was repeated three times. Then Mother Francisca stood in front of Teresa and asked the first question of the *professio*: "What do you desire?"

"I desire God's mercy and the company of my sisters in perpetual enclosure," answered Teresa. Her voice did not falter. For reasons I can't grasp even now, I began to sob uncontrollably. Was it because I thought I'd never see her again? Was it the sheer power of the ritual? I knew that the words "perpetual enclosure" were only symbolic. Encarnación nuns were not only allowed to receive visitors, they could leave the convent, and many of them visited their families regularly. Still, I had the terrible feeling that I was losing Teresa forever.

After she'd finished asking the questions, Madre Francisca read the Constitutions of the Order. Then Teresa, in a clear, firm voice, pronounced her holy vows of chastity, poverty, and obedience. Following each, the sisters responded, "Amen." Teresa's eyes were radiant, her face flushed. What did she feel? Excitement? Fear? Both? Long afterward, she told me that her profession had been the most painful moment of her life, even more painful than when her mother died. "Why, Teresa?" I asked her. "Why?" But she only looked out into nothingness and smiled.

Now the sisters led her behind the open grille. As though in a trance, she approached the altar of the interior church, embraced it, and declared, "I offer and sacrifice myself entirely as a living host."

Mother Francisca, a bit tired-looking, fastened a black veil on her head. "As a sign of your contempt for the world," she said. It was done.

After a wedding there's always a party, and no matter how miserable Don Alonso felt, he was determined Teresa would have a spectacular wedding feast. How he must have wished it were a real wedding feast for a real wedding! He was a somber man, but he knew how to host a bash. He'd already made generous gifts to the convent—a monetary donation and a fine linen coif for each sister. Now he offered a great collation and dinner to which even the family servants were invited, although, of course, they didn't eat with the nobility. Paid musicians played the flute and the *vihuela*, and Teresa played the tambourine. Everyone danced. Teresa, recovered from the strain of the ceremony, smiled and chatted and giggled. Guests crowded around her. They wished her well and kissed her cheeks. She had charmed even the sourest of the old nuns.

I looked around for Don Javier. I didn't see him at first. He wasn't laughing and gossiping among Teresa's cousins, and he wasn't dancing. Finally, I spotted him leaning against the convent wall, his expression dark and brooding. Instead of his usual black suit and white ruff, he was wearing a deep blood-red velvet ensemble, with cording of the same shade along the vest. His white hat was wide and graceful, with a plume of yellow—yellow, the color of death. I thought it was strange attire for a nun's profession. I'd never been to such a celebration before, of course, but the other men were all wearing black. Don Javier squinted at the festivities out of sullen eyes, then lifted his chin with an air of defiance. He wasn't even going to pretend to be enjoying himself.

Suddenly, Teresa called across the patio, "Don Javier! I'm so happy to see you!" At the tinkle of her voice, a hush settled over the crowd. She strode toward him. Her carriage was self-assured, regal. Every eye was on the young man and woman who could have been a couple.

He grimaced and turned toward her. "Doña Teresa, please accept my congratulations," he whispered, struggling to steady his voice. "I . . . I wish you the greatest happiness."

"Thank you, Javier," she said softly.

They peered into each other's eyes. What if he kisses her, I thought. What if he takes her in his arms in front of all these people? A terrible tension filled the courtyard, and I felt suddenly as though I were dying. But their gazes came unglued in an instant. Javier bowed deeply, sweeping his hat across his chest with a great flourish. His jaw tightened; his features hardened. Teresa bowed her head and went back to her friends.

Servants brought in stews of kid and lamb cooked over a slow fire with onions, garlic, leeks, carrots, and spices. There was also an *olla podrida,* a succulent and spicy pork dish, as well as *comida blanca,* a poultry dish with a sauce of milk, sugar, and rice flour—a favorite of the king himself, according to what the gentlemen were saying. People ate heartily, dipping bread into gravy. The men drank wine and the women, iced juices or *aloja,* a beverage made from water, honey, and spices. Don Javier wasn't eating. In fact, he wasn't there. He had disappeared.

We left before the festivities were over. We could hardly be considered friends of the family, and to stay too long would have been unseemly. I didn't approach Teresa to kiss her and tell her how much I would miss her. I didn't even say good-bye. She was surrounded by people of her own class. Don Alonso had welcomed us graciously, but we knew we were out of place.

That evening before dusk a messenger came from Anselmo. The cartwright and his son were anxious to pay a visit, the boy said.

"It's time to formalize this relationship," said Tía Cati. Although Anselmo and my mother had come to a tentative agreement, the cartwright wanted Basilio and me to have a chance to meet each other.

My mother looked confused. "I don't think it's a good idea," she said finally.

"Why not?" said Tía Cati. "Pancracia's not such a homely girl, and she's got a dowry. He'll like her well enough."

"I don't know," answered my mother. "I don't think this bodes well for us."

"She's a good seamstress; he'll never have to go without a decent set of clothes. If he's got any sense in his head, he'll realize this is a good match. There's no reason why anything should go amiss."

The messenger, a child of eleven or twelve, stood there looking bored.

"I have a bad feeling about it," said my mother. "I thought the thing was settled."

"It's settled," said Tía Cati. "This is just a formality."

Nobody asked me what I thought, but, for the record, I had no objection to talking to Basilio. I thought it was considerate of Anselmo to want us to meet each other.

"We should just finalize this and bring in the priest. What does she have to meet him now for?" growled my mother. "She'll have plenty of time to get to know him after they're married."

"They should at least have the chance to talk. What if they don't like each other?"

"What of it? Plenty of married couples don't like each other."

"Tell them to come over tomorrow," my aunt said to the messenger boy.

"They'd like to come over this evening."

My aunt and mother argued about whether or not such a visit was appropriate, especially on such short notice. After all, we had been to a profession that morning. We were exhausted. On the other hand, we were still wearing our best clothes, so it was a good time to receive guests. Finally, Tía Cati instructed the messenger to tell them to come.

Basilio was a tall, dark-complected boy with sleepy eyes and a firm chin. I liked his strong arms and long fingers, and I liked his deep auburn hair, which fell into a gentle wave over his eyebrow when he bowed his head. I especially liked the way he turned to look and grin at me when he caught sight of me at a festival. He wasn't the proud aristocrat I'd once dreamed of, but he would do very nicely. I was older now, and more practical. Better to sleep in a cartwright's cottage next to a boy like Basilio, I thought, than to sleep alone in a cold, naked convent cell.

They weren't long in coming. Basilio wore long, loose pants of some nondescript color between brown and moss green. Perhaps they had once been tan, but work, sweat, and countless washings had robbed their hue of its distinctness. His shirt was homespun, and over his shoulders he'd swung a course, flannel cape. He wore a wide-brimmed, droopy hat, which he kept on when he came into the house, as was the custom. Even though he and his father were simple folk, they were mannerly and soft-spoken.

We didn't have a formal drawing room, of course. Ours wasn't a house like Don Alonso's. We invited them into a little room that served as a parlor and eating area, in which we had three chairs, a rug I'd woven myself, and several bins where we stored remnants and sewing supplies. Tía Cati brought an extra lamp. Basilio remained standing, since there was nowhere for him to sit. For a few moments we just looked at one another, feeling awkward. No one seemed to have anything to say.

"Well," began Tía Cati, "my niece Pancracia is a very capable girl. She can sew and embroider as well as any lady. She knows how to cook, and, of course, she knows her prayers."

Basilio's cheeks turned pink.

"She'll have help in the house, of course," said Anselmo. "My sister's daughter lives with us. She's a rural girl, very strong and good-tempered. She's been keeping house for us since my wife died, and she'll lend Pancracia a hand, too."

"That will be fine," said my mother. "Especially after the babies start to arrive. A woman needs help caring for her babies." I could tell she liked the idea of having a servant to boss around when she went to live with us. Basilio's color deepened at the mention of babies.

"What do you say, child?" said Tía Cati. She took me by surprise. I hadn't expected to be asked to contribute to the conversation. I looked down at my hands, rough and angular.

"I can make you both a new set of clothes," I whispered. A shadow of annoyance passed over Basilio's face. Did he think I was implying his clothes weren't good enough? "If you want," I added shyly.

We didn't talk about money or about the supply of linens in my hope chest. The negotiations had begun in private between Anselmo and my aunt and mother, and they would continue in private. Anselmo opened his mouth to say something, and then thought better of it. My aunt started to cough a deep, wet, angry cough. What was wrong with her? I wondered. This had been going on for too long. Why didn't she go to the priest? He could tell her the right prayers to say to get rid of it. Or there was a blind man who sometimes begged in front of the cathedral. He had prayers and amulets for everything.

"We went to a profession at Encarnación Convent," I said finally. "Teresa de Ahumada took her vows."

"Ah, the beautiful little princess," said Anselmo. "I'm sure it was sad for her father."

"Yes," I said. "I guess . . ."

"He doesn't like priests."

"No . . . I don't know."

"And neither do I. Money-grubbing leaches. Always after the girls. I'm glad I have sons."

I bit my lip. I hoped my mother wasn't going to say anything about Don Alonso being a *converso*. "I used to be Teresa's maid." I murmured in order to cut her off.

"You? I knew you knew the Cepeda Ahumadas, but . . ."

"Yes, at Nuestra Señora de la Gracia. I learned to read there." I turned to Basilio. "I can read you stories. I have a book about knights and ladies full of romantic tales. Teresa gave it to me. I can read to you every night by the fire."

Basilio's eyes clouded. I was perplexed. He seemed angry, but I didn't understand why. "I can cook, I can sew, I can spin, and I can read!" I said hopefully.

Basilio leaned over and said something to his father. Then he excused himself clumsily and disappeared into the night.

We chatted a while longer, but the conversation had turned sour. My mother was glancing around frantically, as though she were looking for something she had misplaced. "Pancracia, leave the room," she commanded suddenly.

"What's going on?" I asked.

I knew I was out of line. It wasn't my place to question her. She stood up and stared at me, grimacing. She could look very imposing when she raised her chin and set her jaw. I saw her hand twitch, and I thought she was going to strike me right there in front of Anselmo. But before she could, the cartwright said matter-of-factly, "It's clear we can't go ahead with this marriage."

My mother spun around. "Why not? We have plenty of money."

Anselmo looked at her as though she were a stupid, disobedient child.

"What young artisan's son wants to marry a seamstress who knows how to read? Basilio doesn't, and I don't blame him." He spoke very slowly, as though he were addressing morons.

"What?" I gasped.

"A girl of humble lineage who knows how to read is a problem. People should remember who they are. They shouldn't go around putting on airs. Especially a woman."

"But we have . . ."

"Yes, Inés, I know. You have money. A fixed sum of money that Don Alonso gave you for a dowry. But you're poor, Inés. You don't even have a place of your own to drop dead in. If it weren't for your sister . . ." Anselmo's face was the color of communion wine. "And this girl and her dirty books . . ."

"Dirty books!"

"Those books about *caballeros* and their women humping by the river. I know what's in those books you like so much, *Doña* Pancracia. I don't always trust the priests, but I'm a good Christian. I respect my obligations. I go to church. And I hear what the preachers say about those romances. That they're immoral and dangerous for women. That they lead women into sinfulness, which isn't hard, because women are the Devil's spawn to begin with. Women read those books and get ideas. The next thing you know, they're opening their legs for the butcher, the farrier, and the brewer too. That's what those books do to women! They make them into whores!"

"But . . ." spluttered my mother. "But we have money!"

"Other people have money too, Inés," growled Anselmo. His jaw was quivering with rage. "A smart father finds a way to put together a dowry. Men borrow money. Or else they send their sons to work for free for their future father-in-law. Good husbands are scarce, Inés. All the young men have gone to Peru. Today a fit young man doesn't have to settle for a book-reading whore for a wife!"

My mother stood there, stunned.

"What you have isn't so attractive, Inés," said Anselmo, lowering his voice a notch or two. "An ugly daughter and a couple of coins." He turned to leave.

"I have . . ." She sounded as though she were choking.

"You have no land and no sons to come and help me in my workshop. We can do better."

I didn't know what to think. I knew I was homely and poor, but I thought I had something to offer. I had thought reading was the prize that would ensure my future. I was confused.

When he had gone, my mother stood immobile, speechless, crazed. Then suddenly she pivoted on her heals and looked at me with a hatred that was positively—how can I say it?—diabolical. Her eyes were red, red like fire, and—I'm ashamed to write this—Satanic. It was as though she were possessed by the Demon himself. He can do that, of course. He can seize people's souls, and I think at that moment he seized my mother's. She approached me—I think her mouth was actually foaming—and drawing her hand back as if to throw a very heavy horseshoe, she smacked me so hard the inside of my cheek knocked against a tooth and instantly spurted blood. I could taste it in my mouth, but I was paralyzed. I couldn't react.

"You had to go and tell him you knew how to read!" shrieked my mother. "You had to pass yourself off as Queen Isabella's pet horse. You idiot! You're as dense as mule turd!"

"I didn't . . ." My jaw throbbed horribly. I was suffocating. I understood vaguely that I had just ruined my own chances for marriage and my mother's chances for a comfortable old age, but I just couldn't put all the pieces together.

That night I cried myself to sleep. "I am stupid," I kept telling myself. "I'm really stupid. I'm as dense as mule turd."

The next morning, before my mother and Tía Cati were awake, I snuck out of the house and made the trek to Encarnación. It wasn't that I wanted to become a nun. I didn't even expect to stay. All I wanted was to talk to Teresa, to tell her what had happened. She was the closest thing I had to a sister. Who else could I talk to? Maybe she would help me figure out what to do. I wanted to hear her soothing voice. I wanted to cry on her shoulder and feel her stroke my hair.

But on the way I began to have second thoughts. What if she didn't want to see me? I remembered that at Santa María de la Gracia there were strict rules stipulating who could visit and when. I knew that Encarnación had a more liberal visitors' policy, but still I wondered, "What if they don't let me in? What if they turn me away?"

I knocked at the door. The extern—the nun who welcomed outsiders—

greeted me as if my visit were the most natural thing in the world. She sat me in the parlor and sent for Teresa.

It was a shock for me to see her in Carmelite garb. Of course, I had just been at her clothing and profession, but somehow it hadn't really sunk in that she'd be wearing a habit forever and ever. The same drab dress every day. What would happen to her lovely ball gowns and the fine jewels her mother had left her? "Are you happy?" were the first words out of my mouth.

"Very happy!" Her eyes were gleaming—out of joy I thought at the time.

I told her what had happened with Basilio, and she burst out laughing.

"How can you laugh, Teresa? My life is ruined, and it's my own fault?" I started to sob.

She put her arm around my shoulders. "No, silly, your life isn't ruined. Your mother will find another boy for you, someone who isn't so small-minded."

"I'll wind up a spinster. I'll have to go into a convent. I mean, it's fine for you, Teresa. You want to be a nun. But I haven't heard God's call. I just want to get married and have a family like a regular woman."

"Listen," she said. "Once a farmer had a mule . . ."

"Who cares? What does that have to do with anything? It's your fault, Teresa. If you hadn't told Sister María Briseño to teach me how to read, my mother and aunt would be sitting in the *estrado* stitching my wedding dress right now."

"Just listen, Pancracia. A farmer had a mule that he didn't think was good for much. One day the mule fell into a well and started braying. The farmer heard it and went to see what the matter was. Poor thing, it was stuck in the bottom of the well squealing "Eee-aw, eee-aw." Well, the farmer felt sorry for it, but he didn't know what to do. Finally, he decided to put it out of its misery by burying it alive. He started shoveling dirt into the well."

"That was stupid. He's ruining his own well."

"The mule started to howl and wail. Everything was ruined, and all because he had made one wrong move. But then, all of a sudden, it occurred to him that every time a shovel of dirt fell on him, he should shake it off and step on top of it. The farmer went to get his three sons, and they shoveled as fast as they could. Every time a wad of dirt hit the mule, the animal shook it off and stepped on top of it. It went on like that all day. Shake it off, step up. Shake it off, step up. Even when the falling pebbles stung his flesh, the mule shook them off and stepped up. Little by little, he worked his way to the top of the hole and stepped out onto the grass."

Now I was laughing.

"You see, when muck falls on you, sometimes you just have to shake it off. Then you can move up. But you're right about the farmer. He ruined his own well. Just like Basilio. He threw dirt at you, but he's the loser. He missed the opportunity to marry a fine-looking girl who's smart and skillful to boot."

"I'm not fine-looking. I'm scrawny and red-faced, with dull, straw-like hair. "

"You're perfectly lovely, Pancracia. And God has something even better than Basilio planned for you." I felt better. "Listen," she said. "Why don't you stay here with me a while?"

"I don't want to be a nun."

"Not as a nun. As a boarder."

"I don't have the money. All I have is my dowry, and I have to keep it in case my mother finds another boy for me."

"But you can sew, Pancracia. Mother Francisca sometimes takes in girls with special talents even if they can't pay. I'll talk to her."

"I don't know . . ."

But Teresa always gets her way, and so before I knew it, it was arranged. I began to think that staying at the convent a while really was the best solution. I didn't want to go back home and face my mother's wrath. This would give me some time to think things over, and it would give her time to calm down. "So be it," I said to myself. *"Así sea."*

The prioress sent a message to my mother that I would stay in the convent until she could negotiate another marriage for me. In payment, I would sew habits and embroider altarpieces.

After three months, I still hadn't heard a word from home. I didn't expect my mother or Tía Cati to visit me. They had work to do and besides, it was a long trek to Encarnación. But they might have sent a boy to say your mother wishes you happiness, or your mother wishes you well, or even your mother is still mad as hell at you. It's true they'd never sent a message to Nuestra Señora de la Gracia when I was there, but still, I kept hoping.

And then, someone did come. But what he said was not what I expected. What he said was, "You must come quickly. Your mother is dead."

"Dead?" I felt myself reel. "Dead? My mother? My *mother*?"

Thoughts of home collided in my head. My mother sitting on her cushion in the *estrado*. My mother stitching the hem of a gown. Gossiping with the neighbors. Folding freshly ironed linens. Lifting her hand. Lifting her hand . . . healthy. Not ill. My mother was never ill. Tía Cati was the one who was ailing, not my mother. Tía Cati was the one who was always coughing.

"There's some mistake," I said to the boy. I heard my voice quivering, and somehow, I knew there was no mistake. It was true. My mother was dead. I felt queasy.

I started to sob. Noisy, heaving groans seemed to come from some faraway place. Invisible hands guided me to a banquette by the window and eased me down. I heard liquid pouring from a jug and then felt a cool ceramic cup against my lips. "Teresa," I whispered.

"The Blessed Virgin will be your mother now. Pray to her."

"Oh God, oh God, oh God," I wailed.

"Dear Lord, take Señora Inés to Your bosom and keep her in Your loving embrace forever." I must have whispered "amen," but I can't be sure. Things grew murky. Icons, candlesticks, chairs, and cabinets seemed to melt into the shadows. I felt myself sink down onto the bench. I remember resting my head on a welcoming lap, while soft hands stroked my forehead. After that, everything went dark.

Angélica del Sagrado Corazón, Carmelite
Toledo, 30 June 1576

CHAPTER 4

Encarnación

THE TRUTH IS, I NEVER LOVED MY MOTHER. I KNOW I SHOULD HAVE LOVED her, but she was such a sour, angry woman. Was it my fault my father died young and left us without a penny, or that I was plain and therefore unlovable? Was it my fault I was smart enough to learn to read? Tía Cati was a kinder, more *motherly* woman, and she had a sense of humor. So I have to admit it: I loved Tía Cati, but I never loved my mother.

Why, then, was I so devastated when she died? When I saw her stretched out in our *estrado*, a white coif on her head and a rose-petal rosary in her fingers, I nearly collapsed. I felt wounded, as though all the oozing gashes in Jesus's body were my own. She had belittled me. She had thwacked me on the ear. But she was my mother, and the only images that came to mind at that moment were happy ones: the three of us—Mother, Tía Cati, and I—in the *estrado,* laughing and sewing and telling stories. Now the *estrado* was silent.

According to my aunt, my mother had just keeled over and died. "I don't know what happened," said Tía Cati. "A moan, a groan, and she collapsed."

I looked at her.

"Well," she said, "you know how your mother was. She wasn't shy about complaining. But the only thing she said was that her chest was bothering her a bit. She thought it was indigestion and asked me to prepare her an infusion of peppermint water."

The funeral was simple. Tía Cati's daughters, Catalina and Irene, came from Madrid with their husbands and children. The women from the *estrado* and their families attended. Teresa was there. Don Alonso didn't come, but he supplied refreshments—almond cakes and fruit juices. Later, we ate a meal prepared by Tía Cati's sewing friends. I thought my cousins would stay awhile, but as soon as it was over, they left for Madrid.

God forgive me, but the only thing I could think of was what would become of *me*? I shouldn't have been thinking of myself at a time like that, but I was young and self-centered. I hadn't lived for decades in a convent, where you have to put everyone else before yourself. I tossed different ideas around in my mind. Should I return to Encarnación? Should I stay with Tía Cati? She was alone now, and if I got married, perhaps she would allow me to stay in the house with my husband. It was a nice house, much nicer than Anselmo the cartwright's. If she arranged a marriage to another boy from the same sort of family, perhaps he would just as soon live with my aunt as with his parents. And if we were occupying the house, I might stand to inherit it, and then I could stay there forever. I know these were sinful thoughts. God forgive me.

As it turned out, I didn't need to worry. Within three months of my mother's death, Tía Cati took to bed with a terrible cough. I brought in a *curandera,* a healer, to prescribe a potion and a barber to bleed her, but nothing worked. One night she was overcome by a fit of wheezing. She hacked and rasped, as though her chest were full of demons she was struggling to expel. Then, all of a sudden, she was quiet. She was quiet because she was dead.

Both my mother and my aunt, dead within three months of each other. God have mercy.

Well, I thought, I can just stay here. I have work. I have skills. I can make enough money to live. Besides, I have my dowry. I'll ask Don Alonso to negotiate a marriage for me. After all, he'd given me the dowry. Why couldn't he find the husband as well?

But, as I always say, you never know when you get up in the morning what the dusk will bring. As it turned out, Catalina and Irene lost no time in informing me that their mother's house was not mine to keep. No sooner did they have the *alguacil* serve notice on me to vacate than their husbands sued each other for possession of the property. They contested everything, not only the house but also the furniture, the rugs, the loom, the pots and pans, even the pins and thimbles. Then, to complicate things further, the widows of Celso and Felipe made claims on Tía Cati's belongings on behalf of her male *criollo* grandchildren, now sailing back from Peru with their mothers on the swiftest caravels available. Who would wind up with the house? One thing was clear: it wouldn't be me. I needed a place to live, so I packed my belongings and trekked back to Encarnación. The only thing I took from Tía Cati's was the discolored green cushion I'd used since childhood to sit by the brazier and sew and my dowry money.

They let me in right away, but Teresa didn't come to the vestibule to greet me, even though I asked for her quite a few times. I didn't know what to do. I'd spent three months at Encarnación and knew several of the nuns, but I'd been allowed in as a boarder only because Teresa claimed me as a friend. Now, standing there in my faded grey dress, my head covered with a black coif like a widow's, I felt like a leftover scrap of cloth. Nuns scurried by, some holding hands and chattering, but they looked right through me. Had I become invisible?

I asked to speak with Madre Francisca, and an elderly nun led me through a long corridor, up some stairs, and into a kind of waiting room. Madre Francisca's amanuensis, a woman with enormous hands and thin, tight lips, told me to wait and instantly forgot about me. I hadn't seen this sister before. She was one of the convent's many recorders—chroniclers, bookkeepers, registrars, and the like—a no-nonsense type for whom a vow of silence wasn't necessary. She was copying figures into a large book, perhaps a ledger.

"Excuse me, Sister," I said after a while. "Do you know Teresa de Ahumada?"

"Who is Teresa de Ahumada?" She put down the magnifying glass she was using to read the numbers and looked at me as though I had suddenly materialized out of nowhere. She blinked a few times, as if wondering how I could possibly have gotten into the room.

"She's a sister in this convent."

"Oh," she said, going back to her work. Then, after a pause, she added. "With two hundred women living at Encarnación, I can't know everyone." She picked up another book—a hefty tome bound in cream-colored kid—and leafed through it. It appeared to be a registry of all the convent's inhabitants since its founding. "She's not here," she said finally. "What I mean is, yes, she's a sister in this convent, but she's not here now. We sent her home a few days ago."

Mischievous Teresa, I thought. What had she done? Fart in chapel or shoot peas at the prioress from the balcony. "Why?" I asked. "What did she do?"

"She didn't do anything. She had a bad fever, so we sent her home to her father."

"She's ill?" I said stupidly. I remembered that overheated look Teresa often had. I'd thought it was passion, excitement, exhilaration, but no, it was a run-of-the-mill fever. She wasn't aflame with the love of God. She just had an ongoing cold.

At last, Madre Francisca called me in. I explained my situation—my mother's death, my aunt's death, the litigation concerning the house.

"And you want to continue boarding here until a marriage can be arranged?"

Yes, I thought. That's what I want. Which is why I couldn't believe my own ears when I heard myself say, "No, Mother, I want to profess."

Mother Francisca raised her eyebrows. "Wait a while," she said. "Don't rush into anything. You should never make a decision while you're upset."

"I'm not upset," I said, biting my lip.

"Well, you should never make a decision after something . . . how shall I say it? . . . after something distressing happens. It's better to wait until you can think more clearly."

"I have nowhere to go."

"You can stay here, of course. Teresa will be back in a few days. Her father says she's feeling better. Wait awhile. Talk it over with her. Then decide."

Panic gripped me. Basilio's rejection had demolished my confidence. What if nobody wanted to marry me? And if I did marry some cobbler or chandler, would he forbid me to read? Would I have to go through life pretending not to know what I'd struggled so painstakingly to learn? I imagined myself wrinkled and haggard, surrounded by squalling children, my mind blank as fresh parchment.

"I wouldn't be a charity case. I wouldn't have to sew to earn my keep. I have a dowry."

"Oh?"

"Yes. Don Alonso de Cepeda gave me a marriage dowry. I could use it for the convent."

Doña Francisca sighed and concentrated hard, as though she were doing sums in her head. "All the same," she said finally, "wait awhile. Taking the habit is a lifelong commitment. It means you want to devote your entire life to God. You have to be sure."

"Yes, Mother," I said. But my mind was made up. If they wouldn't take me in this convent, I'd find another. Basilio had snubbed me. I wouldn't give some other bumpkin the chance to do the same.

Teresa returned in a day or two. She looked pale, but her eyes no longer blazed with fever. I told her I had decided to take vows.

"Do you think they'll accept me here?" I asked breathlessly.

"Are you thinking of becoming . . ." She paused, as if looking for the most delicate way to say something difficult. "The thing is, Pancracia, Mother Francisca is taking in very few lay sisters. The convent is so full that we just can't afford to . . ."

"I understand. I have a dowry."

I didn't want to enter as a tertiary, a white-veiled nun. The black-veiled nuns—the dowered sisters—looked down on white-veiled nuns, the charity cases. Some of these were kitchen nuns who shelled peas and washed pots. Some were laborer nuns who did carpentry or took care of the chickens or pigs. Then, there were the women who were poor but had special talents: the master seamstresses who sewed habits and chasubles or designed gowns for the plaster saints in the sanctuary; talented singers or composers who enriched the house's musical activity; artists who produced paintings for the chapel. The other sisters held them in contempt. I'd experienced the hierarchy at Nuestra Señora de la Gracia, and I didn't want to be a second-class nun.

"I have the dowry Don Alonso gave me," I said again. The look of surprise on Teresa's face made it obvious she didn't know her father had supplied my marriage offering.

"Are you sure you want to do this, Pancracia?" she said finally. "If you have money, you could get yourself a husband easily enough. Just because it didn't work out with Basilio . . ."

"I don't want to go through that again. And I don't want to pretend to be stupid and ignorant so some pigherd can lord it over me."

She looked at me a long time. Then a smile blossomed on her lips. She leaned over and kissed me on the cheek. "Good girl," she whispered.

We embraced. Now we were truly going to be sisters. Real sisters, at last.

Well, for once everything turned out right. Mother Francisca accepted me as a novice almost right away, and I took my vows on a cold, autumn morning when the leaves had almost all fallen, blanketing the convent garden with splotches of red, orange, brown, and gold. They crackled under my feet as I processed into the chapel toward the altar. The only person to come see me was Don Alonso, looking less stiff and grim than during Teresa's profession. I asked to take a new name, and so, on that morning, Pancracia Soto died and Sister Angélica was born.

At Encarnación I felt for the first time that I belonged somewhere. I'd grown up in my aunt's house, and, although Tía Cati made us welcome, my mother always insisted we were just poor relatives, that we had a roof over our heads thanks only to the grace of God and the benevolence of her sister.

At Nuestra Señora de la Gracia, I had lived in Teresa's room and only enjoyed the benefits of the place thanks to her. Now I had my own cell in a convent that was really a home. I had sisters and a Mother Superior. I had entered with a dowry—a gift from Don Alonso, it was true, but a gift belongs to the recipient. With that money, I had paid my own way, and now I was a full-fledged Carmelite, a black-veiled nun, just like Teresa.

Now, after all these years, I ask myself why I really took the habit. Certainly, the immediate reason was Basilio's rejection. It stung terribly. But why else? Because I was lonely? Because I was frightened? Because I wanted to be near Teresa? Of one thing I'm sure: It wasn't out of the desire to serve Jesus. To be honest, serving Jesus never entered my mind. That came later.

I loved the convent from the very beginning, mostly because it gave me the chance to study. As a novice, I spent long hours pouring over books that told about the history of our order. I wasn't allowed to read books of chivalry like *Amadís de Gaula*. (I had hidden away Teresa's copy, which she had given me before her profession.) But these stories were even better. They were full of adventures. There were devout monks and hermits, to be sure, but also bloody battles, daring heroes, and wicked women. Take, for example, the prophet Elijah, considered the founder of the Carmelite order even though he lived before the coming of Our Savior. Elijah saved God's people from the wicked Jezebel, conquering the idolaters at Mount Carmel in a ferocious battle just like the ones in *Amadís*. Later, in the 1200s, lay hermits formed a community on one of the slopes of Mount Carmel and built an oratory to the Virgin on the very spot where Elijah had fought. That was the beginning of the order.

Encarnación wasn't the strictest convent in the world, but it wasn't the laxest. We celebrated the Divine Office with great magnificence and solemnity. We sang psalms at each of the Divine Hours and the Te Deum at Matins on feast days. I have to admit I enjoyed it for all the wrong reasons. I loved the harmonies, the voices raised in exaltation, not because they made me feel one with God, but simply because they were beautiful. But who knows, maybe that was God's way of calling me to Him. He made me love music. And because I loved music, I sang. And because I sang, I prayed. And praying, I felt His presence.

The convent parlor was our window to the world. Originally, it was supposed to be just for family members, but by the time I got to Encarnación, priests, gentlemen, musicians, even courtesans gathered there to socialize and do business. The sisters stayed behind the grille observing, gossiping with visitors, passing notes to friends and admirers. Even though we were stuck behind closed doors most of the time, we knew what was going on because the salon was an endless source of information. Teresa had chosen Encarnación because one of her favorite cousins, Juana Isabel Suárez, had already professed there. Juana Isabel had convinced her that Encarnación, with its relaxed rules and active social life, offered a more pleasant environment than the stricter Augustinian house where she had been before. It was, I thought, a good choice.

One day a *zahorí* wandered into the parlor and demanded permission to search the convent grounds. He was a bizarre-looking fellow dressed in gypsy garb, with a brightly embroidered shirt, voluminous red trousers fastened at the ankle, a black sash around his waist, a bandanna on his head, and count-less chains and baubles dangling from his neck. When he moved, his trinkets tinkled like fairies laughing. All the rich ladies who had come to visit gath-ered around him, and they tittered as he eyed them suggestively. He was extraordinarily handsome, with intense black eyes and a robust mustache. *Zahorís* are able to locate underground springs, sometimes with a divining rod, sometimes with a pendulum. Some can find hidden treasure or even tell where the corpse of a murder victim is buried. A few can see into the future.

Mother Francisca tried to shoo the man out, but he kept insisting that a great treasure was buried somewhere on the convent grounds.

"I must walk in your gardens," he told her. "I must walk until I feel the vibration of the riches hidden beneath the topsoil. Then I must dig."

"What you must do is leave!" commanded the prioress.

"I must dig!"

"You must leave!"

The man took a step backward. He looked up and rolled his eyes, as though he were listening to celestial music. His countenance became serene, then rapturous. "I hear something," he whispered. "I have received a message from God."

"Bullshit," muttered Mother Francisca under her breath. "Someone get him out of here."

"From this blessed house," he said, as though in a trance, "a great *santa* will emerge." *Santa* was what we called holy woman who was a nun. Laywomen could be holy, too, but they were called *beatas*.

The visitors hushed. A charged silence filled the parlor. All eyes were on the *zahorí*.

"Her name is . . ." He paused dramatically. "Her name is Teresa." Everyone gasped.

"Teresa?" one said to the other. "Teresa de Ahumada?"

"Go!" commanded Mother Francisca. "Get out of here. That's all I need, some gypsy sowing discord, predicting one of my nuns will be a great *santa*. The minute one of these girls thinks she's holier than the rest, she becomes impossible." She pushed the *zahorí* out the door.

Immediately, arguments erupted. "She already thinks she's the last chunk of mutton in the stewpot. Now she's going to walk around pretending to be Santa Justina."

For a while there was great anger. Great yelling and snorting. Who was this stupid *zahorí*? people asked. Where did he come from? How did he come off predicting that Teresa de Ahumada would be a *santa*? But then it died down. The townsfolk went back to gossiping in the parlor and the gallants to flirting with the prettiest sisters, ladies on pedestals just like in the novels: beautiful, virginal, and inaccessible.

Most of the young men flirted unabashedly with the several novices at a time, addressing a *piropo* first to one, then another. "Such pretty flowers in the convent garden," they'd say. "I'd like to tend them all!" Some of the visitors brought bouquets for the refectory; some brought sweets. One young Portuguese always brought *brinquillos,* a delicious candy from his native country, or *mantequillas,* a pastry made from sugar, butter, and eggs. The novices and young nuns sat by the grille chatting and giggling, savoring their youth, gazing into the eyes of men who were not their lovers. Some surely hungered for the touch of a masculine hand, for the warmth of a mustachioed lip. Some dreamed of sumptuous weddings and humid beds that would never be. I had no admirers. Sunday after Sunday, I sat by the grille and waited for visitors that did not come. As I embroidered, images of Basilio insinuated themselves into my thoughts. Broad shoulders. Wavy hair. I pushed them away. "I'm better off without him," I told myself. And still, there were times when I had to bite my lip and sniff back tears.

A young man named Don Lope caught my eye. No, I don't mean he caught my eye in that way. What I mean is, I noticed him because he was devoted to just one girl. He was unusual in that way. He didn't flirt indiscriminately. In fact, he didn't flirt at all. He came every Sunday evening just after Vespers and asked for the novice Rosa. Always Rosa. They sat at the farthest side of the grille and lost themselves in conversation. They whispered and twittered until Sister Escolástica came out and chased all the visitors away, and then they took leave of each other with long, languid gazes, sighs and tears that made me think of Amadís and his beloved Oriana. How could the other sisters fail to notice that something was going on between these two? It was just a matter of time, I thought, before someone reported Rosa to Mother Francisca, who would certainly punish the girl. What could I do? I had to warn her.

"You'll be caught," I told her earnestly. "This has got to stop. I'm telling you for your own good." She must have been about fifteen or sixteen years old. She was aptly named, because her skin was as delicate and creamy as the petal of a pale, pink rose. She had thick, flaxen hair, so luminous that the thought of her tonsure made me wince, and eyes like emeralds. She was the sixth daughter in a family of eight girls, and her parents had put her and her two younger sisters in Encarnación when they were no taller than lambs.

"But why?" she said. "What are we doing that's wrong?"

"You're going to be a consecrated virgin, Rosa. You're going to be a spouse of God. You can't be moaning and drooling over some lovesick cub."

"I don't want to be a consecrated virgin. Nobody ever asked me if I wanted to be a nun."

"Well, we don't get to choose our lot in life."

I expected her to react with defiance. I expected her to say something like, "Well, I'm going to choose mine." But she didn't. She just looked at me as Isaac must have looked at Abraham as he raised his knife. She was right, I thought. Nobody had asked her if she wanted to be a consecrated virgin. How could she be a good nun if she was taking the habit against her will? What sense did it make for a girl like Rosa to profess? And yet, what choice did she have?

"You're going to be a nun," I said gently. "You have to tell him to go away. He's overstepping the bounds of decorum."

"I love him."

"You can't love him," I said. "You can talk to him, but you can't love him. He can bring you cakes and trinkets, and you can accept them, but you can't love him."

"I want to get out of here," she said matter-of-factly. Her voice was inflectionless. It was as though she had said, "I want to spin awhile," or "I want to walk in the garden."

"Do you think your father will take you back? You've been here for ten years."

"I don't want to go back to my father's house. I want to be with Don Lope."

"But you'd have to go home so your father could make marriage arrangements."

"I don't need for him to make arrangements. Don Lope and I are already married."

"What?"

"We've made vows to each other. That's all that matters."

"Don't be silly."

But then I thought, perhaps they really are already married, and if they are, what's to be done? Let me write down for the sake of clarity that this all happened before the great council, I mean the Council of Trent. In the old days, before the council, all a man and woman had to do to be married was make vows to each other. You didn't need a priest. You didn't need a ceremony. You didn't even need to tell your parents. Of course, most people had weddings, but a wedding wasn't absolutely essential. If a man and a woman promised themselves to each other, that was it. They were married. They could do all those things that married people do. What I mean is, they could lie together. They could have children together.

After the council, things were different. Too many men were promising to marry girls just in order to enjoy them. And what happened after they'd had their fill? They abandoned them, of course. Then what did those poor girls do? They entered convents—that is, if their fathers didn't do away with them. To solve the problem, the council declared that in order for a couple to be really married, they had to make their vows in public, in front of a priest and witnesses. Private vows didn't count anymore. So when Rosa told me she and Don Lope were already married, I believed her. Why wouldn't I? The Council of Trent hadn't happened yet. Still, there was one thing—one major thing—that didn't ring true: the marriage couldn't possibly have been consummated.

"You aren't married, Rosa," I said. "You're still a virgin."

"What do you mean?"

"I mean you haven't . . . you haven't lain with Don Lope."

"I don't understand. I love him."

How was I going to explain to her what I meant? This child had spent her entire life in a convent, but she didn't even understand what was virginal about the Virgin Mary.

"Do you know how babies are made, Rosa?"

"No."

"A man has to lie with a woman. It's what makes people married. I mean, really married. They sleep in the same bed."

"Then I really have to get out of here. They'll never let Don Lope into my cell so he can sleep with me on my cot. Are you sure that's necessary?"

I knew it was my duty to go to Madre Francisca, but those emerald eyes were so entreating. What should I do? It occurred to me to ask Teresa, but then I decided against it. I didn't know if I could trust her with a secret like this. Teresa was beginning to change. She spent long hours in the chapel praying, and she'd taken to flagellating herself at night. She was making a fetish of being submissive. She had started fawning over Mother Francisca. "Yes, Mother. Of course, Mother. Can I help you with anything, Mother?" She was playing the saint again, just as she had at Nuestra Señora de la Gracia. How could I trust her with Rosa's secret?

"Look," I said to Rosa. "Sisters leave the convent all the time to visit their families. All you have to do is ask for permission to go home for a few days."

The convent was so overcrowded, it was too expensive to feed everyone. In addition to nuns, there were boarders, servants, orphans, and lay sisters—women who lived at Encarnación without actually professing. Some wealthy sisters moved in with their own maids and slaves. Women of means provided their own food, but those without a regular income had to eat whatever there was in the refectory, and there usually wasn't much. The solution was to let nuns take meals at home.

"Just tell Mother Francisca you want to visit your family."

"She'll never believe me."

"Why not?"

"I never visit my family. When was the last time they sent for me or my sisters? They've forgotten about us."

It was true. Rosa never went out, nor did any relative come to visit her.

"Look," I said. "What if you got a letter saying they needed you at home for a few days?"

"No one has ever written to me. Who's going to write a letter like that?"

"Me."

She looked at me blankly. "This child really is dumb," I said to myself.

"Look, Rosa, I'll write a letter. We'll pretend it's from your mother. What's her name?"

"Eulalia Eustacia Martínez de Santa Cruz."

"I'll write a letter and sign her name. I'll say you're needed at home for a few days. Then you can have your tryst with Lope. Once you're really married, no one can force you to stay in this convent."

Suddenly Rosa flung her arms around my neck and covered my cheeks with kisses. "Lope and I can escape and live somewhere far away. We can lie together, just like you said!"

I felt queasy. Was I doing the right thing? I have to admit that in a way, I wished I were Rosa, in love with someone who was in love with me. I wished I were the one escaping with a handsome young man who would take me in his arms and kiss me. Someone like Basilio, but without Basilio's stupid prejudices. But then, I put the thought out of my mind. I had cast my lot with God. Now I had to concentrate on helping this child. I had to write the letter. If Mother Francisca found out, she'd certainly throw me out of the convent. Then where would I go? I was risking my own future to help this silly little cabbage-head. But she was crying for joy, hiccoughing and hopping up and down. How could I go back on my word?

"Rosa," I said. "You must promise me one thing. If you're caught, you must never tell who wrote the letter."

"Never!"

I walked back to my cell and lay down. They were ringing the bell for Vespers. I didn't want to go, but I was afraid that if I was absent, it would rouse suspicion.

The next morning, while the others were spinning, I sharpened my quill and wrote:

To Mother Francisca, Prioress of the Convent of the Encarnación:
> *I am writing you because I am very ill, and I need Rosa to come home at once. Please allow her to leave the convent this afternoon.*
> > *Your unworthy servant,*
> > *Eulalia Eustacia Martínez de Santa Cruz*

Wasting paper is a sin, but I tore that one up. Then I wadded the pieces into a ball and threw it into the fire. Who was going to believe a letter like that? In the first place, why would Doña Eulalia call for Rosa and not for her two younger sisters? And why wouldn't she send a coach for her, or at least a servant? No mother would expect the prioress simply to open the gate and send a postulant gallivanting through the streets on her own. Mother

Francisca was sure to send a messenger to Doña Eulalia's house to check the authenticity of the note.

"This is not going to work," I told Rosa. "We'll have to think of something else."

The child began to pout. "You promised!" she whined.

"Look," I said. "If I manage to sneak you out of here, could you get a message to Lope to wait for you by the convent wall?"

"All I have to do is ask him when he comes."

"You'll have to be very careful. If anyone hears you . . ."

"How will you sneak me out?"

I thought a moment. I'd have to outsmart the extern—the nun who held the key to the convent and manned the turn through which we received packages and messages. "Listen, Rosa," I said, "I know where the extern leaves the key. When they march the postulants into the chapel to pray the Office, tell the novice mistress that you don't feel well and have to lie down. When you exit, wait for me in the vestibule. I'll meet you there, grab the key and let you out. Tell Lope to be waiting with a change of clothes." I was the assistant head of the sewing room now, as well as an apprentice apothecary. In the morning, I oversaw the sewing. When the others left for chapel, I could stay behind, pretending to straighten up.

I felt as though I were participating in a great adventure. I was uniting Amadís with Oriana. I was serving the cause of true love. I was a fairy godmother! What I was doing wasn't sinful, it was heroic! I yearned to tell Teresa, but I was afraid. In the old days, when she was still naughty and fun, she might have helped me, but now, who knew how she might react.

"I'll tell Lope on Sunday, when he comes," said Rosa. "We'll work it out then."

Well, as they say, *El hombre propone, pero Dios dispone.* Man proposes, but God disposes. In other words, nothing ever turns out the way you expect.

On Friday I spent my free time scouting out hiding places near the vestibule. After Rosa left the chapel, she'd need a place to wait for me, or, if I got there first, I'd be the one to hide. I also had to figure out how to sneak back into the chapel after letting her out. I was nervous all morning. I pricked my finger while stitching an ornate altarpiece. I pressed a tiny remnant against the wound and watched the blood weave paths among the threads. It spread in all directions, reminding me of a spider with outstretched legs. A red spider. A bad omen. In the early afternoon, Teresa's cousin Juana Isabel came to find me in the infirmary, where Sister Josefa was teaching me to make pastilles for rheumatism. "It's Teresa," she said. "She's sick again."

"Bring her in," said Sister Josefa. She was a feline-faced nun in her forties, lean and nimble, with slanted, panther-like eyes and pointed, menacing teeth. In spite of her intimidating appearance, she was witty and good natured, the kind of woman whose deadpan humor always caught you off-guard. A demanding but patient teacher, she had already taught me the rudiments of chemistry. Thanks to her, before long I would be mixing potions on my own.

"She's fainted three times already today, Sister," said Juana Isabel. "Maybe we should send her home. I think she needs a doctor."

"She should have been a Dominican," said Josefa. "They're richer and eat better. They don't get sick as often." She brushed her hand against her lip, like a panther cleaning its whiskers. "I'll go see her. You stay here and tend the poison," she said to me.

"It's all that flagellating and fasting," I said. "She was already fragile, and now she's completely ruined her health."

"Flagellating and fasting? God have mercy."

"Father Benedicto recommended mortifications."

"I'll mortify him, that bastard," said Sister Josefa, gathering concoctions into her apothecary bag. "On second thought, you come with me, Angélica. You know her better than anyone. You'll be able to advise me."

Teresa had a terrible fever. Josefa, Juana Isabel, and I sat with her all through the night, but couldn't get it to break. The next morning Mother Francisca summoned Don Alonso to come and fetch Teresa. Juana Isabel and I carried her out to the vestibule. Don Alonso turned ashen when he saw her. His beloved daughter. She looked as though she were about to die. Her skin was clammy, her eyes were glazed and unfocused, and her lips were parched. Her arms dangled like a rag doll's . . . I shuddered and looked away.

We lifted her into the coach gently, gently.

Don Alonso turned to me. "Please, come with us, Sister Angélica," he said pleadingly.

"Of course," I said. I had forgotten all about Rosa.

Angélica del Sagrado Corazón
Toledo, 2 July 1576

CHAPTER 5

New Directions

THE SOCIAL SEASON HAD BEGUN IN ÁVILA, AND TERESA'S COUSINS WERE BUSY with *paseos,* parties, and bullfights. They sent liveried messengers with invitations, but the revelries of Ávila's tight-knit *converso* community brought no sparkle to Teresa's eye. A carriage came with a coachman decked out in a midnight blue cape and a wide-brimmed, plumed hat, but Teresa sent him away with a gracious smile and sad eyes. One piece of news did cause her to catch her breath, though: Don Javier would be wearing kid gloves and ruffs no more. He was going to take vows. He'd already left to study in Salamanca. He planned to join the Dominican order.

We gleaned snippets of information from here and there. The maids knew more about it than anyone. They gossiped with other maids in the marketplace and carried tales back to Doña Teresa's *estrado.* According to the town tattlers, Teresa's profession had left Don Javier crestfallen. The usually witty and sociable young man hid in his quarters for days at a time. Servants who brought him his meals said his skin had taken on the pallor of a mollusk and that he hardly spoke. His father, Don Tello, thought the best cure would be to get him out into the social whirl. Fairs and balls would give him something to look forward to. After some thought, he came up with the perfect solution: an engagement.

Engagements in Ávila are drawn-out affairs involving myriad events— horse races, *corridas,* picnics, dinner parties, and formal dances. Without consulting Javier, Don Tello entered into marriage negotiations on his behalf with an Old Christian landholder named Cardenio Mendizábal. The future bride had a cleft lip, but Mendizábal was offering a magnificent dowry. His motivation was clear: he had no sons and was anxious for a male heir. He probably knew that Don Javier was from a *converso* family, but all the

Sánchezes had patents of nobility, and if *they* were willing to overlook his daughter's imperfection, *he* was willing to overlook theirs.

Once Javier learned he would soon be getting married, he came out of his funk and threw himself into the preparations with gusto. He commissioned a new suit of black velvet with elegant brocade sleeves trimmed with a ruche. He purchased cream-colored silk hose and ordered an ample lace ruff all the way from Amsterdam. He seemed to be himself again. At gatherings he greeted guests warmly. He bowed to the ladies. He drank wine from silver goblets. He danced the galliard. He smiled at his homely bride-to-be with gently teasing eyes. One thing was strange, though: he always wore the same yellow hat plume we'd seen at Teresa's profession. No one could accuse Don Javier of ignorance of fashion, so why was he sporting a feather more suitable for a funeral than for the celebration of an impending marriage? Some people saw it as a sign of defiance. They thought Javier resented Don Tello's choice of a bride and saw his upcoming wedding as a kind of interment. Others thought he was grieving for the lost Teresa, buried forever in a convent.

Perhaps they were both right—because what happened next seemed to be an act of revenge and desperation. On the day of the proposed wedding, all the guests were gathered in the Cathedral of Ávila—the bishop, a gaggle of priests, the mayor, the aldermen, family members, courtiers, and society ladies. Everyone but the groom. The groom was nowhere to be found.

Don Tello was livid. He sent his henchmen to hunt him down. He ordered them to search the town, from the brothels, taverns, and gaming houses to the churches and monasteries. "One way or another," he commanded, "bring him back. Use force, if necessary." But to no avail. Don Javier had disappeared. Don Tello bowed his head in shame. He begged his guests to partake of the marriage feast he had prepared, then left the premises quietly. The bride collapsed in tears and announced her intension of joining the Poor Clares.

About six weeks later a messenger appeared before Don Tello with a note from his son. He was sorry, said Don Javier. He had had every intension of doing his father's bidding, but he had heard the call of God. He was now in Salamanca, studying theology with the great Dominican scholar Melchor Cano. He was going to be ordained a Dominican priest.

How could Don Tello protest? Was he going to tell his son not to obey God's command?

The news sent shudders through the *converso* community. Everyone knew that Melchor Cano stood among the most radical, conservative, and anti-Jewish theologians, and that the Dominicans were in charge of the Inquisition. Had Javier become a traitor to his own people?

Teresa listened impassively to the maids' reports. Perhaps she was just too sick to care. "He has found God," was all she said. "He must follow his heart."

Before long the maids brought another piece of news from the market-place: Basilio had married. His bride was a journeyman's daughter, plain and plump as a brood hen, and just as dumb. Just what he deserves, I thought. I'm sure he'll be happy. For an instant, the old sting came back, but I had too many other worries to dwell on it for long.

It had been Teresa's idea to return to Castellanos de la Cañada to visit her sister María. "Maybe a change of air," she murmured.

Don Alonso thought it was a good idea too. There was a healer in Becedas he knew about. Teresa could stay with María a while and then go on to the neighboring town for the cure. This time, there was no question about my accompanying her. When she was well enough to travel, we climbed into the carriage. Don Alonso threw a blanket over Teresa's knees and kissed her delicately on both cheeks.

"Please come visit, *Papá*," she said. Don Alonso nodded and kissed her again.

The carriage lurched and quivered, then began its wobbly way out of Ávila. Teresa was breathing heavily, gasping at times. A neighbor had recommended sarsaparilla water, reputedly good for the chest, but it hadn't helped at all. In fact, I thought it had aggravated her condition. I was an apprentice apothecary, and I knew something about the properties of sarsaparilla water. Sarsaparilla purifies the blood, cleanses the stomach, and heals skin conditions such as hives, warts, and rashes. It can't clear your chest.

I recommended aromatic vapors of olive oil with vetch, coriander, lavender, and rosemary, a concoction I'd learned about from Sister Josefa. Don Alonso looked skeptical. Perhaps he still saw me as the little girl who tagged along after Tía Cati when she came to take measurements for Teresa's ball gowns. Nevertheless, I prepared the mixture and set it over the fire to produce steam. Eventually, Teresa's fever went down and the congestion diminished. After that, Don Alonso took my advice more seriously.

"I'm counting on you to take care of her," he told me. "None of this nonsense about flagellation and fasting. That kind of twaddle could be dea . . .

could be dangerous." He didn't want to say "deadly." He didn't want to think about where this illness might lead.

Teresa dozed fitfully during the first leg of the journey. I looked at her hand lying limply on the blanket. That beautiful, fragile, white hand, an ailing dove. We'd have to stop at Don Pedro's house in Hortigosa before going on to Castellanos de la Cañada. Teresa was too weak to go the whole distance without resting. Besides, she was anxious to see her favorite uncle. She seemed to find that stern-looking man with his no-nonsense manner strangely reassuring.

Why did I write "strangely"? Why "strangely reassuring"? I guess because Don Pedro did not seem reassuring to me. To me he seemed aloof and intimidating. He was both very rich and a *converso*, two things that made me uncomfortable. It's true I'd lost my fear of Don Alonso, but that's because he'd been kind to me. Anyway, I was used to Don Alonso. But Don Pedro, well, I found him off-putting, with his too-perfectly trimmed mustache and his velvet breeches.

Don Pedro's house was a sprawling affair with countless bedrooms arranged around a vast patio. In spite of the palatial dimensions of the place, the furnishings were simple. There was nothing dainty about Don Pedro's house. It was, like its master, virile, rugged, and austere. Aside from the paneling on the doors and shutters, no ornamentation cluttered the rooms—a reflection of Don Pedro's aversion to triviality. The furniture was made of rich walnut, with upholstery of tooled leather or elegant brocade. It was beautiful and imposing, not pretty.

The library was the largest I'd ever seen, and I'd seen several fine homes when I accompanied my aunt on fittings. It was furnished more elaborately than the other rooms, although no less solemnly. A writing desk with many little drawers and a chair inlaid with ivory stood on one side. On the other stood an ornately carved cabinet hatched with gilt and bone. The ceiling was Moorish style, with repetitive, symmetrical paneling and polychrome tiles. Perhaps it had actually been built by Moorish craftsmen, for many *moriscos*—Christianized Moors—worked for wealthy, Christian patrons. The stone floor was covered with carpets, also Moorish style, with solid backgrounds and intricate designs of blue and yellow.

Don Pedro greeted me more amicably than I expected. He explained that his wife had gone out with her sister, but would be home shortly. "This will be your room, Sister Angélica," he said. It's the habit, I thought. He's showing respect for the habit.

"And, of course," he went on, "the library is at your disposal. Don Alonso tells me you're an herbalist. Feel free to take anything you need from the hothouse to treat Sister Teresa."

Sister Angélica, he said. *Sister Teresa.* I liked the way those words sounded on his lips.

"Belisarda will be your maid while you are here," he added.

Belisarda? My maid? Was I to have a maid then? I, who had once been a maid? But now I was a Carmelite nun, Teresa's sister in religion, and an herbalist. An herbalist! I had never heard myself called that before, but I liked the idea. Herbalist was a highly respected occupation.

"Thank you, sir," I said, trying to sound self-confident.

In the days that followed, Teresa showed signs of recovery, even though she often resisted my medicines. "I'm not that sick," she'd say. "You don't need to baby me, Angélica!" She'd throw a shawl around her shoulders and walk in the patio. She read. She chatted for hours with her uncle. In the meantime, I wandered around the library. Although it was vast, I was disappointed. Don Pedro owned a copy of the letters of Saint Jerome and many hagiographies—Saint Catherine, Saint Perpetua, Saint Lucy. All those martyrs who lost their eyes and guts. A wonderful thing, to be martyred, Teresa always said, but I could never see it. Of course, I understand our lives belong to God and we should be willing to sacrifice everything for the faith, but . . . Well, I don't want to write anything that will land me in Hell, but the truth is, I preferred stories like *Amadís de Gaula.* I'd brought along the copy Teresa had given me, and since there was no prioress to keep an eye on me, I sometimes snuck it out and read to my heart's content.

I liked giving Belisarda orders. She was a fleshy country girl with a wart on her nose and huge, audacious breasts that forever seemed ready to bound off on their own. It was fun having someone at my beck and call. "Belisarda, bring me some dried mint!" Or "Belisarda, I need hibiscus flowers!" Belisarda would scamper off to do my bidding and moments later, whatever I had asked for would appear like magic on my worktable.

Teresa and her uncle talked and talked. I knew what they were talking about. Teresa had been complaining for weeks that she couldn't pray. "I just can't concentrate," she told me. "It's embarrassing, but when I say the rosary, I forget where I am. Sometimes I drift off right in the middle of the *Pater Noster.*" I knew what she meant. I had days like that, too. I still do. But I've never lost sleep worrying about it. This is a rich girl's problem, I thought.

Poor girls like me learn to work from the time they're little. Poor girls are afraid if they aren't useful, nobody will want them around. They don't bother fretting over whether they're saying the rosary perfectly.

"You're just overtired," I told her. "When you feel better, it'll come back."

Me, I was never much for praying the rosary. Saying the same thing over and over puts me to sleep. After the third *Salve María* I'm snoring like a pig. What I like is images. You can kneel before a picture in a chapel or sit with an open book in your lap, and you just know God is there. And music. I learned to feel Jesus's love in voices lifted in choir.

"Try praying the Office the way we do at the convent," I suggested, just to show I was paying attention. "Maybe that will help."

"I try, but I just don't feel God is listening." She lowered her voice. "I just don't feel God is really *there*." I knew she was troubled, but I didn't have any answers.

"What does Don Pedro say?" I asked.

"He doesn't understand," she said impatiently. "Nobody understands."

"I'll make you some tea," I said. "It will help you relax."

Suddenly all the emotions she had tethered up inside bucked and stampeded. "You don't care a thing about me!" she screamed. "I've lost God, don't you understand? I've lost *God*! And all you can think of is making tea!"

"Your fever has returned, Teresa," I said, struggling to keep my temper in check.

"You idiot!" She ran to her room. Later, when I walked by, I heard her sobbing.

"What a bitch," Belisarda whispered. "Thinks she's the last drop of water in the kettle."

"She's sick," I said.

"I'll say."

I turned and glowered, and Belisarda understood she had overstepped her bounds. I puffed out my chest and hardened my jaw. She bowed her head and grunted, "Sorry, Sister." Then she made a rough curtsy and left.

The midday meal was a glorious affair, with a well-seasoned mutton stew with carrots, onions and celery, a hearty loaf of bread, and plenty of fruits and cheese for dessert—a real treat after the scanty fare provided at Encarnación by the penurious cellaress. I ate with gusto. Don Pedro took his meals in his room, so only women were present—Don Pedro's wife, sister, and sister-in-law. I relaxed and enjoyed myself, putting out of my mind Tía Cati's admonition never to appear ravenous in front of rich folks. However, I did have qualms about asking for seconds. I was hoping Teresa would say, "Have another helping, Angélica," but she was picking at her food, oblivious to what was going on around her. I didn't want to be gluttonous. "Lead me not into temptation," I prayed under my breath. Mutton stew was a temptation. "For Christ's sake," I'm sure I heard God answer. "That refers to balling priests, not to mutton stew. One more serving won't make you a glutton." "Thank you, Lord," I whispered. "May I please have a bit more?" I said out loud. A servant filled my plate, and soon I was lost in that magnificent blend of moist, succulent meat and spices.

Well, maybe that's not exactly what God said, but it was something like that. I shouldn't write this down, but the truth is, the God I know understands the craving of a seamstress's daughter for a good dinner. Teresa's eyes didn't light up at the sight of the fleshy oranges, dates, and figs heaped on the porcelain dessert tray. The husky walnuts and tart goat's milk cheese didn't peak her interest, either. But I ate my fill. Later, I heard her talking to Don Pedro in the library, but I didn't bother to eavesdrop. The meal had made me sleepy. I lay down for a *siesta*.

By the evening, Teresa had calmed down. "I'm sorry, Angélica," she said. She bit her lip. "I'm sorry I was so impatient with you this morning." I shrugged. She reached out and took my hand. "I don't know what's the matter with me. It's just that . . ."

"What?"

"At first, I thought that God had guided my steps into the convent, but now He seems to have forgotten me. Don't you ever feel that way, Angélica? Like God has abandoned you?"

"No."

"You're lucky."

"It's just that I don't think about it that much."

"That's a gift. I think God loves you more than anyone. You're blessed."

"You're the one He loves. That's why you think about Him all the time."

"I pray and pray. I say the rosary over and over. I recite the psalms."

"Maybe you're trying too hard, Teresa."

"That's what Uncle Pedro says."

"You can't force God's hand. Leave things alone for a little while. Don't try to do God's work for Him, Teresa. God knows what He's doing. Leave things to Him."

The next day, while we were sewing, Don Pedro stuck his head in the door and held a book out to Teresa. "Read this," he said. "I think it will help you." Teresa took the heavy leather-bound volume and leafed through it.

"What is it?" I asked, when we were alone. She showed it to me. The title was written on the spine in deep red ink: *The Third Spiritual Alphabet,* by Francisco Osuna.

For the next several days she hardly moved from the cushion by the window. She sat turning pages as though mesmerized. The autumn sun sent muted beams through the pane, bathing her forehead in a gentle light, softening her sharp features, giving her an almost ethereal glow. It was the first time in weeks her skin looked healthy, not drab and wan.

When she wasn't reading, she wandered through the house with the dazed look of a girl enamored. The book went with her everywhere. It was better than a lover. It went to bed with her. It accompanied her into the garden. Into the chapel. Into the sewing room. It even stayed nearby when she attended to her toilette. She was so captivated by it that she talked about postponing our journey to Castellanos de la Cañada until she had finished it. What she needs is a real lover, I thought. God forgive me, but the notion surfaced in my mind before I could steel myself against it. And then another thought shot into my consciousness. A real lover. No, I wasn't thinking about Teresa and her cousin Javier. In fact, I wasn't thinking about Teresa at all. I was thinking about Rosa. Rosa and her beloved Don Lope.

Rosa! I'd forgotten her for weeks. I'd left her waiting for me in the vestibule when I dashed out of the convent to accompany Teresa home. Teresa was ill. That's all I could think about at the time. Poor Rosa. I imagined her crouching in a cramped space, listening to the beat of her heart. I'd promised to open the door for her, but I hadn't shown up. I imagined her lingering, reluctant to accept that I wasn't coming, unwilling to believe I'd betrayed her, and then dragging herself back to her cell in tears. I imagined her pacing, trying to make sense of it. Now there was no way out for Rosa. She'd have taken vows by now, I thought. For her, the door to happiness was closed forever. I'd write to her. I'd explain, but she would never forgive me. And how could I tell a confessor I'd failed a friend, a girl I was going *help escape from the convent!* What priest would absolve me of something so hideous?

Teresa had decided to write to her father for permission to stay in Hortigosa until she'd finished Osuna's book. That was good news. It meant

Don Pedro would hire a messenger to take the letter. I could slip the man a coin to take another message to Encarnación. It wouldn't be so far out of his way. At least I could write to Rosa and try to explain things. But could I trust one of Don Pedro's couriers with a secret mission? I had no choice. I wrote the letter and waited. When the messenger appeared, I breathed a sigh of relief. He was a thick old muleteer, the kind of man who doesn't ask too many questions. I warned him to be careful to whom he gave my note. I didn't tell him that if it got into the wrong hands, it could land both Rosa and me in the convent prison. That would only spark his curiosity.

One day, out of boredom, I asked Teresa about the book she was reading. I'd finished *Amadís de Gaula* for the third time and couldn't find anything else to occupy my mind. Maybe, I thought, since Teresa found Osuna's book so fascinating, I'd have a look at it.

Osuna wanted to introduce a new kind of spirituality based on the practice of recollection, explained Teresa. "That means movement inward," she clarified. "Osuna believes in a simpler, more authentic kind of Christianity. He teaches us to seek God within ourselves, within our own souls. He believes in mental prayer, not in reciting prayers mechanically."

I had no idea what she was talking about. For me, Christ was the Son of God, and He was hanging on His Cross in the Cathedral of Ávila. If I wanted to find Him, all I had to do was cross the plaza and go through the cathedral doors, and there He'd be. Or else, I could kneel before the crucifix in my cell or in the convent chapel. You didn't have to invent new ways to find God, you just had to look at His image.

Every so often she'd say to me, "Look, Angélica, read this." But I'd already lost interest in Osuna. I went into the library and picked up the *The Golden Legend,* a book on the lives of the saints. I was delighted. The stories turned out to be as good as *Amadís*. Some of them were pretty juicy—ravaged maidens, giants, and monsters. That's where I found the story of Saint Mary the Egyptian, a public woman who accompanied some sailors to the Holy Land and saw the Virgin in a church in Jerusalem. When Our Lady promised her she could be saved, Mary the Egyptian did penance by wandering around naked in the desert for the rest of her life. After she died, a lion came along and, instead of eating her body, very respectfully dug her grave. That's right! With his paws! Stories like that are interesting to read. They're full of surprises.

One morning Teresa shoved a section from the end of the book under my nose and ordered me to look at it. "Go away," I snapped. "I prefer Mary the Egyptian."

"Just read it, Angélica." She pointed at the passage.

I hated it when she was bossy like that. Nevertheless, I read out loud, "I think it best to search for God in our hearts, for it is written: 'I found much wisdom in myself, and I profited much from it.'" I stopped reading and looked at Teresa. "So?" I said.

"Isn't it wonderful?"

"What's so wonderful about it?"

"Don't you understand what it means, Angélica?"

I had no idea what it meant.

"It means that God is within us. God isn't in all the empty rituals we perform without thinking or in all the prayers we recite mechanically. When we say the Our Father without paying attention to what we're saying, we're not praying at all."

"If we say the prayers, we're praying," I said stubbornly.

"Look, Angélica, do you ever just recite the words unconsciously, without concentrating on their meaning?"

"All the time."

"Well, that's just going through the motions." She laid her hand gently on my wrist to show she wasn't reprimanding me. "Real prayer means turning inward. Blocking out all the distractions, all the intrusive thoughts, all the sounds and sights that prevent us from concentrating. Real prayer means quieting the soul so God can come in. Osuna wants us to find God in our own hearts and really listen to His words."

I thought about it a moment. "Well, isn't that what I told you before?" I said finally. "You can't force God's hand. You can recite all the Hail Marys in the world, but you can't make God come into your heart."

"Exactly, Angélica. You were right."

"I was?" I couldn't believe she was giving me credit for some insight. The truth is, I'd never really thought about these things before. My mother had taught me to pray the rosary, so I did it. To me, praying was praying, and that was the end of it. Images helped. Music helped. Those things gave you a special feeling, but even if you didn't have that feeling, you said what you were supposed to say and that was good enough.

"Anyone can find God, Angélica. Anyone. All you have to do is make a space for him. You don't have to be a priest or a nun. God loves everyone."

I was quiet. I was listening. But then I thought: This is a trick. "Even Jews?" I said.

"I pray that all people will find God's grace," she said placidly. I didn't think she had answered my question, but I didn't say anything. After a pause she went on. "There's nothing wrong with those vocal prayers we practice. They can lead us to God, too. But only if we think about what we're saying. Only if our hearts are in it. For some people, vocal prayer, practiced consci"entiously, is enough, but Osuna says that mental prayer takes us to a higher plane. Mental prayer requires sustained attention. It requires awareness. At first, when you're just learning, you can meditate on a crucifix or a passage from Scripture, but you have to really concentrate on them, forcing your mind back to its object whenever it wanders. What I mean is, you can't just let yourself slip into a comfortable fog. You have to stay alert. Later, as you progress, you learn to transcend words and images. You let your senses grow numb and clear your mind completely. You lose yourself in darkness."

"You mean, you fall asleep?"

"No, you can't let yourself fall asleep. You have to stay awake and aware. You have to be attentive to all your interior experiences. You can't lose your focus. Then, if God wills it, in that absolute, quintessential darkness, you reach the light—a state of illumination or insight in which you *know* God. I don't mean knowing in the way you know what you learn in books, I mean . . . how can I put it? . . . You're one with God."

It was too much to take in. I couldn't fit it all into my head. Teresa was quiet, lost in thought, so I got up to find a place where I could read my own book undisturbed. I had already read the story of Mary the Egyptian a dozen times, but there were other good stories in *The Golden Legend*.

Hours later, I found her sitting exactly where I had left her, *The Third Spiritual Alphabet* on her lap. Her face was so serene and luminous. Now, when I look back on that day, I think that was perhaps the first time I ever saw Teresa in ecstasy.

By the time we left for Castellanos de la Cañada, Teresa's condition had started to deteriorate. Her nagging cough reminded me of Tía Cati's. It frightened me. It had started out as a dry hacking, but lately she had been spitting up yellow, blood-streaked sputum. She struggled for breath, gulping and wheezing as though she had a bellows in her chest. She complained of pains in her upper torso, near her heart, and in her back, her side and her neck.

"I'm sorry for being such a nuisance," she'd say, dissolving into a fit of coughing so terrible I was afraid she'd choke on her own pasty saliva. Often she couldn't sleep, and I'd sit by her bed reading to her. "I'm burning alive, Angélica," she told me. "I think God is giving me a taste of the Hell that's waiting for me. It's because I'm wicked and don't let you sleep."

"Hush," I said. "You're not wicked, and you'd have to do something far worse than keep me up all night with that croaky cough of yours for God to send you to Hell."

She smiled through her fever. "I'm very wicked," she said. "I'm the wickedest of the wicked. I don't even pray right."

"You're only mildly wicked," I laughed. "Don't flatter yourself."

I remembered Teresa's sin, the one she'd committed with her cousin Javier, but I was sure that whatever it was, it wasn't terrible enough to cause such physical suffering. Plenty of people sinned, and you didn't see them coughing up blood. Besides, she had confessed that sin, and I supposed the priest had absolved her—especially since he'd told her the offense wasn't mortal. I reached over to touch her forehead, but before I laid my hand on her skin, I felt the heat radiating from her body. She was ablaze.

"Your hand feels so cool," she said. "It's like an angel wing fluttering across my face."

I made cold compresses of lavender water to bring down the fever and chamomile infusions to relax her, but she was growing weaker. Don Pedro was beside himself. He wanted to keep her with him, but she clearly needed medical attention. The healer in Becedas was known for her herbal cures. We had to leave for Doña María's and then go on to the neighboring town.

The snows started before we reached the Guzmán home—a sprawling estate surrounded by fields and hills, now white like mounds of meringue, to the northwest of Ávila. Thickets of cork oak dotted the landscape. They stood like gloomy Goliaths against a gloomy sky. These trees, with their tough, airtight bark, impervious to rain and indifferent to heat, are like the people of the Castilian Meseta, robust and roughhewn, yet giving. They produce flooring for houses and stoppers for wine bottles. In the summer, the peasants harvest and market the cork, but for now the trees stood in clusters, huddled together like families, each solidly rooted but reaching out to the others with its brawny, beckoning arms. Some cork oaks were over four hundred years old. Noble and steadfast, I thought, like the folks this earth produces. The community consisted of ten or twelve houses, all clustered around Don Martín's. In small rural communities like this one, landholders and peasants are like kin. The Guzmáns were godparents to most of the neighbors' children. A large fountain stood in the patio. Probably in the summer it was filled with splashing birds, but now it was empty and still. What resonated most in those parts was the silence. The silence of a snowflake fluttering to the earth. The silence of the moon hanging low in the sky. Once in a great while you could hear sheep-bells in the distance, as flocks moved from field to field in search of pasture, but most of the time silence reigned—silence so crisp it seemed brittle, like the diaphanous ice panes that formed on ledges and steps.

Doña María had settled gracefully into domesticity. Her silhouette had softened, and her bosom had become full and spongy from nursing. "Sister Angélica," she said, "we appreciate your coming. Father has told us what a help you've been to Teresa."

Was she kidding? Was she being sarcastic? Was she being nice because now I was a sister? Or had marriage really changed her? I'd always had the impression she found me rather bothersome, but now her voice was as warm as fresh muffins.

"You know how much I love Teresa," I said smoothly.

She gave me a large, light-filled room next to Teresa's with a comfortable bed, a chest filled with linens, a basin, and a pitcher. "Let me know if you need anything," she said.

Martín de Guzmán y Barriento didn't share his wife's enthusiasm for visitors. He greeted Teresa with forced cordiality. Me he hardly greeted at all—just a cursory bow and a nod. He was a nervous man, perpetually angry, prone to fly off the handle for the slightest thing. He was jealous of the shadow that hugged his wife's steps and of the petticoats that stroked her thighs. Addicted to litigation, he brought suit against surgeons and tailors, merchants and scribes. If he thought a vintner had watered the wine, he went straight to the town council. He avoided lawyers, preferring to represent himself. He thought all *alguaciles* and judges were corrupt, yet his unremitting proceedings kept him always in their midst.

He treated me like a suspect from the start, eyeing me as I prepared infusions, breathing down my neck as I folded linens. Doña María had servants, of course, but there was so much to do in a country house—stitching and spinning as in any house, but also caring for animals, preserving and brewing, chopping wood and making candles. And then, there was Teresa to care for, as well as Doña María's babies. I was busy all the time, too busy to think about Don Martín. But then, all of a sudden I'd look up and see him staring at me.

One day I was putting away some bedclothes I'd just mended when I came across a strange object at the bottom of a chest. Lying under the sheets and comforters was a spice holder—a small, silver, two-storey tower with a pyramid roof and a circular base. By lifting the roof, you could place different kinds of spices—cinnamon, cloves, nutmeg, coriander, cumin—into the body of the device. The perfume of the spices would diffuse through the grated openings or "windows" along the sides. I lifted the object out from under the fabric and noticed some strange inscriptions on the crown and the base, squared-off characters with little foot-like tips. I'd seen that kind of markings before, but where? I stuck my hand under the cloth and felt around. My fingers touched something hard and smooth. I pulled it out and looked at it. It was a platter of some sort, highly decorated in greens, browns, yellows, and oranges. Along the rim were flowers and birds of paradise, and in the center, a large Hand of Fatima with a six-pointed star in the center. I turned the plate around, and on the back I saw the same kind of symbols as on the spice holder. There was nothing unusual about the geometric figures. Hands of Fatima and six-pointed stars were common. Both Old Christians and *moriscos* used them. But those letters . . .

Suddenly I became aware of another person in the room. I felt my hands grow clammy and my throat tighten. The muscles in my upper back seemed to turn to cord, then knot and tangle. I looked up. Don Martín stood staring at me. "Put that down," he commanded. There was something about the way he looked at me . . . it reminded me of . . . what could it be? "Put it down and leave this room." His voice was steady, firm.

All at once I remembered. I put the dish down on top of the bedclothes next to the spice holder without bothering to bury them. That look . . . Don Alonso had looked at me that way long ago, when he realized I'd overheard him profane the name of Our Lord. Those strange letters, I had glimpsed them on a piece of fabric—a shawl or a streamer of some kind—in Don Alonso's library. I couldn't know at the time that the spice holder was used in the Havdala, the ceremony closing the Jews' Sabbath, or that the dish was for their commemoration of the Exodus. I found out about those things later, when inquisitors produced such objects, commanding me to identify them, and—praise be to God—I couldn't. Did Teresa know her sister concealed paraphernalia used for heretical rituals in her linen chest?

"Teresa," I said, even though she was showing no sign of feeling better, "I think we should leave for Becedas as soon as possible."

"Why?"

"We came here for the *curandera,* and you haven't seen her even once."

"I can't, Angélica. I can hardly get out of bed, and there's still snow on the ground."

It was true. It had been a treacherous winter, and although April was approaching, the fields were as barren as faraway moonscapes. Even so, I was anxious to be out of that house. If the Guzmáns were practicing heretical rites, or even if Doña María was just guarding heirlooms from her father's Jewish past, the place was contaminated. If anyone found out about those secret objects, we would all be subject to investigation. "All right," I said, "but in a week or so . . ."

"We'll see." And she drifted off to sleep.

Occasionally messengers came from Ávila bearing letters, but not many, and none brought a response to the note I'd sent Rosa. After a while, I stopped thinking about her. I had my own problems. Teresa was my primary concern. Her cough was getting deeper and stickier. I made plasters and eucalyptus rubs, but their effects were temporary. I was running out of ideas.

Every day I walked over the frosted earth to do my chores, pulling my cape tightly around my body and harboring the hope that some valiant flower would push up and show itself. The meadows had to be dreaming of violets and bluebells and poppies, just as I was. Sometimes I could feel Don Martín's steely gaze on me as I threw grain to the chickens. Inside the house, I felt like I was being stalked. Sometimes I'd look up from swaddling María's baby, and there he'd be. Or else I'd feel a sudden hot breath on my arm while I was concocting an infusion in the kitchen.

"I don't like having that girl from the convent around," I overheard him say to his wife. "She snoops around too much."

"You're dreaming, Martín."

"Stay away from her. Keep your trap shut and don't tell her anything. You women are all gossips. Don't know how to keep your maws shut."

The next time I went to burp the baby, Doña María snatched her from me.

"Please, don't trouble yourself," she said, trying to sound gentle. "I'll take care of it."

Then, almost overnight, it happened. The sun caressed the pastures, and mantles of emerald materialized miraculously. Wildflowers blossomed on the hills, producing splotches of blue and yellow and pink. Birds shattered the silence of winter. Roads became passable, and a messenger came. He handed a letter to Teresa, and, on the sly, another to me. It wasn't from Rosa, but the handwriting looked familiar. I slipped it into my sleeve and snuck off to read it.

Ávila, April 27, 1538

Jesus be with you, Sister Angélica,

May this letter find you content and with God's light in your heart. The person to whom you wrote is no longer here at Encarnación. I intercepted your note and kept it in order to prevent its falling into unsympathetic hands. I have not found an opportune moment to respond until now. As you know, it is not always easy to find a courier in the convent.

The intended recipient of your missive vanished shortly after you left to attend to Sister Teresa in her illness. Mother Prioress notified her father, and we fully expected him to storm the convent demanding an explanation for his child's disappearance. It was, after all, reprehensible on our part to allow her to escape. However, he has taken no action against Encarnación and, in fact, has not even replied to Mother Prioress's communications. I have no further information.

I beg you not to respond to this note. If your message were intercepted, you could be implicated in this unpleasant affair.

Your Sister in Christ,
Juana Isabel Suárez, Carmelite

I felt nauseous. Shivers radiated from the base of my neck down my back and along my arms. I felt as though armies of inchworms were slinking over my body. Disappeared? How could that be? Did she make a pact with one of the externs? Did she conjure the Devil? Or did she simply follow one of the sisters through the door? And where was she? Did she take off with Don Lope? And if so, did he marry her, or did he have his way with her and abandon her in some godforsaken clump of underbrush, the way so many young men did with their "ladies" once they had enjoyed them? It was all my fault, I thought, for encouraging her, for talking about lying with lovers. She was just a child, an innocent novice. How could I put those dirty ideas into her head? I knelt in front of the crucifix on my bedroom wall and asked God to forgive me.

That evening Teresa told me, "*Papá* says we can go to Becedas now. I received a letter today. He has made arrangements for us to stay with the *curandera*. My cousin Juana Isabel will join us later. That will make things a bit easier on you, Angélica. I know I'm not . . . well, I'm not so easy to deal with sometimes."

"That's putting it mildly."

"I can be pigheaded."

"Worse than a jealous husband," I said. I tried to smile and not think of Don Martín.

Angélica del Sagrado Corazón
Toledo, 8 July 1576

CHAPTER 6

"Blessed Are Those Who Mourn"

THE *CURANDERA* BEGAN BLEEDING TERESA THE DAY WE ARRIVED. RAQUEL Córdoba was a large woman with a billowing bosom and blond hair harnessed by a neat little coif. Everyone called her Tía Raquel. Her eyes were set narrow, too narrow for her ample face. Her mouth reminded me of an unripe strawberry, white, compact, and puckered. She wore a sensible apron with a blue bib and a sash she tied firmly over her hefty rump. Her tray of hellish-looking instruments—bistouries of varying sizes—lay on a tray in orderly fashion. She was chillingly efficient with a knife, slicing Teresa's arm deftly, pressing, squeezing, then collecting the contaminated blood in cups she emptied in her flower garden. No wonder her roses bloomed with such exuberance.

Tía Raquel was proud of her craft, which she'd learned from her mother and grandmother. Her methods were conventional: bleeding, purges, potions, and herbs. She bragged that she was better versed in her art than the barber-surgeons. Like them, she prepared syrupy concoctions that served for a variety of ailments, from typhus to love sickness—some people call it *el mal francés*—which French sailors brought back from the new lands across the sea.

Tía Raquel was known for her powerful diuretics and sudorifics, which left her patients jumpy or languorous, depending. She disliked interference and didn't care a whit that I was an apprentice apothecary or that Don Pedro had called me an herbalist. To her I was just a nuisance—a meddlesome girl who thought she knew something about cures. I held my peace as long as I could, but when I saw her treatments begin affecting Teresa adversely, I had to speak out. "It's enough, Tía," I finally said to her one day. Blood was dribbling over Teresa's wrist in a sticky little rivulet, then trickling in globules into the cup. This was the second time Tía Raquel had bled her in a week. I watched her bandage Teresa's arm. The wound was too deep. Blood seeped from the incision through the gauzy material, forming the outline of a squashed insect. "She can't take any more, Tía," I insisted.

The *curandera* looked at me with disgust. She forced a mug of purl to Teresa's lips. "To build your strength back up," she barked. "New blood is what you need. Healthy blood."

"Tía . . ." I began.

"This child has sinned," she snapped. "She has a demon lodged in her body, and until I can coax it out, she won't get better. Eventually, it will flow out with the noxious blood." She looked at me as though I were an idiot. "They certainly didn't teach you a thimble's worth of medicine in that convent," she added sourly.

Teresa was growing weaker. It was clear she had a chest ailment of some sort—her lungs, her heart, I wasn't sure. But so much bleeding was doing her no good, and the laxatives Tía Raquel fed her were turning her stomach inside out. The room stank like a pigsty. I dowsed Teresa in lavender water to keep her from puking at her own stench.

"I feel like a piece of rancid meat," she complained hoarsely. "I feel putrid." I hung a pomander by her bed and opened a window.

Instinctively, Teresa knew she had to get out of the house. She felt better when she got up and walked around. At last, she summoned the courage to escape for an hour or two a day.

"My head has cleared a bit, Tía," she told the *curandera*. "I'm going to church to thank God for your care. Sister Angélica will accompany me. Don't worry. We'll be back before long."

Raquel Córdoba shot me a dirty look, as though I'd put her up to it. I perfumed Teresa from head to toe to disguise the odors of disease. She helped me, turning this way and that way so I could scent her temples, her wrists, the inside of her elbows. She moved slowly, but with a determination that surprised me. "How do I look?" she asked.

"What difference does it make? You're sick. You're a nun. You're not going to a party."

She smiled. In the soft morning light, her face shone in spite of her infirmity.

"Yes, I am," she said weakly. "Mass is a banquet, a celebration! A lady puts on her finery and paints her lips to meet her husband. Why shouldn't I pretty myself up for my Spouse?"

I shook my head. "There's some twisted logic there somewhere, Teresa." But just thinking about getting out of the house seemed to be doing her good, I thought.

"Lying to Tía Raquel like that," she whispered. "I feel guilty." She giggled like a naughty child who had just put one over on the nanny.

"You're not lying, Teresa. You really are going to church."

"You think I'm going to give thanks for finding myself in the clutches of that old witch? I'm going to pray she has a heart attack."

"Teresa!"

She'd been bedridden much of the winter, but in Castellanos de la Cañada a local priest had trudged through the snow to say Mass daily at the Guzmán's private chapel. Teresa had taken communion in her room when she was too sick to get up. But now, in Becedas, she didn't want visitors, not even a pastor. The bloody rags. The stinking chamber pot. It was humiliating for a girl like Teresa, the town beauty, who had always been as spirited and lively as a brook. I held up a looking glass for her. She winced at the waxy pallor of her own cheeks.

The little church of Becedas was only a stone's throw from Raquel Córdoba's house. The first day, Teresa walked slowly, leaning on my arm. The next, we repeated the trek, Teresa still holding on to me, but moving a bit more freely now. Every day we made our way to the little church of San Honorat, but soon it became clear that God wasn't the only draw. There was also Father Alejo.

I met Father Alejo almost forty years ago, long before I'd tried chocolate. If I'd known that delicious substance then, I would have realized that Father Alejo was just like chocolate—full-bodied, smooth, sticky, sweet, and sensual. His eyes were the color of cacao beans, a deep, rich brown that made you feel warm and yet somehow embarrassed. Whenever he looked at me, I had to lower my eyes. In his presence, I felt all tingly, as though fairies were running all over my body with their tiny, tickly feet. No wonder the Church was suspicious of chocolate.

The presence of two new parishioners—young nuns from Ávila—attracted the priest's attention right away. He engaged us in conversation the very first day. He made small talk.

"You must miss your sisters," he said.

"Oh, yes, Father."

"What a lovely April we're having."

"Oh, yes, Father."

Teresa was immediately taken with him. He had an easy smile and a rich, sweet voice. There was a gentleness about him, a vulnerability that made you want to take his hand and squeeze it. After we met him, even I began to adopt a sunnier outlook—at least, for a while. When Teresa was with him, something of her old verve came back. Before I knew it, she was going to confession every other day, then every day. At first, I'd wait for her in the back of the church, but then I began to grow impatient. What did she have to confess that took so long? My confessions were over in a flash. *Uno, dos, tres, absolución.* I watched them. They sat together in a corner, in full view. Confessionals weren't yet common in our churches. She'd kneel beside him, head bowed, but they seemed more like two people engaged in conversation than confessor and penitent. Sometimes it seemed like he was doing all the talking. I stopped waiting for her. I started going back to Tía Raquel's house right after Mass.

Teresa's interminable confessions were raising eyebrows. Father Alejo had a bad reputation. He was living with a woman, people said. She had him bewitched, and now he was trying to seduce the little nun from Ávila. Or maybe she was seducing him.

"She'd better watch her step," said Tía Raquel, who brought home gossip from the marketplace, along with blades and toad's livers for her treatments. "If she causes a scandal, they'll run her out of town or worse. But before that happens, I'll get rid of her. I can't have some little tart of a nun ruining the reputation of my establishment." I shuddered. Get rid of her?

I began to fret constantly. What if they found out she was from a *converso* family? They'd accuse her of sorcery and lechery and who knows what else? After Mass, *conversos* reputedly washed the baptismal waters off their skin in elaborate ceremonies. They performed ghastly Jewish rituals with the blood of Christian infants in windowless rooms or deep in the forest. And everyone said Jews were lascivious, that Jewish women were capable of casting spells on Christian men that caused them to abandon God and ally themselves with the Devil. They especially loved to corrupt priests, people said.

Once the rumors reached the Holy Brotherhood, the inquisitors would be after Teresa in no time with their torches. I thought of the Hand of Fatima and the six-pointed star in the Guzmáns' chest. If the authorities went after Teresa, they'd surely investigate me, too. What if it came out that I knew all along her sister and brother-in-law were hiding tools for Jewish rites? It would do me no good at all to testify that a priest came several times a week to say Mass and hear confessions. Everyone knew that Judaizing *conversos* just pretended to perform the rites required by our Holy Mother Church. They made a great show of taking communion, then locked themselves in shadowy cellars where they performed their wretched ceremonies.

I had to get Teresa away from Father Alejo, but how? She came back from her confessions beaming. Talking to the priest seemed to be good for her. Tía Raquel was weakening her with her bloodletting, but the priest was strengthening her with his . . . what? Spiritual guidance? Friendship? Or . . . was something else going on between them? It wouldn't be the first time a confessor had ensnared a penitent. Mother Francisca was always warning us to be on the lookout. A suggestive remark. A languid look. And Father Alejo, with his scrumptious cacao-colored eyes, his muscles flexing subtly under his cassock, his luscious smile. Oh, God, I thought. Oh, God, no.

I pushed the idea out of my mind. He was perhaps a lax and lustful priest, but he wasn't out to trap Teresa. What would he want with her? She was hardly a Salomé. She was just a sick girl, happy to spend a few pleasant hours away from Tía Raquel. Poor Teresa. I felt guilty for having such thoughts. After all, why shouldn't she delight in Father Alejo's company? She was as ashen and weedy as ever, and she still coughed up bloody mucus at night, but at least now she had a reason to get up in the morning, to leave the house, to put one foot in front of the other. She had a smile on her lips, and the grace and wit that had never completely left her shone with a new intensity. She was even beautiful, just like the moon—pallid, yet radiant. Still, I worried.

"Teresa," I began, "Father Alejo . . ."

"Oh, that poor thing. He's as good as fresh-baked bread. It's terrible how they gossip about him."

"But Teresa, everyone knows he lives with a woman."

"It's not his fault," she said seriously. "She put a hex on him. Really, she's a sorceress."

"Teresa, you can't believe that."

"But it's true. She makes him wear an amulet under his shirt. I've seen it. He took it out and showed it to me. A little idol, a Venus." She lowered her voice. "With no clothes on . . . just a tiny conch over her . . . you know . . . her pudendum."

"You mean her cunt?" I said, suddenly annoyed and wanting to mortify her. Who used fancy words like "pudendum"? Spoiled ladies with brocade bodices or moneyed nuns with swansdown habits.

"Yes," she said, looking me straight in the eye. "Cunt."

"Well," I said, "take it away from him and get rid of it."

"I'm trying, but every time I ask for it, he starts to cry. He thinks he'll become weak and . . . you know . . . unmanly . . . if he gives it up."

"He's a priest. What difference does it make if he's impotent?"

"No man wants to feel swishy, even if he's a priest."

"Well, this can't go on. People are saying . . ."

"I know, I know. I'm working on it."

Every day she'd come back to Tía Raquel's more excited. "Really, you wouldn't believe how good he is, Angélica. He's a saint. He's so afraid this woman . . . her name is Porcia . . . he's so afraid that if people get their hands on her, they'll tie her to a cart and drag her through the streets until she's dead. That's why he can't turn her out. 'She's in God's hands,' I keep telling him. 'You have to think of your own soul.' But he's under her spell."

"So it's not because he's such a good person that he doesn't get rid of her. It's because he's enchanted."

"Well, yes but . . . He really is a *pan de Dios,* Angélica. He's a morsel of God's goodness right here on earth. He's so remorseful about the way he's been living. He just sobs and sobs."

I wondered who was confessing to whom, but I didn't say anything. That night, as I lay in bed in my white muslin shift, I thought about Porcia. I wondered what she looked like. I imagined her with abundant, copper-colored hair, unbound and flying about, her breasts exposed, and her skirts hiked up, just like Mary Magdalene's in a painting I'd once seen. What was she doing at that moment? I imagined her running her hand under Father Alejo's nightshirt. Did the tingly tiny fairies dance all over his body, as they had mine? I imagined her working her hand downward, downward, then fingering his cock. I imagined him, oh so compunctious, yet obligated to satisfy Porcia in order to protect his masculinity, mustering a heroic erection.

My breathing grew heavy. My chest hurt. I was about to do something sinful. I tried to think of Jesus, to imagine Jesus looking at me with profound disappointment, but that only stimulated me more. Jesus, the voyeur. It was perversely exciting. I brought my hand up under my shift and caressed my nipples, then my waist, my belly, the hair around my sex. Finally, I allowed my fingers to satisfy my physical yearning.

Afterward, I should have felt ashamed. What was I going to tell my confessor? What was I going to tell Father Alejo? That I had fallen asleep thinking about him, with my hand between my legs? And yet, instead of scruples I felt something different. What was it? A prickle, a quiver, a profound sense of peace.

One day when I came back from picking mint for tea, I found Teresa gleefully putting together a little package.

"This is it!" she squealed, before I could ask what she was doing. "I've got it!"

She held out a tiny, naked Venus with pointy nipples and wavy hair.

"The amulet! How did you get him to give it to you?"

"I begged, I nagged, I teased, and finally, I just snatched it from him!" She giggled. "I'm tying it up in this cloth with a bunch of pebbles. I'm going to throw it in the river."

We told Raquel Córdoba we were going to church, but instead, took the road that led past the cobbler's shop, behind the marketplace, and out through the meadow. We crossed the clearing slowly, in order to conserve Teresa's energy. When we finally reached the river, Teresa took the little parcel, held it a moment, and said a prayer for its speedy submersion.

"Here," she said, handing it to me. "You're stronger. You throw it."

I pulled my arm back like a boy throwing a ball and sent the amulet flying. It fell with a dazzling splash. Spattering droplets caught the sun's light, then cascaded downward and dissolved into the river.

"He's free," she said.

"Yes. Let's see if he leaves her."

He did leave her. And then, unexpectedly, he died. Just like that. Without any warning, not more than a few days after we had disposed of the Venus. A heart attack, they said. He just keeled over while dressing for Mass. Maybe his system couldn't take abstinence. Or maybe, as Teresa said, God was waiting for him to mend his evil ways before He called him. "He died in a state of grace," Teresa told me. "I saw him ascend into Heaven." I thought the fevers were making her say crazy things. Either that, or she was making up stories to impress me.

Juana Isabel Suárez arrived about two weeks after Father Alejo's funeral. I was happy to see her and anxious for news from the convent. The last few months had left me exhausted. The intimidating Don Martín (were the Guzmáns *Judaizantes*?), the lascivious Father Alejo (was he really up there cavorting with angels?), and Tía Raquel (was she a wise woman or a quack?)— all of it had taken its toll on me. I was exhausted, but I tried to keep my thoughts coherent. I prayed. God answered my prayers. Juana Isabel came.

But the solemn sister who appeared in Becedas that June afternoon was not the bubbly nun I had left in Ávila. The minute she climbed out of the smart-looking coach they had sent from the convent, I knew something was wrong. "What now?" I said to myself wearily.

It was a beautiful early-summer day, hot but not scorching. The sky was so blue it took your breath away. Diaphanous clouds hung in space, like gossamer veils shed by angels. Two elderly priests accompanied Juana Isabel. They greeted Teresa and me courteously, deposited their charge, and disappeared down the road in search of an inn and a good meal.

I stood in the dust until they had gone. The pastures spread outward in every direction like a jeweled mantel glittering in the sunlight. The flocks looked like clusters of pearls amid the intermingling of emerald, tourmaline, and jade. I hated to go inside. I would rather have climbed to the top of the church bell tower to drink in the view. I didn't want to hear any more bad news.

Juana Isabel found Teresa looking haggard and wan. Raquel Córdoba had intensified her treatments. Without Father Alejo to distract her, Teresa seemed to be losing her vitality. Juana Isabel didn't wait for me to ask what news she brought from the convent.

"I have something sad to tell you," she said. "I'm sorry to be the bearer of bad tidings, but . . . it's about Rosa."

My heart dropped into my stomach. "Is she ill?"

Juana Isabel looked down. "She's dead."

My temples began to throb and my fingers turned to icicles. "Dead . . ." I whispered.

"She escaped. Probably slipped out behind some of the girls who were visiting relatives."

"Yes, I received your letter. Did her father go looking for her?"

"Don Rogelio has so many daughters . . . It wasn't as though he cared much about Rosa and her little sisters. He never visited."

"Did he come to her profession?"

"She didn't profess."

"She must have married. She had a young man . . . Don Lope. She confided in me." Now I was the one who lowered her eyes. I was ashamed. I should have told.

"They had it planned. He was waiting for her. He had a mule ready. They took off toward Salamanca. There was no priest, no ceremony, but well, secret nuptials are not so uncommon. The Church recognizes them. It could have been all right." She bit her lip and then went on. "Apparently, Lope had stolen some money from home. He was going to settle in a town near Salamanca, where the family had property, then write his father, Don Félix, and tell him that he'd married for love. Lope was sure his father would pardon him and give the couple his blessing. What Lope didn't know was that Don Félix had made arrangements for him to marry someone else, the only daughter of a rich farmer. The girl didn't have a title, but she had an impressive dowry, and since Lope wasn't the eldest son, the bride's pedigree wasn't so important. The way Don Félix saw it, both he and the girl's father had made a good deal. She'd marry a nobleman, and Lope would net a small fortune."

"But if Lope was already married to Rosa, what could Don Félix do about it?"

"When Don Félix heard that his son had run off with a silly little novice with no money, he flew into a rage. He went thundering over to Don Rogelio's house. He screamed that his daughter had dishonored him, that she was living in sin. It couldn't be a real marriage, he said, since Lope was promised to someone else. Don Rogelio would have let it go. He didn't care much whether Rosa was married to God or Don Lope or the Devil, provided he didn't have to provide for her. As long as the neighbors weren't talking, what difference did it make if she were living with some boy who was willing to call her his wife? But Don Félix was making a lot of noise. He was accusing Don Rogelio openly. A man can't allow his name to be dragged through the mud. Now that Rosa's escape had become a public scandal, Don Rogelio had to take action. Rosa had dishonored him. He'd be the laughingstock of the town."

I felt my heart sinking. A story like this could have only one outcome. This was all my fault, I thought. I could have prevented it.

"The two men, Don Félix and Don Rogelio, rode off together to the town where their children were living. According to the gossips in the convent parlor, they surprised Rosa with her embroidery in her hand. Don Félix held Don Lope fast, while Don Rogelio drew his sword. Without so much as a tear or a prayer, he murdered his daughter. The child was wearing a pretty little dress with a white ruffled bodice. When he brought her back to us, the fabric was drenched with red. She reminded me of a slaughtered swan, its blood seeping through its feathers."

"He brought her back to you?" I exclaimed through my sobs.

"He laid her body on the floor of the vestibule. 'I entrusted her to you,' he hissed at Mother Francisca. 'And look how you took care of her.' 'God entrusted her to *you*,' Mother Francisca hissed back. 'You placed the law of honor above His law: Thou shalt not kill.'

"He was trembling with rage. 'I paid a dowry for her to enter this convent,' he snarled. 'Wait,' said Mother Francisca. She disappeared into the interior and came back with a small black pouch. 'Here,' she said, hurling it at him. Ducats went flying through the air.

"We buried Rosa in the convent. Her two younger sisters were hysterical with grief, poor things. The littlest one—she's about eight—squatted on the floor and wet her shift. The other one lifted up the hem of her habit and buried her face in it. Mother Francisca didn't say a thing. She just let her be. Don Rogelio didn't come to the Mass. He didn't even pay the funeral expenses. A couple months later, we heard Don Lope had married a blue-eyed beauty from a nearby farm."

I made myself a tea of valerian and chamomile and went into my room to lie down. I knew the herbs would put me out for hours. All I wanted was to sink into darkness. I couldn't bear to think about Don Rogelio, about Rosa. And yet, the image of that poor child, her soul as pure as rainwater . . . What flashed through her mind when she saw her father standing before her, sword unsheathed? Did she understand she was going to die? Did she cry for her mother? Did she curse me, the friend who had allowed this to happen? I would have to confess. I had committed a mortal sin. But I couldn't compose my thoughts. I could only surrender to the valerian.

The priest who replaced Father Alejo at the church of Becedas was ancient, with a face like a dried apricot and no teeth. Decrepit and dull, he seemed an ideal confessor. He probably wouldn't live much longer, I thought. I could get it over with and never see him again.

Juana Isabel wrote to Don Alonso right away. Teresa was getting worse, she said. He should send for her. He should bring her home.

Within days, Don Alonso's coach arrived in Becedas with Don Alonso in it. He looked older. The creases around his eyes had deepened and his hair was graying. His clothes, as always, spoke of refined austerity. He was still a handsome man.

The stink and gloom of Raquel Córdoba's house momentarily overwhelmed him. He glanced around and took it all in: the bloody mugs, still unwashed from the morning's bleeding, the containers of leeches, the blades, the pincers, the potions. The crease between his brows lengthened, and his jaw tensed. He spoke with measured syllables, "Where is my daughter?"

"Oh, Don Alonso, we weren't expecting you today."

"I know. That's why I came today. Where is my daughter?"

"She's much better, *señor*. The treatments have done her a world of good."

"Excuse me for speaking out of turn, Don Alonso," I said, lowering my eyes, "but Teresa is very ill. I think it best . . . I would suggest . . ."

"Get her out of here at once, Uncle," interrupted Juana Isabel. "This hag is killing her!"

"Sister Juana Isabel . . ." said Raquel, feigning humility, "how can you say such a thing? I'm trying to help. Don Alonso has unwavering confidence in me. Isn't that so, *señor*?"

"Let me see Teresa," he commanded. His voice was resolute, controlled.

"I don't know if she's ready . . . ," the healer began.

"She's upstairs," I said. Don Alonso pushed past Raquel as though she were an insignificant object—a broom or a mop—and climbed the stairs two by two.

He didn't find Teresa in bed, as we all expected, but kneeling, lost in prayer. He stepped out discreetly. Finally, she looked up and saw us in the doorway.

"*Papá!*" she cried, stumbling to him and collapsing into his arms.

"I was praying for Rosa," she whispered. "We must all pray."

Don Alonso looked at me askance. I nodded slightly, but said nothing.

"Let's pray that now she's safe and free. And we must pray for Don Rogelio and Don Félix as well. May they see the evil of their deed, may they repent, and may God forgive them."

Don Alonso stood there uncomprehending. No one offered him an explanation.

How could she be so good, I wondered, praying for those bastards who deserved to rot in Hell? I had no intention of praying for Don Rogelio and Don Félix. As far as I was concerned, they could both spend eternity on the coals.

Don Alonso turned to Juana Isabel and me. "Sisters," he said, "please help Teresa get her things together. We should leave as soon as possible."

He wanted to carry Teresa downstairs, but she balked. "I can walk," she insisted. Haggard as she was, she forced a smile. "In fact, I bet I can beat you! Let's race, *Papá!*"

He took her by the hand, and she eased herself gracefully downstairs. As pale as a fine pearl, I thought, and just as luminous. Her glow came from within. The pallor of illness only served to highlight the perfection of her features.

Don Alonso brought her home, where he could care for her himself. Juana Isabel and I went back to Encarnación, but we visited almost every day.

We were in the hellish month of July, and a blazing film floated low in the atmosphere. I worried about Teresa. How could a girl in her condition stand that heat? She always greeted us with a laugh—that tinkling laugh that reminded me of crystal shattering—but it was clear she was struggling.

During the winter months the people of Ávila hoard ice in a huge, underground deposit. In the summer, they withdraw portions of slush to make iced drinks, which they flavor with fruit juice. Every day Don Alonso's servants trudged to the deposit, lugging back heavy ceramic containers filled with rime to make tangy ices for Teresa.

"*Papá* is so good to me," she whispered. "And you know, he's making a lot of spiritual progress. I'm really delighted."

She laid her hand on my wrist. The feel of her clammy fingers through my habit made me shudder. I'd already lost one friend that summer—two, with Father Alejo. I couldn't bear to think of Teresa growing weaker and weaker until she . . .

"We've been talking about mental prayer, the kind Osuna describes in *The Third Spiritual Alphabet*. When I feel up to it, we chat under that big oak in the garden at dusk. *Papá* has been trying recollection—you know, sitting alone with God, blocking out everything around you and allowing yourself to melt into the stillness within."

It sounded beautiful. I felt peaceful just hearing about it. I didn't realize at the time how dangerous those ideas were. I didn't realize that someday they'd get Teresa into trouble.

"*Papá* says that since he's been practicing recollection, he can pray for the first time in years. That makes me so happy, Angélica." She seemed so serene. She'll get better, I thought. She's making progress, too. I went home feeling more hopeful than I had in a long while.

"An intimate, personal relationship with God," I told my sisters. "That's what faith is really all about. It's not about reciting prayers you don't understand, but about knowing God in a profoundly personal way." I began to feel it too, that special, close relationship with God. But it was hard to explain. I kept looking for comparisons. "It's like falling in love," I told them. "It's like falling off a mountain peak and feeling yourself gliding, floating, borne by seraphim." Some listened. Some shrugged and went back to their spinning or their gossiping. Juana Isabel and I started praying together during the recreation periods. Not going to the chapel and reciting the rosary, but sitting in the garden and meditating. I thought my confessor would be thrilled.

Father Tomé was a young Dominican, only twenty-five but already portly and balding. His tightlipped grimace gave him a constipated look. He didn't like confessing women, which he thought beneath him, and was irritated that his superiors had assigned him to Encarnación. He was one of four convent confessors, which meant that he and his companions each had to hear some fifty confessions a week. He assigned light penances—a couple of Hail Marys or a twitch or two with the switch—unless a nun claimed to see visions. Then he'd do a more thorough interrogation because visions could mean a woman was possessed by the Devil. But for someone like me, with banal sins and little imagination, confessions were short and perfunctory.

Until I said, "Do you know what I desire most, Father?"

"What, daughter?"

"What I desire most, Father, is an intimate, personal relationship with God."

"*An intimate, personal relationship with God?*" Father Tomé lowered his brow. His eyes became cloudy and suspicious. "What the Holy Mother Church demands of us is that we carry out all our obligations, that we keep our vows, that we chant the Office, that we . . ."

"But the purpose of all that is to know God. To know God intimately." He looked at me as though I were a recalcitrant little girl refusing to put down a toy. "Where did you get such notions, child?"

Child? It's true I was only eighteen, but he was acting as though he were my grandfather. Still, he was a priest, so I swallowed my pride. I told him about Teresa and her Uncle Pedro, about Osuna and recollection, about God shining through the darkness of the soul. "Teresa says that through mental prayer, Don Alonso has made tremendous spiritual progress," I said.

Father Tomé started to twitch like a nervous pony. "Those ideas come from the Devil!" he snapped.

I was flabbergasted. I should have bit my tongue. I should have said yes, Father, and gone back to my cell. Instead, I said, "But Teresa says her father can pray for the first time in years."

"I don't doubt it," he said dryly.

"But isn't that a good thing, Father? He feels truly connected to God in a way he never did before."

"That's the way Jews pray."

"What?"

"Directly to God. Without the rites of Our Holy Mother Church.

Without priests. I don't doubt Don Alonso prefers mental prayer. He's a Jew. He prays like a Jew."

"No, Father . . . Forgive me . . . He goes to Mass."

"He goes to Mass, but he continues to pray like a Jew. Those people are never at home in church. They'd much rather sit on a rock and do it all themselves. They're arrogant. They think they don't need the ordained ministers of the *one holy catholic and apostolic Church*." His face had turned the color of raw liver.

Images came tumbling back into my mind. Images from long ago, from days in the *estrado*. Tía Cati's descriptions of autos-da-fe. Jews parading down the streets in *sambenitos*. Townspeople hurling rotting vegetables, fruits, stones. No wonder *conversos*—even those who sincerely loved Our Lord Jesus—felt more comfortable praying mentally than genuflecting in church with the neighbors who had abused them. No wonder they wanted a personal, intimate relationship with God.

"Tell me something, daughter . . . have you ever heard Teresa or anyone in her family say anything . . . you know . . . questionable? I mean, aside from this business about mental prayer."

"Questionable, Father?"

"You know what I mean. Suspect. Something that might indicate they weren't truly Christian?"

"No, Father."

"Have you ever seen them do anything unusual? Prepare meals on Friday for the next day, for example? Or keep objects in their houses that might be used for unorthodox practices?"

I remembered the spice holder with strange letters, the platter with the Hand of Fatima and the six-pointed star. I looked straight at Father Tomé. He had a large pimple on his nose.

"Objects, Father?"

"Yes, objects that might be used for rituals Mother Church might not approve of."

"No, Father."

"Think hard, Angélica. You've spent a lot of time with the Cepeda Ahumada family."

"No, Father. I haven't seen any strange objects. I'm absolutely sure."

I went to Mother Francisca and asked her if I could change confessors.

"Why, daughter?" she asked.

"He has bad breath, Mother. He stinks like a farting sow. I can't stand to be near him." She should have punished me. I don't know why she didn't.

Mother Francisca arranged for a new confessor. Braulio Estévez looked like an angel—the kind you see in paintings of the Annunciation. Soft blond hair and eyes like pools of liquid sapphire. A manly jaw, broad shoulders, strong hands with long, shapely fingers. The only thing missing were those feathery wings artists always paint coming out of the white robe—wings that look as though they were sewn onto the garment. It doesn't make sense. The wings grow out of angels' backs, not out of their clothes. It would be tricky to insert openings in the back of a robe small enough so you couldn't see any skin and large enough to pop through two broad, functional wings. You'd have to drape the fabric over the wings or else slit the cloth, turn up the edge, run it along either side of the wings and sew it up. I should know. I'm a seam-stress. Anyhow, Fray Braulio didn't have wings. As a matter of fact, if I had thought to look under his habit, I might have discovered hoofs.

He was a Carmelite and wore his habit with elegance and grace. Few men wear a dress so well. He had a reputation for being a good and gentle listener. He was allegedly something of a lady's man, but I was so glad to be rid of Father Tomé that I attached little importance to the wagging of evil tongues. They say you should never listen to gossip, but in this case, not lis-tening was a mistake. Most of the younger nuns liked him and wanted to confess to him, but Mother Francisca was usually careful to assign him pen-itents who were past the age of temptation. (Or, at least, that's what she thought.) She must have thought I was strong enough to resist his easy smile, or perhaps that I was too plain for him to want me.

I didn't talk to him about mental prayer. I avoided issues that might lead to conversations about Judaizers and heretics. Anyhow, he didn't seem partic-ularly interested in my prayer life. When I spoke to him of wanting to be closer to Mary, he grew distracted. Instead, he liked to hear stories of scandal and tragedy, so that's what I gave him. I told him about Rosa and Don Lope, about how sinful I felt for not having reported their affair. "Oh Father," I moaned, "how can God forgive me?" I liked the way his eyes sparkled when the details got juicy. I liked the way he looked at me, the intensity of his gaze." I told him about Teresa and Father Alejo. "Even though it all worked out for the best, Father, I should have prevented her from becoming involved." He looked at me with such compassion, such tenderness. I pre-tended I thought he was just being kind. After all, I told myself, he was my father confessor. It was natural for him to be caring. But, well, I guess I have to admit that I knew we were both playing games.

I didn't tell him I'd once been in love with Don Javier, though. Not because Don Javier had been Teresa's suitor, but because he was now a priest, and Fray Braulio might know him.

Teresa's fevers and coughing persisted, and the pains in her chest continued to grow worse. Don Alonso brought in doctors, not quacks like Raquel Córdoba, but real doctors. They bled Teresa, but in moderation. They placed leeches on her back and fed her sugary compounds. But even if they saved her, I thought, Father Tomé could kill her. He could accuse her of unorthodox prayer practices before the Inquisition. What could I do? All I could do was pray.

The stifling August air hung over Ávila like a mantle. Breathing was a chore, even for the healthy. Yet the sewing room buzzed with excited antici-pation. The *Pausatio,* the feast of the Assumption, was approaching, and we were adorning the convent for the joyous event. We were Carmelites, after all, named for Our Lady of the Carmel. What happier occasion for us than the joyful departure of Mother Mary from this life and the assumption of her most blessed body into Heaven! There were statues to be dressed and altars to be adorned. On the eve of the Assumption, we would fill the chapel with summer flowers—white roses for Our Lady's purity, yellow for her death, red for her son's precious blood. We would gather bouquets of amaryllises, hibis-cuses, and nasturtiums to lift our spirits and pay homage to the beauty and diversity of God's world.

Teresa planned to share the day with us. She asked her father for permis-sion to say her confession in preparation for the Mass. Why had Don Alonso refused? Did he fear his daughter wasn't up to it? Did he have a premonition that confession might turn into extreme unction?

Don Alonso's messenger arrived at the convent early in the morning on the 15th. Teresa has done it again, I thought. She always gets her own way. She must have said her confession last night, and now, here's the courier to tell us the carriage will bring her within the hour. The man asked to see Mother Francisca. Ah, I thought, she's going to make a grand entrance. She'll be a bit wobbly on her feet, but that will only make it all the more dramatic. "How brave she is," everyone will say. "She's so ill, but she has mustered up her strength for this special day. A real martyr," they'll say. Well, it's okay, I thought. She needs distractions. Let her play the saint.

Mother Francisca dismissed the messenger and called a group of us to her. Instead of the expected grin, she wore a grimace. A tear like a sliver of silver glistened in the corner of her eye.

"Mother," I murmured, "what's wrong?"

She seemed unable to focus. Her lips trembled almost imperceptibly.

"Mother?" The prioress looked as though she were going to disintegrate.

"Don Alonso's messenger says . . ." She caught her breath. "He says Sister Teresa is dead."

Dead! *¡Muerta!* The word struck me like a metal object.

"It can't be," I whispered. "It can't be." My stomach was churning. I felt as though my insides would explode.

¡Muerta! The bloody bandages. The stench of the sickroom. Suddenly, I felt as though I were thrashing in a sea of vomit, hurled this way and that by malodorous waves. A moan surged from my aching bosom.

A cool hand pressed the small of my back and steered me toward my cell. Soft, loving hands swabbed my face and neck, then pressed an infusion to my lips.

I don't remember the feast of the Assumption. I don't remember the aroma of the roses or kneeling before the altar in joyous celebration. What I remember is Teresa stretched out before us on her bed, inert, peaceful, all fatigue gone from her beautiful face. The black veil against the blush of her cheek. The satin pillow. She looked like a sleeping princess awaiting the magic kiss. Don Alonso, as pale as the moon on a winter's night, refused to let us dress her for burial.

"No," he said softly. "No." He didn't want to believe she was dead.

I closed my eyes and prayed:

Blessed are those who mourn:
they shall be comforted.

Angélica del Sagrado Corazón
Toledo, 15 July 1576

CHAPTER 7

Awakenings

WE COULDN'T PUT OFF THE BURIAL ANY LONGER. THREE DAYS HAD PASSED, and Teresa's body was still at her father's house, stretched out on the bed, her arms folded over her chest. I remembered what Lazarus's sister Mary said to Jesus when He asked her to open Lazarus's tomb: "I can't, Lord. He's been dead more than three days. He stinketh." The thing is, a corpse stinks after three days, especially in the summer, when even live people stink from sweat. Animals go around panting and their breath smells rancid. You have to take out the chamber pots as soon as there's a drop in them because in the heat shit—including the shit of nuns and fancy ladies—reeks. And even then, you have to cover it up with parsley just to keep from puking.

Curiously, Teresa's body emitted an almost imperceptible aroma of roses instead of rotting meat. You could smell it if you got very close to her. I didn't say anything to anybody about it. Something about the idea frightened me.

Don Alonso still refused to allow us to wash and shroud Teresa's body. Every once in a while he held a mirror to her lips to see if her breath misted the glass. It never did.

"Come," I whispered, nudging him gently toward the door. "The time has come."

"She's not dead," he kept murmuring. "I know she's not dead." He refused to go out of the room. He was afraid to leave us alone with her.

"Yes," echoed Mother Francisca. "The time has come."

"It has not come!" he bristled. "You will not dress her for the grave!"

In spite of the August heat, candles burned in holders on chests on either side of the room. Don Alonso picked one up and brought it close to Teresa's face, searching for signs of life. With the meticulousness of a doctor examining a patient, he moved it from her chin to her ear, then upward toward her forehead. The light moved eerily from feature to feature without provoking a reaction. Suddenly, a drop of hot wax dripped onto Teresa's eyelid. I flinched, squinted, and moved my hand instinctively to my own lashes. I expected Don Alonso to curse the candle, but instead, a spark of hope glimmered fleetingly in his eye. He stared at his daughter as though he thought the power of his gaze would force a response. But Teresa didn't blink. Her face showed no hint of consciousness. Don Alonso looked away.

Poor man, I thought, he just can't accept it.

The candles sent graceful, vaporous ribbons into the air. I'd opened several windows to let in the evening breeze, but Don Alonso ordered the curtains closed so that the light and noises from outside wouldn't disturb his sleeping daughter.

"Let her sleep," he said, tiptoeing around the room. "Let her rest." My eyes met Juana Isabel's, then Mother Francisca's. No one wanted to tell him she would sleep forever.

In a corner of the room, a bouquet of lavender stood rotting in a vase. Flies buzzed about, drawn—curiously, I thought—more to the decaying blooms than to the dead girl. I picked up the flowers and threw them out. Don Alonso watched me as if to protest, but said nothing.

Now the scent of roses emanating from Teresa's body became more noticeable.

"I smell an odd perfume," remarked Mother Francisca.

"I don't," snapped Don Alonso, uncharacteristically prickly.

Night fell late in August, but it was growing dark. "You should go back to the convent," said Don Alonso. His outward serenity had returned.

We didn't go back. At midnight, we were still standing around the bed watching Teresa, begging God for a sign of life, knowing there would be none.

"Lorenzo will stay with her tonight," said Don Alonso, seeing my eyelids droop. Lorenzo was planning to embark for Peru, but his sister's illness had caused him to put off the trip.

Finally, Juana Isabel and Mother Francisca climbed into Don Alonso's carriage. I collapsed into a chair in the corner and dozed. Lorenzo sat across the room, next to a chest on top of which two tapers burned dimly in low, silver holders. I opened my eyes for a second and saw Teresa's inert profile in the muted light. Her brow and forehead looked unexpectedly flushed. Lorenzo was snoring softly. It was unseemly for the two of us—a bachelor and a nun—to be sleeping there together in a room, especially a room with a corpse, but we were too exhausted to care about decorum. I must have fallen into a deep slumber, because the next thing I remember was a blood-curdling scream.

It sounded as though it came from a woman, but it was Lorenzo.

My eyes snapped open and I sprang toward the bed. Flames leapt from the covers.

"Water!" I yelled. "Water!"

I thrashed at the bedclothes with my shawl, trying to smother the blaze. My hands smarted from the heat. Teresa's face was all aglow, a dazzling angel amid Satan's flares.

"Move her!" I screamed at Lorenzo. "Move Teresa!" He stood there gasping, staring at me with uncomprehending eyes. "Grab her by the shoulders!" I screamed. "Pull her off the bed!"

Silvia rushed in, recoiled at the blazing bedclothes, and ran back out. Seconds later, she returned with a bucket of water she had drawn for the next day's wash. A tongue of flame lapped the air, catching the hem of Teresa's skirt.

"Holy Jesus!" screamed Silvia. "Holy Mary mother of God! Get her out of here!"

Don Alonso burst into the room and yanked Teresa out of his son's arms. Silvia went for more water. Within minutes, we had put out the flames. Silvia stood there, two empty buckets in her hands, and looked from Don Alonso to the limp body he held. Tears trickled from her eyes. Teresa hadn't stirred.

The maid didn't have to say a word. She bowed her head and, uttering a *Pater Noster*, left the room. Moments later, another maid came in with fresh linens. When she was done changing the bedclothes, Don Alonso laid his beloved daughter gently on the sheets and crumpled into the same chair I had occupied. He sat there sobbing for a long time. Finally, he pulled himself upright and fixed his eyes on Teresa. "All right," he whispered. "Tomorrow you will dress her."

As soon as Mother Francisca returned the next morning, she sent word to the convent that a grave should be dug.

I dreaded what had to come next. Gently, lovingly, I slipped my arm under Teresa's back and eased her into a sitting position. Her head fell heavily onto my shoulder, and I placed my cheek against her forehead. Her skin didn't have the dank, clammy feel of dead flesh. Instead, it was tepid. Silvia came in with a basin, her tears dripping into the water, and Juana Isabel began to sponge and perfume Teresa's delicate feet. How many times had I washed those lovely ankles with lavender water when we were girls? I pulled the shift up above Teresa's knees, and Sister Francisca slipped some rags under the body so we wouldn't dampen the bed. Teresa's legs were shapely, white and firm in spite of her long illness. She reminded me of the statues of the goddess Diana—robes flung open to reveal fine limbs—that adorned the parks of fine houses.

Juana Isabel's sponge moved swiftly over the curve of Teresa's thighs and hips, but when Mother Francisca lifted the shift up over her head to expose her sex and breasts, Juana Isabel looked away. I took the sponge from her, dipped it in the water, and dabbed gently around her secret parts. *Pudendum*, I thought. Teresa's *pudendum*.

"*Cunt!*" I heard Teresa blurt out, her eyes dancing with mirth. "Go ahead and say it, you ninny!" I looked at Teresa's inert body, her lifeless features, her closed eyes. I swallowed hard.

I had helped Teresa bathe countless times, but she had always kept her shift on. Seeing her exposed like that . . . I don't know . . . it was somehow shocking. Her pubic hair, soft and reddish and curly. Her breasts, firm and large. Her nipples, pink as rosebuds. She was beautiful, more beautiful than the naked Venus in the Count of Mollén's garden.

Together Mother Francisca and I removed Teresa's shift. She lay there, bare and innocent as God made her. A terrible thought occurred to me. I could examine Teresa. Mother Francisca and Juana Isabel wouldn't suspect a thing. I could just slip my hand up into . . . I could find out the answer to the question that had gnawed at me for years: Had Teresa and her cousin Javier been lovers? Had she entered the convent a virgin? I began to wash her inner thigh, slowly, carefully, working the sponge toward her exposed sex. I held my breath.

The Mother Superior had left the bedside and was preparing the shroud, a soft, black sheet of silk and wool. Juana Isabel was unfolding the clean habit in which Teresa would be buried. It would be easy for me to do what I was planning to do. It would take a split second.

But then, suddenly, I pulled my hand away. I felt ashamed. Was I going to violate my sister's body? Was I going to expose her secret now, in the hour of her death? I pulled a fresh shift down over her head and torso, then covered her up with a blanket. Gently, I brushed her hair. It was as short as an animal's pelt, yet longer than weeks before, when it had still been covered by a wimple. It had grown during her illness and continued to grow now, in death.

We dressed her and sealed her eyes with candle wax. I winced as I watched the hot wax drip onto her pale eyelids and dark lashes. Don Alonso came in and stood by her side, grasping the bedpost for support. He gazed at Teresa's face, placid and still, then placed his hand on her wrist. "She has a pulse," he whispered. "I'm sure of it."

I touched his arm. It would have been audacious under other circumstances, but now, what did it matter? He was just a wretched being in need of human warmth. "Soon the other sisters will be here," I said gently. "Eat something, Don Alonso. You haven't eaten in days."

About thirty nuns from Encarnación streamed into the house in the afternoon. They had come to bear away Teresa's body. The grave was ready. The funeral would be the following morning in the convent church.

That night we held a vigil. Mother Francisca, Juana Isabel, and I had turned the room into a *capilla ardiente,* a provisional chapel ablaze with candlelight. Tapers lined Teresa's tiny oratory and stood along her dressers and chests, on her night table and secretary. Her face glowed like an angel's. She's already in Heaven, I thought.

Teresa's older sister María had come in from the country, and her younger sister Juana had come back from Encarnación, where she was staying. We all knelt by Teresa's bed, and Father Braulio prayed over her body. As he made the sign of the Cross, his eye held mine. I felt my heart riddled with an indescribable longing. I caught my breath. At about five in the morning, we got ready to lift her onto the litter. Don Alonso was wailing, "No! She's not ready to be put in the ground! I can feel her pulse!"

"Poor, demented man," muttered Mother Francisca.

"She's with God now, Uncle," said Juana Isabel softly. "She's at peace. Rejoice for her."

"She's moving!" wailed Don Alonso.

"No, Uncle. She's with God."

I looked at Teresa and felt something like tiny stabs up and down my arm. I was certain her eyelids had fluttered under the cold candle wax. I'm as demented as he is, I thought.

But Juana Isabel had seen it, too.

"It looks like she's trying to open her eyes," she whispered. Her hands were trembling.

"She's moving!" stammered Don Alonso. He reached over her body and gently removed the wax seals. Teresa opened her eyes. All around her, candles were burning. The voices of the nuns chanted in unison, "Blessed are those who mourn: they shall be comforted." The flickering flames against the murky wall, the chorus of voices . . . She must have thought she really was in another world. "Teresa!" whispered Don Alonso.

She stared at him, then looked around at me, at Juana Isabel, at Mother Francisca and the other sisters. "Why did you call me back? I was so happy where I was." Her voice was weak, but perfectly audible.

"Where were you, Teresa?"

"I was in Heaven."

Again, Juana Isabel and I exchanged glances. "It would be better not to make her talk," I said, assuming authority. After all, I had been her nurse.

But Juana Isabel couldn't rein in her curiosity. "Did you see God?"

"Yes, He said He had work for me to do on earth." She closed her eyes. A shadow of fear darkened Don Alonso's face. He must have thought she might slip away again.

But she kept talking. Something about convents. Something about foundations.

"I saw Hell, too," she whispered, without opening her eyes. "It was terrible. Flames and burning bodies. Just like in the pictures." She was thinking, no doubt, about a huge painting of the damned plunging into Hell that hung in the convent corridor. Had she really smelled the crackling flesh, or had she dreamt the whole thing, reworking familiar images in her delirium?

"Teresa, my darling Teresa." Don Alonso was weeping quietly and rubbing Teresa's hands. "Don't tire yourself."

"It was so beautiful, *Papá*" whispered Teresa. "I saw the Virgin Mary, and I saw *Mamá*, too. *Mamá* was surrounded by angels. She asked about you and about my baby sister, Juana."

"Did she ask about me, the other Juana?" said Juana Isabel.

"She asked about all of you."

Don Alonso invited the nuns to break their nighttime fast and showed them into the *estrado.* He asked Silvia to have bread and cold meats brought from the kitchen. Then he returned to Teresa's bedroom, where Juana Isabel and I were dismantling the *capilla ardiente.*

"We thought you were dead," Juana Isabel said quietly.

"You'll know I'm dead when you see my body covered with a cloth of gold," said Teresa. What had she meant by that? I wondered. Her voice sounded as though it came from a long ways off. It occurred to me that she was still on the other side.

Don Alonso sat on the bed and tried to pull her toward him, but the instant he touched her, she whimpered. The pain was unbearable. The slightest movement caused her agony. She couldn't lie on her back. Instead, she had to curl up in a ball, contracting her stomach, tucking her legs to her chest. In order to change the bed linen, Juana Isabel and I had to place her carefully in the middle of a sheet, then lift the corners to form a litter. Gently, we carried her across the room and placed her on a divan, setting her down as though she were made of glass.

The rest of the nuns went back to the convent. Only Juana Isabel and I stayed on, along with Teresa's older sister. Eventually, María left, too. She had to get back to her family.

"I think she's paralyzed." Juana Isabel's voice was so low, it was as though she'd only mouthed the words. But Teresa heard her.

"I'm not paralyzed," she protested, emitting tiny squeaks. It was painful for her to speak, but she ran her finger over the sheet to show she could move it.

I caressed her hair, careful not to press her skin. She closed her eyes to show she liked it.

"I love you, Teresa," I whispered. "Please get better." A droplet formed on her eyelid. "Dear God," I prayed, "please let her get better."

Fall came. The foliage turned red and ginger. Laborers gathered wheat and kitchen maids preserved fruits and stored vegetables for the winter to come. The days passed. The skies dimmed and the fields became a palette of chestnut and charcoal. Trees, stunning in their starkness, formed dark silhouettes against a dreary firmament.

Teresa lay motionless on her bed. Juana Isabel had returned to Encarnación, and only I was left to care for her. She could move her arms now, but her legs remained immobile, like two dead snakes hanging from a withered tree trunk. Day after day I sponged her forehead, brushed her mushrooming curls, no longer bound under a wimple, and passed her bedpan to Silvia. "Pudendum? You mean cunt?" I heard her say in my mind. I laughed.

The winter was long and tedious. I stitched a blue silk dress for the Virgin in the convent chapel, then embroidered the skirt with a vine pattern.

I made new bed linens for Don Alonso. But mostly I prayed and read to
Teresa. Occasionally I returned to Encarnación for an afternoon, but I didn't
like to leave Teresa in anyone else's care. She was my responsibility.

The Feast of the Magi came and went. Now the days were growing
longer and the fields were awakening. Purple saffron flowers pushed their
little heads up defiantly through the snow. Delicate leaves appeared on
branches that had seemed dead only days before. Children sang *rondas* and
frolicked in the mud without shawls or mantles, oblivious to the icy spring
air. In Don Alfonso's kitchen the cook was busy planning the Easter meal.
The aroma of cinnamon bread and *pan de Pascua* wafted through the house.

Teresa was making progress. She was able to talk. She could sit up for
longer and longer periods, although her legs were still limp. I massaged her
hands and rubbed her back with pomades of animal fat and lavender water.
I made compresses of camphor and eucalyptus. The doctor came every day
and prescribed medicines, which I prepared in the kitchen. They were working, I thought. Teresa's eyes were brighter and her breathing was smoother.

"I want to go back to the convent," Teresa told me one day, quite suddenly. I was sitting on the bed, preparing to read to her from Laredo's *Ascent
to Mount Zion.*

"How are you going to go back? You can't even walk."

"I'm bored here," she said. "I want to see my sisters."

"I'll ask them to visit."

"They do visit, but it's not enough." There was no sense in arguing.
Once she got an idea into her head, she was like a goat that butts and butts
until it knocks open the gate.

"No, Teresa," pleaded Don Alonso. "You're not ready. Wait until it's
warmer. Wait until summer. If you catch a chill now, you may never get well."

But the Sunday preceding Holy Week he accompanied us back to
Encarnación, trying the whole way to dissuade her.

Easter Vigil at the convent is the most beautiful of all Masses. That night
I was so overcome with gratitude for Teresa's recovery that I felt almost—how
can I say it?—almost transported. Even now, after all these years, I can close
my eyes and relive the moment. Hours after nightfall we line up outside the
chapel, each with a taper in her hand. The deacon, imposing in his sparkling
white dalmatic, lights the paschal candle, and we file in, chanting, gliding
like specters in the shadows. Each nun ignites her taper from the paschal
flame, and soon the chapel is radiant with candlelight. The deacon begins the

Exsultet, the song in praise of the paschal candle: *Dominus sit in corde tuo, ut digne et competenter annunties suum Paschale praeconium.* "May the Lord be on thy heart and on thy lips, that thou mayest worthily and fittingly proclaim His Paschal praise." He has a deep, melodious singing voice that holds you in its embrace and makes you feel as though gentle, loving arms are lifting you off the ground. At the words *incensi hujus sacrificium,* he releases five grains of incense and a pungent aroma fills the air. The Virgin, crowned in light, smiles at me, her darling daughter, and I feel such tenderness for her I want to kiss her feet. Jesus, more radiant still, looks with love at me, His bride, and I know He sees everything I hide in my heart. I feel His gaze on my brow. He is thanking me for caring for Teresa, and I am thanking Him for sparing her life.

That night, in my cell, I pray a new prayer—one that I heard Don Alonso chant every night from behind the closed door of his bedroom, when he thought we had all gone to bed: *Hear, oh Israel, the Lord our God, the Lord is one.* And then he chanted something else in a foreign language, maybe Arabic or maybe . . . something like *Chemá Yisroel, Adonai Elojenu, Adonai Echad.* He chanted with a voice full of emotion, as though he were sobbing and laughing and making love all at the same time. I can't get that prayer out of my head, and so that night, after the Vigil, I chant it, too, but not out loud, of course. What harm can there be in a prayer?

What I'm going to write now is, well, nasty, I admit it. If I have to testify at Teresa's beatification, I'll just leave this part out. I think I've made it perfectly clear that I loved Teresa, but the fact is, after we got back to the convent and settled into our daily routine, she got to be something of a pest. She was sick, of course, and her legs were paralyzed. You have to make allowances for people with problems like that, but even so, and I'll write this down one more time, she got to be a real pest. Not because she was mean. She wasn't. On the contrary, because she was good. So good, so sweet, so pious that nobody could stand her.

Teresa had a large, two-storey suite at Encarnación. Nuns with money could have quarters like that. I had a cell down the hall, a nice one, I'm not complaining, but nothing as elaborate as Teresa's. Don Alonso had insisted that Silvia move in with her in order to bathe and groom her, but it was my job to make sure she took her medicine, got enough rest, and ate properly. She couldn't keep to the same schedule as the other nuns, of course. She was too fragile.

She did get up at five in the summer, six in the winter, just like the rest of us. In the morning I'd go to her cell to get her ready for the day, hoping, praying, that she was done vomiting for the morning. Even though I was her nurse and used to it, it was a nasty way to start the day. I'd sponge her forehead and her lips with rosewater and slip an anis pastille under her tongue. Her breath was so acrid I had to turn away. She'd see me and start to cry.

"I disgust everyone," she'd say. "Why didn't God let me stay in Heaven with Him?"

After her stomach settled, we'd pray an hour, and then I'd take her to the chapel for Divine Office. I'd have to carry her because she was still too weak to walk. I'd pick her up in my arms like a pile of dirty bed linen and tramp down the hall singing "It's off to the river I go, I go. It's off to the river to wash." Teresa would giggle, and I'd feel so . . . I don't know . . . so useful. I loved to see her happy, to hear her silvery laugh. On those mornings I felt as though I really were Teresa's little sister. I felt I was doing something special for her, something no one else could do.

But then, one morning, when I got to Teresa's room, she wasn't there. I looked around. The silk sheets were crumpled on the bed, and the fine, flannel blankets were piled up on top of them. The fluffy, feather pillows were thrown to the side. The curtains were open. Sunlight flooded the room, illuminating the delicately carved bone crucifix her brother Fernando had sent from Colombia. Everything was in its place: the gilded statue of the Virgin that stood by the intricately carved prie-dieu, the ornate silver candle-holder she kept on her night table, the copy of Laredo's book, the painting of the Annunciation on the wall.

Silvia came in and began to tidy up the room. "Where's Teresa?" I asked, worried.

"In the chapel."

"Did you take her?"

"No, she crawled there. To show her appreciation to God."

I hurried toward the chapel. In the corridor, about twenty *varas* from the door, I caught up with her. There she was, sitting on the floor, dragging her limp body along with her hands. First she'd stretch out her palms and place them flat on the floor, then she'd ease herself down on one elbow and pull herself forward, and finally, she'd grab her legs, limp as rags, and tuck them underneath her. Three or four sisters stood around her, watching.

"Such devotion," one of them whispered. "She's a saint."

"Come on, Teresa," I said to her. "I'll carry you the rest of the way."

"No. I'm doing this for God, as an act of gratitude."

"You'll wear yourself out."

"No!" she snapped as I bent down to help her. "Leave me alone!"

I walked on ahead and left her to her own devices.

Every day after that, Silvia would attend to Teresa in the morning. That was fine with me. I was sick of cleaning up her puke. I preferred to pray in my own spotless cell. As soon as Teresa was dressed, she'd begin her pilgrimage down the hall, inching along like some kind of an exotic black reptile. As time went on, her ambulation became more dramatic. She added sound. She grunted and moaned. She perfected her crawling—reach, crouch, drag, reach, crouch, drag. She learned to look up at the ceiling and roll her eyes, as though she'd just seen Jesus blow her a kiss. Her audience was growing. At first, only a few nuns came out to watch the spectacle. Then there were six or seven. Then ten. Then fifteen. Then thirty.

"She's a saint! She'll bring glory to this convent!"

Someone remembered the *zahorí* who had predicted the appearance of a great holy woman named Teresa at Encarnación. "It was foreseen!" exclaimed her admirers.

But a growing number of sisters resented the daily morning brouhaha. "Such antics," huffed an ancient nun. "She's a hypocrite. All she wants is attention."

"The early morning is for prayer," Mother Francisca chided Teresa. "The sisters are supposed to be praying to God. They're not supposed to be watching you." Mother Francisca had always befriended her. She'd cared for her when she was ill. Her words stung.

"I'm sorry," whispered Teresa. Her face was turning splotchy and her eyes were welling up. She bowed her head in a sign of repentance. But then she glanced up, and the look that flashed across her face wasn't remorse but defiance. Had anyone else caught that flicker in her eye? "You're not sorry at all, you little bitch," I muttered under my breath.

Mother Francisca turned to me. "Sister Angélica," she said. "Take Sister Teresa into the chapel and seat her in her usual place."

That put an end to Teresa's crawling to chapel in the morning, but not to her sanctimonious exhibitionism. Whenever a sister left her white mantle in the choir before leaving for the refectory, Teresa would gather it up and fold it neatly. When the chandler delivered candles, she put them away, lining them up in the bin without being asked. She shucked peas in the kitchen with the servant nuns and kissed the hems of their garments as they processed into the chapel. Well, what was the big sacrifice? She was on the floor anyway.

When Don Alonso brought *yemas,* she'd distribute them among the others, leaving none for herself. "It's better to give than to receive," she cooed, placing a morsel in the open mouth of each nun as though she were giving communion. I thought it was revolting and told her so.

"I'm trying to follow in Christ's footsteps," she said hotly. "I'm modeling love and generosity for the other sisters."

"Who are you to model anything?"

"Well, what did *you* ever do for any of them?"

"I concoct potions that cure them of their hacking coughs, gas pains, and menstrual cramps. I make pastilles that soothe their aching throats. I sew chasubles, so the priests can say Mass for them. I make habits, so they'll have something to wear."

After that, we hardly spoke to each other for about a month or two. But then, in a grandiose act of contrition, she came and asked my forgiveness. During the *recreo.* In front of everybody. What was I going to do? I took her in my arms and hugged her. "Of course, Teresa," I told her. "Of course, I forgive you. I know you appreciate my nursing and sewing skills."

At the grille, she was as charming as ever. "Sister, I saw you in church this morning," gurgled an awestruck young man in a deep green velvet doublet. "You almost made me swoon."

"You should have been paying attention to the priest, not to me," she giggled.

"But Father Raimundo's sermons are so boring, Sister."

"Exactly. They remind us of Heaven."

"Heaven? How so?"

"They go on an eternity!" So witty, so clever! "Earlier today I was praying," Teresa went on. "I said, 'Dear Lord, so far today I've been perfect. I haven't talked back to Mother Prioress, I haven't lost my temper with any of the sisters, I haven't badgered my confessor, I haven't fallen asleep at Mass or had one unwholesome thought. But it must be almost five o'clock in the morning, Heavenly Father, and soon I'm going to have to get out of bed!'"

Peals of laughter. So adorable! So vivacious! But her detractors continued to scowl.

Where did I stand? I wasn't sure. I owed her everything. We'd been friends since childhood. But still. She wore on me.

During the *recreos* six or eight of us would gather in the *estrado* in Teresa's cell. Silvia would serve almond water and pastries, and Teresa would sit on her padded silk chair and preside over the group like a queen over her ladies-in-waiting. She had to sit on a chair because of her legs. The rest of us sat on cushions and sewed and chatted.

I can't remember exactly when it was that the new girl named Cándida came to Encarnación. She had a hunched back and an elongated, greenish face. She reminded me of a turtle, the way she scrunched up her shoulders and snapped back her head, as if to hide under a shell. She had thick arms and legs, with squarish hands and sharp little nails. Her eyes were tiny and lashless, and she rotated her head around to look at you, staring intently without blinking. When she walked, she kind of dragged herself along, first placing one foot ahead of the other, then heaving her body forward the way a turtle does under its carapace. Nobody liked her. Nobody wanted to spend *recreo* with her. When we retired into Teresa's suite, our cushions and our sewing in hand, she would follow us with her sad, turtle eyes, then disappear into the shadows.

"You know," said Teresa one day, "we should invite Cándida to spend the *recreo* with us." By then her legs were stronger, and she was able to sit on a cushion like the rest of us. Juana Isabel was tatting. Her hands, flicking and twisting the shuttle, reminded me of fluttering sparrows. Teresa was sewing a seam. Mother Francisca had asked her to make a gown for the statue of the Virgin in the refectory. Teresa pulled the thread up through a supple swatch of velvet.

"Careful, Teresa," I said a bit sternly. (After all, I was now the head of the sewing room and the convent authority on stitching.) "You're pulling it too tight. You'll make the cloth buckle. You mean that ugly little novice with a hump on her back?"

"She's one of God's children, just as you are. I think this needle's too thick."

"There's nothing wrong with the needle. You're pulling too tight. Here, let me do it. There's something creepy about her, the way she's always staring at you."

"I think she's just lonely. Nobody pays any attention to her. Let me have it now. I get the idea. Stitch and then backstitch, right?"

"You won't have to backstitch if you don't pull so tight. Look, like this. Hold the needle loose in your hand, then make tiny stitches. See? That's right, Teresa. She came to see me once in the infirmary, and it made me shudder just to touch her skin. It's clammy, as though she'd just climbed out of a pond."

"What an awful thing to say. It's not right to ostracize anyone, Angélica. It's not Christian." There she goes again, I thought. The do-gooder.

"Angélica's right," piped in Juana Isabel. "Mother Francisca says you have to *love* everyone, but you don't have to *like* everyone."

"You're pulling too tight again, Teresa," I said. "Look how the material is bunching up. You have to take it out and start over."

"Oh, God, I'm ruining the velvet. Mother Francisca will be furious."

"Let me get it started for you. Look, in, out, in, out, tiny stitches. Hold your needle loose, otherwise you can't control the thread."

"Now let me try. I think we should let her come at least once. Maybe we'll like her."

Of course Teresa got her way. Before we knew it, Cándida was following us around like a pet. She'd appear out of nowhere, sniffing at Teresa's heels—or mine. She was like a wild thing, somehow miraculously domesticated, who feels safe only in the company of its master. She crouched at Teresa's feet during *lectio divina*. During chapel, she stared lovingly at Teresa instead of turning her eyes toward Jesus. And at *recreo*, she crept noiselessly around the sewing room like a trapped reptile, emitting a dank, foul odor. The way she gazed at Teresa, so lovingly, with such devotion . . . it made me uncomfortable. But Teresa didn't seem to mind.

Her charity toward the wretched creature didn't go unnoticed, of course. Nothing went unnoticed in the convent. Teresa's admirers were full of gushy compliments. She was as kind as Saint Martin of Tours, they said, and as patient as Saint Arcadius. Rubbish, said her detractors. What? Just because she lets that wretched humped beast grovel at her feet?

One day the three of us were sewing in Teresa's sitting room. Just the three of us: Teresa and I, plus the turtle. Cándida's stitches looked like the rough, uneven tracks of insects. "Help her, Angélica," Teresa kept saying to me. "She can't get it right." I crouched behind Cándida and stretched my arms around her body. Then I took her hands in mine and guided the needle in and out of the fabric. But the poor girl was so clumsy, she couldn't manage on her own. Her chunky fingers kept losing their grip. Little squeals of desperation emerged from her throat. Finally, she jabbed at the cloth and made a stitch. But the thread knotted on the wrong side of the cloth and stuck. She pulled at it to undo the stitch she had just made, but that only made it worse. She yanked again, and the thread snapped.

I sighed—it must have sounded like a sigh of disgust—and went back to my own sewing. Cándida picked up the delicate embroidery needle in her stubby fingers and tried again. She brought it close to her turtle eye, managed to thread it, but then dropped it. She picked it up and poked the cloth. *¡Por Dios!* She drove the needle right into her finger. A drop of blood glistened on the white fabric, then worked its way into the weave. Tears trickled down the girl's scaly cheeks and her nose filled with snot. She fumbled the embroidery hoop, and her work fell to the floor, but instead of picking it up, she lifted her arm and wiped her nose on her sleeve. She opened her mouth to speak, but only strange animal sounds came out. "Glu . . . glug . . ."

"Help her again, Angélica."

"You help her."

Teresa shot me that pious look of hers. I pursed my lips and didn't move.

"Help her, Angélica," she insisted.

"You help her, Teresa."

Teresa moved behind Cándida and wrapped her arms around her, just as I had. Carefully, she took her fingers in her own and maneuvered the needle into position.

Suddenly, Cándida slumped and turned, sliding down Teresa's chest until her lips were right on her breast. She opened her mouth and then . . . What was she doing? Sucking her like a baby? Kissing her nipple through the soft, woolen habit?

A look of horror flashed across Teresa's face. She placed her hands on the creature's shoulders and gave her a shove with such hatred that it sent her sliding across the floor.

Silence. Teresa sat staring loathingly at Cándida's crumpled body. Without getting up, the girl crawled out of the room, leaving her blood-stained embroidery next to her cushion. Teresa looked down. I'd seen the revulsion in her eyes, and she knew it. She was struggling to compose herself. I took up my work and started to embroider, but my hands were trembling.

"Poor thing," murmured Teresa after a long while. "We have to pray for her." I kept my eyes on my needlework and said nothing. "You have to be compassionate, Angélica," she said. She sounded condescending, like a school mistress berating a wayward child. I bit my lip. "God loves her. We should pray . . ."

"You phony!" I exploded. "We should pray? *You* don't pray at all! You're too busy flitting around pretending to be a *santa*. What happened to your intimate relationship with God? I saw the way you looked at that girl. Not with love, Teresa. Not with pity, but with disgust."

"You saw what she did!"

"Then why don't you say you despise her? Why do you pretend to be so forgiving when you're filled with fury? You're a fraud, Teresa de Ahumada!"

She stared at me, the color draining from her face and her chin quivering. She opened her mouth as though to spit out some expletive, but then, all of a sudden, she crumpled.

"I know," she said suddenly. "I know, Angélica, you're right."

I stared at her a moment, then turned back to my sewing. Was this part of her act, I wondered, or was she speaking from the heart?

"Help me, Angélica." she whispered. "It's true I'm a vile creature. It's true I don't pray. I'm just going through the motions, but I don't know what else to do. I haven't been able to pray for months. I'm afraid to tell my confessor. I felt God's presence so profoundly at Tío Pedro's, when I discovered mental prayer. But now, it's as though God has abandoned me again. I try to pray, but I feel like no one is listening."

I'd known Teresa de Ahumada my whole life, and I knew she was telling the truth.

"Well," I said gently, "it's better to be honest with yourself."

"What shall I do, Angélica?"

"I don't know. I'm not your spiritual director, Teresa."

"But you're my friend."

"Well, I'd say first forgive Cándida. Go to her and comfort her. And then wait. Wait and pray, even if you feel no one is listening. God will come back to you. I know He'll come back. He always does."

Angélica del Sagrado Corazón
Toledo, 18 July 1576

PART II
Teresa in Ecstasy

CHAPTER 8

Dancing with the Devil

"IT WAS SO STILL, IT WAS LIKE BEING CAUGHT IN A PICTURE, WHERE NOTHING moves and time never passes. Not a candle flickered. Not a torch burned. A soft light filled the church, but it came from somewhere else, not from wicks or lamps. A light like an April dawn. No, not like an April dawn. Not like anything you've ever seen on earth. A light like an aura of sanctity. Like a mantle of peace. Yes, peace. It was so peaceful. Peaceful and beautiful, like death. I didn't know what was happening to me, Angélica." I held my breath and waited for her to go on. "I felt enveloped in love. It was like floating in a vapor of love."

"A vapor of love," I whispered.

"And then I saw Him. I mean, I didn't actually see Him. I felt His presence. But it was more than that. It wasn't just—how can I say it?—it wasn't just a feeling. It was something more. It was . . . it was seeing without seeing. I mean, I didn't see Him with my eyes, the way I'm seeing you, Angélica. But I saw Him, I saw Him with my spiritual senses. He was there, right there, with me. Christ was with me, by my side."

"I don't understand. What do you mean, your spiritual senses?"

"I . . . I can't explain. It's like . . . Think of your Tía Cati. Can you see her? Can you see her in your mind? You're not seeing her with your eyes, but you can see her anyway, can't you, Angélica? Well, it's something like that. Not exactly like that but, well, similar."

"You saw Christ, Teresa? You really saw Jesus? Maybe it was just your imagination."

"It wasn't, Angélica. I could never invent anything so beautiful. You have to believe me."

"I do believe you."

"The others won't. I'm sure they won't."

She was right. Nobody believed her. When she finally got up the courage to tell people, no one believed her.

She'd gone to Nuestra Señora de la Anunciación, the big church near the north wall of Ávila, to meet Don Fernando. I mean the pentagonal church with two huge columns at the entrance, the one with the Masonic emblems on the triangular column that supports the pulpit. Everyone used to call it "the Jewish church" because a rich *converso* named Mosén Rubí de Bracamonte had it built. Mother Francisca says it looks more like a lodge of the Scottish freemasons, although how would she know? On the other hand, lots of other people say that, so maybe there's something to it. The pulpit is covered with Masonic emblems, which made the inquisitors so jittery, they ordered Bracamonte to stop construction for a while. But then, they changed their minds. When you've got a lot of money, you can usually convince people to let you do what you want. Teresa had gone there to see a priest, Don Fernando de Guzmán, Bracamonte's son. They're *conversos,* of course, but since the family has given so many ducats to our Holy Church, Don Fernando had no trouble getting ordained.

"What was Jesus doing?" I asked.

"He wasn't doing anything. He was just *there.* I can't explain it, Angélica. Suddenly, I just *knew* He was there."

She'd stood there, mesmerized, she said. Don Fernando was so engrossed in his own words, he didn't even notice. There were times when I thought she was making things up to get attention, but this time, it was different. Something about the awe in her eyes, about the wonderment she conveyed.

At first, she was afraid to tell anybody. Of course she told me, but she didn't tell anyone else, not even her confessor. She had to be careful because the Inquisition had started really cracking down on visionaries. The convents were full of women claiming to see things from the otherworld, but, according to the priests, most of them were just making up stories. They wanted attention, the priests said. They wanted to prove they were God's favorites so that everyone would fawn over them. They'd describe their visions with such passion that they wound up convincing themselves. Then, there were others who really did see visions, not because God sent them, but because they performed such terrible penances—fasting for days and going without sleep—that they wound up seeing things. Their visions, the priests said, were nothing more than projections of their enfeebled minds. But the inquisitors knew how to get the truth out of them.

The inquisitors. Dressed all in black, pointed hoods covering their faces, they glide like ravens in flight. They circle and circle, tracing diminishing rings around their victim, then swoop down, robes flapping like wings. Their voices, distorted by face coverings, are like the cacophonous cawing of ten thousand crows surging up from the fiery bowels of Hell. They ask questions. When they don't get the answers they want, they take measures. They can be very persuasive. They have ingenious instruments, these clever men. They must spend months and years conceiving and constructing them. They have metal cords to tie around a nun's knuckles, cords they twist so tight that the coil cuts through her skin. They twist until blood spurts from her wounds, until the fingers separate from the hand. Or else, they order her to disrobe and hang her by the wrists. They let her dangle until her arms pop out of her shoulder sockets. Finally, the poor sister, shrieking in pain and mortified by the leers on the invisible faces behind the hoods, tells them what they want to hear: that she made up the whole story or, worse yet, that her visions are the work of the Devil.

They have machines for squeezing the fingers till the bones splinter. They have knives and hooks for probing below the nails. They have special pincers for tearing out tongues and sharp-edged spoons for gouging out eyes. They have whips of iron cords with a spike at the end of each for tearing the flesh until the bone is bared. They have clamps with screws that can be tightened until a leg is crushed. They have cradles full of spikes and pulleys to stretch the body. They have boiling pitch to pour down your throat and molten rods to probe between your legs. They're brilliant men. Their imaginations are boundless. We've all heard about these machines. They make sure you hear about them. It's a way of encouraging good behavior. But, of course, this is all for our own good. The inquisitors toil day and night on behalf of Holy Mother Church. They're serving the cause of Christ by protecting us from the Devil.

It's true the Devil can send visions. Lucifer was an angel, but he committed the sin of pride. God cast him out of Heaven, but as a kind of consolation prize, gave him the power to trick people. I could never figure out why God did that. Anyhow, Satan can take any form. He can sneak into your life in the guise of a friendly puppy or a gentle lover or even as Jesus himself. And then, when you least expect it, he ensnares you. If the inquisitors think you've succumbed to the wiles of the Devil, they give you a little taste of what's waiting for you in the hereafter.

That's why Teresa had to be careful. Women visionaries were particularly suspect because they're easy prey for the Devil. That's because women are flighty and hysterical—at least, that's what they say. Women are impetuous. They don't think things through. "*Hysterikos* means 'pertaining to the womb,'" Father Tomé once told me. "Women have wombs. That's why they tend to be hysterical." "Not as hysterical as you, you stupid fart," I thought. But I just said "yes, Father" and changed the subject.

There was a great visionary, an abbess from Córdoba named Magdalena de la Cruz. She belonged to the order of Poor Clares. She was known for her predictions and had foretold the Battle of Pavia, when our king Carlos I, grandson of the most holy Catholic monarchs Fernando and Isabella, won part of Italy away from that wretched Frenchman Francisco I. I once saw Mother Magdalena when she came through Ávila. People ran alongside her carriage, begging her to bless them. They banged on the doors and stuck their arms through the windows until finally, she stepped down, very regally, and held out her hands for people to kiss. Many onlookers knelt on the ground and kissed the hem of her habit. "My precious child," she said to a skinny young mother who stared at her through skeletal eye sockets, "how can I be of service to you?" "Bread," breathed the young woman. "Bread for my children." "Jesus is the bread of life, child," said Magdalena. The girl bowed her head. "I will pray for you, my child." "Oh, thank you, Mother," said the supplicant. People sighed and wept as though she had snatched a loaf of bread out of the air.

She had a huge following. Empress Isabel, King Carlos's wife, was so taken with her that she gave her a portrait of herself. She even granted her the privilege of making the first robe for the baby Prince Felipe. But then, something unexpected happened.

It was on a January 1. Perhaps the year was 1544. I'm getting older now, and my memory isn't as good as it used to be. I do recall it was on the first day of January, though, because people said she didn't want to start the new year in a state of sin. What sin? Gossip ripped through the town. She'd had an affair with a young acolyte, some people said. She had a woman lover, said others: a pretty little novice who was supposed to sleep on a mat by her bed, but who had made her way under the covers. Who knows what really happened. Maybe nothing. Maybe her confessor sowed the seed of guilt in her mind. Maybe he convinced her that she had committed sins she never committed. Confessors sometimes do that. The fact is that on that day

Magdalena de la Cruz confessed publicly that her holiness was all a sham, that she couldn't work miracles at all, and that if she could see into the future, it was because she'd entered into a pact with the Devil. She couldn't stand it anymore, she said. She was sick with remorse. They threw her into prison, where she rotted until the demons came and carried her off to Hell.

After that, everyone looked at everyone else with squinty eyes. Priests ordered prioresses to be on guard for sibyls and mystics. Prioresses gave orders that suspicious chatter was to be reported. And it was worse if you were a *converso* because, people said, *conversos* sometimes faked ecstasies just to prove they were authentic Catholic Christians. *Spurious visions,* the priests called them. "Beware of Satan," thundered Father Tomé from the pulpit. "Beware of *spurious visions.* Keep your eye on your sister! For her own good, report any mention of visits from the beyond. We will examine her and take appropriate measures."

Mother Francisca shook her head in disgust. "*Spurious visions,* indeed," she muttered. "As if I didn't have enough to do. Now I have to be on the lookout for overexcited, addlebrained nuns who go around talking to themselves." But even so, she warned us about the Devil and showed us how to scare him away with a crucifix.

That's why Teresa's didn't tell anyone about her vision. In this climate of hysteria, she certainly wasn't going to advertise that Jesus had appeared to her in Bracamonte's pentagonal Jewish church.

"What if it was a vision sent by the Devil?" she whispered, her eyes as anxious as those of a doe facing a hunter's arrows.

"What if it was sent by God?" I squeezed her hand.

For a week or so, neither of us said anything more about it, but secrets have a way of scrambling out from their hiding places. *Las paredes oyen,* they say. "The walls have ears."

One morning Teresa came to find me in the infirmary. She'd been suffering from nasal congestion, and I was boiling dried eucalyptus leaves to ease her breathing. It was pouring out. You could hear fat drops thwacking the cobblestones by the window. The hem of her habit was drenched and filthy, even though she wore a long cape. "You shouldn't go out in this weather," I snapped. "How can I keep you well if you go running around in the rain?"

"I have to tell you something," she said. Her voice sounded a bit unsteady.

"I'm listening," I said without putting down my tools. Several sisters had sore throats and stuffy noses. A few were running fevers. It was late fall, the season when folks are most vulnerable to colds. Even though we Abulenses are hearty people, the shift from warm to cold weather takes its toll. I'd spent the morning making medicines. I'd ground cherry bark into a powder to make a soothing tea. I'd mixed elder and yarrow flowers with a potpourri of peppermint, rosehip, safflower, and clove to brew a potion for respiratory ailments and salves to break up congestion in the chest. Teresa stood there in the doorway, her nose twitching wildly, as though she were trying to prevent a sneeze. Her eyes had a feral look about them. "Go on," I said.

She shifted her weight from one foot to the other. "It happened again," she whispered. "A vision. Only this time I saw . . . the Devil."

I put down the pestle I was using to grind leaves.

"I'd gone out to the dovecote when I suddenly saw a huge toad standing about two *varas* away from me. It was hideous, Angélica, a grayish-yellow color, all slick and slimy as though it had just come out of the muck. But its skin wasn't like a toad's. It was covered with oozing lesions, like a leper's, and the pus and slime ran together all over its body. Its eyes were sickly and sticky, full of gunk. It looked at me out of those diseased eyes and suddenly it smiled at me—a Satanic smile. I wanted to scream, I wanted to run. I could hardly keep myself from retching. I felt faint. I tried to look away, but wherever I turned my eyes, there it was, with its noxious gaze and revolting smile. Oh God, Angélica, what's happening to me? God is telling me something. He's telling me I'm going to Hell."

"He's telling you something, but I don't think it's that."

"God is angry with me, Angélica. It's because . . . it's because I don't pray." She paused, a pained look in her eyes. "I do try, Angélica, but my mind wanders. I think about my brothers Antonio and Fernando fighting infidels in Peru, risking their lives to spread God's word. If only I could be a soldier too! I think about my father. I'm the one who taught him mental prayer, but when he asked me if I prayed every day, I told him I was too ill. I said that the doctors and even my confessor had told me not to worry about prayer, but just to try to get better. I lied to him, Angélica. I'm a hypocrite and a fraud, just as you said."

"I think you need to go to confession, Teresa."

"Do you know what else I think about? I think about Cándida, about how much I enjoyed pushing her on the floor! I think of ways to make the sisters love me—getting sweets for them and carrying messages from their admirers. I think of jokes to tell at the grille. I think about the silver crucifix my brother Lorenzo sent from America. I think about how much less you have than I do, but how wise and useful you've become. I think how much better you are than I am, and I feel angry, I feel inferior, and I . . . I almost hate you." She started to sob. "No wonder God is punishing me. No wonder He's handed me over to the Devil."

Her words did not give me any sort of satisfaction. I didn't think, ha, you're finally admitting you're a phony. What I felt was pity. "You have to talk to someone about this, Teresa. You need someone wiser than I am to help you. Tell your confessor what you just told me."

"You know what my confessor said? He told me that mental prayer was a sin. He said that's the way . . . certain people . . . pray?"

"What people?"

She looked at her hands and was silent a moment. "*Alumbrados*," she said finally. The word dropped like a brass weight on a crystal goblet. The *alumbrados* are a sect of sinners headed straight for Hell—at least, that's what the priests say. The *alumbrados* believe in direct enlightenment from God. They meet secretly in people's houses, and lay people, even women, lead their prayers. They think you don't need the sacraments, that you can know God through His divine illumination. A lot of them are *conversos* because, I guess, some *conversos* feel more comfortable praying in homes than in churches. The priests say they're as bad as Lutherans!

After that, I expected to see a change in Teresa. I expected loud and ardent demonstrations of her orthodoxy: vocal prayers, tears of contrition, rapt attention to sermons. Instead, things went on just as before. But I couldn't spend all day worrying about Teresa. I had my own problems. I was feeling terribly guilty, but I couldn't go running to my confessor about it. How could I, when my confessor was the thorn stabbing my conscience? Fray Braulio, with his piercing gaze and his silky voice. When he spoke to me, sometimes he leaned so close that I could feel his hot breath on my cheek. I never unburdened my soul. I never discussed my scruples. Instead, I admit it, I confessed just to feel his closeness, just to brush my knee against his, all the time wringing my hands in contrition, acting as though it hadn't happened.

"Father," I whispered, my voice all breathy, "I know it's a sin, but I'm losing patience with my best friend, Teresa."

"Everyone loses patience sometimes, dear."

I pretended not to notice that he had called me dear. It was very improper.

"But Fray Braulio, she's my best friend. And she's very ill."

"You're good, Angélica. At the core of your being, you're as pure as holy water."

"The thing is, Father, she's so . . ."

"Self-centered?"

"I hate to say it, Father."

At that point the Devil must have gotten into my head—it was happening more and more lately—because suddenly I asked, "Father, do you think mental prayer is a sin?"

"What?" He smiled at me, and his smile was so warm and kindhearted I almost melted.

"Mental prayer," I stammered. "Talking directly to God instead of reciting the prayers prescribed by the Church. Or, rather, not instead of, but in addition to."

"What does your conscience tell you, angelic angel?"

"That it's not a sin, Father. That God is deep in our hearts, and we can find Him if we're very, very quiet and listen for His divine word."

"Is that what your friend Teresa told you?"

Suddenly, I was on guard. "No . . . no, it's just something I heard."

"Well," he said softly, taking my hand in his, "don't worry, my sweet Angélica. Your heart is so pure that whatever you do, God will understand."

He left me confused. A man had never caressed my hand like that before. I didn't know what to think. I went back to the infirmary, but instead of mixing concoctions, I curled up in a corner and cried.

As I look back, it's almost impossible to distinguish one point in time from the other. Days, seasons, years and decades melt into one another, forming one amorphous blob. When, exactly, did Cándida come in out of the swamp? I can't remember for sure. It must have been in the early forties—1541 maybe, or 1542. And when, exactly, did Christ appear to Teresa in Anunciación Church? I can't be sure. But one day I do remember is December 21, 1543. I remember the date because every year we celebrate its anniversary.

I'd gone out a little after dawn to gather bark for my medicines. It was snowing and the moon still glimmered faintly on the horizon as though through a milky curtain. The icy air pierced my skin like a million tiny needles. My throat stung. I blinked, and frosty tears burned my cheeks. My feet were growing number with every step. I cupped my hands over my nose and mouth and exhaled forcefully to warm them, then clamped my teeth together to keep them from chattering. Except for the rasp of the falling snow, all was silence. Several white-veiled nuns hauling grain to the dovecote appeared out of nowhere. Even at a short distance they had been indiscernible—their pale figures blending into the pale background. I greeted them with a silent nod and they returned my greeting. Further along another group of lay sisters was gathering snow for water. They moved like specters in the opaque morning light, stooping and standing, stooping and standing to fill their basins. If they spoke, I didn't hear them. The snowflakes were falling faster now, like great globs of soapsuds that hit the ground with a thud.

When I returned to the house, icicles like wolves' teeth were clinging to my mantle and my hood was caked in rime. I flung off mantle and hood and went to the refectory to warm myself by the fire. But there was no time to defrost. The other sisters were lining up for Mass. Still shivering, I took my place among them. The cold air had made me sleepy. My eyelids were leaden, and I had to struggle to keep from dozing. I stood and knelt mechanically, oblivious to the words of the priest. The benches were hard and the choir was uncomfortably cold, but the heady aroma of incense affected me like a soporific. I thought I heard the *sanctus* bell reverberate, but no, we hadn't got to that part of the Mass yet. We were just beginning the Credo. *Credo in unum Deum, Patrem omnipotentem, factorem caeli et terrae, visibilium omnium et invisibilium* . . . "Oh please God," I prayed. "Let this Mass be over." I was too drowsy to realize the sacrilegiousness of my prayer. *Per quem omnia facta sunt* . . .

All of a sudden I was jolted out of my lethargy by a shriek, no not a shriek, more like a gasp, a series of gasps, or a cry. Whatever it was, it came from the section of the church occupied by the public. "What happened?" The question rolled through the choir like a fire through a field. "What happened? What happened?" Teresa, sitting several rows in front of me, had apparently seen where the commotion was occurring. Now she was making her way down to the nave. Typical, I thought crossly. Whatever's going on, she has to be in the middle of it. But then I heard her voice—wavering, fragile, like a voice of a frightened child.

"*Papá!* What's the matter? Look at me, *Papá.*"

I could see the sanctuary, but it wasn't clear what was going on. People were forming clusters around someone—perhaps, judging from the group,

Don Alonso. It was chaotic. Women were standing in the men's section, and no one moved to chase them out. I recognized Don Pedro, his wife, and Doña Guiomar de Ulloa, a prominent society lady who had two daughters at Encarnación. They were bent over a crumpled figure, a man, but I couldn't see his face. The nuns in the choir were scrambling to get downstairs, elbowing each other in their haste.

"Daughters! Stay where you are! Stay in your places!" commanded Mother Francisca. Slowly, reluctantly, some of the nuns moved back toward their seats. Others kept nudging their way toward the nave. "Stay where you are!" commanded Mother Francisca.

"Let me go, Mother!" I implored. "I'm a nurse. I might be able to help!" She nodded, and I hurried downstairs. People kept attaching themselves to the group of onlookers huddling by the slumped figure. "Please, let me through," I begged. "I'm a friend of the family. I'm a nurse!"

When at last I got to Teresa's side, I saw Don Alonso doubled over. He was holding his chest and his face was ashen. "Don Alonso!" I murmured.

He looked up at me with wild, feverish eyes. His breathing was jagged. He retched, but didn't vomit, then crossed his arms tightly in front of him as if struggling to control the impulse to heave.

"*Papá*..." murmured Teresa. She spoke softly, like a mother comforting a crying child.

Suddenly, Don Alonso lurched forward, hitting his head on a bench and collapsing on the ground. He lay there, sprawled on the floor.

"*¡Papá!*" He appeared unconscious. I took his wrist in my hand and tried to get a pulse. At first I felt nothing, but then I detected the weak, uneven rhythm of a dying man.

"Someone bring Father Tomé!" stammered Teresa. "My *Papá* is . . . very ill."

Don Alonso had been a father to me, too. He'd treated me with affection and given me a dowry. He'd entrusted me with the care of his beloved Teresa. I wept like Mary at the foot of the cross when they nailed shut his coffin, even though I knew he was already in Heaven. *Chemá Yisroel, Adonai Elojenu, Adonai Echad,* I prayed softly, certain that God would hear and understand what I did not. *Pater noster, qui es in caelis: sanctificetur nomen tuum; adveniat regnum tuum; fiat voluntas tua, sicut in caelo, et in terra.* "Our Father, who art in Heaven, take Don Alonso to your bosom and keep him with you for all eternity," I prayed. "And bless us, his daughters. Give us the strength to go on without him. And if speaking to you this way, mentally, directly, is a sin, then forgive me, dearest Father. I only ask that you welcome into your Kingdom the only mortal father I ever knew, Don Alonso de Cepeda, a good man. Amen."

After the funeral dinner given by Doña María and her husband, Teresa and I cried in each other's arms all night, our tears mingling and dropping to the floor, soaking through the floorboards and into the ground.

Angélica del Sagrado Corazón
Toledo, 20 July 1576

CHAPTER 9

Still Dancing

THERE ARE SO MANY THINGS I CAN'T REMEMBER. DAYS, MONTHS, EVEN years. What happens to those things that disappear from your mind? It's as though they never happened. You go through your life conscious of the world around you—people who need eucalyptus to help their breathing or instruction on how to embroider a flower with loops and knots. You mix brews and teach tricks with a needle. You welcome a new sister into the convent and bury another. You live in the moment, but then the moment slips away, and later, when you look back on your life, you can't remember if certain things ever happened. It's as though you had lost part of the time allotted to you. It's as though you were dead during those black blotches in your memory.

The other day Sister Radegunda said to me, "Do you remember that towheaded girl Mother Francisca rejected because she had a scar over her eye?"

"No," I said.

"It was about twelve years ago. She had a big, red and black scar over her eye like a caterpillar. Mother Francisca had made arrangements to send her back home to Medina del Campo, I think, but she came down with a fever. You sat up with her all night. You were still Sister Josefa's apprentice, and Sister Josefa had recommended compresses. You made some and put them on the girl's forehead, but were very careful not to touch the scar. Don't you remember?"

"No."

"She was fond of you. You kept telling her that you were sure God had other plans for her, that she shouldn't be sad about having to leave the convent."

"What happened to her?"

"She died. They came for her body and buried her in the family mausoleum. I don't remember her name, but I'll never forget her face, especially that terrible caterpillar she had crawling over her eyebrow. I can't believe you don't remember."

But I didn't, and I still don't. I've sat up all night with so many girls with fevers, I just can't remember all of them. For me it's as though that girl with the scar never existed, as though I were dead through the whole incident. How many things have vanished from my mind without leaving a trace? Sometimes I think I've only been alive during about a quarter of my life. What I mean is, if you don't remember something, is it really yours? And if I can't even remember my own life, how can I remember Teresa's? Well, I'll just have to tell what does remain. I want to put as much down on paper as possible, just in case I have to testify if . . . *when* she's beatified. And if I die before that happens, whoever finds this testimony can use it to further the cause.

What I do remember is that after they buried Don Alonso, Teresa slipped into melancholy. She kept saying it was her fault he died. "Father Sergio says God is punishing me because I pray all wrong," she sobbed, "like a Lutheran or an *alumbrado*. He says if I keep on praying mentally, I could go straight to Hell."

An idea began to obsess her: Had she herself sent her beloved father to Hell by teaching him mental prayer? She suffered nightmares. She bit her fingernails. Finally, she decided to go see her father's old confessor, a Dominican named Fray Vicente Barrón. Maybe he'd reassure her, she thought. But what if he said Fray Sergio was right? Did that mean Don Alonso would spend eternity tortured by demons? She was terrified. She kept putting off her visit. Either the weather was too stormy or she was too weak from illness or something else got in the way. Finally, toward the beginning of February, she set off over the sparkling, ice-studded fields for the Dominican monastery of Santo Tomás.

I don't remember what she told me about the meeting, but Fray Vicente must have put her mind at ease, because afterward, she calmed down. She was less weepy, less edgy. She went back to mental prayer, and so did I. She guided me. She taught me the art of recollection. You have to be very still, she told me. You have to turn inward, shut out all distractions, erase the external world and eradicate all images and sounds from your mind. And in that darkness deep inside, that's where you'll find God's light.

I tried hard. I didn't hear God's voice the way she did, but I did find a sense of peace, a peace like you experience when you go out alone on a winter morning, and the air is clean and raw. You can sense God's presence in the blueness of the sky, in the unsullied water of the frozen stream, in the starkness of the trees. You can feel God's hand on your temples.

It was about then that the terrible letter came from America telling about Antonio's death in Iñaquito. It hadn't been that long ago that Don Alonso had died, and now Teresa's younger brother was with him in Heaven. Antonio, with his soft brown eyes and chestnut hair, his square jaw and sturdy shoulders. I remember Don Alonso chasing him out of the room when I went with Tía Cati to fit Teresa's gowns. I remember how I giggled when he tickled my neck with a little white rabbit he kept in a hutch in the garden. He was just my age: twenty-six. I imagined Antonio at twenty-six—strong, broad-shouldered, soldierly. "It's the Lord's will," murmured Teresa with resignation. "He died a hero, bringing our holy Catholic faith to the godless. I only wish I could serve Christ as he did."

But when I thought of Antonio, it wasn't his service to God that stirred me. Instead, it was a kind of yearning for something I dared not name. I was a nun, a consecrated virgin, not to mention spawn of the humble classes. I knew I had no business thinking about Antonio, my benefactor's son, in . . . let's say . . . an amorous way. And yet, sometimes at night, lying in my bed, I closed my eyes and dreamed about Antonio with his soldierly stance, and Father Alejo with his chocolaty eyes, and Basilio with his broad shoulders and wavy hair, and Father Braulio with his soft fingers and languid gazes, and I did what I had done that time in Becedas when images—terrible images, delicious images—crept into my head. Images of Father Alejo, of Don Lope and Rosa lying in each other's arms. Images of Basilio and his new wife. Images of Don Javier, the soon-to-be ordained priest, tenderly kissing a woman. What woman? Me.

I didn't know what to tell Father Braulio about my sinful thoughts. At first, I said nothing. But something about the gentleness in his eyes made me think he'd be understanding. Of course, I couldn't tell him everything. I approached the subject gingerly, like a cat inching along a banister, advancing one step at a time on its little feline feet.

"You know, Father Braulio," I told him, "once I was engaged." He raised his eyebrow, suddenly interested. "The boy's name was Basilio. I had a nice dowry and everything. But I decided to serve God instead."

It was a lie. I lied to my confessor. Well, it wasn't exactly a lie, but it was certainly a misrepresentation. I didn't exactly run gleefully from Basilio's arms into the convent. I left out the significant detail that my betrothed had called the whole thing off because I knew how to read.

"Are you sorry?"

"No, of course I'm not sorry. But sometimes . . ." I hesitated. I didn't know how to go on.

"Do you sometimes miss—how shall I say it?—do you sometimes miss male company?"

"I have plenty of male company. I confess to you twice a week, Father Braulio."

He grinned in a teasing sort of way. "And that's enough for you?"

"Oh yes, Father. That's enough for me."

He licked his lips in what seemed at the time an innocent gesture. "But don't you pine for—let's say—the joys of marriage?"

"Do you mean children? There are plenty of little girls in the convent. The nursery is full of toddlers whose parents brought them here for us to raise."

"I mean marital relations, angelic Angélica."

"How can I miss what I've never known, Father?"

He broke into laughter. "Of course, of course," he said, taking my hand. I felt a jolt and a tingle. "But do you sometimes think about those things?" he whispered. There was something suggestive about his voice. Also something exciting. A man had never looked at me the way Father Braulio was looking at me just then. I felt my cheeks grow hot and my head become as buoyant as a bubble about to burst. What if Basilio didn't want me, I thought. Fray Braulio was refined and worldly, and he seemed to like me. "Such thoughts are natural, Angélica," he whispered. His breath was like cinnamon and orange blossoms.

"They're sinful, Father."

"Sinful? Why?"

"Women must submit to their husbands for the sake of procreation, Father, but no woman yearns for the indignity of . . . of . . ."

"You're as pure as light, my little Angélica. As pure as light. But it might surprise you to know that there are some women who actually enjoy submitting to a man." I felt dizzy and, for reasons I couldn't fathom, short of breath. I knew he was telling the truth though, because I knew that given a chance, I would be one of those women.

Suddenly, he got up, and as he did, his habit—the front part of his habit—brushed against me. I felt—I'm ashamed to write this, but I'll write it anyway because it's what happened—I felt the part of a man that grows hard when he's excited. It's true. I felt his sex brush against my shoulder. I jerked away and looked down at my fingers, all rough and calloused from cutting bark for cough remedies.

I was about to say something else about sinfulness, but I couldn't speak. It was as though the words were caught in my throat. I looked up at him. A grin crossed his lips. A grin or maybe a leer. But then it disappeared, and he looked straight at me, his gaze steady and sober.

"I wouldn't worry about it, Angélica," he said, making his voice sound very serious. "Finding evil in every thought and act is infinitely more sinful than showing a healthy interest in how a man can pleasure a woman. Confessing constantly, stroking one's guilt—those are sins of scrupulosity. Don't fall into the trap of feeling forever culpable. It's a trap the Devil lays for the pure of heart."

I looked at him.

"It's a trap the Devil lays for girls like you."

By the time I got back to the infirmary, my head was spinning. That day was Tuesday. My next confession would be on Friday. In all the maze of blurry details from that time in my life, details that fade into one another and disappear into chaos, that's one detail I remember clearly. I confessed on Tuesdays and Fridays. The day that Father Braulio did what he did, that was a Tuesday.

How would I confess to him on Friday? I shuddered whenever I thought of it. How would I tell him that what he did, even if it was an accident, was reprehensible? How would I tell him that . . . that I liked it, that I wished he'd do it again, that I'd tried to put it out of my mind, to be angry, to remember the holy chastity of our Virgin Mother, but that I couldn't help wishing, wishing until my head felt as though it would explode, that I could feel him close to me, close, close, rubbing against me. "Oh, God!" I prayed. "Help me know what to do!"

But Friday never came. Well, of course it came, but I didn't confess to Father Braulio. The Council of Trent had begun not long before. The pope— it was Paulo III—had called it to confront the accusations that had led to the Lutheran rebellion. Everywhere, churchmen were meeting. Issues had to be articulated. Agendas had to be made. Representatives had to be chosen.

Father Braulio had to travel to Toledo to meet with Carmelite officials on the important business of what part the Order was to play in the council that had begun in Trent the previous December.

Instead of Father Braulio, a doddering skeleton of a priest confessed me—a man with cavernous, cobwebby eye sockets who must have been at least a hundred and six. "I've had some unholy thoughts in the last couple of days, Father," I told him. He appeared to be dozing. "Father?" I coaxed. He opened his eyes long enough to absolve me, then fell back asleep.

At the grille the women gossiped lazily, but the men were keyed up over the newly convened assembly. The idea, as I understand it—and it's true I'm only a woman and the daughter of a seamstress—was to address some of those problems that made Luther rebel in the first place. Not that Luther was justified. Not at all. I would never say that. It would be a sacrilege! But you'd have to be blind not to see that there were certain abuses—well, maybe "abuses" is too strong a word, but I'll just write "abuses" for now—that had caused concern for years. Things like priests who amassed fortunes by demanding contributions from their parishioners. And things like priests who kept a mistress in every village, each one surrounded by a gaggle of bastard children. (I wondered if Father Braulio would opine on confessors who stroked their penitents' hands and called them dear.) The council was also to deal with bishops who overstepped their authority, clergy more interested in their benefices than their sermons, and seminarians who didn't bother to learn Latin.

One of the topics that interested us women was clandestine marriage. Before the Council of Trent, a promise of marriage was supposed to be as binding as a marriage itself. After all, marriage was simply a promise made between two people in the presence of God. Even though we were cloistered, we knew the consequences of this doctrine. There were girls like Rosa in every convent—girls who ran off to be married secretly. More common still were the girls who gave themselves to lovers who promised to marry them only to take their pleasure and disappear. Where were the cads who played husband for one night? Far away in America or Italy or the Low Countries. Or perhaps married to someone else. What was to be done with such girls? They were no longer virgins and therefore no longer marriageable. There was no place for them to go but the convent. Encarnación was bulging with such girls. Something had to be done. It was the job of the Council of Trent to figure out what.

To be honest, though, I wasn't losing sleep over the meetings in Trent. I didn't realize at the time that the findings of the great council would some-day set the Inquisition on Teresa's heels—and mine—by making an issue of our way of praying. What did keep me awake was Father Braulio. Did he want what I thought he wanted? If he made a move, how would I react? The thought of Braulio's touch, the scent of his perfumed breath, his flaxen hair, his sensual pucker, his languorous gaze—all these things filled me with con-fusion and anxiety. I should have repented. I should have told everything to my ancient confessor. Instead, I sat for hours staring into space, daydream-ing about Braulio.

I was no longer interested in mental prayer. I was interested in Braulio. I didn't tell Teresa, though. She had her own troubles. She was still mourn-ing her father and Antonio when a new letter came from America. Her brother Fernando had been wounded in Iñaquito. Teresa read the short missive with dry eyes. "*Que se haga tu voluntad,*" was all she said. "Thy will be done."

Not everything that happened that year was bad. Teresa's little sister Juana, who had shared her cell at Encarnación, had a suitor! I can't remem-ber exactly how Juan de Ovalle appeared on the scene. It seems to me he vis-ited the grille one afternoon with his brother Gonzalo. Juana was about twenty then. She wasn't the beauty Teresa had been, but she was a sweet girl with a gentle disposition. She had soft, chestnut eyes and an easy smile. Juan de Ovalle was a nondescript young man, one of many that buzzed around the convent. He seemed rather smug and self-centered to me. He talked inces-santly about his skill with a sword. He'd studied with one of the best fencing masters in Alba de Tormes, he said, and could outmaneuver any of Juana's brothers, even though they'd fought in the Americas and he'd never ventured beyond the city gates or handled a weapon more dangerous than a blunt foil. He was obstinate, too, arguing that the Jesuits, a new order of priests that the pope had sanctioned less than a decade earlier, would never amount to anything. There was no arguing with him. He had all the answers.

Teresa pooh-poohed my reservations about Juan de Ovalle. "He's just young," she said. "He'll calm down." To me he seemed absurdly childish. Still, he didn't drink immoderately or swear. And he wasn't given to gam-bling—that scourge that had brought down so many families.

It was Teresa who negotiated the marriage contract. Both her father and Antonio were dead, and Fernando, Rodrigo, Lorenzo, Jerónimo, and

Pedro were all in the Americas. Agustín was still in Spain, but he was too young and too wild to take charge. And so it was up to Teresa, as the head of the family, to secure Juana's future.

The Ovalles from Alba de Tormes were the kind of people we called *hidalgos de gotera,* "gutter nobles"—third-class aristocrats, proud of their titles but poor as cockroaches. Lords and ladies only in their own hamlets, they struggled to keep up appearances in run-down manor houses with family crests over the front gate. Although the elder Juan de Ovalle was poor, he had a bit of property, a respectable last name and some distant cousins at court. As for the purity of his lineage, Teresa (daughter of a *converso,* after all) knew better than to make an issue of such things. Using the negotiating talents that would serve her so well later in life, she managed to bargain a tiny allowance and the gift of a nice tract of land for the young couple.

The tower of Alba de Tormes was constructed by King Fernando, husband of our most Catholic Queen Isabella. Now the Duke of Alba is turning it into a castle. He has brought the most gifted Arab stonemasons, bricklayers and glasscutters to create . . . Wait, did I write "Arab"? No, I meant *morisco.* There are no more Arabs in Spain, only *moriscos,* Moors who have seen the light and embraced our most holy Catholic faith. (Although, I've heard that most of them still bow down to Allah in secret.) They're wonderful architects and artisans, crafting intricate designs out of brick and stone in a style we call *mudéjar.* Such beautiful patterns, such original plays of symmetry and light. Walls that remind you of spun sugar, ceilings that remind you of whirls of flower petals.

Juan de Ovalle's lands lay in the shadow of the tower, on the other side of the River Tormes. Juana and Juan were married in the Church of Santiago, a lovely *mudéjar* construction with the nave joined to a sanctuary formed by a presbytery and apse composed of brick arcades. Above the walls of the presbytery, trefoil arches reach toward heaven. After the wedding Mass, the elder Juan gave a repast that scarcely revealed the sorry state of his purse. Capons and suckling pigs, kid and meat pies—everything seasoned to perfection and beautifully served. Only the after-dinner entertainments were lacking—a few shoddy musicians, including a four-fingered rebeck player (probably a Jew, like most such performers), and a clumsy juggler.

Once Teresa had married off Juana, she turned her attention to other family matters. Don Alonso had died heavily in debt, having made some imprudent real estate deals that nearly bankrupted his estate. The one wise thing he did before leaving this earth was to make Teresa co-executor of his will. Unfortunately, the other co-executor was María's husband, Martín de Guzmán. Everybody had a claim on Don Alonso's estate. The man from whom he'd bought a farm that turned out to have no water supply wanted to be paid anyway. The man to whom he sold a piece of property had occupied the land and now refused to cough up the money. The sisters of some small cloister on the outskirts of Toledo claimed that Don Alonso had promised them a tract, now mortgaged to someone else, and demanded its value in cash.

Things went from bad to horrible when Martín de Guzmán insisted that María was entitled to a full half of her father's estate, since she was married and had produced heirs. Teresa tried to reason with him. She convinced two of her brothers—I can't remember which ones—to relinquish their inheritance in favor of María, but even that didn't satisfy the greedy Don Martín. He wound up suing her—his own sister-in-law!—and Teresa was forced to hire a lawyer and go to court. Doña Guiomar de Ulloa, with whom she had gotten friendly, not only comforted and consoled her, but also introduced her to a competent attorney able to guide her through the legal labyrinth. At last they got the whole thing settled, but all that scrapping with claimants, attorneys, and judges took a toll on everyone. I'd never liked Don Martín—the creepy way he always seemed to be spying on me—and now I liked him even less.

Doña Guiomar had made hefty contributions to Encarnación, so when she started inviting Teresa to her home, sometimes to spend days at a time, Mother Francisca granted permission easily. The Ulloa palace was always filled with people of influence—people like Francisco de Salcedo and his wife, Doña Mencía del Águila, the theologian Father Gaspar Daza, and the brilliant orator Father Juan de Ávila. They were all good Christians, devout people, as grave as judges except for the good-humored young matron herself. Doña Guiomar was fabulously wealthy and fond of the attention of prominent men. She could be giggly and cloying, but she was sincere about her faith and clever enough to keep her bubbly personality in check with the stern masters of theology. Teresa was still grappling with her spiritual anxiety, and she liked spending time with Doña Guiomar's friends, all of them ardent practitioners of mental prayer.

Teresa had grown especially fond of Don Francisco de Salcedo, whom she called "the Holy Cavalier." An older gentleman with sparse white hair and crooked teeth, he was a frequent visitor at Encarnación, where he came to chat with Teresa and other nuns about spiritual matters. He was related to Teresa by marriage: his wife, Doña Mencía del Águila, was a first cousin of Teresa's Tío Pedro. Don Francisco was one of those people born for the monastery, even though he was married and had a family. Quiet, sober, and always chivalrous, he'd spent forty years in prayer and study and twenty attending lectures at the Dominican monastery of Santo Tomás. After Doña Mencía died, he became a priest. To be honest, I couldn't stand him.

Don Francisco's humility was exemplary . . . and nauseating. "I'm the most wretched of sinners," he'd say, wringing his hands. If you challenged him, he'd become irritated. Soon Teresa was following his lead. I had images in my head of both of them up in Heaven after they died, fighting over who was more abject. Salcedo: "*I'm* the lowliest creature ever born!" Teresa: "No, *I* am!" Salcedo: "No, *I* am." I couldn't imagine why she wasted time talking to him.

Sometimes I pouted that Teresa no longer bothered with me now that she had new friends. But the truth is, *I* had pulled away from *her*. Doña Guiomar's forward-thinking circle was interested in Teresa's spiritual grappling, but I wasn't. All I could think about was Braulio. How long would he be gone? What would happen when he came back? Would he hold my hand and call me his angelic Angélica? What if he kissed me? What if he . . . ? I was in no state to talk about God. I was headed straight for the Devil, and I knew it.

We never spent our *recreos* together anymore. She went to her *estrado*, and I went to the sewing room or played ball with the other nuns in the patio. But one day she called out to me as I was walking in the garden. I was surprised.

"Come," she said. "Come sit with me awhile. It's been so long since we've talked."

Spring had come. Azaleas, daffodils, hyacinths, dogwoods, magnolias—everything was exploding with color. But Teresa's mood didn't match nature's exuberance.

"Have you been all right?" she asked anxiously, laying her hand on my wrist. "You've hardly spoken to me in weeks."

"I'm fine," I lied. "I've just been busy."

"That's good," she murmured. "I've been . . . I'm frightened, Angélica."

"We're all frightened," I said impatiently. "The Devil is everywhere."

She turned to me, astonished. "You know then?"

What was she talking about? I searched her face for a clue. "Know what?" I asked finally.

"What they're saying about me."

"Look, Teresa," I said. "What makes you think everyone is talking about you? What makes you think everything in this convent revolves around Teresa de Ahumada?"

I expected her to get all huffy, but instead she just sighed. "I'm sorry," she said. "I wasn't even thinking about the convent."

I was sorry I'd said what I said, but the words were out of my mouth, and you can't take back words. It's hard enough to scribble out what you've written. You just can't do it without making a mess, and it's even worse with words you've spoken.

"The Holy Cavalier thinks I'm possessed by the Devil," she said quietly.

"Don Francisco? That old wreck of a man!"

I thought: Why am I being so horrible to her? It's not her fault I've fallen in love with my father confessor. And the minute I thought it, I knew it was true. I was in love. I'd never before dared to articulate my feelings for Braulio, but now there was no turning back.

"Forgive me, Teresa," I stammered. "I haven't been myself lately."

"Maybe you're working too hard," she said gently.

"What did Don Francisco say?"

"He thinks the Devil might be sending me visions. He told me to consult with Father Gaspar Daza. He's very knowledgeable about such things." I was stunned. She'd vowed never to mention those visions to anyone but me and her confessor. "Why did you tell him?" I asked.

"He's such a sweet, kind man, and he's studied theology. I thought he could help me."

I was furious with Salcedo. That detestable little mouse, all sugar and meekness. That soppy piece of milquetoast and his twittering wife, so easily swayed by talk of demons and spirits. The inquisitors were putting ideas in people's heads. Folks like Salcedo saw the Devil's hoof everywhere, in every stubbed toe, every nervous tic, every sleepless night. Every frenzied woman could be a heretic. Every prayerful monk could be an *alumbrado*. Even a vision of Jesus could be the work of the Devil. Of course, the Devil could tempt you. I knew that. He'd tempted me, and he'd caught me. I was headed straight for the flames. But did the Devil really send images of Our

Lord Jesus Christ, or did he send handsome, blond, square-jawed friars with melodious voices and eyes like oceans?

A few days later Salcedo accompanied Teresa to meet with Daza, one of the most highly respected theologians in Ávila. I can imagine the scene. Daza, somber and hook-nosed, thin as a knife, reeking of incense. Teresa, timid and squirming as though her habit were infested with fleas. Daza, his lipless mouth in constant metamorphosis, like some gelatinous animal. Teresa, her pallid hands stiff as strangled doves. Yes, Father. No, Father. Of course, Father. Daza, a Mephistophelian scowl like a nightmare.

Not only did Daza conclude that Teresa's visions came from the Devil, he spread the news all over town. It wasn't because of her method of praying, he said. They all practiced mental prayer. Spiritual renewal movements were popping up all over Spain (much to the dismay of conservative theologians), and many were based on mental prayer. But just because he was a spiritual trendsetter, said Daza, didn't mean he could be duped by some misguided woman visionary. Teresa was a weak, vain female, he said. Women like her already thought they were in direct contact with God, so all the Devil had to do was send them visions of Our Lord. They'd get so excited they'd think they were saints and become bloated with pride. Then the Devil could snatch them. Daza was so pumped up with his spiritual perspicacity that he blabbed about Teresa wherever he went. These hysterical females had to be silenced, he warned. They were undermining the faith. People thought these women were holy and flocked to them in search of advice and blessings. But they were all frauds, just like Magdalena de la Cruz! Daza's calumnies took their toll. Teresa began to lose weight and color.

One morning I went out to gather herbs to make her a cough remedy. The spring was like a maiden in all her glory, full of life and energy, but I felt bedraggled. For weeks I'd been immersed in my own problems, but now I was worrying about Teresa again. The worst of it was that Daza's rumors had reached the other nuns. Teresa had always had admirers and detractors, but now even her friends were going over to the other side.

I was lost in thought when I heard a rustling in the shrubbery. I thought it was the breeze, and went back to picking mint. But then I felt a presence near me. A bird, I thought. Or a squirrel. Some animal. I glanced at the flora and saw not a wild rabbit but the hem of a cassock. Braulio was standing about two arm-lengths away. I shrank back in amazement.

"Braulio!" I whispered. "I mean, Father Braulio. What are you doing here?"

"I was looking for you, my little angel."

"You're on convent grounds!"

"So? I'm your father confessor."

I was pressing an apronful of mint against my midriff. I was so flabbergasted, I didn't know whether I was happy to see him. My heart began to pound wildly, but was it out of joy, desire, or apprehension?

"Are you going to the Council in Trent?" I asked stupidly.

He burst out laughing. "Aren't you glad to see me? Put that down and come with me."

I hesitated. Something in me wanted desperately to follow him, but an ominous mist hung in the air.

"Where?"

"Never mind. Just come." He took me by the hand, and I didn't pull away. I knew we weren't going to the chapel to pray. His hand was strong, virile. I felt a rush of excitement I didn't try to smother. I let him lead me. I knew the Devil guided our steps, but for that one moment—I admit it— I didn't care.

He took me to the gardener's shed at the end of the orchard. It smelled musty, of moist earth and rotting wood. The floor was muddy and covered with tools, so you had to be careful where you stepped. Hoes, shovels, scythes, and clippers leaned against the walls. Containers of seeds were stacked in corners, and bulbs for planting in the fall were buried under rags.

"How did you know where to find me?"

"The deformed little nun with droopy eyelids told me. The one who looks like a turtle."

"Cándida?"

"I don't know what her name is."

"Her name is Cándida."

He slipped his arm around my waist and held me against him. I felt so lightheaded I could hardly keep my balance. It was as though the muscles in my legs had turned liquid.

"Father Braulio . . ." I murmured.

"Sh . . . Sh . . ."

"What if someone comes? What if . . . ?"

I didn't finish the sentence. Suddenly, his mouth was on mine. I felt soft cat feet pattering up my spine. My body was a limp rag in his arms. He eased me back against a post that stank of decomposing wood, and somehow it made me giddy. I had never been drunk before, but I imagined it must be like this. The scent of his breath was different from what I remembered, not cinnamon and orange blossoms but, I don't know, slightly sulphurous.

He was working his fingers up under my shift, and I felt a surge of panic. Still, I didn't push him away. He moved his hands deftly over my hips, my buttocks, stroking gently. He knew what he was doing. He didn't fumble or struggle with ties. Before he entered me, I saw him slip something over his sex—an animal membrane fashioned to fit over the cock. I relaxed. I knew I wouldn't get pregnant. I was grateful to him for his foresight.

He was riding me now, moving rhythmically like an expert horseman. It was painful and exhilarating all at once. I felt as though I were soaring over the valley, galvanized, breathless, free! I opened my eyes long enough to see a giant rat scurry across the floorboards. Satan, I thought. I closed my eyes again and let passion take its course.

Braulio could come and go without arousing suspicion, since he was confessor to scores of nuns. He knew secret places where we could be alone—closets in the sacristy, lean-tos in the garden. Besides, his family had a house in Ávila they left vacant much of the time, preferring the wider expanses of their country estate. As for me, I left the convent freely to purchase supplies for the infirmary. From medical manuals I learned that a paste of mashed dates, acacia bark, and honey would prevent pregnancy and that caps of lemon or other citrus fruits placed at the entrance to my womb would kill Braulio's seed. I didn't breathe a word about any of this to Teresa. She was still struggling with her visions and locutions. How could I reveal my depravity to an innocent like her? We were both victims of passion, by mine was evil, while hers was divine.

One afternoon I heard the most alarming sounds coming from Teresa's cell. A hiss like a whip slicing the air, then a terrible crack followed by a moan. I stood by the door and listened. Ssss. Crack. Moan. And then again and again, except now the moans were shrieks. Ssss. Crack. And then a blood-curdling scream that brought forth mental images of a torture victim on the rack. I pushed opened the door. What I saw caused me to crumple against the wall. Teresa, nude from the waist up, wielded a sturdy horse whip. Rhythmically, she spun it above her head, then brought it down with all the force she could muster on her bloody back.

I grabbed the whip and struggled to wrest it from her.

"No!" she screamed. She fought me, but she was so weak that I overpowered her easily.

"Stop, Teresa!" I yelled at her. "If you need to punish yourself, use one of the switches Mother Francisca provides for the purpose. You'll shred your flesh with this thing."

She'd collapsed on the floor, sobbing. "Father Daza says I need mortifications! I have to shred my flesh. I have to beat the Devil out of my body. Satan is filling my head with spurious images. I'll burn in Hell unless I can rid myself of evil." I picked her up and put her in bed.

"Have you eaten yet today, Teresa?"

She hadn't. She never ate in the morning because of her stomach problems, but it was already past the midday meal. I suspected Daza had demanded fasting as well as flagellation.

"Your health doesn't permit this nonsense," I snapped. What good was it for me to hover over her to protect her health, I thought, if Daza was going to prescribe mortifications?

"Put that down," she whispered, pointing to the whip I held in my hand.

"No! You'll destroy your body!"

"The soul is more important than the body!"

I should have taken it to Mother Francisca and explained, as a nurse, that Teresa was in no state to torture herself with horse whips. Instead I shrugged and dropped it on the floor. I was anxious to go to Braulio. I was a sinner.

I fell into the routine of the hypocrite, praying the Divine Office, meeting Braulio twice a week for "confession." It was delicious . . . for nearly eight years. Imagine, eight years of fornication and lies! But then, in 1554, something happened. So much time has passed since Braulio loved me. Twenty-two winters. I was a young woman then, and now I'm in my fifties. But I remember the date clearly because it was that year that the Jesuits opened their school in Ávila.

Teresa and I were entering the oratory that morning, when suddenly Teresa fell to her knees before an *ecce homo,* a polychrome statue of the wounded Christ. She started to wail, "Oh, my Lord and my God! Those terrible wounds you endured for us!" I don't need to describe the scene because she described it herself in her *Life,* a copy of which is still, in this year of Our Lord 1576, in the hands of the Inquisition. I have a duplicate, though, one I copied out myself. This is what she wrote: "I felt so keenly aware of how poorly I thanked Him for those wounds that, it seems to me, my heart broke. Beseeching Him to strengthen me once and for all that I might not offend Him, I threw myself down before Him with the greatest outpouring of tears."

And that's exactly what happened. She cried, lying there at Christ's feet, as though the floodgates of her soul had burst open. I didn't know what to do. I just stood there and watched.

Teresa came to see that moment as a turning point. "My conversion," she called it, because at that instant she experienced a profound transformation. After eight years of being tortured by Salcedo and Daza, she finally understood that she was indeed in God's hands, not the Devil's. She knew that at that moment she had experienced the overwhelming, awe-inspiring presence of God's grace and self-revelation. She felt that from then on, she would be a new person, wholly committed to loving and worshipping God. At that moment—the moment at which she knew firsthand God's love and redeeming power—she felt a new strength, a strength that enabled her to fight against Daza and his slurs.

But the curious thing is, I felt it too. "Whatever you've done," I told myself, "God will forgive you, provided you repent wholeheartedly and change your ways. God loves the sinner, and faith liberates her from her wickedness."

I determined to end my relationship with Braulio, but it turned out to be not so easy.

Angélica del Sagrado Corazón
Toledo, 25 July 1576

CHAPTER 10

Enter the Jesuits

BLACK AND YELLOW ARE THE COLORS OF DEATH, AND THE NEWLY WIDOWED Doña Guiomar wore them regally. That evening she appeared in a costume of deep gold taffeta trimmed in ebony. The skirt, which cascaded downward over her petticoats, was supported by a farthingale consisting of three horse-hair hoops. A stiff corset transformed her upper torso into a long, inverted cone balanced on top of the broad pyramid formed by the underskirt. Her mutton-shaped sleeves blossomed into tufts of black lace at the wrist. Over her gown she wore a black, sleeveless surcoat, richly embroidered with gold and pearls.

That afternoon I had overseen the ironing of her enormous gold-tone ruff, whose delicate fluting was starched stiff and propped up with wires. I instructed the hairdresser how to curl her hair and pile it into a chignon, then position the black, peaked widow's coif on her head. It was I, not her maid, who fastened the bracelets around her wrists. Ever since I'd started accompanying Teresa to her house, Doña Guiomar wanted me to dress her. Only me. I hadn't sewn gowns in years, but I was still an expert seamstress and understood the construction of clothes. I could make a pleat lie flat and tie a bow to perfection.

Not long after Teresa had collapsed in tears before the *ecce homo,* I started accompanying her to Doña Guiomar's. I wanted to get out of the convent, to hide in a place where Braulio couldn't find me. Besides, I liked Doña Guiomar. Her husband had died a few months before, and she'd gone from *dama de sociedad* to subdued widow in a matter of days. Yet she was still an affable, open young woman who loved company. She didn't go to balls anymore, but she did entertain. I spent hours at her side discussing fabrics and fashion. She had bought some perpetuana, a woolen fabric with a twill weave, for a cape, and she wanted me to suggest a trim. Would popinjay blue (so stylish) be appropriate for a widow? What about gingerline? Were horsehair hoops better than the new metal ones? Was a sausage-like bolster fastened at either hip better than hoops? Visiting her took me back to the days when I accompanied my mother and Tía Cati to the homes of aristocratic ladies, where we fitted magnificent dresses and drank almond water with the maids in the kitchen. But now I wasn't relegated to the kitchen. Now I was a dowered nun at Encarnación, invited into the hall to chat with the guests.

It wouldn't be long before the callers arrived. Lamps flickered. Shadows caressed the walls coquettishly. In spite of her sorrow, the grieving widow was clearly excited. She rang for the kitchen maid, and an ancient woman appeared, wrinkled as a raisin. "Have you checked the crystal, Maridíaz? Does it sparkle?" "*Sí, señora.*" "Are you sure there are no water stains on the silver?" "*Sí, señora.*" The screech of wheels and the whinnying of horses prompted Doña Guiomar to shoo Maridíaz out of the room and settle back on the divan. The widow took a short, sharp breath and smiled as though she were posing for a portrait.

"They're coming from just across the way," said Teresa. "They don't need a carriage."

Doña Guiomar relaxed her facial muscles. "I know that," she said curtly.

My stomach was tight with anticipation. In order to have something to do, I bent over and petted Doña Guiomar's fluffy, white dog. The animal jumped onto my knees and licked my face. I cringed. I didn't know whether or not it was appropriate for me to hold it there. Just in case it wasn't, I tried to coax it off. The dog leapt to the ground, then hopped back onto my knees.

A male voice called. "*¡Ah de la casa!*" Doña Guiomar tweaked her skirt again, and a manservant showed in two clerics, one very young and the other, middle-aged and avuncular. Doña Guiomar began to flutter like an overwrought butterfly. Teresa looked down at her hands.

"Don Diego! Don Miguel!" Doña Guiomar, radiating charm and excitement, made the introductions. Both men were Jesuits, priests of the radical new order that had started in 1540 with just a handful of men, and now, only fourteen years later, boasted over a thousand. Known as the Society of Jesus, they had just started a school in Ávila, the *colegio* of San Gil. Ignacio de Loyola, founder of the Society, stressed education, explained the older man. He saw schools as the means to create an enlightened and moral clergy, a goal being promoted at Trent.

Doña Guiomar had been confessing with Jesuits since they'd come to Ávila the year before, and her devotion to the order bordered on veneration. She'd brought Teresa to meet Father Diego de Cetina and Father Miguel de Torres because, she said, Daza had turned out to be a fraud and Teresa needed a new confessor. Someone smarter, more perceptive. It was a delicate situation because Daza himself was in tight with the Society of Jesus. It had been one of Daza's friends, Hernando Álvarez de Águila, a *converso* Jesuit and distant cousin of Teresa's, who had obtained papal permission to found the *colegio* in the first place.

Father Miguel. He was magnetic. He drew you in. He was talking about Father Ignacio's plans to send missionaries all over the globe—to India, Japan, even America. Father Francisco Xavier had already left for Goa, he said, and other Jesuits were getting ready to set up missions in the New World. "Men are so lucky," breathed Teresa. "I wish I could serve God as a missionary." I have to admit it, I couldn't take my eyes off of Father Miguel. I hardly noticed his young companion, Father Diego. He was just a boy, really, only twenty-three years old. He didn't talk much, and when he did, his tone was hushed and deferential. Whenever he opened his mouth, he looked at Father Miguel, as though asking for permission. Doña Guiomar glanced at him every once in a while, causing him to blush and twitch. I couldn't imagine him preaching.

We ate in the great hall, as was the custom in palatial residences like Doña Guiomar's, on tables arranged for the purpose. Doña Guiomar's servants brought in plates of kid, fowl, and vegetables. All of a sudden the dog jumped onto Teresa's lap.

"Barque!" shrieked Doña Guiomar. "Get down from there! Maridíaz! Come get Barque!" She pronounced it Bar-kay. I thought it was a strange name for a dog.

"It's an English name," explained Doña Guiomar demurely. "I mean, it's not a name at all, it's the sound a dog makes in English. That's what my husband—*Requiescat in pace*—told me. He's the one who bought me the dog."

"Bark," said Father Miguel. "What a dog does in English is *bark*."

"Yes," said Doña Guiomar, *bar-kay*." She giggled, covering her mouth with her hand.

Teresa glimpsed at the older priest with flirtatious eyes. I wondered for an instant if she was going to fall in love with him. I thought of Braulio and tensed. Women fell into the clutches of their confessors all the time, and

Teresa, although almost forty, was still a beauty. It could happen, I thought. He was charming and sophisticated. She was energetic and intelligent. And it was clear they were beginning to like each other.

A few days later Sister Radegunda accompanied Teresa to San Gil, where she was going to meet with her new Jesuit confessor. I was busy in the sewing room when one of the novices came to announce that someone was asking for me.

"Who?"

"Father Braulio."

I felt as though I had suddenly gone from a warm kitchen into an ice deposit.

"Tell him I'm ill."

The girl's eyes opened wide.

"You have to go," she said. "He's your confessor." A smile crept across her lips, a smile that could easily have been a sneer. Did this girl know something she shouldn't? I wondered.

"I've been confessing with someone else lately," I snapped.

"Really? That's not what he said. He said he was your confessor and you had to go."

It wasn't true I'd been confessing with someone else. I hadn't been confessing at all. I'd say I was going to confession, then slip away and hide in my cell or in one of the countless nooks in the convent, a labyrinth of obscure passageways and secret spots. The audacity of the bastard, I thought, to send one of the novices to look for me.

"He's waiting for you in the chapel," said the girl self-importantly.

If I didn't go, she'd have plenty to tell Mother Francisca and the other nuns. In a flash everyone would know something was going on between Sister Angélica and her confessor. Something had to be going on for a nun to refuse a visit from her spiritual guide. I gathered my sewing into a basket. The novice stood there watching.

"Run along," I snapped. "You don't have to wait for me."

"He told me to wait for you. He told me to accompany you to the door of the chapel."

I flushed in humiliation. He had put this stupid child in charge of me.

The chapel was almost dark. No candles were burning, and little light came in through the stained glass windows on either side of the nave. Braulio was sitting toward the front.

"I haven't seen you for so long, my angel," he said softly. "You've been avoiding me." He gestured to me to sit beside him.

I looked down. He took my hand in his and began to massage my fingers tenderly. Right there, in front of Our Crucified Lord. "Braulio," I whispered. "This can't continue."

He kissed my palms, my wrists. He ran his hand up my arm to my elbow, then slowly, gently, began to caress my upper arm. "No, Braulio," I breathed. "Please!"

He leaned over and kissed my cheek, then placed his hand on my breast and felt for my nipple under the cloth of my habit. I pulled back. "No!"

"Why not, my precious Angélica? I love you. You know that."

"It's a sin, Braulio!"

"Why, darling? Why is it a sin? God gave us feelings and bodies. All this glorious passion comes from God."

"We both took vows, Braulio. I'm a consecrated virgin of . . ."

"You're no virgin!" He burst out laughing. "You? A virgin? You've been sleeping with me for almost eight years! You can't get it back once you've lost it, Angélica."

I must have turned crimson. I must have trembled in shame.

He grabbed me by the wrist and pulled me toward him. With his free hand he reached under my habit and grabbed my inner thigh. Suddenly, he pinched so hard I felt a pain shoot from my knee to my hip. I let out a short, muted shriek, and he snorted. I wriggled away from him and started to run, but he seized me from behind by the waist.

"Let me go!" I screamed, struggling to get free.

"Shut up, you idiot!" he snarled.

He grabbed my wrist and twisted so hard I felt as though my arm would pop out of its socket. Tears spurted from my eyes and I bit my lip in order not to cry out. He dragged me into the sacristy. A vague aroma of incense and wilting flowers permeated the air. Priestly vestments hung here and there, made visible by dim window light. Their eerie, irregular shapes made me think of ghosts. He pinned me against the wall with one hand and held me in place with his knee. I tried to lunge forward and bite his shoulder, but he kicked my shin with such force that my leg went limp under me. I let out a scream. "I told you to shut up!" he growled. I saw his free hand rise like a flying gargoyle, then plunge toward me. I heard a nauseating crack. My mouth filled with blood. The gargoyle covered my face, and still I thrashed. Braulio was struggling to pinion my head against the wall. With his hand plastering my mouth, he dug into one cheek with his thumb, into the other with his fingers. Then he rammed my skull against the stone surface. Fireworks burst inside my brain, rockets like the ones they send up for the feast of Santiago. My shin, jaw, and head were throbbing horribly. My whole body was a mass of earsplitting screams. Enraged, Braulio was tearing at my skirts.

I opened my eyes and saw a statue of Christ on a chest, placid, unmoving.

"God, help me!" I moaned.

Braulio yanked off my undergarments and thrust himself into me. He sank and rose, sank and rose for about a minute. His movements were rough, irregular. Then it was over. Tears were streaming down my cheeks. My lips and jaw were swelling and blood was dripping onto my habit.

"You bastard!" I whispered through my sobs.

"From now on, you little bitch, you give me whatever I want whenever I want it," he hissed. "Whenever I want it, you understand?"

"I'll tell. I'll go to Mother Francisca."

He burst out laughing. "Go ahead. I have so much shit against you, I could have them throw you into the pit tomorrow."

"I'll tell them you raped me!"

"Don't you know I can bring charges against you before the Inquisition, you imbecile! All I have to tell them is that you're an *alumbrada*. All that shit about mental prayer! All that slop about talking to Jesus!"

"You can't tell anything I said during confession!"

"Since when do you play by the rules, little angel? You haven't played by the rules since you started fucking your father confessor!"

"You have no evidence. You have no witnesses!"

"I control half the women in this convent! All I have to do is order them to testify you've been praying like a Jew. You'll be roasting in no time, and I'll piss on your ashes."

"I'll bring you down with me! I'll tell them what you did to me. I'll tell them you seduced me, you raped me!"

"Who do you think the father inquisitors are going to believe, Sister Angélica? Me, a priest, or you, a woman?"

"They can examine me," I shouted. "They'll see I'm not a virgin!"

He raised his hand again, but it was only a threat. "Shut up," he hissed. "How are they going to know when you lost your pretty little jewel? Maybe you entered the convent without it."

"I'll go right now! Your seed is all over me."

"I'll tell them it's the Devil's seed. You've been fucking the Devil! You're nothing but a Jew-loving, Devil-fucking heretic. Listen," he said, more calmly. "Don't make problems for yourself. Keep your mouth shut and your legs open. Everything will be fine." He was straightening his clothing. "Unless you cross me," he added coldly. "In that case, I'll have you killed."

"Go ahead," I whispered hoarsely. The throbbing was unbearable. "Who'll miss me? All I am is a seamstress's daughter. No one cares what happens to me."

"Really? Well, that's probably true. You're certainly nothing to look at. You sure as hell won't be missed for your looks." He snickered. "But just think of spiked chains piercing your flesh, my little angel. Think of metal clamps slicing your titties. Or else think of the eyes of the whole town on your naked body while your limbs are being harnessed to four horses, then pulled in different directions. That's the usual punishment for whores like you."

"I don't care," I hissed. "I don't care what you do to me. We all have to die. I'd rather die like a martyr than give in to you ever again. I'm not committing any more sins of the flesh."

"Oh, I think you will. Because if you don't, your friend Teresa will be out there on the barbecue with you."

A shiver crept like a centipede up the back of my neck. "What does Teresa have to do with any of this?"

"Oh, I have more on her than you can imagine. She's a Jew and she prays like a Jew. And Daza planted the idea in everybody's head that she's possessed by the Devil. It would be easy."

I was speechless.

"So, my little angel, do we have an understanding? You don't want to be responsible for your friend turning into roast meat, do you?" He winked. I felt my insides roil.

I tore away from him. I groped my way back to my cell and crumpled onto the fresh, white sheets of my bed. I felt like a pile of rotting garbage. It was sinful, I thought, to defile the bedclothes with my repulsive body. The laundry sisters had washed the sheets in lavender. I closed my eyes and lost myself in the sweetness of the fabric.

When I didn't show up for the Divine Office, Mother Francisca sent a novice to find me. I saw her enter the room like a specter and heard her voice as though through water. I hid my face. "I can't get up," I whispered. "I'm ill."

In a while the girl came back. "Mother Francisca wants you to go to the infirmary."

"I can't get up." My voice sounded like that of an old woman. "I'm ill."

I slipped into a troubled sleep. I felt Braulio's hand, huge and hairy like a bear's paw, crushing my face. Jackals licked blood from the sacristy floor, while a frenzied Hydra yanked holy objects from drawers and hurled them against the stone walls. Braulio disappeared, and in his place an incubus materialized. It rubbed against me and chuckled lasciviously. Somewhere in the distance Teresa, engulfed in flames, was shrieking.

When I opened my eyes, Sister Josefa was standing by my bed. She was old now. Nearly two decades had passed since I had gone to work as her apprentice in the infirmary. Tiny grooves radiated outward from the corners of her eyes like sunrays, and her chin was crinkly and ill-defined, but her hands were still strong and competent. She was looking down at me, her gaze shrewd and steady. My head still hurt, but I was wearing a clean nightshirt, and my wounds were dressed. There were pillows under my head in place of the mound of straw I usually slept on.

"You're awake," she said matter-of-factly. "You have to eat. I've had a broth prepared."

"I don't feel like eating."

She propped me up against the pillows and rubbed some salve on my head. She was gentle, but I winced at her touch. When the broth came, she placed her arm around my shoulders and spooned the liquid into my mouth. I didn't resist. Instead, I allowed it to trickle down my throat slowly. I inhaled and detected the tang of onions and carrots that had simmered for hours with meat. I detected thyme and bay leaves, garlic and pepper. A broth fit for aristocrats.

"Thank you," I whispered. "It's very good."

"Who did this to you?" she asked without preface. I turned over and buried my face in the pillows. How could I tell her? I pulled the sheets up around my neck.

"What son-of-a-bitch did this to you?"

I didn't know what to say. I squeezed my eyes shut and didn't say anything.

"What *hijo de puta* did this to you?" she asked again. Her tone was unnerving.

"Braulio."

"Here," she said, holding a cup to my lips. "Drink this. It will calm you, make you sleep."

I slipped into a sweet darkness. When I awoke, my head was no longer throbbing. The curtain was drawn. All that was visible was a small candle burning next to something—a form—on the windowsill. It took a moment before I realized that someone was seated next to the bed. She was turned away from me, her head resting on her arm, which was supported by the back of the chair. I reached out to tug gently on her habit.

"Angélica!" she said softly. "You're awake. Thank God!" It was Teresa.

"Have you been here long?"

"Hours. Days. I don't know. Sister Josefa keeps it dark in here. You can't tell day from night. I've lost track. A couple of days, I think. Thank God you've come to."

"What's going on?"

"You've been ill. Very ill. It happened suddenly. One morning you were fine and then, in the afternoon, when I went to look for you, they told me you were ailing. Sister Josefa said not to awaken you. She said to keep the curtain closed and to leave you covered up. She won't tell me what the matter is. She's been very mysterious. How do you feel?" She leaned over to kiss me on the forehead. "We've all been so worried," she said, taking my hand. "I've been praying to Our Lord day and night. If anything ever happened to you, Angélica, I'd just . . . I couldn't stand it." She wiped a tear off her lid. "I brought you some tea this morning, but it's cold now. I'll ask Silvia to get some more."

"Thank you."

She got up to summon the maid. I could make out the form on the sill now. It was a statue of Christ. It looked like that same one that had been in the sacristy. She saw me blinking at it and sat back down again. "I brought it in here to keep you company," she said.

Silvia came in with the tea, a combination of chamomile and peppermint. I sipped it in silence and before long dozed off again.

Days passed before I could get out of bed, but at last the swelling eased and I could hobble around the garden on Teresa's arm.

"What happened to you, Angélica?" she said as she eased me into the swing in the patio.

"I don't know. It's strange. I hardly ever get sick."

She looked right at me with her cool, dark eyes. "No," she said. "What really happened? You're covered with bruises. You had compresses all over your face and Sister Josefa bandaged your leg. It looks like you fell out of a tree."

"Maybe I did."

"Or maybe someone pushed you."

I looked down at the dusty path. The flowers had wilted, and the summer sun had singed the tips of the leaves. An enormous calico cat lay on a bench, stretched out like a pasha.

"What did Sister Josefa tell you?" I said finally.

"Nothing. She didn't tell me anything, but I'm not blind."

"Braulio," I said simply. She raised her eyebrows. I bit my lip.

"They have so many ways to hurt you," she said finally.

"What are you talking about?"

"Confessors. They have so many ways to hurt you."

I didn't say anything. "You don't have to tell me what happened," she said finally, "but if you want to, I'll do whatever I can to help."

For the next couple weeks I tiptoed around the convent, terrified I'd run into Braulio in the chapel, the parlor, or some forgotten corridor. What was to prevent him from hiding behind a statue and pulling me into the vestment cabinet? Or from pushing me into a linen closet and coming down on me among the sheets and coverlets? I refused to go outside for fear he'd be waiting for me on some forgotten path. Hadn't he once snuck into the garden and lured me into the gardener's shed? I stopped going to Doña Guiomar's house. Instead, I spent afternoons with Sister Josefa, who changed my bandages and did her best to calm my nerves. It was she who acted as my confessor —yes, I realize it's a sin to confess to a nun, that only a priest can administer the sacraments—but I had to talk to someone, and it was easier to talk to Sister Josefa (God forgive me for saying this) than some man. How could a man understand the loneliness of a plain woman, a seamstress once rejected by a suitor, who enters a convent because she has nowhere else to go? How could a man understand the elation of an ugly hatchling that a prince charming like Braulio suddenly calls his "angel"? Can a man understand a woman's passion, a woman's longing? Sister Josefa, with her lined temples and her puckered jowl, understood everything. I told her the whole story. I told her how I had given myself to Braulio, how we had been lovers for eight years, and how I had tried to break it off after Teresa's conversion before the *ecce homo*. I told her about everything except Braulio's threat. His threat to Teresa, I mean. I couldn't tell her about that without revealing Teresa's secret: the fact that her father had been a *converso*.

I wondered if Sister Josefa would go to Mother Francisca and ask her to file a complaint with the Provincial. But all she said was, "Be patient, put it in God's hands."

Every minute of every day I lived in terror. I kept thinking that at any moment Braulio would appear out of nowhere, pin me against a wall, and make the demand, "Give me what I want, or whatever happens to Teresa will be your fault."

I couldn't sleep at night without a draft of valerian. Sister Josefa would mix it with apple juice and honey to camouflage the bitter taste. Every night the nightmares grew worse. Black-robed prelates wreaking carnage. Blood flowing in torrents down walls, through ruts, over my feet, between my toes. Incubuses tearing off the habits of sleeping novices, lacerating their flesh with spiky fingernails, thrusting penises like swords into their virgin sexes. Teresa floating upward, upward, over a bonfire, then shot down by a blunderbuss and plunging gracelessly into the flames like a slain fowl. I was terrified to sleep. I was terrified to stay awake.

When Braulio said Mass, his eyes swept over the congregation, over the choir. Was he searching for me? In the parlor he looked at me with an insinuating leer. Once he caught me on the way to Office and hissed something in my ear, but I wrenched myself away. I could hardly work. I agonized incessantly. Was he hiding in the gardener's shed or waiting for me at the grille? Would he send the stupid little novice to get me from the sewing room? Would he complain to Mother Francisca that I wasn't complying with my holy obligations?

I wanted the sacrament of reconciliation. I wanted to confess, to make peace with God, but how could I tell Mother Francisca that I needed a new confessor? How could I explain that I had to get away from Braulio? If she called him in and questioned him, he'd know I'd betrayed his secret and would carry out his horrible threat.

And of course, I couldn't talk to Teresa. How could I tell her that because of me—me, her friend and her sister—her own life was in danger?

Angélica del Sagrado Corazón
Toledo, 27 July 1576

CHAPTER 11

Confessions

I WAS SO WRAPPED UP IN MY OWN MISERY THAT I FORGOT ABOUT EVERYTHING else, including Doña Guiomar's beautiful dresses and the Jesuits of San Gil. Teresa was careful not to ask too many questions. She was discreet. She didn't pry. Who knows how much of the story she'd cobbled together?

But one day, she ventured cautiously, "Doña Guiomar asks about you all the time, Angélica. She misses you. She doesn't understand why you stopped visiting."

"Oh," I stammered. "There's so much to do around here." We were in Teresa's *estrado* sewing. I sat on the same faded cushion I'd used in Tía Cati's house decades ago.

Her thread caught, making an unsightly knot. "Damn!" she growled. "I'll never be as good at this as you."

"Never," I agreed. I took the embroidery from her, cut the thread, and loosened the stitches. Then I went back over her work with a fresh thread, fastening the slack strand and covering the mistake. "Here, try again," I said, handing back the cloth, "although frankly, Teresa, you're a lost cause. If you don't know how to make a loop stitch at forty, you never will."

"I'm not forty quite yet," she laughed. "There's still hope!"

I shrugged. "Well, I'm not surprised you like your new confessor," I said. "I was sure you and Don Miguel would get on well together."

"Don Miguel? Oh, no. Father Diego is my confessor. Diego de Cetina."

I looked at her in amazement. "Father Diego! That kid?" I conjured up a mental image of Diego de Cetina. Bobbing head, nervous eyes, pimply chin, diffident demeanor.

"I admit, I had to get used to the idea. But then I just decided, well, this is the hand God dealt me, so He must have His reasons. God doesn't make mistakes." She smiled, and I noticed that delicate lines were forming around her eyes. "He says he thinks my visions are from God, but he's not absolutely sure. He wants some of the older Jesuits to examine me. The thing is, he believes in me, Angélica. It's true he's just a boy, but at least he's given me hope."

"And Don Miguel?" I wondered how the handsome Jesuit who had looked at Teresa with such warmth had consented to hand her over to an underling.

"Don Miguel . . . Ah, that wouldn't have worked. At least, he doesn't think so. He says I'm too impressionable, that I let Daza overwhelm me and before that, Fray Sergio. He said I'd do better with someone with a less imposing personality, someone I'd obey out of humility, not out of fear. I do have to learn humility, Angélica."

"Yes, you do," I agreed. "You're quite pig-headed."

She pinched me on the arm and burst out laughing. Of course I wound up telling her all about Braulio. How could I keep my secret from Teresa de Ahumada, my best friend, my sister? The only thing I didn't tell her was the part about him calling her a Jew who prayed like a Jew. That was something we couldn't talk about. To Teresa de Ahumada, my best friend of twenty-five years, I couldn't mention the word *judío* or the word *israelita* or the word *converso*. Even between sisters, there are certain things you just can't talk about.

She convinced me to go to Mother Francisca and tell her the whole story. "She may punish you, Angélica. She may even send you to the convent jail for a few months. But at least you'll be able to do your penance and get it over with."

The idea of spending three months in the damp, stinking Encarnación dungeon hardly appealed to me. The cold weather would soon set in, and the subterranean vault would be freezing. If one had to do time, the summer months were more survivable. I decided not to go to Mother Francisca right away. She was busy, I told myself. Several new postulants had come in, two of them from wealthy families able to pay hefty dowries, and Mother Francisca was deep in negotiations. I convinced myself that the whole Braulio thing would blow over. Weeks had gone by and he hadn't sent for me. Not only that, he hadn't complained to Mother Francisca about my not showing up for confession. Maybe he was tired of me, I thought. Maybe I was done with him once and for all. Maybe I should just sit tight and wait to see what happened.

The only person I felt comfortable confiding in was Sister Josefa. To my astonishment, she agreed with me. "I'd wait a while," she said. "Mother Francisca is so busy right now. And, to be honest, I don't think Braulio will be bothering you anymore."

"Why is that?"

"Oh, you know, men like that come and go," she said enigmatically.

"But I need a new confessor."

"Ah yes. Be patient, my lamb. God provides."

I settled into an uneasy routine, working in the infirmary in the morning and the sewing room in the afternoon, accompanying Teresa on her visits to Doña Guiomar, tiptoeing through the corridors in dread of Braulio. However, Braulio was making himself scarce. He said Mass a few times a week, but never called for me. I took communion, even in my unconfessed state of sin, in order not to attract attention. It was wicked, I know, but what else could I do?

"I can't go on like this," I told Sister Josefa. "I need a confessor."

"All things come to she who waits. You'll see."

She was right. In a few weeks Mother Francisca called me to her office and told me that she had assigned me a new confessor: Father Sergio. "He has a slot," she said. "Your friend Teresa no longer sees him. She goes to the Jesuits for confession."

I wasn't happy about it—Fray Sergio was the one who had told Teresa that mental prayer was a sin—but fortunately the days that followed were full of distractions. The official opening of San Gil took place in May, and Father Francisco de Borja, once one of the most powerful men in Spain, came to town for the event. Older people still remembered him as the Marqués de Lombay, Grand Duke of Gandía. The direct descendent of a pope, he had inherited riches beyond measure and become a potent political force. But then, shortly after he had become Viceroy of Catalonia, the king ordered him to accompany the remains of his recently deceased wife, Empress Isabel of Portugal, reputedly the most beautiful woman in Christendom, to the royal sepulture in Granada.

The grand duke had seen the empress many times bedecked with diamonds, emeralds, and rubies, her slender frame clothed in velvet, her sumptuous tresses interwoven with strands of pearls. Now, he would see her one last time. Ritual required him to open the coffin and identify her body. Slowly, painstakingly, the royal morticians lifted the lid, and when they did, the blood drained from the duke's lips. The empress, King Carlos's exquisite flower, was a mass of rot and worms. Mortified, Borja uttered the resolution that would reverberate throughout Spain and the entire Christian world: never again would he serve a mortal master. "All that lives, perishes," he whispered. "All earthly goods are vanity. Only God is eternal."

He kept his word. A few years later, after his wife died, he became a Jesuit.

And now, here he was in Ávila. Grandfathers and grandmothers who remembered him in his finery were anxious to see him in his plain black soutane. Would he look sad, now that he'd forsaken the treasures of the world, or serene and pious? The town council organized a magnificent procession, with giants and jugglers, jesters and acrobats. The guilds paraded with their banners, their members in official colors. Blue for the bakers, green for the grocers, red for the carpenters, black for the farriers. Musicians played flutes and lutes, Italian chitarras, tambourines, and bells. The ladies wore wide, satin gowns that turned them into walking mushrooms. The streets were ablaze with color, and at night, so were the skies. The councilmen had brought in Italian pyrotechnicians to set off multicolored fireworks. After dark the crowds gathered in the plaza to oooh and aaah as rockets exploded into dazzling chrysanthemums that shimmered among the stars.

Among the throngs I caught sight of a familiar face. A rotund, bald man in his forties, with sagging jowls and sunken eyes. Who was he? I was sure I knew him, but I couldn't place his face. He carried a brown robe thrown over his arm. Perhaps he had marched in a procession with his guild brothers, I thought. Brown. I tried to remember. What guild wore brown? Suddenly, it came to me. Brown was the official color of the cartwrights. It was Basilio! A heavyset woman, haggard and graying, stood beside him. She held a little girl of about six or seven by the hand. The child kept coughing, a wet, angry cough. I approached the mother cautiously.

"Excuse me, *señora*," I said respectfully. "Perhaps I can be of service to you. I have some pastilles that might help your child's cough."

Basilio stared at me suspiciously.

"I'm a nurse at Encarnación Convent. If you want, come to the turn tomorrow morning and ask for Sister Angélica. I'll have them ready for you."

Basilio's look had changed from suspicion to curiosity. He was eyeing my habit. He didn't want to look right at my face—that would have been rude— but he must have thought I looked familiar. He opened his mouth as if to say something, but I turned and moved swiftly away. What did I feel? I felt nothing. Absolutely nothing.

I joined the other sisters in the crowd and together with hundreds of others carrying candles or torches we trudged to San Gil. Borja, still a fine-looking man, with a long, aquiline nose and merry eyes, greeted the townsfolk warmly from the balcony of the *colegio*.

Father Miguel used his influence to arrange a meeting for Teresa with the duke—now Father Francisco. There was an interesting nun at Encarnación Convent, he must have told him. She had visions she thought came from God, and her confessor agreed, but he, Father Miguel, wanted the opinion of a person of authority.

Teresa returned from her interview with the great Borja euphoric. "He said he thought my visions came from God," she told me, "and that I should stop struggling against them. He told me to always start my prayer with a meditation on the Passion, and then, if the Lord should rise up in my spirit, not to resist."

Very nice, I thought. Her problem is solved. The support of a man like Borja would get the doubters off her back. Now she could enjoy her visions in peace. But what about me? Braulio was still there haunting the convent salon, and something told me it was only a matter of time before he made his next move.

Not long after that, I saw him at the grille with one of the young nuns, a pretty redhead—at least, she'd been a redhead before we sheared and veiled her—with look-at-me cheekbones. Her name was Ramona. He was standing rather too close to her and speaking rather too low. He stroked the bars, and I saw their hands touch—a swift, delicate kiss of the fingertips that sent a quiver up my arm. I should have left the room, but instead, I stood there fascinated. Braulio turned and saw me, and his lips parted into a smirk. Then he turned back to Sister Ramona and whispered something that made her blush and titter.

I wish I could write that at the moment I felt concern for the well-being of my sister, that I was fearful she'd fall into the same trap I had and suffer the same consequences, but the truth is, what I felt wasn't fear for Sister Ramona's immortal soul. What I felt was rage. A surge of fury ripped through my body that left me reeling. He was still there! He was still seducing women! And she, the little imbecile, was lapping it up! And now, the two of them were mocking me!

I knew it wasn't fair to blame Ramona. After all, hadn't I fallen for Braulio? The truth is that I, the homely girl that no other man had ever wanted, had delighted in Braulio's sweet words and gentle caresses. But I was in no mood to be reasonable.

"Looks like you've been replaced." The voice seemed to come from under water. A gravelly, irritating frog's croak. I looked down. It was Cándida.

I was speechless. How did she know about Braulio and me? Mortified, I spun on my heel and bolted from the room. I had the feeling all of them were watching me and laughing.

I went to find Sister Josefa, but she wasn't in the infirmary or in her cell. She'd gone to visit her niece in Cáceres, Sister Radegunda told me, and wouldn't be back for days. The only other person I could talk to was Teresa, but she was with Doña Guiomar. I had to unburden myself, so I went to Fray Sergio and told him everything. It was torture. I felt as though I were standing before him naked, exposing my hideous, sinning body. He prescribed mortifications, so I got a switch and flagellated myself, then knelt outside on a gravel walkway until the stones pierced my knees. Little by little I regained my powers of concentration. I went back to brewing herbs, sewing altarpieces, praying. Still, that image kept returning to haunt me. Braulio and Ramona. That exquisite moment when fingertip met fingertip.

One day, while I was in the chapel undressing a statue of Our Lady of Mount Carmel to repair her gown, a hand like a vise grabbed my arm. I knew that grip, and the sweet, seductive fragrance of orange blossoms that emanated from the body it was attached to. I thought he'd forgotten me, so he took me completely by surprise. "Let go or I'll scream," I said firmly. I had rehearsed this moment over and over in my mind.

"You won't scream," Braulio said, manacling me with one hand and covering my mouth with the other. I struggled to get loose. "You bitch," he hissed. "You're the one who got me sent away." I squirmed until I caught the fleshy part of his palm between my teeth and bit hard. He uncovered my mouth.

"I don't know what you're talking about."

"Yes, you do. You went whining to them, and now they're sending me north to get killed. That's what they do with people they want to get rid of. They ship them off to France or Holland or England, places where heretics are slitting Catholics' throats."

"How could I get you sent away? I don't have any power or connections."

He loosened his grip. "Yes . . ." he said haltingly. "That's true. You're a nobody. But . . . you could have gone to Mother Francisca."

"Well, I didn't," I hissed. My heart was pounding.

He looked perplexed. "Somebody betrayed me. Somebody . . ."

"Somebody betrayed *you*? You've been violating the women of this convent for years. I didn't turn you in, but I'm glad one of my sisters did, you bastard." I glared at him, certain he would slap me. How could I have loved this man? I wondered. How could I have felt angry at Ramona? Now all I felt for her was pity. And for him, disgust.

"Let me go," I whispered. "I have work to do." I twisted myself free of him.

"Wait . . ." He grabbed my wrist, but not brutally. "Do you know who . . . told them?"

"No."

The blood drained from his face. He stood there looking at me, suddenly contrite, his features contorted. I thought it was a trick. "Angélica," he whispered, "you could help me. Every day the heretics invade monasteries and massacre friars. It's dangerous."

"It's in God's hands, not mine," I said dryly.

"You could go to them. You could tell them it's not true. You could say the allegations against me are lies. They'd believe you. You're such an angel, no one would suspect you of . . . Please, Angélica. I know I've been . . . I've been unkind to you. I've been wicked, brutal even. But I've begged God for forgiveness." He crumpled against the wall. His cheeks were damp and his lips quivered. "Do you know what they do to Catholic martyrs in England, Angélica? They tie them to a post and disembowel them while they're still alive. It's true. The wretched creatures have to watch their own entrails fall out of their bodies!"

"I have no idea what allegations have been brought against you. God's will be done, Braulio. Be brave. It's an honor to be martyred for the faith." I admit I felt a bit smug.

"Angélica, I'm sorry for everything terrible I did to you. Forgive me! Help me!"

"I'll pray for your immortal soul, Braulio," I said. I walked away.

Braulio was already gone by the time Sister Josefa returned to Ávila. I didn't have to use a *cilicio* anymore to torment my flesh. I was cured of my desire for men, at least . . . I was cured of my desire for Braulio. That doesn't mean I didn't think about him anymore, though. His fair hair and sea-blue eyes still worked their way into my consciousness. I wavered between anger and melancholy, hurt and loneliness. Sometimes I wanted to crawl into bed and sleep forever.

"You know, Sister Josefa," I said one day when we were mixing potions, "Braulio thought I was the one who complained to the Provincial and got him sent north."

The old herbalist smiled. "How could it have been you? It would have to be a sister with *enchufe*. Someone with clout. Someone with an uncle or cousin or brother in the hierarchy."

"Do you know who it was?"

"Of course."

"Ramona?"

She chuckled. "No, child, not Ramona. Sister Ramona's the daughter of a farrier. She has no power aside from her pretty face."

"Then who was it?"

"Can't you guess? It was Cándida."

I was astounded.

"Think, Angélica. Why would Mother Francisca allow a wreck like Cándida into this convent if the girl didn't have money and pull? You know how picky she is about looks. Don't you remember the girl with a scar like a caterpillar over her eye? Francisca sent her away!" I still didn't remember that girl. "Well, Cándida is a troll, but she's a Valdivieso, one of the most aristocratic families in the country. Now, a family like that can't have an embarrassment like Cándida hanging around. Think of the gold it would take to try to marry her off! So they hid her in a convent. But Cándida is a very powerful young woman, the niece of the Grand Inquisitor of Toledo. When she decided to get rid of Braulio, all she had to do was write to her uncle."

"But . . . why did she want to get rid of him?"

"She was jealous."

"Of Braulio?"

It took me a moment to absorb what Sister Josefa was suggesting. "You mean . . . ?"

"Sister Cándida is in love with you, yes. It happens." Sister Josefa's voice was as calm as if she were explaining the properties of eucalyptus leaves.

"But I'm a woman, just like she is. It's impossible!"

"It's . . . let's say . . . an aberration, but as I said, it happens."

"I thought . . . What I mean is, if she's in love with anyone, it's Teresa."

"At first she liked Teresa, but you were kinder to her. You tried to teach her how to sew. Teresa was very cross with her, so now you're the one she loves." I didn't know what to say. "Just treat her kindly, Angélica. She's a lonely creature, shunned by everyone. Women are so superstitious. They think an ugly face means an ugly soul, but that's nonsense. She won't hurt you. Anyhow, she's done you a favor. You wanted to be free of Braulio, didn't you?"

"What did she accuse him of?"

"Of improper conduct with nuns. Of carnality. You weren't his only victim, Angélica. There were many over the years. Cándida lurks in the shadows watching. She knows everything that goes on. When she made her accusation, she had all the data she needed. She gave names and dates, of course, but she was careful to protect you. Anyway, they're not going to conduct an involved investigation."

My head was spinning. It took me days to grasp that Braulio was really gone and that I owed this favor to Cándida. I still tiptoed down corridors, peeking behind doors, peeping into closets. I had to get used to the idea that all this time Cándida had been spying on me in the refectory, the sewing room, the garden—her turtle's head extending from its shell, swiveling this way and that so that her sleepy eyes, situated, it seemed, on either side of her skull, could focus. But Sister Josefa was right. Cándida meant no harm, and I soon realized that a smile or a kind word were, for her, treasures to be cherished. I grew used to her sitting motionless at my feet while I sewed and to accept her quiet, reptilian ways. Years later, when she died, I shed tears and prayed for her soul. It was harder for Teresa to accept her. She had an aristocrat's sense of propriety. But even she learned to appreciate the girl's undying loyalty and the great service she'd done the convent by getting rid of that insect, Braulio. Turtles are good for destroying insects.

It was about then that Teresa had to change confessors, too. Father Diego de Cetina was a sickly boy, and his superiors decided the cruel Castilian winters were too much for his frail constitution. They sent him to Italy, where for once in his short, unnoteworthy life, he enjoyed God's earthly gifts—smiling skies, redolent cheeses, and dates bursting with sweet, sticky juices. Well, I hope he enjoyed those things. Maybe he expired in a dark, roach-infested hospital, coughing up blood and burning with fever. But I prefer to think he slipped into paradise while savoring a creamy fig pudding. For the faithful, of course, there are only happy endings, but those last days before one steps into eternity can be wretched. I pray that Diego's were filled with peace and sunlight. As soon as he left Ávila, his Jesuit brothers forgot all about him. At least, I never heard anyone mention him again until, months later, a letter came saying he had died.

The Jesuits have produced many great men. Father Francisco Xavier has brought the faith to India and Japan and Father Peter Canisius is busy reconverting Germany back to Catholicism. They'll be saints someday, remembered forever. But Father Diego de Cetina will disappear into obscurity unless I rescue him with this testimony. That's why I have to write down that he was, in his own way, an important man. He believed in Teresa, and in that way, he changed her life. That's why I can't let him be forgotten.

Juan de Prádanos, the priest who replaced Cetina, had only been a Jesuit for a year, but he was very knowledgeable about mental prayer. He was about twenty-seven and attractive enough, although with a long, horse-like face and undisciplined eyebrows that reminded me of underbrush. He was an attentive listener, and when you spoke to him, he looked right at you, nodding or interjecting exclamations—ah!, I see!, quite so!—that allowed him to respond without interrupting your flow of speech. Teresa adored him.

It was Juan de Prádanos who taught Teresa the *Spiritual Exercises*—how to use images to kindle the spirit. He suggested she start out by looking at an image—a picture, a crucifix, a statue—or else, read a passage from some inspirational book. Then, he told her to imagine a scene from Scripture, using all her senses. "See the sky, feel the heat, smell the sweat!" he told her. The point is to lose yourself in the scene so that before you know it, you're right there with Jesus, lost in His love. She told me all about it. One day he read Teresa a passage about an encounter with Jesus on the road, then instructed her to imagine her own meeting with Him.

"I closed my eyes and saw Jesus wearing pilgrim's garb," she told me. "He didn't seem at all surprised to see me. He started a conversation right away. He was easy to talk to and a good listener. His hair was long and wavy, just like in the painting by Pedro Berruguete in the cathedral, but He didn't have that beatific look He has in the picture.

"'Teresa,' he said. 'I'd like to spend some time talking with you.' I invited him home, to my father's house, the house I grew up in. I went home to prepare, but as I approached my house, a dry, bleak garden came slowly into focus. It looked familiar, but I couldn't quite place it. Ugly roots poked up through the earth. Bugs crept over rocks and dirt. Trash lay everywhere—bits of glass, scraps of pottery, rope, paper. Here and there a dead bird, carrion for worms, decayed among drab twigs. Carcasses of roses hung over a trellis like strangled mice. When had those roses withered? Only weeds found life here. Was this my father's garden, the garden he'd left me in charge of tending? It was. I had neglected it so long, it had gone to waste.

"I set to work weeding and watering. I seized the stems of those terrible plants that wanted to slice my fingers. Yanking them out was backbreaking business, but Jesus was coming. I heaved up buckets of water from the well and lugged them to the garden. As I was making my way, a pail in either hand, I noticed an old irrigation ditch running through the property. Would it still work? I filled it with water, which trickled in a slow but steady stream over the hardened earth, softening it. Soon I would be able to plant. I looked for a hoe.

"Suddenly, rain clouds formed above the scorched patch and a calm, steady, healing rain fell from the sky. Fingers of water gently massaged the earth. The sun came out. Vegetation popped up—lush plants covered with flowers of every hue—yellow, pink, lilac, red, fuchsia, orange. A carpet of periwinkle. Exuberant roses. Cheerful day lilies. Assertive peonies. I carried armfuls of flowers into the house and filled vases with bulging bouquets.

"Jesus came just when He said He would. He was wearing the same pilgrim's robe and sandals as before, and had that same engaging smile. We sat in the *estrado*. I served peppermint tea from my own garden. We breathed in the heady perfume of the flowers, and we talked. 'Let's talk like this a while every day, Teresa,' He said. 'I don't mean praying the Office or reciting the *Te Deum*. I mean just chatting like good friends. Can we do that?' I promised Him I'd try."

I was weeping. "Mental prayer," I whispered. "That's what it is. Chatting with God."

"Yes," said Teresa softly, "that's what it is." It was the Jesuits who really taught her how to pray. The *Spiritual Exercises* turned her life around.

But a spiritual journey doesn't happen on a straight road. Sometimes you make detours. Sometimes you seem not to be going anywhere at all.

Angélica del Sagrado Corazón
Toledo, 30 July 15 1576

CHAPTER 12

Farewells

DEEP FURROWS CROSSED HER FOREHEAD AS LONG AS I'D KNOWN HER, BUT now they had softened, and the skin above her brows was almost as smooth and luminous as a girl's. Her lips were full and supple, as if ready to spread into a smile. Her closed eyes were slightly sunken, but not at all ghoulish. Teresa, Sister Josefa, and I had laid her out on a divan, crossed her hands on her breast, and placed a rosary in her fingers. The gold crucifix caught the sunlight from the window and glittered among the folds of her habit. The portrait painter set up his easel and brought in a stool. Following his instructions, I placed a richly embroidered silk cushion under her head and draped a piece of blue satin over the back of the sofa. Teresa arranged roses—red, pink, yellow, and white—on her chest and around her face. The painter stood back and assessed the scene, then made some adjustments. The color of the satin contrasted too harshly with the flowers, he said. A deeper shade of blue would be better. He situated the body just as he wanted it, and I ran off to the sewing room to find a remnant I thought would be more to his liking. When I brought it to him, he arranged the fabric on the divan and sat down to work.

I sighed. "Just last week she was begging me to sew an altarpiece. Who would have believed that today they'd be painting Mother Francisca's funeral portrait!"

"It happened so suddenly. You never know when God will call you to His side."

"You never know."

"When Death says your name, you have to be ready to go," said Sister Josefa.

Teresa watched, fascinated by the forms emerging on the canvas. The amorphous blobs of color slowly took shape. A wimple, beads, a rose. A face. Teresa shook her head. "I'll bet Mother Francisca will get things all organized up there in Heaven. She'll have some souls darning and some washing dishes. She'll tell them, 'You feed the chickens and you sweep the walk, you shell the almonds and you kneed the dough.'"

"Darning? Kneading dough? That doesn't sound like Heaven to me, Teresa." I said.

"Oh, the souls that are working, those souls are in Hell. But Mother Francisca is in Heaven. Getting to boss everybody around forever, that's her Heaven."

"Stop chattering," growled the painter. "You're distracting me."

I knelt before Mother Francisca's body and said a prayer. I would miss her. I had dressed many bodies for burial, including Teresa's, but when I saw Mother Francisca's stretched out in the infirmary, I fled the room in tears. For years the prioress had been the only mother I knew. In a way, I loved her more than my own mother. She was more patient and more forgiving. She'd given me a home. Teresa squeezed my wrist. The painter signaled us to leave.

Mother Francisca's wealthy Castilian family had insisted on a sumptuous funeral portrait, as was the custom for people of her class. They would donate it to the convent, a testimony of their devotion to the order and to God. The painter would paint the body first, since it had to be removed soon for burial. Then he would add the family crest in the lower right-hand corner and bare-bottomed angels among fluffy white clouds.

Soon we'd have an election for the next prioress. Everybody knew that Sister Josefa would win, even though she said she was too old to take on the job. "Choose Angélica instead," she said. "She's not yet forty and full of energy." But we both knew I could never be prioress. The noblewomen in our convent would die before taking orders from a seamstress's daughter. Anyhow, I wasn't fit to govern. Braulio had left a stain on my soul as well as on my body. In spite of her age, Sister Josefa was perfect. Wise, tough, yet compassionate, she'd been a nun for forty years and understood women. Besides, she was an astute judge of character and wasn't afraid of priests. She knew how to deal with overzealous confessors and nosy provincials.

It was just before the election—which Sister Josefa won handily—that someone gave Teresa the small engraving in black and white of the wounded Jesus, His head bowed and His hair falling over His precious face. It wasn't much bigger than my hand. At first, Teresa carried it around with her everywhere. Then, she propped it up on a chest in her cell and knelt before it every morning and evening to pray. Some sisters thought she was overdoing it. They said Teresa carried everything to extremes. If a priest prescribed five minutes of mortification, she thrashed her back for an hour. If he told her to fast for one meal, she fasted for a day. They thought, she's an actress playing to the crowd, like the performers in the traveling troupes that put on shows in the plaza. Now she's got a new audience, the Jesuits, and she's acting up a storm for them. It's true there was something in Teresa that made her want to outflagellate and outfast everybody else. She was a competitive sufferer. But what the others didn't understand was that Teresa was wrestling with her own personal demons.

"What's gotten into you?" snapped Sister Caridad one day. "Why are you pretending to be the penitent Magdalene!"

Teresa bowed her head. "I love Mary Magdalene," she murmured. "She sets an example for us all." Sister Caridad grunted and marched off in a huff.

One day, Teresa called for me. She'd developed a nasty rash on her back and needed a salve. I wasn't surprised she was suffering from skin irritations. Nervousness does that to you. I've seen lots of overwrought women break out in hives. I prepared a salve of garlic oil and flour and brought it to her room.

The doors of convent cells don't have locks, but I always knock before entering, not like some people I know who just barge in with no consideration for the possibility you might be sitting on your chamber pot. I rapped lightly and stood there a moment, waiting for a response. I could hear moaning coming from the room. Alarmed, I peeked in. Teresa was sprawled out on the floor before the image of the wounded Christ, banging her head on the boards and pleading, "Dear Jesus, set me free of the chains that bind me! Set me free!"

I stepped backward and closed the door noiselessly. She hadn't seen me. I had to catch my breath. I'd witnessed her mortifications before, but this was different. This was heartrending. It made me shiver, like the sound of a delicate fabric ripping. This was no act. It was a cry from the soul. But what was it that tormented her so? What were the chains that bound her? At that moment I knew that the others were wrong. Her spiritual anguish was real.

Later on in the day, when I was checking her rash, she confided, "Thanks to Father Juan, I've been learning how to face my own imperfections and deal with them. I've discovered something horrible about myself, Angélica: I'm vain."

I burst out laughing. "I could have told you that! You didn't need a priest!"

She smiled. "I suppose so. But I needed to discover it for myself. Now, with Father Juan's guidance, I'm ready to come to terms with it."

"If you want a list of your flaws," I said, "just come to me. I know them all."

That's when I realized Teresa was struggling to control an evil passion: her craving for attention. On the one hand, she believed God was calling her. Hadn't He blessed her with visions? But narcissism was hindering her spiritual progress. The Jesuits had taught her that transformation began with self-knowledge and humility. While the Council of Trent was reforming the church from the outside—defining structures and organizational relationships—the Jesuits were reforming the church from the inside, effecting personal renewal in one soul at a time. But the other nuns just didn't understand. Teresa was a phony, they said. She wore a fine worsted habit, but had taken to laundering other women's undergarments. She curtseyed to postulants half her age, and she spoke in a whisper, like a remorseful schoolboy. She walked around with the face of a condemned Jew. She never played chess any more during the *recreo*, and she never took up her tambourine, which she'd always loved to rattle during feast day celebrations. She was becoming a perfect bore, they said. Worst of all, she spent a scandalous amount of time at San Gil. Weren't Carmelite confessors good enough? They didn't understand that Teresa was cultivating humility—sincerely, this time.

One afternoon, when we filed into the chapel, Teresa was already there, deep in meditation. The *Veni Creator* began:

Veni Creator Spiritus,	*Come, Holy Ghost, Creator, come.*
Mentes tuorum visita,	*From thy bright heavenly throne!*
Imple superna gratia,	*Come, take possession of our souls,*
Quae tu creasti, pectora.	*And make them all Thine Own!*
Qui diceris Paraclitus,	*Thou who art called the Paraclete,*
Altissimi donum Dei,	*Best gift of God above,*
Fons vivus, ignis, caritas,	*The Living Spring, The Living Fire,*
Et spiritalis unctio.	*Sweet Unction, and True Love!*

In the middle of "Fons vivus, ignis, caritas" a collective gasp undulated through the sea of nuns. I looked around, strangely conscious of a floral scent that seemed to come, not from the flowers that adorned the altar, but somewhere else. The place was bathed in a soft, rose-colored light that made me think of Eden before the fall. The air was charged with that pregnant stillness that precedes a storm.

Teresa, who had been sitting a few rows in front of me, had slumped down on the ground and was gently writhing as though—oh God, forgive me for writing this!—as though she were making love to an invisible lover to whom she had completely surrendered. Some of the nuns had gathered around her. They stared, horrified or mesmerized, unable to grasp what was happening. Teresa's breath was shallow and uneven. Her face was turned upward, her trembling lips slightly parted as if awaiting a kiss. Her long eyelashes fluttered softly. Her shoulders twitched and her breasts heaved. She moaned. Her face was flush. A tiny bead of sweat had formed on her forehead, just where her wimple met her skin. Then, suddenly, for no apparent reason she began to weep violently, wailing and flailing as tears gushed from her eyes. She was panting heavily now, as if trying to catch her breath. Finally, her body went limp, and she was silent. What was happening? Was she having some sort of seizure? Was she dreaming? Or was she in a trance?

One of the sisters approached her—I think it was Radegunda—and held out her arms as if to clutch Teresa's shoulders. "Teresa!" she called softly. "Teresa, wake up!" But Mother Josefa gently pulled her away. "No," she whispered. "Don't touch her. Don't call her. Leave her alone."

Teresa quivered and sighed and hiccoughed a few times. Slowly her sobbing subsided. Her limbs stiffened, then relaxed. She opened her eyes gradually, but seemed unaware of her surroundings. She looked extraordinarily serene, as though she had awakened from a refreshing sleep. Her lips moved, almost imperceptibly at first. Then a few words became decipherable. Something about Jesus. Something about intense darkness and blinding light. Something about seeing and not seeing.

At last the words flowed intelligibly. "I was with Jesus. I saw . . . I didn't exactly see, but I felt Christ beside me. I didn't really see Him, not with the eyes of my body, but I know He was there. How can I explain it? I didn't really see the way you see a chair or a table or a tree or the sky. What I mean is, I didn't see any form, and still, don't ask me how I know, but I do know I saw Him, clearer than sunlight, with that knowledge that burns within. It's not something you can put into words. You have to experience it." She was silent a moment, then went on. "All I can tell you is this: I saw Him. I was with Him. And He spoke to me. He said, 'From now on, Teresa, it is my will that you no longer converse with men, but with angels.' It's not something you can understand with the intellect, so don't trouble your heads about it. Just believe . . ."

I had witnessed all kinds of convulsions, but I'd never seen anything like this before. I was terrified and shocked. There was something so sensual about the way she had . . . what's the word? . . . yielded to whatever it was she had seen. And yet, there was something eerily reassuring about her words. "Just believe . . . Just believe . . ." I didn't know what to think.

Teresa squinted and then, as though gripped by the ferocious claw of awareness, passed her gaze from one sister to the next. The calm in her eyes turned to horror. She looked down and realized she was sprawled on the floor. She tucked her feet under her body and steadied herself on the bench in order to pull herself up. "Forgive me, sisters," she whispered. "Forgive me, Mother Josefa. Forgive me, forgive me."

The prioress put her arm around Teresa's shoulders and led her out of the chapel. The rest of us stood there in silence. Sister Radegunda tried to recommence the recitation, but we were too dazed to respond.

"What happened to her?" someone said finally.

"She saw God!" It was Cándida. Her croaky voice rose above the whispers.

"This is awful!" people began to murmur. "This is just awful! *Terrible. Un desastre.*"

We all knew what the event we had just witnessed meant: that there'd be an investigation of the convent. We'd all be suspect. The Council of Trent had taken a stand against "esoteric beliefs," and the inquisitors were growing antsy over what they called "mystical outbreaks" in the female orders. The "mystical malady" was contagious. It was like the pox. When one nun got it, it spread all through the house, causing "mystical mayhem"—sisters falling over statues of the agonizing Christ, having themselves nailed to trees, writhing and thrashing about on the floor. The inquisitors were sick of dealing with female hysteria, but they couldn't just let it go. Ecstasies might be the work of the Devil.

"And what if Teresa really did see Jesus?" gurgled Cándida.

Well then, exoneration would come in due time. The way the Inquisition worked, you were guilty until proven innocent. The proceedings could be long and arduous. You had to gather documentation, make sure everyone told the same story. The best thing would be to keep Teresa's rapture a secret. But with two hundred women in Encarnación, how could we?

"You must not talk to anyone about what you saw here today!" ordered Sister Radegunda. "We have to keep this quiet until we find out what really happened. If one of us is suspect, all of us are suspect!" Hushed whispers filled the chapel. One by one the nuns joined the recitation of psalms. "God is a shield that protects me / saving the honest of heart."

Resentment against Teresa intensified. She might be possessed or she might be putting on an act to show how holy she was. Either way, the sisters said, she was a menace to the well-being of the group. Some wanted to hand her over to the Inquisition. Others wanted to send her away.

"This isn't good for her and it isn't good for Encarnación," sighed Mother Josefa. In spite of her multitudinous administrative duties, she liked to visit me in the infirmary and putter around with powders and salves. "This resentment is going to eat a hole in the gut of the convent. It's like a cancer."

"But how can you get it to stop?"

"Doña Guiomar de Ulloa has invited Teresa to stay with her a while. You know Doña Guiomar, that rich widow who's thick with the Jesuits. Well, I'm going to let Teresa go. But I want you to go, too."

I put down the basil root from which I was extracting oil—very effective for respiratory infections—and looked at her.

"Teresa hasn't said a word about this to me. Anyway, Doña Guiomar didn't invite me."

"She will, and you owe me a favor, *preciosa*. Who do you think put the bug in Cándida's ear about getting rid of Braulio? Time to pay up."

I was speechless. Mother Josefa was the one who had maneuvered Braulio out of my life? She must have read "Why?" in my arched eyebrows because she said, "Let's just say I couldn't have my best apprentice abused by some two-bit friar."

"What about the infirmary and the sewing room?" I finally stammered.

"Radegunda is an excellent seamstress, and I'm always here to supervise the infirmary."

"You don't have time. You're the prioress now." I stopped and looked her in the eye. "You mean you told Cándida to ask her uncle to send Braulio north?"

"Well, it was easier than slipping belladonna into his wine. Although I was prepared to do it if I couldn't win over Cándida."

"Poison him? You were prepared to poison him with belladonna? You? A consecrated virgin of the holy Roman catholic apostolic Church?"

"Don't change the subject. I want you to go to Doña Guiomar's and report back to me about what's going on."

"In other words, you want me to spy."

"It's for Teresa's own good. I have to be able to yank her back if things get out of hand."

Within a day or so we were packing our bags. I didn't mind going to live with Doña Guiomar. I'd visited palaces with my aunt and mother to make gowns for rich ladies, but living in one would be a new experience. Besides, Doña Guiomar had a famous *beata*—a holy woman—living with her, and I was anxious to meet her. They called her Maridíaz, and I'd seen her the night we had dinner at Doña Guiomar's. The night we met the Jesuits, Don Miguel, and Diego de Cetina. The night that silly little dog named Barque jumped onto my lap. At the grille, Maridíaz was on everyone's lips. The whole town seemed fascinated with the strange woman Doña Guiomar had taken in as a maid out of charity. This would be a chance to find out what all the fuss was about.

Life at Doña Guiomar's wasn't what we expected. News of Teresa's rapture or ecstasy . . . or fainting spell, as some people called it . . . had spread through Ávila in spite of our efforts to keep it secret. Once it got out that there were two holy women staying with the pretty widow, the curious sent letters requesting audiences with Doña Teresa and Maridíaz as though they were lady popes. Teresa tried to stay away from the crowds. She wanted time to think and pray, and she wanted to be close to San Gil so she could consult Father Juan de Prádanos as often as she needed to. But Doña Guiomar was delighted with her new position as patroness of holy women. She encouraged callers, especially if they were people of influence.

When the chatter and clamor got to be too much for Teresa, she'd duck out to the oratory, leaving Doña Guiomar's guests so engrossed in their noisy piety that they didn't even miss her. Once, during a strident conversation about the religious wars in the north—that is, France and the Low Countries—she grabbed me by the arm and nudged me toward the doorway.

"Where are we going?"

"I have to get out of here. I can't stand to hear Daza say one more time that we should gather up the Lutherans and burn them alive in their churches."

"Well, what do you think we should do with them?"

"We should pray for them, of course. If we kill them, we won't have much chance of bringing them back to the faith, now will we? I'd wish I could be like those Jesuit missionaries who evangelize in the north and lead apostates back to God. It's a shame women can't preach."

We were crossing the garden toward a small stone structure with an ample smokestack. As in most large houses, Doña Guiomar's kitchen occupied a separate building so that in case of fire, no damage would be done to the main residence. As a little girl I'd spent plenty of time in kitchens while my mother and aunt took measurements for dresses, but I no longer felt myself on a level with the maids who skinned rabbits and peeled carrots. I wanted to go back to the hall.

"I don't want to go in there," I said. "What business do we have in the kitchen?"

Teresa didn't answer. She just eased me through the door. The staff must have been occupied in the main building serving dinner because no one was there except for a hunched old woman squatting on a cushion with a bowl next to her. It was Maridíaz.

"Mother, you remember Sister Angélica, don't you?" said Teresa respectfully.

"Ah," said Maridíaz without looking up. "I'm eating broth. Do you want some?" She took a sip and wiped her mouth with her hand. Her jowls were droopy, and her neck, soft and puckered. I thought she must have been in her seventies. All of a sudden, she jerked her head around and looked at me. "Of course I remember Sister Angélica," she snapped. "Do you think I'm feebleminded?"

Teresa reached for two cushions lying against the wall and handed me one.

"Go ahead and take the stool," muttered Maridíaz, nodding toward a low stool near the fire. A large, black pot that smelled of mutton hung over the flames. We both sat down on cushions and waited for her to say something, but she seemed to have forgotten us. She just kept slurping broth from her bowl. Two minutes went by . . . five . . . ten.

"I was born poor and I'll die poorer," she said abruptly. I stared at her. She didn't seem like a holy woman to me. She was gruff and coarse, like the peasant she was.

"The whole town reveres you, Mother," said Teresa.

"I just tell people what God tells me. I'm a messenger. I relay messages."

"Doña Guiomar holds you in very high esteem."

"I'm her servant," said Maridíaz curtly. "Her kitchen maid." Again she became involved in her broth, gulping loudly, wiping her mouth, gulping again. For a while, no one spoke.

"What brought you to Ávila?" Teresa asked finally.

Maridíaz burped noisily, then ran a crust of bread around the rim of her bowl and popped it into her mouth. "What?" she asked with her mouth full.

"What brought you here from the country?"

"The sermons." She burped again and let out a long, leisurely fart, very high pitched, like air escaping from a wineskin. A fetid odor wafted over our heads. Maridíaz seemed not to notice.

"There are so many churches and monasteries here in Ávila, you can always find a good orator," said Teresa, trying to move the conversation along.

"My parents wanted me to marry. They even arranged my engagement, but I wasn't interested. I don't like men and won't pretend to." Maridíaz wiped the rest of the bowl with the bread. Slowly and systematically, she rubbed the crust over the bottom, then over one side, then over the other. When she was done, she licked her fingers one by one. Finally, she closed her eyes and seemed to doze. I signaled Teresa that we should go, but just as we were about to get up, she spoke again. "When they died I came here. I took private vows of poverty and chastity. I didn't join any order. What do I need an order for? Do I need some prioress telling me what to do? Only God tells me what to do. I gave away everything I owned. My black woolen dress, my grey cotton dress and my aprons. Also my heavy black cape and my home-spun sheets. I gave everything to people needier than I. For myself I saved only this dress, a shawl, and a grey cloak, and now I've given that away, too. I don't need clothes and sheets and money. I'm happy with my rags and a bowl of broth a day, or maybe an onion and a piece of hard bread. All I really need is God. Do you understand me, sisters? All you need in this world is God! I lived alone in a hovel in the Vacas section of town. I didn't care what people said about a woman living alone. I don't care what people think! I only care what God thinks!"

Her eyes were round and glazed, like those of a chicken facing a butcher knife. She didn't look at us as she spoke. Instead, she hurled her words at some imaginary interlocutor on the other side of the room, spit flying from her mouth.

"The problem was," she went on, "I couldn't find a good confessor, someone who would be tough on me and help me purge my soul of all the rot, all the putrefaction, all the pus and excrement. Because we're sinful, sisters! We're all sinful! And I'm the worst of all! A lowly worm, that's what I am. A cockroach! A maggot! But I couldn't find anybody to help me, to really take me seriously, until the Jesuits came. Prayer and mortification, that's what it takes, sisters! Father Baltasar is the one who sent me to live here with Doña Guiomar. It's a form of penance."

I didn't know who Father Baltasar was, but I thought Maridíaz must be crazy. Compared to the poverty of Vacas, Doña Guiomar's kitchen was luxurious. Teresa was looking down at her hands, as though deeply humbled. Either that, or she was just afraid of being spat on.

"Pure mortification, sisters! Praise the Lord!" Now that Maridíaz had started talking, there was no stopping her. "The other servants hate me. They hit me, and once they even burned me with a hot iron. Look at this scar!" She rolled up her sleeve to show her forearm. "That's where the cook threw scalding water at me. And look at this bruise! That's where the cook's assistant punched me for dropping a bag of flour. They're impure, you see, and they don't like having a *beata* in their midst. They're fornicators and liars and thieves. They have men, and they steal from the kitchen and gossip about the mistress." She lowered her voice. "Doña Guiomar doesn't know they abuse me, and I won't tell her because I welcome these punishments. This is part of God's plan to purify me, to purify my soul! I've been blessed, you see. It's my lot to suffer for Jesus, just as Jesus suffered for me. Do you understand, sisters?

"The other servants see that I strive to be holy, that I pray and confess my sins. And my sins are many, sisters. You can't erase the blackness from the human heart. But sinner that I am, I can still help others. People come from all around to ask me to pray for them. When I walk down the street, people call out to me. They ask for my advice. I've cured people who are dying. I've counseled widows to remarry and virgins to enter the convent. I once prayed over a woman who hadn't been able to conceive for five years, and two months later, she was pregnant! I know the secrets of the universe, sisters, not because I'm wise, but because God gives me knowledge!

"I don't care whether a person is a lord or a beggar," Maridíaz rambled on. "I serve all of humanity! Ladies and whores. Dukes and hoodlums. Christ died for all of us, not just for the rich and powerful. That's why I'm going to leave this house. Bishop Álvaro de Mendoza has given me permission. I'm going to live in absolute poverty in the tiny room in front of the main altar of the Church of San Millán. Like a hermit! Like the desert fathers of long ago! I'll teach the little boys their prayers, and if any fancy ladies want to see me, why, they can visit me there. All these new groups with their new ways of praying. Well, they're okay. But it's not just how you pray, sisters. It's how you live. Do you understand me? It's how you live!"

Suddenly, she was quiet. I didn't know what to do.

"Thank you, Mother," said Teresa, after a minute or two. "We'd better go now."

Maridíaz took no notice of us. She sat there, looking into empty space. We walked back toward the house. "For a holy woman," I grumbled, "she seems to complain an awful lot."

But Teresa was lost in thought. Something Maridíaz had said touched her profoundly.

Sister Angélica del Sagrado Corazón
Toledo, 12 August 1576

CHAPTER 13

Madwoman or Saint?

"HOW CAN I DESCRIBE IT? GOD, IN HIS MOST SACRED HUMANITY, WAS represented to me."

"You mean, you saw Jesus."

"No, that's not exactly what I mean. If I say, 'I saw Jesus,' you'll think I saw Him standing there, the way I see you and you see me. It's true God's humanity was represented to me as it is in paintings—think of that canvas in the cathedral of the marriage at Cana—but with such exquisite beauty and majesty that it defies description."

"You mean, you saw Jesus as He looks in paintings, only more magnificent."

"It's that I can't describe this vision without ruining it, Angélica. I wish I'd seen it with my eyes, my bodily eyes, so I could explain it to you in a way you could understand. I saw . . . experienced . . . such splendor, but not a splendor that dazzles. It's like something . . . a light infused with a soft white-ness. It produces a shivering delight. It's a light that doesn't tire the eyes, a light so different from earthly light that the sun's brightness appears tarnished in comparison, and we perceive it in a way that makes ordinary seeing seem deficient. It's like the difference between sparkling, clear water flowing over crystal, reflecting the sun, and cloudy, muddy water flowing along the ground. That doesn't mean that the sun is merely 'represented' and isn't there, or that the light in the water merely 'resembles' sunlight. How can I put it into words, Angélica? It *seems* like natural light, and yet, in comparison, the light that fills our everyday world is artificial, fake. Divine light is light that has no night; nothing detracts from it. It's a light you could never imagine, no mat-ter how hard you tried. Am I making any sense at all, Angélica?"

"No."

"It's that I'm so ignorant, I just don't have the words."

"How do you know you didn't just imagine it, Teresa?"

"Because something you just make up, after a while you forget it. But this I'll never forget. It will stay with me forever."

"What did you feel?"

"At first, I felt a terrible fear. I didn't know what was happening. But then, I became completely serene, as though I were floating in a calm, warm pool, buoyed by the weight of the water."

I'm writing these words just as she spoke them. Or at least, as I remember she spoke them. But of course, this happened a long time ago, in 1558. Almost twenty years ago. Still, I'm trying to be as accurate as I can so I can tell them what Teresa said about seeing Jesus when I'm called to testify at her beatification, provided I'm still alive when that day comes. I'll read this over right before I testify so that I have it all fresh in my mind and won't waver.

To be honest, at the time I didn't know what to think. This was the friend I'd grown up with, played with, helped make dresses for. This was the sister I'd dressed for death and nursed back to health, the sister I shared confidences with my whole life. And now I looked at her and didn't recognize her. She was speaking a language I didn't understand. What was she? God's creature? An angel? A fraud? Or just a befuddled woman?

Teresa had gone through a lot that past year. Her darling younger brother Rodrigo, the playmate of her childhood, had died fighting Indians in Chile. When someone you love dies, it's worse when you're not there. She had nightmares. Rodrigo's head bashed open, blood and brains seeping into the rocks. Rodrigo's limp body lying on the sand, pierced by an Araucanian arrow. Rodrigo, Rodrigo . . . There was no comforting her.

And then Father Juan de Prádanos, who had guided her spiritually for over a year, fell ill and had to leave San Gil. It was his heart, they said. Doña Guiomar begged the Jesuits to send him to one of her nearby estates, and, thank God, they acceded. Doña Guiomar herself went to care for him. "Oh, God, what will become of me without Father Juan?" wailed Teresa.

It was all too much for her, I thought. That's why it occurred to me—God forgive me—that perhaps this last rapture, or vision, or hallucination, was simply the consequence of all the strain, all the heartbreak she'd gone through. Perhaps it wasn't a mystical experience at all. Sometimes when terrible things happen one after the other, you become disoriented, you see things that aren't there. Anyway, to me it didn't matter whether she was a visionary or a madwoman. She was my best friend, my sister. I had to stick with her.

We'd just returned to Encarnación from Doña Guiomar's. I remember it was on the feast of Saint Paul, January 25, because I'd sewn a pretty little pincushion for Sister Paulina, a gift for her saint's day. We were at Mass, when without warning, Teresa moved away from the other nuns and glided like a ghost toward the back of the chapel. She turned to face the altar, then fell to her knees, arms outstretched, palms upward, before the crucifix. Her pupils rolled back into her head, leaving only the whites of her eyes visible. She reminded me of one of those statues of martyrs with their gaze turned toward heaven, except that her face wasn't lifeless and dull like a statue's, but glowing, ethereal. Her whole body quivered. Then she sank back backwards onto the ground as if in a state of utter surrender. The sisters gasped and stared.

Sister Caridad hissed, "I thought her stay with Doña Guiomar was supposed to cure her of these antics." Caridad was a dark, corpulent nun who was friends with Ramona.

Some of the other women shrugged or shook their heads in disgust.

The rapture lasted a minute or two. Afterward, Teresa blinked and slowly pulled herself up into a sitting position, as if exhausted. Mother Josefa approached her cautiously, then reached out and helped her up. Teresa seemed confused. Slowly, she regained her equilibrium, drawing her breath in gradually deepening inhalations. "Oh, sisters," she murmured. "I saw something so wondrous, so extraordinary. I saw Jesus!" Caridad moaned out loud.

"Sister Caridad," snapped Mother Josefa, "bow your head and confess to your sisters that you've committed the sin of unkindness."

Caridad bowed her head and recited mechanically, "I confess to almighty God, and to you my sisters, that I have been unkind to Sister Teresa." No one was paying attention.

I helped Teresa back to her cell and sat by the window embroidering in the winter gloom while she rested. "Let's go for a walk in the garden," she said suddenly.

"It's freezing, Teresa," I said without budging. "And your health is still delicate."

She put on her mantle. "Come," she said, holding out her hand. "Just a short walk."

We followed the path to the dovecote. It had snowed, but the fluffy, white flakes hadn't iced the path. Teresa stepped gingerly, like a convalescent.

Suddenly, at a distance, a swarm of nuns materialized. They approached slowly, like fat, black flies. Where had they come from? Had they been waiting in the dovecote? Had they been hiding behind the skeletal trees that dotted the shivering garden? Teresa thought they were coming to greet her. She waved and scuttled toward them, then halted abruptly. Even at a distance, it was clear to me that the intentions of these women were not friendly.

As they drew nearer, they seemed to swell in size, their bodies made bulkier by heavy, black, hooded mantles. Finally, they positioned themselves in front of us. They'd metamorphosed from flies to an army of gigantic, black crows. Teresa blinked, her eyes runny from the cold.

"Sisters, good afternoon."

The women pressed around us, forming a semicircle and penning us in. I can't remember everyone who was there. Sister Ana Martínez, Sister Brígida, Sister Elena, Sister Lucía, and Sister Caridad . . . Who else? Sister Ramona. Teresa's detractors, the faction that pooh-poohed her raptures. It's true I had doubts, too, but I wasn't going to let them push her around.

Sister Caridad was the leader. A large-bosomed woman of Andalusian peasant stock, she was foul mouthed and tough. She'd entered Encarnación as a charity case and earned her keep scrubbing floors and emptying chamber pots. She enjoyed intimidating the novices. A small, scarlet scar underneath her left eye—the kind that would have kept her out of the convent if Mother Francisca were still in charge—created a perpetual squint. She stood directly in front of Teresa, her dark, square-jawed face threateningly close. Her wide stance and hands on hips gave her the appearance of a crow with outstretched wings. She stared at Teresa as if ready to peck out her eyes. She was breathing heavily, and when she exhaled, puffs of vapor burst from her mouth.

"Teresa de Ahumada," she hissed. Like all southerners, she pronounced the *s* with too much sibilance.

"Yes, Sister?" Teresa looked into Sister Caridad's eyes without flinching.

"This bullshit has to stop, Teresa de Ahumada. You're jeopardizing the entire convent."

"*Sí, sí,*" squawked the others. "You're going to get us all in trouble."

"What are you talking about?" A stray snowflake settled on Teresa's high cheekbone.

"Don't play dumb, Teresa de Ahumada. Everybody in Ávila is talking about your fits, and it won't be long before the grand inquisitor swoops down and flings us all into the dungeon. I know a fraud when I see one.

Do you have to practice making your eyeballs all white like that, or does it come easily?"

Teresa stood looking at her a long time, so long, in fact, that the other women began to grow nervous. They fidgeted and adjusted their capes.

"How could I bring the wrath of God down on you?" Teresa said calmly. "Do you think I have so much power?" She made her voice sweet and innocent, like a schoolgirl's.

"Don't play games, you bitch. You're just out for attention. Or else, you're in bed with the Devil. Either way, you're attracting the notice of the authorities, and when they come to interrogate you, they'll make life miserable for the rest of us as well." Swirls of vapor spewed from Sister Caridad's mouth.

"It's not my fault Jesus chose to appear to me, Sister. It's not a favor I asked for."

"Jesus didn't appear to you, you pampered little lapdog. I say the same prayers you do, and I never saw Christ in the bedsheets."

The other women snickered. "Jesus came to me, Jesus came to me, Jesus came all over me," chanted Sister Ramona in a sing-song voice. She looked right at me.

"I'm sorry," said Teresa. She took a step forward, as though to push through the line and continue down the path.

"Not so fast, lapdog," hissed Sister Caridad. With her left hand she grabbed Teresa's wrist. Then she raised her muscular, cape-covered right arm and sent her hand flying against Teresa's jaw. Blood trickled from the corner of Teresa's lip toward the bottom of her chin. I pulled a remnant of cloth I used as a handkerchief from my sleeve and patted her face.

"Leave her alone," I snapped.

But Sister Caridad didn't even look at me. She grabbed Teresa's arm just above the elbow and squeezed it tight. She was a farm girl, and she had a grip like a wrench.

"I want this to stop," she snarled.

"It's not in my power to make it stop," said Teresa firmly. She showed no sign of fear.

"Nonsense!"

"Yes, nonsense."

She looked at the other women. "This bitch is making fun of me!"

"Better not do that," said Sister Lucía. It was a threat.

"I said 'nonsense,'" said Teresa, "because this is something you can't make sense out of. It's non-sense. What I mean is, it's beyond our ability to understand or control. Now, please let us continue on our way."

Sister Caridad looked confused. She loosened her grip slightly. "I don't know what the hell you're talking about, Teresa de Ahumada."

With a quick twist of the arm Teresa snapped free and pushed her way through the line. She took off briskly in the direction of the dovecote. I followed her.

"These phony visions better not happen again," yelled Sister Caridad. But she didn't chase after us.

Teresa kept on walking without quickening her pace. I heard someone scampering to catch up with us. It was Ramona. She ran around in front of me and stood there, arms crossed. "I can get you into big trouble," she whispered. "Braulio told me all about you. I know everything."

I froze in my tracks. I felt as though someone had thrown snow in my face. My lips went cold, and I began to tremble.

"So does Mother Josefa," said Teresa evenly. "You won't be telling her anything she doesn't already know. Now, go back home, little girl."

It was a command. Bewilderment replaced hostility on Ramona's face. She turned on her heels and hurried to catch up with the other women. I didn't bother to watch them disappear into the house, but soon their squawking ceased and I knew they were gone.

Sister Caridad wasn't the only one who wanted Teresa to put an end to her visions. Teresa's new confessor, Baltasar Álvarez (the same Father Baltasar who confessed Maridíaz), nagged her constantly, and it's not hard to figure out why. If his penitent turned out to be a fraud or, worse yet, a dupe of the Devil, his neck would be on the line. Until then, the Jesuits had been supportive of Teresa, but Álvarez was an insecure little man who was terrified of making a mistake. He had faith in her, he kept insisting, but others were urging caution. To make matters worse, Salcedo was back in the picture, and he wanted to have her exorcized. Álvarez said he was *concerned*. He was just being *vigilant*. With his concern and vigilance, he was making a wreck out of her.

"Imagine," Teresa told me, "Salcedo told Father Baltasar that the safest thing was to put me through the exorcism ritual. That way, they'd be sure I was clean."

"And will he?"

"I hope not." She shuddered. "But maybe they'll have to. Jesus cured demoniacs."

"And Jesus said to the demon, 'Be quiet! Come out of him! And the unclean spirit threw the man into convulsions and with a loud cry went flying out of him. Mark 1:25-26."

"I'm terrified of convulsions," whispered Teresa. "I've heard that during exorcisms, people sometimes foam at the mouth or bite like rabid dogs. That's because they have demons in them, and those demons have to come out. What if I really do have demons in me?"

"Your visions don't come from Satan, Teresa."

"I believe they come from God. But what if I'm wrong? Being certain you're right is the sin of pride!"

Álvarez ordered Teresa to stifle her visions. "When you see an image," he said, "give it the fig!" (Boys "give the fig" to other boys who cut them off on the road or say nasty things about their sisters. It's a vulgar gesture made by pressing the thumb between the middle and the index fingers.)

For a while she seemed to see Jesus everywhere—in the chapel, in the garden, in the soup. No, no, I shouldn't be making jokes. There was nothing funny about the way she suddenly lost control of herself, sometimes slumping over and hitting her head against a cabinet or the foot of a table. She would lie there seemingly lifeless for a moment or two, then open her eyes. Later, she would tell me what she'd experienced. It was always different, yet always the same. Sometimes she would see Jesus, and sometimes she wouldn't, but she still knew He was there. When she did see Him, it wasn't with her corporeal eyes, but with her spiritual eyes. I know it sounds crazy, but I can only write what I saw with my eyes and heard from Teresa.

One gloomy All Souls Eve Doña Guiomar sent her carriage for us. It was snowing hard, and icy winds pierced your chest. We were glad to arrive at Doña Guiomar's palace and warm ourselves at her hearth. Doña Guiomar called for Maridíaz, and the four of us retired to the palace chapel, where we knelt at prie-dieus and prayed silently for the souls in Purgatory. I prayed for my mother, Tía Cati, Don Alonso, and Teresa's brothers Antonio and Rodrigo. I thought about Braulio and wondered if he had died in the violence in the north, and if so, if by some wily ruse he had wormed himself into Purgatory, instead of staying in Hell, where he belonged.

Suddenly, Teresa shrieked. Then she jumped up, ran to the font, and started splashing holy water at the place where she had been kneeling.

"Doña Teresa!" cried Doña Guiomar. "What's wrong? What are you doing?"

But Teresa seemed oblivious to everything except that one spot on her prie-dieu. "Go!" she hissed. *"Vade Retro!"*

Doña Guiomar stood up, but I signaled her to stay where she was. "She sees something," I said softly. "Leave her alone."

"Go, go, go away!" At last Teresa stopped and stood still. Her sleeves were soaking. So were the breviary and the stone floor around the prie-dieu. She looked at us curiously. "Didn't you see him?" she asked. "It was the Devil. He was perched right there on top of my prayer book, then he jumped down and stood at my left side. Didn't anyone else see him? He spoke to me. 'Teresa,' he said. 'Teressssa!' His mouth was like an ink blob, with tiny little pointed teeth—many more than a person has—all over his gums in uneven rows. A huge flame, as bright as the sun and without a shadow, burned all over his body. 'Teresssssa,' he said. 'You escaped from me once, but you won't get away again!' 'Oh Holy Jesus,' I prayed, 'make him go away!' And I ran to fling holy water at him. Didn't you see him?"

"No."

"Oh," she said softly, her eyes still fixed on the place where she had knelt. "You must think I'm mad. But . . . but I saw him. I really saw him. You have to believe me, Angélica! Do you? Do you believe me?"

"Did he go away?" I asked.

"Yes," she said. "He went away."

I bit my lip and looked at the puddles. "Dear God," I prayed, "help her." I felt as though she were slipping away from me, as though she were drifting off into some other dimension.

She didn't say anything more about visions for the next couple of weeks. Perhaps she was having them but was afraid to tell anyone. Then, one night she woke up writhing in her bed. Silvia, her maid, came running to get me.

"Be careful what you say to her," Silvia cautioned me. "She's very sick. She's in terrible pain, and she thinks she might be possessed. Salcedo's still talking about having her exorcized. She's terrified." Silvia's candle flickered.

"Slow down!" I whispered. "I can hardly see where I'm going. What do you think?"

"About what? About the exorcism?"

"Yes. Would it be better to get it over with once and for all?"

"She's not possessed. There's something wrong with her. Something physical. Heart problems or some kind of infection. I've known her since she was born, and she's always been sickly. If you ask me, Salcedo's the one who's possessed."

Teresa was thrashing around in bed. "Oh, God," she wailed. "Is all this pain serving you in some way? If so, please, I beg of you, give me the strength to endure it."

I placed my hand on her forehead. It was scorching. "Teresa," I said, "you have a fever. It's too dark to go out for ice, but I'll make you an infusion."

"No," she whispered. "Let me suffer. Let me suffer until the end of the world. It's my way of serving Jesus."

"Jesus doesn't want you to suffer," I said with as much authority as I could muster. "He wants you to be well."

"How do you know?"

"I know because He told me," I lied. "He said, 'I have great plans for Teresa, but first she has to feel better.'"

"But you didn't know I was sick tonight."

"Yes, I did. Jesus told me."

"Silvia told you."

"Jesus told me before Silvia even came to my cell. In fact, I was waiting for her."

"That's right," muttered Silvia. "She was waiting for me."

"I have terrible pains in my uterus and in my lower back," stammered Teresa. She spoke with enormous difficulty, as if she were tearing each word out of her flesh with her nails. Awkwardly, she rolled over on her side, searching for a more comfortable position. "Oh God," she moaned. "Thank you for this . . ." A surge of pain cut short the sentence. "Oh, God, it hurts."

I took her hand in mine. "When it hurts again, squeeze. Silvia," I turned to the maid, "run and get me a cold, wet cloth."

"Oh, my heavenly Father," whispered Teresa. "Thank you for this sign."

"What sign, Teresa? You think these horrible cramps are a *sign from God*? I'm scared to death they're a sign you've got a uterine infection."

She lay there, grasping my hand. In the candlelight, her eyelids appeared raw, but her cheeks had cooled. I placed my hand on her forehead again. The fever was breaking up.

"There! That sign there!" she whispered. "That little creature." Suddenly, she started to giggle. "Don't you see him? That nasty little black creature!" She was laughing almost hysterically now, hiccoughing through her pain. "It hurts!" She crossed her hands over her uterus as though to hold in her insides, but still she kept laughing, gulping the air and trembling. Tears dripped into the bedclothes. She's hysterical, I thought.

"It's . . . it's the Devil." She could hardly get the words out. She was panting, struggling to catch her breath. "I'm not afraid," she said finally. "It's a sign God is sending me so that I'll know this agony doesn't come from Him, but from the forces of darkness. But he's gone now. The little Devil, I mean. He's disappeared. When you laugh, it makes the Devil go away. It's not as good as holy water, but it works. I'll bet he's angry he lost me!"

Oh, God, I thought. What's happening to her? "Teresa," I said softly. "Drink something." Silvia had returned with the wet cloth and some almond water.

But instead of taking the cup Silvia held out to her, Teresa picked up a *disciplina,* a small switch she kept by the side of her bed.

"Teresa," I snapped, trying to wrest it away from her, "what are you doing?" I thought she really was losing her mind.

In spite of her illness, she had a strong grip. I couldn't yank it away. She began to strike herself on her head, bare back, and shaking arms.

"Stop, Teresa!" Silvia and I both tried to get the switch away from her "This is no time for mortifications." The welts left by the switch were visible on her feverish skin.

"Yes it is," she gasped. "I need to keep the Devil away. I have to!"

"Fling some holy water on him."

"I don't have any left."

"Silvia will go for holy water. Go, Silvia, go to the chapel."

"No," whispered Teresa. "No, no. I don't want the others to know. Especially Caridad."

What could I do? At last she tired herself out. She let the *disciplina* drop and dozed off. Light was filtering in through the window, and I could hear the other sisters filing past the door on their way to the chapel, but I decided to let her sleep. I went to tell Mother Josefa that Teresa would miss Lauds.

But the next time it happened, there was no keeping it secret. We were gathered in the refectory for the midday meal. It was a long, rectangular room, with short, wooden seats attached to the wall, each with a small table in front of it. On each table were a plate, a glass for almond water or ale, and a skull to remind us that even as we fed the body, the flesh withered. Sister

Radegunda was sitting at one end of the hall reading from Fray Luis de Granada's *Book of Prayer and Meditation*. Her voice droned on.

Suddenly, Teresa, who was sitting next to me, fell sideward against my shoulder. Then she rose, took a step or two, and slid to the ground, in front of my table. Sister Caridad, who was sitting across the room from me, crossed her arms and rested them on the shelf of her bosom. She shot me a look that said, "Not again!" and shook her head. I looked away.

I knew better than to touch Teresa, so I sat there, watching her. Her face was tilted upward, all aglow, as if illuminated by a celestial beam. I searched the room for the source of the light, but the rays from the window landed on Radegunda's reading table, on the other side of the room. Teresa's eyes were shut lightly—sometimes they blinked—and her mouth was slightly open, as though she slept. The folds of her habit fell softly around her, discretely covering her feet, as if arranged by an artist. Her hands lay inert by her sides. Then, after a while, she lifted her arm and with her right index finger pointed to some invisible being. I looked in the direction she pointed, but saw nothing. A moment later, she clutched her heart. She moaned as though in agony—not . . . how can I explain this? . . . not the kind of agony . . . I'd better start over. She didn't look as though she felt pain, at least, not hurtful pain, but the exquisite pain of love.

She saw an angel. Afterward, she described him to us, but there's no need for me to try to remember what she said because she wrote it all down in her *Life*.

The angel was not large, but small; he was very beautiful, and his face was so aflame that he seemed to be one of those very sublime angels that appear to be all afire. I saw in his hands a large golden dart and at the end of the iron tip there appeared to be a little fire. It seemed to me this angel plunged the dart several times into my heart and that it reached deep within me. When he drew it out, I thought he was carrying off with him the deepest part of me; and he left me all on fire with great love of God. The pain was so great that it made me moan, and the sweetness this great pain caused me was so superabundant that there is no desire capable of taking it away; nor is the soul content with less than God.

I'm glad she put down this vision in writing because I would never be able to describe it. I think you have to have experienced something like this in order to tell about it, and me, I don't see angels standing over me with fiery darts in their hands. All I see are baskets of cloth to be cut into albs or soutanes or chasubles, then hemmed and embroidered. Or containers of charcoal to be ground into powder for diarrhea.

When she opened her eyes, a smile illuminated her face. I'd never seen her look so beautiful. Her eyes were glowing and her face was radiant, blissful. The women gathered around her.

"What did you see, Teresa?" "What did you feel?" There must have been ten or fifteen sisters groping at her.

"I don't know how to explain it," she said with a sigh. She looked a little disoriented, as though she were still elsewhere. "I felt myself rising, I felt myself . . . I don't know . . . almost flying, but not the way a bird flies. I was surrounded by angels, those very sublime angels they call cherubim. The angel with the dart . . . he must have been one of them. I don't know if I'm making any sense at all. Maybe . . . maybe I'm . . . maybe I'm crazy, but I saw an angel, an angel all ablaze, a cherubim. I can't explain it any other way. That's what I saw."

"Come, Teresa," said Sister Josefa, leading her away. "You need to rest."

I knew she wasn't making it up. She was too timid about describing her experiences. This was not a Magdalena de la Cruz, avid for notoriety. But what was going on?

"She felt herself rising," whispered Sister Lucía. "Did you hear her?"

"Bullshit," snapped Sister Caridad.

"I *saw* her rising," whispered Sister Lucía, even more softly than before. "I'm sure of it."

"So did I," confirmed Sister Remedios.

"She levitates!" said Sister Escolástica.

I looked from one to the other, amazed. "Did you see her levitate?" I asked.

"Just a tiny bit," said Sister Escolástica. She looked around at the others for reassurance.

"Once I saw her levitate a full *vara* off the floor," piped up Sister Ramona.

"You did not," growled Sister Caridad. "You never said anything to me about it."

"I was afraid to tell anyone, but I saw her."

"So did I," said Sister Ana Martínez.

"This is rot!" snarled Sister Caridad. But she didn't look so sure. Her dark, Andalusian face had paled, and she was rubbing her hands together nervously. She turned to me. "Did you ever see her levitate?" Her pinched eyebrows produced a ragged gash above her nose.

"No," I said truthfully.

I sat down to finish my meal: cold duck with carrots and parsnips. I used bread to maneuver a piece of fowl off the plate and into my mouth. I chewed slowly, without looking at them.

"Well, I have," insisted Sister Escolástica.

"She levitates all right!" confirmed Sister Ramona.

"She's not of this world," murmured Sister Brígida. "She's one of God's chosen."

"She's a saint," whispered Sister Lucía. *Una santa.*

An echo filled the hall. "A saint! A saint!" Sister Caridad's eyes darted around the room, doubt and trepidation clouding her gaze. She stepped back, perhaps considering what to do in the face of her disappearing power base.

Mother Josefa returned and ordered the nuns back to their places. Sister Radegunda took her seat by the window and began to read. "What madness it is that Adam's children build their grandiose towers on such fragile foundations, unaware that they're building on sand, and that any moment the wind will knock down what is inadequately anchored!"

By the end of the day the convent was buzzing with news of Teresa's levitations.

"Have you heard?" Sister Brígida asked Father Baltasar, who had come to the convent to say Mass. "Sister Teresa levitates!"

The priest took out a handkerchief and blew his nose. "I think not, Sister," he said matter-of-factly. He sniffled and shuffled off toward the chapel.

"Yes, she does," Brígida called after him.

Father Baltasar stopped and pivoted on his heel. His nose was crimson and his eyes, drippy. "Have you seen her?" He sounded like a bullfrog.

She paused. "Others have seen her."

"How many?"

"Several." She paused again. "A few." She turned to Sister Remedios. "Did you see her?"

"Escolástica did. She says she looked beautiful floating up there all aglow by the ceiling."

Father Baltasar cleared his throat and shook his head, but didn't contradict her.

"With all due respect, Your Reverend," I said cautiously. "I think you're too hoarse to say Mass. Would you like me to prepare you some cherry bark tea?"

He didn't answer. He just stood there looking at the ground, then turned and disappeared into the chapel.

"Tell me, Angélica," Teresa said one day. We were in the infirmary with María de Ocampo, Teresa's niece, who was recovering from a soar throat. "Did you ever see me levitate?"

"No."

"Are you sure?"

"Yes. Absolutely sure." I thought she looked a little disappointed.

"Lots of other people have seen it," croaked María de Ocampo.

I ignored her. "I'm not saying it didn't happen, Teresa. I'm just saying I didn't see it."

Teresa picked up a small, squat, white vessel with the word "Laudanum" printed on the label hanging from its neck. She squinted, and the tiny lines around her eyes deepened. Her chin was growing spongy, less defined. Minuscule crevices feathered out from her lips. Fissures descended from her nose to the corners of her mouth and from there, downward, giving her a slightly marionette-like appearance. They weren't deep yet, but even in the soft light of the late afternoon, they were visible. Teresa was forty-five. She was still beautiful, but she was aging.

"This is awful, Angélica. It has to stop."

"I know."

"What has to stop?" whispered María. She was an impulsive, spontaneous girl, an orphan whom Teresa had taken under her wing to educate.

"This craziness . . . this nonsense about me being a saint . . . about my levitating." María stared at Teresa, wide-eyed. "I can't stay here, Angélica," Teresa went on. "There's too much chatter. There's no time for mental prayer. No place to be alone with God."

I sighed. "Where would you go, Teresa? Another convent? It would be the same as here."

"You could start your own convent!" piped up María.

Teresa looked at her, startled, as though María had read her thoughts.

"Angélica," said Teresa, her voice quivering with a sense of urgency. "Do you think my visions are real?"

"I do, Teresa."

"And do you think they come from God?"

"I do." And at that moment, I did.

"Well . . . if I told you that God asked me to do something for Him, would you help me?"

"How do I know He wants me in on the project?"

"What María just suggested . . . I was thinking about it myself. What if we started a new convent, one where women could really devote themselves to God, living in silence and poverty, with no distractions? A place where, once you entered, you'd never leave. When you wed God, you'd be His alone. No salon full of gossips, just a tiny locutorium for meeting with relatives and holy people. No babble. No noise. In a house like that, you could really feel God's love."

"I don't know, Teresa. Has God given you a floor plan?"

She was silent for a long moment, and then she began to speak softly. "To the world, what is a woman, Angélica? Poets sing about her beauty, her golden hair, her emerald eyes. But do they ever talk about her soul or her mind? To them, a woman is nothing but an empty casing, a beautiful shell that inspires and excites. What I'm thinking of is a new kind of convent, where women could divorce themselves from everything worldly. There would be no titles, not even *doña* and *señora*. A woman would just be herself, her soul, her heart. Status wouldn't matter. Money wouldn't matter. No woman would be turned away because she didn't have a dowry." Teresa's eyes shone like jet. María stared at her in awe.

"A woman would be appreciated for her spirit, not for her father's name and wealth. We'd return to the primitive rule of Carmel. We'd live like the desert hermits who founded the order—poor and barefoot. Remember what Maridíaz said: 'It's not just how you pray, but how you live.'" She paused again. "We'd call ourselves discalced Carmelites. Being discalced—barefoot—would be a sign of our detachment from the comforts of the material world. God wants me to do this, Angélica."

"How do you know?"

"He told me. Not with words you can hear with your bodily ears, Angélica. He communicated the message directly to my mind. He infused my intellect with His will."

"I can help!" rasped María. "I have my inheritance. It's not much, but it's yours!"

I put down the apothecary jar and looked from one to the other. "You're a madwoman," I said to Teresa. "Either that or a saint." She put her arms around me and kissed my cheek, then went over to María de Ocampo and squeezed her shoulders.

"You'll help me, won't you Angélica?" she said. It wasn't a question.

"Yes," I said. "I'll help you." How was I to know that this particular piece of madness would change not only my own life, but also the history of Spain and of our holy Catholic faith?

Angélica del Sagrado Corazón
Toledo, 20 August 1576

CHAPTER 14

Hazardous Roads

SPRING HAD COME, AND I WAS PLANTING HERBS IN THE GARDEN: PEPPERMINT, dill, coriander, parsley. All of a sudden I felt his eyes on me. My wrist trembled and the shoots I was holding tumbled out of my hand. I swiveled slightly and saw two worn boots and the hem of a habit. I didn't have to look up to know it was Braulio.

"You," I whispered. "What are you doing here?"

"No hello? No kiss?"

"I thought you were in the north. In Paris or Brussels."

"I was in Paris, but I've been back for months."

I put down my tools and stood up, but not too close to him. I felt like a doe cornered by a hunter. Instinctively, I glanced around for an escape route.

He clasped his hands together, as if to show he had no malevolent intentions. "I don't want anything," he said softly. He looked older, more subdued. His face was wan, his eyes, tired. "I just came here to warn you."

"About what?"

"I was in Valladolid for the autos-da-fe. Everyone is talking about the *santa* of Ávila, even in Valladolid, five hundred leagues to the north. Your friend Teresa is going to get herself killed." His voice was steady. He wasn't making a threat, just conveying information.

"What the hell are you talking about?"

"The new king is a madman, and he's out for her kind."

Felipe II had ascended to the throne in 1556, inheriting Spain and the Low Countries from his father, Carlos. The old king had been born in Flanders and wasn't so scandalized by the new ideas from the north. For him, confronting the Protestants was more a question of political expediency than of orthodoxy. His son, on the other hand, was reputedly a religious fanatic.

"She has protectors," I said. "Powerful people like Doña Guiomar de Ulloa."

"Look what happened to Carranza de Miranda, the queen's confessor. King Felipe got it into his head that Carranza's views were unorthodox and had the Inquisition arrest him."

"I don't believe you. You're trying to intimidate me."

"No, I'm trying to help you. I feel bad about . . . the things that happened."

"About raping me?"

"Listen to me, Angélica. Teresa is in danger. Do you know who Constantino Ponce de la Fuente is . . . was? He was the court preacher. They discovered he was secretly a Lutheran, so they arrested him—barged into his house one night while he was playing chess with his wife. They threw him into a dungeon in the old Augustinian monastery. Now he's dead. He committed suicide, hung himself with his own shirt."

I cringed. "Why are you telling me these things? To see me squirm?"

"In Valladolid they found out that Lutherans were meeting at midnight at the home of Father Agustín Cazalla, a professor of theology from the University of Salamanca."

"I've never heard of him," I said nervously. My heart was beginning to pound.

"I saw him burn, Angélica. I heard his shrieks when the flames touched his flesh. The king was in attendance, and all the court gentlemen and ladies. The sweetest little girl was there—she was so blond and fair. A cherub, really, in a frilly, silk dress with lace cuffs. 'When will they burn them, *Papá?*' she kept saying. Her eyes glowed with excitement. A huge crowd gathered. Thousands of commoners. Whole families with children, all there for the entertainment. You know what they do, Angélica? First they singe the cheeks of the condemned, just to titillate the crowd. Then they set the torch to the hay around their feet."

"But surely a woman . . ."

"Oh, being a woman won't save Teresa. Don't you know about the Jeronymite nuns from San Isidro Convent in Seville? People said they read the Bible, like Lutherans. The inquisitors decided they were contaminating not only other convents, but even the lay people."

"Teresa isn't a Lutheran."

"Anything they don't understand is Protestant, Angélica. It's a word they use for whatever is strange and new. In King Felipe's sick, depraved mind, anyone who thinks, reads, or feels is a heretic. I don't have time to explain this to you now, Angélica. I just came to warn you. Your friend's in danger. If you love her, tell her to lie low. She's attracting too much attention."

"But so far away, in Valladolid? It can't be!"

"Have you ever seen an auto-da-fe, Angélica? They do it on Sunday, the holiest day of the week, so more people can attend. The prisoners march to the stakes in their yellow robes and pointed caps, tears rolling down their cheeks. I was close enough to see the veins bulging in their necks, the beads of sweat on their foreheads, the trembling hands. A priest walks on either side of each one, encouraging him to confess his sins, to save his soul. 'Renounce your evil ways, my son,' they say. 'Recant, my daughter. Death will be less painful.' If the victim accepts, the executioners do him the favor of strangling him before laying the torch on his body. If he doesn't . . ."

"Stop, Braulio! Stop! You're terrifying me!"

"I want to terrify you. I want you to see that this is no game, Angélica. The king has given the Inquisition orders to be fast, thorough, and severe. No more long, drawn out trials. He wants to clear Spain of heretics right now! And the *conversos*, Angélica, he hates them. He thinks they're responsible for all Spain's ills. Every misfortune that happens, he blames on the *conversos*. If the country is crawling with Lutherans, it's their fault. If he's suffering an attack of gout, it's their fault. The man is obsessed. He doesn't really know the difference between a Lutheran and a *converso* or between a *converso* and a porcupine. Although there's some truth to what he says. The reform movements are attracting a lot of Jewish converts. Churches with no images, less pomp, less genuflecting . . . that sort of thing appeals to them. Anyway, tell Teresa to be careful. And you be careful, too. They'll see you as an accomplice." He sounded sincere. A strange thought came to me: In some sick way, he still cared about me. Otherwise, why would it matter to him that Teresa's fame might put me in danger?

"The worst of the inquisitors is a man from here. That makes him doubly dangerous because he might know something about Teresa's family. Javier Sánchez Colón. A Dominican."

I trembled like a violet in a cold wind. Javier Sánchez Colón. Teresa's handsome cousin Javier. Everything changes, I thought. Braulio is my protector. Basilio is a fat, bald cartwright. Javier—once so tender and sensitive— is a cruel inquisitor who oversees public executions.

"The Dominicans have taken a stand against everything your friend

Teresa believes in," Braulio went on. They think people who seek a personal relationship with God reject the sacraments. They think mental prayer leads to heresy. Melchor Cano is their leader, and Sánchez Colón studied with Cano. This Sánchez is a dangerous man, Angélica. Try to keep Doña Teresa out of his clutches."

I dropped the rest of the coriander and began to wring my hands with such force that I nearly dislocated a thumb. I felt as though I had a wad of raw dough in my stomach. A hot, wet stream trickled down my leg. I locked my knees together, praying that my underskirts would absorb the urine. A wave of nausea came over me, and I had to struggle to steady myself. I locked gazes with Braulio in order to keep his eyes off the ground. What if he realized what had happened? What if I had left a puddle under my feet?

"Are you . . . are you back in Ávila for good?" I stammered.

"I'm leaving for Paris tonight. Goodbye, Angélica. God protect you."

He turned and disappeared into the foliage. He knew every secret passage in the convent garden, every hiding place. They wouldn't catch him. I gathered up my tools and darted back to my cell to change my wet underskirts.

I began to have nightmares about autos-da-fe, only instead of Cazalla or Ponce de la Fuente, it was Teresa who was being escorted to the stake, Álvarez on one side of her, Daza on the other. And lighting the torch, the Dominican Inquisitor Javier Sánchez Colón.

I didn't say anything to Teresa about what Braulio had told me. The thought of starting a new convent had galvanized her, and I didn't want to ruin her happiness. I hadn't seen her so excited since she was a girl. Her idea was to create a real community of women. Not a dumping ground for girls who had no place else to go, but a small, dynamic beehive where sisters could pray and learn. It would be her way of fighting what plagued the faith—the apathy and empty ritualism, as well as the epidemic of skepticism fostered by the Lutherans. Her nuns would be fighters. She didn't see prayer as passivity, but as a form of assertiveness. She would save the heretics by praying for them. Her brothers were battling pagans in the New World, and she would battle the church's foes in the old. Men could be priests and soldiers, but women could be active, too. She'd known for years that God had a mission for her. Now she knew what it was. This would be her apostolate. Seeing her so fired up, how could I warn her to be cautious?

I don't know how the rumors about the new convent began to spread, but they did. I heard people whispering at the grille and, when I went out to buy medicine, chattering in the plaza. Father Baltasar grew antsy. He was an inexperienced confessor, only twenty-seven years old, ordained just the year before. Juan de Prádanos, Teresa's former confessor, had been young, too, but some people have a natural gift for spiritual direction. Father Baltasar was unsure of himself. Teresa's reputation intimidated him. People were calling her a saint, but Salcedo was still demanding exorcism. Father Baltasar didn't know what to do. He was afraid to take chances. He began to torture her.

"You're a worm!" he screamed. "Yes, Father." "Uncover your face! Look at me! You're a piece of slime!" "Yes, Father." "I'm saving you from yourself. Your soul is like a festering sore. You have to scoop out the rot." "Yes, Father." "This nonsense about a new convent has to stop!" Silence. She was convinced that God himself had demanded she move forward with her plan. There was no way she could give it up.

Álvarez knew that if the Inquisition set Teresa ablaze, they'd throw him into the flames after her. After all, it's a confessor's job to ensure his penitent's orthodoxy. Believe me, there's no demon as terrible as an insecure confessor. He prescribed new mortifications. Teresa prayed the rosary lying face down on gravel. She allowed two sisters to tie her to a cross and hung there until her arms went numb. I begged her to ask for a new confessor, but she refused. She had to prove her humility, demonstrate her obedience.

Finally, he forbade her to read. It was the last straw. Teresa had always been a reader. She didn't hide novels in the bedclothes the way I did—and still do—but she often had a book in her hand. The year before, in 1559, the Inquisitor-General Fernando de Valdés had issued an Index of Prohibited Books—the longest ever. It included 253 titles—fourteen editions of the Bible, editions of the New Testament in Spanish, and over fifty books of Hours. The Jesuits had a library at San Gil, and before the Index, sometimes they'd lend her a volume—Juan de Cazalla's *Light of the Soul* or *Audi, filia,* by our very own Juan de Ávila. But now, every book about mental prayer or recollection was forbidden, under pain of excommunication. Especially if it was written in Spanish. Books in Latin were considered less dangerous because only learned men could read them, and they knew how to interpret them correctly. But books in Spanish were accessible to less educated people, women, for example, and who knew what a woman might do with a book about finding God in her own heart? She might turn into an *alumbrada* or a Protestant.

And now Teresa couldn't even read the two or three books that were still permitted to the rest of us. Well, she'd had enough of Álvarez. He'd commanded her to wear a hair shirt for an entire week. She went to Mother Josefa and got one, then brought it back to her cell to put on. But instead of placing it under her shift, where it would chafe her skin and cleanse her soul, she tied it over her habit. "He said to wear it," she chuckled. "He didn't say where."

"Take that off," he snapped when he saw her. "What will people think?"

"You care too much what people think, Father," she retorted. "What people think is less important than what God thinks." I could see that Maridíaz had had an effect on her.

To make matters worse, Teresa's visions were growing more frequent and elaborate. Father Baltasar sat by the grille, twisting and untwisting the hem of his cassock. Did her visions come from the Devil or God, he was surely wondering. The Devil or God? The Devil or God? Thedevilorgod? If they came from the Devil, he had to put a stop to them. But if they came from God, by tethering Teresa, he would be working against the divine will.

One morning I was ironing furiously in the laundry room. Mother Josefa had given me some tassels, fringe and ribbons to sew onto vestments destined for a monastery in Salamanca, which I was now pressing into place. My stitching was so fine that priests from all over Spain ordered attire from me, and since Mother Josefa considered this a great honor for Encarnación, I never refused a request. Juana Isabel and I were getting the garments ready to return to the priests. I used three irons. Two warmed while I wielded the third, pressing down hard on the material, then shifting it carefully over the ironing table. When that iron cooled, I put it back over the fire, picked up a hot one, and continued my work. In the meantime, Juana Isabel folded each newly pressed vestment carefully, packed it in straw, and placed it in the crate the messenger would hoist into the cart to take north.

Teresa's sister Juana came in. She was five months pregnant and already waddled like a goose. Nevertheless, she did her best to make herself useful, testing the irons to make sure they weren't so hot they'd scorch the fabric. She'd wet her index finger and touch the metal, declaring her verdict on each instrument. To be honest, the poor child was so clumsy, I'd have preferred she just watch, but I didn't want to hurt her feelings, so I just kept an eye on her and prayed she wouldn't drop a heavy iron on her foot. I needn't have worried. In a short time she grew tired and sat down to rest. She took some yarn out of a satchel and began to knit a bootie—knit, knit, purl, knit, knit, purl. We were laughing over the feminine ways of priests—so fastidious about their bobbles and trimmings—when Teresa rushed into the room.

She'd hardly embraced her sister when the words gushed from her mouth. "It was so marvelous! It was like nothing you could ever imagine. He spoke to me! He touched me! I can't explain it. It was different from the other times. He gave me something, a token of His love, a sign, a proof that it was really He." And then, something about a rosary, a crucifix, jewels.

I understood she'd had another vision, but the syllables spilled out so fast, I could hardly grasp her meaning. "Slow down, Teresa," I said, still ironing. The messenger would leave soon for Salamanca. Sister Escolástica, the cellaress, had ordered he be given meat and ale out in the carriage house, but as soon as he was done eating, he'd want to be on his way.

Teresa sat down next to her sister. "I was praying in the chapel, when all of a sudden I became aware of His most holy presence."

"Christ was there in his Divine Humanity," I said automatically.

"In his Divine Humanity!" echoed Juana excitedly.

"But I was afraid. I remembered what Father Baltasar said—to give him the fig—and so I raised my hand to make the gesture."

"That's awful!" exclaimed Juana Isabel.

"He was understanding," said Teresa. "He knew I was just following Baltasar's orders. He assured me my visions didn't come from the Devil and promised to give me proof they really were from God."

"What did you do?" asked Juana, wide-eyed.

"I was still afraid. I thought those sweet words might be a trick to get me to let down my guard, so I held up the ebony crucifix at the end of my rosary and pointed it right at Him. You know, the Devil can't abide the sign of the cross. One glimpse of a cross, and he flees."

"And then?" I'd put down the iron.

"He asked for the crucifix. He held out his blessed hand, and I placed the cross in it. His fingers were long and white and as soft as the catkins of pussy willows."

"I always gather pussy willows for Saint John's Day," said Juana stupidly.

"He held it for a while. Then He took my hand in one of His and placed my ebony crucifix in it. When I looked down, I saw that it was adorned with four large stones of indescribable beauty. Stones more gorgeous than diamonds, more exquisite than any earthly gem. A diamond would look cheap next to these treasures."

"Do you have the crucifix?" asked Juana excitedly. "Will you show it to us?"

Teresa plunged her hand into the folds of her habit and took it out. She held it gently, as if she were afraid of dropping it and loosening the stones. She stared at it a moment, her eyes wide with awe. "Oh, my Lord and my God," she whispered. "It's so magnificent." Juana Isabel and I exchanged a quick glance. What she held out to us was a standard rosary with a plain black crucifix—the same one each of us carried in her pocket. There were no priceless jewels.

"Oh, I know what you're thinking," said Teresa softly. "But no one can see them but me. The same thing happened to Saint Catherine. Jesus placed a gold ring with precious pearls on her finger, but no one else could see it. Don't trouble yourselves about it." She smiled blissfully.

"Can I have it?" begged Juana.

"Of course, Juanita." Without hesitating, Teresa handed her the precious object. Juana's face lit up. She threw her arms around Teresa's neck and kissed her. "Thank you, Teresita," she cooed. Then she wrapped the rosary in a handkerchief and placed it tenderly in her knitting bag.

I didn't know whether Teresa was crazy or truly blessed. I mean, when someone tells you something is there, and you can clearly see it's not there, what are you supposed to think? But I guess that rosary really was miraculous because, after Juana took it to Alba, the parish priest laid it on the eyes of Doña Iria de Toledo, an aristocratic lady who suffered from cataracts, and she was cured. It's true. Many people, including Doña Iria's surgeon, swear it.

Suddenly, I smelled the awful odor of something burning. "Oh, my God!" I cried. I had scorched the hem of a chasuble. "Oh, no," I moaned. "Now what will I do?"

Teresa took the material in her hand. "I'm sorry, Angélica. This is all my fault. But look, it's just a little piece at the bottom. You can snip some from an inside seam and cover it up."

If you're really a saint, I thought, why don't you perform a miracle here and now? Make this cloth whole again! Instead, I said, "Go ask Escolástica to give the courier more ale, and I'll try to fix this." She strode to the door as briskly as a girl. "Don't tell anyone else about the crucifix," I called after her.

She didn't follow my advice. She went right to Father Baltasar, who hemmed and hawed and finally told her that even the gem-studded crucifix was no proof that her visions were authentic, especially since no one else could see the stones. "Keep on giving those visions the fig," he told her.

But Teresa was shrewd. At the time, the Dominicans were waging a campaign against mental prayer. They considered the teachings of men like Osuna misguided, if not heretical. Praying, they said, should be done by rote, in the traditional way and supervised by priests. And as for visions, locutions, and ecstasies, it was all rubbish. A few of God's chosen might enjoy such favors, they conceded, but for the most part, visionaries were frauds. Especially women visionaries. You'd think Teresa would avoid Dominicans like the plague, but instead, she faced the enemy head-on. She sought out a brilliant Dominican theologian named Domingo Báñez and asked him his advice. I guess she thought that if she could get him to defend her, everyone else would leave her alone. But Báñez was noncommittal. He didn't back Álvarez, but neither did he discount the possibility that Teresa's visions came from the Devil. What he told her was that giving the fig to the Lord was a sin. "An image of Jesus should always be venerated," he said. "A beautiful picture, even though it was painted by a scoundrel, is still precious. It's the image you're honoring, not the source of the image." Poor Teresa. They pulled her this way and that way until she nearly lost her mind. The one who finally put a stop to it was Pedro de Alcántara.

I'd heard of Fray Pedro—he was famous even when I was a child—but I'd never seen him. Some people venerated him as a saint, even in his lifetime. Others said he was a lunatic who carried austerity to such unhealthy extremes that he made a mockery of monastic life. He was a Franciscan, a discalced friar in some small town I'd never heard of. He zigzagged across Spain barefoot, wearing only sackcloth and a girdle of plate. He ate only leaves and berries and went for days without sleeping. When he did sleep, it was rarely for more than an hour at a time and usually in a trough so short he had to remain curled up or on his knees. In the monastery his cell was only a *vara* and a half long, much less than the length of his body, and there he slept with his head against a board. People said he never wore his hood, no matter how hot the sun or cold the wind. He rarely raised his eyes. In fact, he lived in the same monastery for three years without ever seeing the face of a single one of his brothers. He hardly ever spoke to women. He preached among the poor in the worst neighborhoods, those inhabited by thieves and assassins, but since he lived in abject poverty, what did he have they'd want to steal?

The news that Fray Pedro was coming to town made Álvarez nervous. "A nut case," he said. "An extremist. There's no reason why a holy man can't take a bath once a year. And a good meal now and then never made a person less virtuous." But Teresa was anxious to meet him. His ideas about returning monastic life to its primitive origins were akin to her own.

With Mother Josefa's permission, she and I, accompanied by Father Baltasar, went to find him in the Church of Nuestra Señora de la Anunciación.

A wisp of a man, Fray Pedro was sixty-one years old, but looked ninety-one. His face was rough and knotty, like a gnarled root. His body was stooped from his walking with his eyes on the ground. His tattered clothing—I can hardly call his garment a habit or a soutane—was as rigid and coarse as tree bark. I expected a vinegary character, cured by a life of abstinence and solitude, but in fact he hardly spoke at all, and when he did, he radiated kindness. He smiled often, the corners of his cracked lips turning upward like a crescent moon, his tiny eyes disappearing into his rumpled visage, his knobby cheeks bulging. "Sometimes I run through the woods singing for sheer joy," he told us. "I'm the Lord's town crier!"

Father Baltasar and I left Teresa to kneel at his feet and say her confession. She was with him a long time, perhaps an hour or more. In the meantime, Father Baltasar sat with me in the vestibule at the back of the church. "Let's hope he talked her out of this harebrained idea to start a new convent," he grumbled. "After all, a nun can't just walk away from her convent and start a new one."

My mind began to wander. I wondered if Braulio really felt remorse for what he had done to me. I wondered where he was. I started to fidget. Father Baltasar glared at me.

Finally, Teresa and Fray Pedro rose and moved down the side aisle toward the rear pews. She walked behind him, her head bowed, her lips moving.

"Well, Father," said Fray Pedro, addressing Baltasar. There was a touch of irony in the way he called the younger man "Father." I shifted my weight nervously. I was afraid there might be a fight. Baltasar Álvarez was a heavyset young man with a porcine face and a ruddy complexion. When he was upset, he grew crimson from the top of his forehead to the tips of his fingers. At the moment, he was as red as a suckling pig roasted and candied for Christmas. He chewed his tongue and bit his lip. I thought he was going to make a petulant remark, but instead, he exhaled noisily. Teresa kept her eyes glued to the floor.

"Father Baltasar," said the aged friar purposefully. I was amazed at the resonance of his voice. "Sister Teresa's visions and locutions come from God.

The mortifications to which you're subjecting her serve no purpose. They must stop. And so must this nonsense about exorcism."

Álvarez's lips quivered. "Yes, Father," he said, almost inaudibly.

"Another thing, Father. Her plan to start a new convent that follows the primitive rule is an excellent one. Christ calls us to reject worldly values and follow Him." His voice was calm and his eyes steady. Nothing about his demeanor suggested anger, but Álvarez tensed. The old man's words surely stung. The men of San Gil were gaining a reputation for high living. "I have experience dealing with the Holy Father, our blessed Pope Pius IV," Fray Pedro continued. "I know about starting religious houses—patents, permissions, that sort of thing. I will help Sister Teresa, Father Baltasar, and you will not stand in the way." He still looked completely unruffled.

"Yes, Father," murmured Álvarez.

He got the message, I thought. He won't make trouble. I felt suddenly exhilarated. "My God," I said to myself, "this is really going to happen." I looked at Teresa. She was beaming.

At that moment, I felt such love for my sister. She was about to set out on a great adventure! She was doing the will of God! It's true that when she first talked of starting a new convent, I vacillated, but once we got to work, I threw myself into the project. And I have to say this, even though it might sound like pride, Lucifer's sin: She couldn't have done it without me. My name may not go down in history, but Teresa de Ahumada would never have succeeded if it hadn't been for me.

Angélica del Sagrado Corazón, Carmelite
Toledo, 22 August 1576

CHAPTER 15

The Jewel of Spain

"What shall I call her, Your Highness or Your Grace?"

"I don't know, Teresa. You're the lady. I'm just the daughter of a seamstress."

"Should I call her Your Most Illustrious Duchess Doña Luisa? This is torture. I should get reduced time in Purgatory for this."

We were supposed to stay hidden, but I couldn't resist peeping out the carriage window. I'd never seen such a huge metropolis. They called Toledo the jewel of Spain, and no wonder. Tradesmen scurried here and there with bolts of fabric, reams of lace, colorfully painted earthenware jugs, exquisitely carved boxes. *Moriscos* bedecked in gold chains hurried down the street, pots and pans and all kinds of trinkets tied to their waists. They were forbidden to wear Arab headgear, but you could recognize them by their garish colors and dark skin. And the traffic! I'd never seen anything like it. Carriages, carts, barrows, dollies, wagons, mules, horses, donkeys. Ávila was a sleepy town in comparison. Carlos V had held court in Toledo, but his son Felipe II made Madrid his capital. Toledo was too small, he said, to support his vast administrative apparatus. Too small! If Toledo is too small, I thought, imagine what Madrid must be like.

We had entered through the Puerta de Bisagra, an ancient Moorish gate shaped like a horseshoe. Everywhere graceful *mudéjar* structures with symmetrical arches and intricate stonework shone like crystals in the white winter sunlight. "That's the Plaza de Zocodover," said Juan de Ovalle, pulling back the curtain a finger or two just for a moment. "It's the central market." In spite of the cold, merchants hawked their wares to eager buyers. Meat hung from giant hooks. Bins of dried nuts, beans, lentils, and peas lined stalls. Colorful soaps, flasks of olive oil, spices, thread, buttons, pins, and ribbons lay in heaps on tables. My eyes bulged at the displays of velvet, brocade, satin, and taffeta. Tía Cati would have loved this city.

"Should I call her Your Charity?"

"Your Charity isn't used for great ladies!" cried Juana Isabel. "Call her Your Grace."

"Your Ladyship is the correct form for a duchess," pronounced Juan de Ovalle. "She's the daughter of the second Duke of Medinaceli. You should call her Your Ladyship."

"Good afternoon, Your Ladyship," said Teresa, practicing. "So nice to make your acquaintance, Your Ladyship. So lovely to be here with you, Your Ladyship."

"Look, Teresa!" I squealed. We were passing through the Calle Comercio, where shop after shop displayed exquisitely worked silver, magnificent swords, candles, tapestries, chess sets, plates, and jugs brightly painted with birds, flowers, and vines.

Teresa pulled her shawl tighter around her shoulders. "I'm freezing," she moaned. "It's so cold that even the angels in Heaven are wearing cloaks."

"I'd rather be cold in Toledo than warm in Ávila. Look at that gorgeous church!" To the side stood a magnificent *mudejar* edifice, with graceful arches and lacy ornamental moldings.

"That's Santa María la Blanca," said Juan de Ovalle importantly. "It was once a synagogue. This place used to be crawling with Jews. Still is, only now they perform their nasty rites behind closed doors."

"What nasty rites?" I asked, eying Teresa. I remembered my aunt Cati had said that Teresa's grandfather was from Toledo. They even called him *El Toledano*. Juan Sánchez was one of those Jews with which Toledo had once been crawling.

"Those disgusting blood rituals," snapped Ovalle, "like killing Christian babies. I always tell the maids, 'Be careful with little Gonzalo and Beatriz. Don't let them out of your sight.'"

Teresa's stared at her hands with studied impassiveness. "There are no longer any Jews in Spain," she said softly.

"Now they pass themselves off as *conversos*," Ovalle retorted.

"Jesus teaches us to look to our own sinfulness and not criticize others."

Juan de Ovalle glared at her as though she'd sprouted fangs. "You go out of your way to be outrageous, don't you, Teresa?"

Teresa looked out the window. "Good afternoon, Your Ladyship." Her demeanor was cool, unruffled, but her twitching, upturned lips betrayed a smirk.

Juana Isabel was struggling to get a good look at the building, whose elegant geometric designs disappeared as the carriage rounded a corner and headed uphill.

"You're too close to the window," barked Juan de Ovalle. "Someone might see you."

What were we doing in Toledo? We were being tucked out of view, secreted out of town so no one could find us. In Ávila, our whispers resonated like roars, roars so loud that Ángel de Salazar, the Carmelite provincial, thought he had to get Teresa out of the way before she shamed the whole order. But he had to be careful. Teresa had admirers, important people like Doña Guiomar and the revered Pedro de Alcántara. Flinging her into prison could provoke a catastrophe. Besides, what if God really was on her side? It was so hard to know about God.

The whole town was up in arms over Teresa's plan to leave Encarnación and start a new convent. What do you think, Reader, whoever you are? That people greeted the possibility of a new religious house in Ávila with shouts of Alleluia? Do you think the townspeople kissed our feet and cried, "Congratulations, Teresa de Ahumada, congratulations, Angélica!" No, they did not. Let me go back to the beginning.

Fray Pedro de Alcántara had commanded Father Baltasar Álvarez to keep his mouth shut, and for a few weeks the Jesuit obeyed. But then he got nervous. Teresa said she was following God's instructions, but, he must have asked himself, who was she to chitchat with God? And who was this weird Friar Pedro to give him orders? Seething (I imagine he was seething), he went running to Daza and Salcedo to see what they thought he should do. Well, Daza was never one for keeping a secret. If people were whispering before, now all of Ávila was abuzz.

Fortunately, the townspeople hadn't yet guessed where Teresa was planning to found her new convent. If they had, they'd have stormed the little house, bashed in the walls, smashed the windows, torn up the garden, thrown animal feces on the floors, and stoned us all—Teresa, me, and Doña Guiomar, whom they saw as Teresa's co-conspirator. "Did this Teresa think she was too holy for her own convent?" people asked. Weren't her sisters good enough for her? The Encarnación nuns were furious. Some of the noblest families had relatives in Encarnación, and now this upstart, this daughter of a silk merchant, found the place lacking. The ladies in brocade dresses and diamond earrings lowered their voices and asked, "Who is this *conversa,* this daughter of a Jew?" What the city fathers wanted to know was this: Who was going to support the new convent? Teresa said she was going to found it in poverty, without sponsors. That meant the townspeople would have to give alms. There were already scores of religious houses in Ávila, many of them requiring charity. The last thing the city needed was a new convent to maintain.

One afternoon Teresa, Doña Guiomar, and I were walking down the street, when all of a sudden an egg hit me squarely on the chest. It was a mistake. The thrower had been aiming for Teresa. The gooey mess ran down the front of my habit.

"Keep walking," ordered Teresa. "Don't stop to quarrel."

"There's the nun who thinks she's a saint!" a young man called out.

Others joined him. "You took vows, Sister! Now go back to your cell and pray!"

A glob of raw dough came flying through the air and caught the elegant Doña Guiomar in the eye. "Why don't you tend to your household, widow? Go take care of your children."

"Keep moving," instructed Teresa. But Doña Guiomar was too stunned to take another step. She stood there, the pasty substance stuck to her left cheek. The side of her face looked like a whitewashed melon. Her lashes and the hair around her temple were gummy. I thought she was going to cry, but then, she straightened up and hissed, "Better they should have a mother who walks with a saint. They don't need me to be their nursemaid. They have nannies enough already." Teresa took her by the arm and, with inappropriate familiarity, coaxed her away.

Usually I didn't go with them, but when I did, people left me alone because I wasn't important. If they noticed me at all, they thought I was Teresa's servant. It was better that way. It gave me more freedom. I could run errands and carry messages for Teresa and Doña Guiomar without anyone raising an eyebrow.

I knew that Daza and Salcedo were the ones stirring things up. "That Teresa de Ahumada is a troublemaker," they told Álvarez. Well, maybe those weren't their exact words, but that's the gist of it. Suddenly, Álvarez was refusing to grant Teresa absolution. Her very own confessor! It's clear what he was up to. He was trying to get into the good graces of his superior, Father Dionisio Vázquez, the new rector of San Gil.

Vázquez was a peculiar sort, taciturn and melancholic. A tall, skeletal man, with a long, purplish face, he looked like one of those ancient hybrids —a griffin (part eagle and part lion) or a centaur (part man and part horse). Father Vázquez was part man and part eggplant. A mix between a human and an aubergine. A hubergine, or something like that. His most salient characteristic was his rotting teeth—tiny, crooked, black hooks that always seemed to want to latch onto something, like an arm or a throat. When he talked, which wasn't often, his mouth gave off a putrid odor. To me, he never said a word. Not even a perfunctory *Salve María* when I came to the door with Teresa. Back when he was a young Jesuit and had a full set of white teeth, he had shown promise, people said. He had even been confessor to Francisco Borja. But he was too ambitious. He rubbed people the wrong way, and things had gone badly for him.

Once Álvarez had told Vázquez about Teresa's plans, the rector had to take a stand. The Society of Jesus had met with tremendous success in Ávila, but now things were deteriorating. Father Ignacio had died several years before, in 1556, and the new breed of Jesuits was reputedly more concerned with the quality of wine at table than with serving Our Lord. There was another problem, too. In this tight-knit little band—some twenty-seven or twenty-eight men—the vast majority were *conversos*. Father Ignacio had never cared about the lineage of his disciples. Everybody knew that some of those closest to him were of Jewish ancestry. In fact, the Society of Jesus was one of the most liberal orders with respect to admitting *conversos*. But the political climate had changed. King Felipe II was tightening the screws. If the *conversos* of San Gil backed this controversial *converso* nun, people would see the order as tainted. They might even run the Jesuits out of town. Vázquez couldn't afford to anger the people of Ávila, and if he sided with Teresa, he'd do just that. Teresa had counted on the Society of Jesus for years, but now she found herself without Jesuit allies.

One afternoon I found her in the garden peeling an orange. With consummate skill she slipped the blade through the rind just by the navel. Then, rotating the fruit carefully, she inched the knife downward, slicing the peel into a perfect spiral, which dropped to the ground. She broke the fruit in sections and gave a chunk to me. I was feeling gloomy. It seemed as though everyone but Doña Guiomar had abandoned us. I put a section of orange to my lips, bit the rind, and sucked out the juicy pulp. "Maybe this isn't the right time to start a new convent, Teresa," I ventured.

"Do you think we should give up?"

"It's a crazy idea, isn't it? I mean, leaving a convent where we've lived for twenty-four years to go off and form a new one. We have no backing, no allies. We'd have a better chance of converting the grand Turk Saladin than of making this work."

"What would you do if you didn't have oranges to eat, Angélica?" she asked, sticking her knife into the rind of another piece of fruit.

"What do you mean? What does that have to do with starting a convent?"

"Just think about it. What do you do in the winter, when there are no oranges?"

"I eat something else."

"Well, if the Jesuits won't support us, maybe we should look for spiritual nourishment somewhere else."

"Like where?"

"After my father died, when everyone was telling me that mental prayer was a sin, Fray Vicente Barrón came to my rescue. Maybe I should go back to the Dominicans. I have a friend at Santo Tomás, Father García de Toledo. He's an influential man. I bet he'll take my side."

"You can't just go from one priest to another until you find one who tells you what you want to hear."

She stuffed a section of orange into her mouth and chewed slowly. "Why not?"

"You took a vow of obedience. Obedience, chastity, and poverty. Remember?

"I'm obeying God."

"You're supposed to obey God through your superiors."

"I will . . . when I find a superior who understands what God wants me to do."

That was her strategy. Not only then, but always. When one priest refused to take her side, she'd find another one who would. She was clever that way. She could follow the rules and break them at the same time. I wish I were shrewd like Teresa. If I were, I'd be on my way to sainthood too. Because being a saint isn't so much about being good. I mean, it is. But it's also about getting things done. And Teresa knew how to get things done.

I shook my head. "Alright, Teresa. I suppose it's worth a try. Go talk to Father García de Toledo. I'll go with you."

Santo Tomás was a sprawling monastery founded by Doña María Dávila, widow of the treasurer of our most glorious Catholic monarchs, Fernando and Isabella. The king and queen loved this monastery so much, they spent their summers there, and when their poor son Don Juan died at nineteen, they had him buried there. You can see his sepulcher in the center of the chapel, his beautiful, serene, young face carved in alabaster, the folds of his robe as delicate and fluid as if they were real. The Santo Tomás chapel is strange in that the main altar is high up, at choir-level. It's adorned with five large tablets framed in gold that depict the life of Saint Thomas. The choir, in a style they've just started to call Gothic, is so delicately carved in walnut that it looks like pointelle lace. I waited in the chapel while Teresa went to talk to García de Toledo.

At forty-six, she was still a charmer, and I thought she'd win him over. But García was noncommittal. Like other Dominicans, he was wary of visionaries. "He said he'd think about it," she said. "I told him I'd leave the matter entirely in his hands, but I did mention that Fray Pedro de Alcántara was in favor of the project."

Very clever, I thought. With a recommendation like that, how could he say no? But it wasn't so easy. Everyone in Ávila from the count to the cobbler's apprentice had an opinion on Teresa's project. People wrote to García to give their advice. Tell that woman yes, tell that woman no, tell that woman to go to Hell. One little Carmelite nun had turned Ávila on its ear!

Fray Ángel, the Carmelite provincial, was livid. Teresa de Ahumada was attracting far too much attention. He had to get rid of her, but how? The solution was Doña Luisa de la Cerda, widow of Don Antonio Arias Pardo de Saavedra, a fabulously wealthy aristocrat.

Fray Ángel must have rubbed his hands together in glee when he heard about Don Arias's death. Doña Luisa, people said, was inconsolable. Well, even the rich have feelings. She spent her days wandering through her magnificent palace like a specter, or else weeping, crumpled in a heap on a velvet cushion in the great hall. Her children were afraid she was going to follow their father into the family crypt. She needed company, they thought, but who could console a lady so great that kings and cardinals called her cousin? Doña Luisa had asked about the *santa* from Ávila that everyone was talking about, so the family contacted Fray Ángel and asked him to arrange for Teresa to visit. Now Fray Ángel could, as my Tía Cati used to say, *matar dos pájaros de un tiro,* kill two birds with one stone. He could whisk Teresa out of town and at the same time get on the good side of the staggeringly powerful Doña Luisa.

For her trip to Toledo Teresa had taken care with her attire. She wore her most tattered habit and a shawl much too flimsy for the weather, darned and patched to cover the holes. It was a clever move. It was a way of putting her sanctity on display—who but a saint could show such distain for material wealth and comfort?—and at the same time place herself on a level with her hostess, or even a notch above. After all, Doña Luisa might be the wealthiest woman in Spain, but Teresa de Ahumada was the most pious. Doña Luisa was in utter awe of the *santa,* while the *santa* felt utter contempt for the duchess. Yet, they needed each other. Doña Luisa needed a saint to console her and impress her friends, and Doña Teresa—she was still *Doña* Teresa— needed the support of influential people if she was ever going to get the reform off the ground.

A majordomo met us at the gate and showed us down a path covered by a stone arcade. A plethora of servants and aides materialized—pages, menservants, maids, ladies-in-waiting—all dressed in the colors of mourning: black, yellow, burgundy, navy. They bowed, they curtsied, they said welcoming words, they gaped at Teresa and smiled at me. They flitted around, taking our bags, offering us warm drinks. We walked down an endless corridor. My roughly shod feet had never touched such a fabulous carpet, a rose-patterned Flanders weave that made me feel as though I were walking over a flowered meadow. My seamstress's eyes took in the ornate archway, bursting, like an interior garden, with sculpted flora, undulating vines, luxuriant foliage. Gigantic candelabra heavy with candles hung from the ceiling like crystal chrysanthemums.

An apparition came into view at the end of the hallway, an apparition that you didn't have to be a saint to see: an opulently dressed woman of about forty or a bit older, with hennaed hair and deep creases at the corners of her eyes, but still attractive. She wore a richly adorned *gamurra,* or outer gown, with gold passementerie up and down the front and around the collar, over a stiff, high, black satin bodice ending in a point at the waist, as was the fashion. The sleeves were puffed from shoulder to elbow, tight from elbow to wrist. Her starched, bell-shaped farthingale made her appear very tall and slim, although she was a woman of normal proportions, a little shorter than I am. Under her skirt she wore a *basquiña,* a black underskirt that peeped out at the hem of her overskirt. The long train of her gown was fastened at her wrist, which was adorned with a row of thick, gold bracelets. On her bosom lay a large, diamond-shaped brooch, black with gold birds, leaves, and flowers, in the traditional Toledano style. Her hair, braided with thick, gold cord and fastened close to her head, was crowned with a velvet coif. Teresa stood next to her brother-in-law, eyes lowered until the duchess was almost in front of her. She didn't curtsy, so neither did I.

"Welcome, welcome!" gushed Doña Luisa.

"Thank you, Your . . . Grace . . . Your Illustrious . . . Your . . ."

"Your Ladyship," erupted Juan de Ovalle, "we're so delighted to . . ." Suddenly, he stopped, awestruck, unable to go on. A nervous silence followed.

Doña Luisa burst out laughing.

"I'm sorry, Your Ladyship," said Teresa softly. "I'm . . . I'm not used to . . ."

"No matter," said Doña Luisa kindly—and I really do think she meant it kindly. "We're all the same in God's eyes."

"You see, Angélica," said Teresa, turning toward me although her comment was obviously meant for the duchess. "Sometimes we're afraid to pray because we just don't know how to address Our Lord. But here, I used the wrong title to address her Ladyship and she just laughed. So why should we be afraid to talk to God, who is all-powerful, yet infinitely merciful?" She said this with a tinge of what seemed something like flirtatiousness, then waited a moment to see if Doña Luisa realized she had just been put in her place.

"This is Sister Angélica," Teresa went on, "and this is Sister Juana Isabel."

Just then a fluffy brown and white dog—one of those ubiquitous ladies' dogs one finds in great houses—came scampering down the hall. He scuttled under Doña Luisa's skirts, then took off again, darting in and out of the maids' petticoats, eluding the valet who was struggling to catch him. All of a sudden he ran up to Teresa, lifted his leg, and peed on the hem of her habit.

Doña Luisa shrieked. "Oh, oh, I'm so sorry! I don't know what's gotten into him. Brutus, you naughty dog! I'm sure he went outside to do his business right before you arrived."

"Yes," said Teresa dryly, "but there's always a little extra for a friend."

An embarrassed valet snatched up the dog and carried him out. A maid got down on all fours and rubbed the edge of Teresa's habit with a damp rag. Then, another maid showed us to our sumptuous quarters.

"This is a new kind of mortification," grumbled Teresa, when we were alone. "All these frills and luxuries, what do we need them for? Women of God need only God."

"Speak for yourself," I said. "You go ahead and sleep on the floor if you want to. I'm looking forward to resting my bones on that big feather bed and letting my head sink into that big feather pillow. And all these heavy blankets! At least we won't be cold tonight."

In spite of the duchess's lugubrious mood, her palace was a whirlwind. Like nearly all important noblewomen, she kept a retinue of ladies-in-waiting, many of them young girls from aristocratic families whose parents sent them to fine houses to be educated. At elegant residences like Doña Luisa's, these girls learned etiquette and fine needlepoint, and often also received instruction in religion, reading, grammar, French or Italian, mathematics, and science. Doña Luisa's charges also learned Latin, which was unusual, since most men of letters thought Latin an inappropriate subject for ladies. María de Salazar, the cleverest of Doña Luisa's ladies, was a bouncy child of fourteen who scampered around like a puppy. Not only was she a beauty with hair like a radiant sunset, but she shone in Latin and French and composed poetry in the Italian style.

In some ways, she reminded me of Teresa as a girl. She loved parties and frilly clothes, and whenever Doña Luisa had guests, she'd spend hours getting ready. Servants would braid her hair with silk ribbon, then undo it and twist it into *moños*. She'd try on her green velvet dress, then her gold satin gown. When she was sure she looked her best, she'd come running to Teresa.

"Am I pretty, Madre?" The fragrance of lavender filled the room when she moved.

"*Ni tan hermosa que mate, ni tan fea que espante.* Not pretty enough to knock them dead, but not ugly enough to scare them."

María de Salazar's bell-like laughter reverberated throughout the chamber. Rumor had it that she was the bastard daughter of one of Doña Luisa's male relatives and that her mother was a *conversa*. Like all the girls, she spied constantly on the famous *santa*. "Will she levitate?" they tittered. "Will she perform a miracle? Will she have a rapture?" They were obsessed with Teresa.

María tired Teresa out with her chatter. "I want to be a nun just like you, Madre. I want to found a convent, just like you. I want to see Jesus, just like you."

"*Cacarear y no poner huevo,*" said Teresa. "A lot of clucking, and no eggs. I see you putting pretty bows in your hair and decorating your wrists with gold bracelets, but I don't see you spending time in the company of the One you say you love." María bowed her head, completely deflated.

For a widow in mourning, Doña Luisa had a prodigious appetite. Usually we took our midday meals in her *estrado,* seated on cushions on the dais. Servants filled drinking bowls of dark green Belgian glass with almond water, which they poured from a prunted beaker. When important guests shared our meal, we ate in the great hall, or *estrado de cumplimiento,* a large room with a fine chimney on either side. In the dead of winter, when quivering birds huddled in tree hollows and the air felt like slivers of glass against your skin, it was almost balmy in the dining chamber. At one end, a sturdy partition attached to the ceiling formed a kind of inner balcony with stairs to the minstrel gallery above, where musicians and singers entertained us. Servants entered through this balcony, which connected with the kitchen and the buttery, where drinks were prepared, and the pantry, where maids transferred food onto huge serving platters. The hall was divided into two parts, one for men and one for women. Doña Luisa employed an army of servants for such occasions.

I'd never seen such abundance. Doña Guiomar's table was meager in comparison. Doña Luisa regaled her guests with an enormous selection of meats—beef flavored with imported mustard and capers, mutton, rabbit, ox-tongue, pork, venison, swan, dove, and chicken. Afterward came boiled salads of eggplant, leeks, endive, cauliflower, and beets, all delicately flavored. Then there were cheeses imported from France or the Low Countries, dried fruits, nuts, and comfits. Knowing Teresa had a sweet tooth, Doña Luisa's bakers did their best to surprise her with tasty delights, such as almond cakes or pies of preserved oranges or plums. Teresa usually ate heartily, sucking her fingers to show how much she appreciated her hostess's hospitality.

The duchess loved to astonish her friends with exotic dishes made of mysterious ingredients. Once, pulpy red berries bursting with juice appeared on the serving tray, accompanied by onions, garlic, artichokes, aubergines, and a dash of ginger. Even before the servants entered the room, the aroma piqued your nostrils. The squishy fruit was a bit sweet, a bit tart. I took a whole one into my mouth, then turned it over on my tongue. It burst, filling my mouth with a flavorsome juice and tiny, bitter seeds. Doña Luisa laughed. "Be careful, Sister," she teased. "It will make you fall in love. It's called a *poma amoris.*"

"Love apple!" squealed María de Salazar.

"They're originally from America, where they call them *tomates* or *jitomates,*" explained Doña Luisa, "but these come from the south of Italy, where they recently started growing them for food. At first they were grown only for decoration because people thought they were poisonous. My cousin the cardinal sent these to me by papal messenger."

After dinner the servants brought in games for the gentlemen—chess, backgammon, cards. The women chatted, then retired to their quarters to read or rest. Although Teresa usually relished conversation, that afternoon she slipped away before the final course was served.

I assumed she wanted to write. Father García de Toledo, concerned about the gossip linking her to *alumbrados* and Protestants, had asked her to compose a memoir describing her spiritual practices so that, if questioned by the Inquisition, she could prove the orthodoxy of her beliefs. The mayhem in Ávila had left her little time to work. Here, she was able to organize her thoughts. But when I went up to our room, she wasn't writing. She was shivering in bed.

"Teresa, what's the matter with you?"

She gulped and moved her lips, but didn't seem to have the strength to speak. She was clutching her chest. I sat on the bed and put my hand on her forehead. It was clammy.

Men were laughing in the great hall. I imagined them drinking brandy and picking their teeth with gold toothpicks. Teresa opened and closed her hand in a pumping motion.

"Squeezing," she whispered. "I feel . . . as though I'm being squeezed to death."

"I'll get a doctor."

"No doctors."

"Don't be obstinate, Teresa!"

"No. No . . . I'm beginning to feel better. See? I can talk now."

"What hurts? Your chest?"

"I'm better now, but I still feel dizzy. I felt nauseous at dinner."

There was a knock at the door. María de Salazar tiptoed in and stood, wide-eyed, staring at Teresa. "Is Sister Teresa ill?" she whispered.

"Yes, run off now. She can't talk to you." María winced as though I'd slapped her. "I'm sorry, child," I apologized. "But something's wrong with Sister. I think it might be her heart."

"It could be the love apples," said María earnestly.

Perhaps an hour after she'd gone, Doña Luisa appeared in the room. She'd changed into a dark, wool gown, simple and elegant, adorned only with a lace collar and cuffs. She arched her neck and stood motionless, as though entering a ballroom. She carried herself with that slightly constipated air cultivated by the rich. In her hands she bore a small, Toledo-style coffer, with a lid worked in gold leaf and mother-of-pearl.

"María says Sister Teresa is ill," she said, without looking at me.

I'd given Teresa some valerian, and she was just beginning to doze off. I wanted Doña Luisa to leave, but she was a duchess and this was her house.

"She's resting, Your Ladyship," I said, trying to make myself sound very respectful.

"I'm feeling better," said Teresa, groggily. "It was a passing malaise."

Damn it, Teresa, I thought. Stop being tough and brave. Tell her to get out of here so you can go to sleep.

"I'm glad to hear that," said Doña Luisa. She smiled, and I thought for a moment her beautiful porcelain face was going to crack. She put down the coffer gently, as though it were a sleeping baby. "Here, I brought you something to cheer you up."

Teresa's eyelids were drooping, but she forced herself to look at the box. I was sincerely curious. What did Doña Luisa keep in that exquisite coffer? Fragrant salts? Some kind of bonbon? If it was something sweet, I would have to step in and prevent her from giving it to Teresa. Candy would have a bad effect on her digestion. The duchess stroked the box tenderly, then took a tiny gold key from her sleeve and opened it.

Teresa looked inside and swallowed hard, as if trying to stifle a laugh. Her chin and the corners of her lips twitched. "Lovely," she gasped. In spite of the pain in her chest, she was overcome with mirth and had to cough violently to camouflage it. I peered inside the box. The duchess's jewelry was arranged in neat little rows: diamond earrings, a garnet ring, thick gold bracelets, an emerald and diamond necklace, and several brooches with sapphires, rubies, and pearls.

Doña Luisa smiled radiantly. "I'm so glad you like it. I thought it would lift your spirits."

"It's beautiful, Your Ladyship. But please excuse me. I'm a bit faint." She sank back into the pillows as though she were overcome with vertigo.

When we were sure she was out of earshot, Teresa broke into laughter, holding her chest with one hand and wiping the tears that rolled down her cheeks with the other. "Imagine," she hiccoughed. "She thought that her jewels would make me feel better. Her *jewels*!" Finally, Teresa regained her composure. "Poor Doña Luisa," she said, after a while "She was just trying to help."

By the time we left Doña Luisa's in early spring, Teresa had finished her memoir—which would someday be known as *The Book of Her Life*. She'd also won over Doña Luisa and some of her powerful friends to the cause of the reform. What a disappointment for Father Ángel de Salazar. He'd sent Teresa to Toledo to undermine her project, but instead he wound up advancing it. As we climbed into the carriage, María de Salazar came running after us. "Take me with you," she begged Teresa. "I want to be a nun!"

"When you devote as much attention to God as you do to your hair ribbons, you'll be welcome in my convent," said Teresa, and she kissed her on the cheek. Who could have suspected at the time that someday Teresa would come to see this frivolous child as her true spiritual daughter and successor?

Angélica del Sagrade Corazón, Carmelite

Toledo, 5 September 1576

CHAPTER 16

Miracles

Is it fair to resort to the Devil's tricks in the struggle against him? I admit that in the beginning we had recourse to subterfuge. Doña Guiomar had found a tiny house in San Roch, a neighborhood on the northern edge of Ávila, outside the city walls. Teresa's brother-in-law Juan de Ovalle left Juana and their two children, Gonzalo and Beatriz, at home in Alba de Tormes and quietly bought the property, then brought his family to occupy it. It seemed a likely enough thing for him to do. Juana was seven months pregnant, and it was only natural that she should want to be near her sister. The neighbors didn't suspect a thing. Every day Teresa told Mother Josefa she was going to Juana's, and indeed, that's where she was going. But the prioress was as shrewd as a cat. She knew something was up.

"My sister needs me, Mother," Teresa said with pretend meekness.

"Of course," said Mother Josefa, without looking up.

With me, she was less accommodating. "Juana's confinement is approaching," I told her, "and with my knowledge of herbs, I could be useful."

"What do you know about midwifery?" she growled. "You've never delivered a baby. Everything you know about medicine, I taught you, and I never taught you to deliver a baby."

"Still, I think I could be useful."

"Maybe you're assisting in some other kind of birth," she retorted. "If so, stop right now. I don't want you involved. Teresa could very well get herself thrown into prison, and I can't afford to have you rotting in some poke beside her, Angélica. You're the convent apothecary and the master seamstress. Teresa is expendable, but you're not. I love you both, but if I have to lose one of you, let it be her."

Once she got to her sister's, Teresa left Juana in my able hands (on the days I managed to go with her) and directed the workmen, who were busily turning the house into a convent. She had designed the chapel, the cells, the locutorium, the chapter room, the kitchen, the refectory, and a garden with tiny hermitages where the nuns could retire to pray. Ovalle had put up most of the money for the house. Doña Guiomar had helped, and María de Ocampo had contributed her small inheritance. Teresa didn't have enough to pay the workmen, but she wasn't worried.

"Saint Joseph himself promised to provide," she told me. "He appeared to me one night, and do you know what he said, Angélica?"

"He said, 'Don't worry, Teresa. I'll send over a dozen angels who'll work for free.'"

"All right, go ahead and make fun of me."

"'They won't eat, so you won't have to feed them, they won't shit, so you won't have to build an outhouse, and they'll wear work clothes, so the neighbors won't even notice them.'"

"Saint Joseph is my favorite saint," she said, ignoring me. "He always comes through."

She was right. Teresa is always right. Well, usually. That's why she's the leader of the reform, and I'm just the leader of the sewing brigade. As a reward for his coming through or maybe just as an expression of her devotion, she named the convent San José and even had a lovely statue of him leading the child Jesus by the hand placed at the entrance. Maybe the work really was done by angels because, even though the masons dug and laid stone and the carpenters hammered and sawed, the neighbors never suspected what they were up to.

As the convent grew, so did the child in Juana's womb. The summer heat had swollen her feet so badly that she almost never left her *estrado*. She slept there, and also ate, sewed, and prayed there. That's also where she received Teresa, me, and Doña Guiomar. There was plenty for us to talk about. News had come from France that in March, the Duke of Guise, one of the most ardent leaders of the Catholic faction, had attacked a Protestant church service at Vassy, in the province of Champagne, and slaughtered more than 1200 people—men, women, and children—all of them unarmed. Fighting was still going on all over the country, and every day innocents were dying. The talk of blood-drenched pews cast a pall over the *estrado*. Those who had died were heretics, of course. Even so, the duke's actions seemed extreme. "Pray for the poor Protestants," lamented Teresa. "Pray they see the light and return to Holy Mother Church."

Juana, once such a giggly little thing, sat in silence. Her wispy, girlish body had become bloated like a bullfrog's, and her skin had taken on a greenish tinge. Her lips had shrunk into a thin, cracked, parchment-like film. She seemed hardly to hear our chatter, but instead, stared into space, opening and closing her mouth in silence, like an aquatic creature floating in a pond. I had forebodings about this pregnancy. It's true, I'd never attended a pregnant woman, but I knew the signs of fatigue and dehydration.

It was early July, and the laborers were making progress on the new convent. I'd just bathed Juana's feet in cold water and rubbed them with salts to make the swelling go down. The screech of crickets sounded like an invasion of devils. That's because it was stifling. Everyone knows you can tell how hot it is by counting the number of chirps a cricket makes in a minute. The more chirps, the more it swelters. Now the crickets were chirping so fast their cry sounded otherworldly. I went to prepare dinner, but Teresa flitted around, unable to contain her excitement. In less than two or three months we'd be able to move into San José.

"Please, Teresa, sit down and eat," gasped Juana.

"You eat. I'll just take a quick peek at the chapel to see how the floor's coming along."

"It's a plain stone floor, Teresa. What is there to check?"

The rest of us sat down to plates of cold meats, artichoke, marigold leaves, and onions. To drink there were iced juices: cider, perry, raspberry. Afterward, a maid brought fruits and cheeses. The perfume of freshly peeled oranges filled the room. I closed my eyes and felt the sweet, sticky juice trickle down my throat. I was excited and happy. It's true we were risking the wrath of a lot of important townspeople, but the meal and iced perry had left me feeling buoyant. Everything would work out, I told myself.

I imagined Teresa kneeling before the pope, her head nearly touching the floor. The pope looked stern, his rheumy eyes fixed on the stooped body before him, his long nose hooked slightly over a broad white mustache that extended from his upper lip to the sides of his face, then burst into a billowy white beard that covered his chin, neck, and chest. In my mind he looked very old and gaunt. He wore a deep red chasuble over a not-quite-white alb and a biretta of the same red color as his chasuble. Suddenly, his lips parted into an unexpected smile. "Teresa, you naughty nun," he said kindly. "You've outsmarted all those pompous prelates. Good for you. Now go in peace and enjoy your new convent. And please, pray for me, my child, poor sinner that I am." Of course, I've never seen the pope. I have no idea what he looks like.

After the meal Juana took her rosary and tottered to her bed and lay down. She always slept with her prayer beads. The rest of us curled up, heads on cushions, and dozed off. Teresa hadn't eaten and still wasn't back from surveying the workmen's progress.

A sudden noise, like rocks crashing to the ground from a very high place, sent Juana's rosary flying to the floor. "My God, what was that!"

Staccato shrieks filled the air like the sputtering of a doused fire. The noise came from the direction of the construction area. I tried to make out the voices. One of them was Teresa's. What if she'd fallen on a loose stone and broken her leg? I thought. What if an unstable wall had collapsed and injured her? Men's voices were becoming audible now. One of them was Juan de Ovalle's, but the others I didn't recognize.

Doña Guiomar and I darted toward the door. Juana was hobbling along behind us, groping at furniture to keep her balance. "Come," I told her. "Take my hand."

Doña Guiomar arrived first. Her scream triggered a stabbing pain that went from my molars to my temples, like when you bite into something too cold. "It's Gonzalo!" she shrieked. "It's little Gonzalo!"

"Oh, no!" whimpered Juana. "Oh God, no! Not my baby!"

I struggled to steady her, pressing against her bulk with my entire body. Her weight against my arm and shoulder made my other arm dance crazily. We made our way down the stairs and through the patio to the construction area. Teresa was stooping over the inert body of five-year-old Gonzalo. Juan de Ovalle and some of the workmen hovered nearby. Juan sobbed softly, his face in his hands, his body bowed like an old man's. *Mi hijo,* he whispered. *Mi hijito está muerto.* My little son is dead. Oh, God, oh God, anything but this. Strike me down instead, God. Don't take little Gonzalo away."

He lifted his head to see his wife standing there, her thin, cracked lips twisted into a silent cry, her eyes fixed on the body of her child, who lay still and white on the recently laid stones.

"My poor Juana," he sobbed. "My poor, poor Juana. Our baby, our Gonzalo . . ."

"We had just returned from our siesta," said the master mason. "We were getting back to work." The man was visibly shaken. "All of a sudden, the retaining wall collapsed right on top of the boy. What was he doing there? He must have been poking his nose into things, the way boys do. But this is no place for a child to be playing."

"Where was Cristina?" wailed Juana. "Where was his nursemaid?" She looked feverish.

"Gonzalo probably snuck out after she lay down for the *siesta*," stammered Juan.

"Bring that woman to me," commanded Juana, her voice suddenly husky. "She murdered my child with her incompetence! She was supposed to be watching him, keeping him safe! Why was she sleeping?" She started to wail uncontrollably.

"No," said Teresa softly.

"No?" snarled Juana. "Who are you to tell me no? What do you know of what a mother feels at a time like this? It's easy for you to play the saint. You don't have to deal with real problems. You don't have children."

"The child will live," said Teresa firmly.

Juana had metamorphosed into some unrecognizable creature. Her veins throbbed in her swollen neck. "What are you talking about? I can see he's dead!" She was shaking convulsively.

I knelt by the limp body, took his wrist in my hand and felt his pulse. I knew Teresa was right. "He'll live," I whispered.

Juana, out of her mind with grief, didn't hear me. Juan slipped his arm around her shoulder and tried to calm her, but she kept on moaning.

The nursemaid, Cristina, came running, tripping over her ham-toed feet. "*¡Dios mío! ¿Qué le ha pasado a Gonzalito?* What happened to little Gonzalo?"

Juana lifted her head and looked at the woman as though she were about to lunge for her throat. Then, suddenly, she sank to the ground, a rumpled heap of flesh and fabric. Her face was a frightening shade of crimson. Globs of mucus spilled from her nose and mouth. She was thrusting the fingernails of her right hand into the soft tissue of her inner left wrist.

"*Tía!*" No one heard the tiny voice except for Teresa and me.

I squatted next to Juana and put my hand on her shoulder. "Look at Gonzalito!" I said. "He's moving!"

Juana looked at me stupidly. "What?"

"Look at your son, Doña Juana! He's moving."

The child was squirming, looking from one adult to the other, trying to figure out what was going on. The master mason, a dark, lanky man with a thick mustache, opened his eyes wide, then fell to his knees. "The little boy is alive," he whispered. "She has saved him. It's true what they say about Doña Teresa. She works miracles." The other workmen imitated him.

Juana looked at her sister, who was still crouching over Gonzalo. "Teresa," she breathed. "Teresa, thank you."

"Give thanks to God, Juana."

"I'm sorry, Teresa. I'm sorry about what I said. I was so frightened."

"I know. Sometimes grief destroys our defenses. Then the Devil gets into our souls and makes us say stupid things. But now you must give thanks to the One who saved your child."

By the next morning the whole town knew that Teresa had performed a miracle: she had raised little Gonzalo from the dead. When she walked down the street, people fell on her like the locusts in the Book of Revelations. They begged for help, grabbing at her garments.

"Please, Mother, my baby is sick. Save him!"

"I don't have permission from the Holy Father in Rome to work miracles!" she told the supplicants, smiling kindly.

Did she know a stone had merely knocked little Gonzalo unconscious, or did she herself think she'd performed a miracle? Or maybe the whole incident was part of God's plan to make people take Teresa seriously. After all, God works in mysterious ways.

One by one Teresa's adversaries were turning into supporters. Daza. Salcedo. Even Álvarez. Or perhaps they just saw the handwriting on the wall. Teresa's fame was growing. News of her supernatural powers spread to Toledo and Valladolid. Those men weren't dimwits. They must have realized the crowds were with Teresa. Not only that, Doña Luisa de la Cerda had marshaled a legion of aristocratic supporters for the reform.

But wait a minute. This isn't a romance of chivalry, where the hero slays the dragon and everything just falls into place. Even though we had allies, Fray Ángel de Salazar, the provincial, was still furious with Teresa, and most of the Encarnación nuns were so resentful, they wouldn't even speak to us. It wasn't long before everything came crashing down with more force than the falling stones that had knocked Gonzalito unconscious. The refectory, the dormitory, and the chapel still weren't ready, and now, suddenly, the laborers seemed to be dragging their feet. In the morning we'd find the construction area vacant. No men. No tools. Nothing. Teresa sent for the master mason.

"I'm sorry, Madre," he apologized. "But we haven't been paid in weeks."

The color drained from Teresa's face. "How can this be? I thought Doña Guiomar was taking care of it."

"Doña Guiomar tells us *mañana, mañana,* but our wives and children need to eat today."

Teresa sighed. "This is God's work, *hijo.*"

The workman pursed his lips and stared straight ahead.

The fact is, Doña Guiomar was nearly out of money. When I went to see Teresa in her cell later that afternoon, I found her sitting on her bed like a man, legs apart and wrists resting on her knees. Her mouth was moving as though she were having a conversation. Every so often she'd sit up and gesticulate, making a point to some invisible interlocutor.

"Who are you talking to, Teresa?"

"Jesus, of course."

"And what does Jesus say? To forget the whole thing?"

"Of course not. He says, 'Don't worry about it, *hija.* I'll take care of everything.'"

"Does He say how?"

"He doesn't have to say how."

The next day Teresa asked Doña Guiomar to write to her mother, Doña Aldonza de Guzmán, for thirty ducats. Doña Guiomar balked.

"We have to finish this project," declared Teresa imperiously. "Jesus wants this done."

For the first time since I'd known her, I saw anger flash across Doña Guiomar's face. "I've given you everything I have, Sister Teresa. I can't give you any more." Her eyes were steady. I was sure she wouldn't back down. "Maybe God doesn't want this convent," she added. "Maybe that's why He allowed that wall to fall."

Teresa held her ground. "The Devil knocked down that wall, not God. And since it was the Devil who knocked it down, I will raise it up again. That is what God wants."

"How do *you* know what God wants?" Rage was thrashing around in Doña Guiomar's breast like a caged animal. The two women stared at each other. "Well," snapped Doña Guiomar, "if that's what God wants, let Him provide the money."

"He has," said Teresa with excruciating calm.

"Really? Where is it?"

"In your mother's purse."

Doña Guiomar took a deep breath, and then began to sob softly. She sat down, wrote a note to Doña Aldonza, and called for a messenger.

Within days, the thirty ducats arrived, and work on the convent continued. "Praise be to God," exulted Teresa. Her friend smiled weakly.

Teresa was talking to Jesus all the time now. He was her personal advisor, architectural consultant, and financial manager. But when Juan de Ovalle looked up to Heaven, he didn't see Our Savior. What he saw was a black cloud hanging right over his house in San Roch. As far as he was concerned, everything was going wrong. The work was shoddy. The workers were behind schedule. The neighbors were beginning to look at him in a funny way. Worst of all, Doña Guiomar had sworn she was not going to endure the humiliation of asking her mother for any more money. Ovalle was beginning to think Teresa should cut her losses and give up.

Teresa paced back and forth in the unfinished refectory, chewing on her lip and making guttural noises. She ran her finger over unfinished walls and kicked loose floor stones out of the way. Work had once again come to a standstill. There was nothing we could do but pray.

One morning we went out to the courtyard to sweep up debris and tidy abandoned piles of granite. Hell couldn't be hotter than Ávila in August. The heat clung to my forehead like a fever, and translucent braids of vapor rose from the ground. On that day, even I, witness to Teresa's conversations with Jesus, was beginning to doubt the sanity of this project.

A maid appeared in the yard. "Sister has callers," she said meekly.

"Callers? I'm not expecting callers," said Teresa. She turned to me and shrugged. We followed the maid into the house.

Two men in merchants' garb were waiting. They appeared to be Spaniards, but spoke Castilian in a strange way, interjecting words we'd never heard before. They wore doublets with wide sleeves adorned with straight slits called *acuchillados*, very fashionable at the time, and thick gold chains with medallions. But the colors of their suits were garish, greens and blues not normally used in Spain. They turned out to be silver merchants whose business had taken them first to Mexico, then to New Granada and Peru. Teresa mustered a smile, wiped the sweat from her cheeks, and ordered the maid to fetch refreshments.

One of the men handed Teresa a package. She turned it over and examined the seal. "It's from my brother Lorenzo," she said. A smile crept to her lips.

When the merchants had left, she sat down and tugged at the covering. The package was wrapped in a coarse cloth, under which a layer of straw protected a pouch. The straw smelled old and damp and moldy. I thought perhaps it had been stored in a dank place—perhaps a ship's hull—for a long time. Teresa ripped the thread that held the pouch shut. At last, she came to a sealed letter and two other pouches, one the size of a coin, the other a bit larger. She undid the catch of the first, and out fell a heavy gold medal worth at least a hundred ducats. "God bless my brother Lorenzo!" she squealed. Then she opened the second purse, and out poured heaps of silver and gold. Finally, she slit the envelope and pulled out Lorenzo's letter. It said she should sell the medal if she needed more cash to finish construction of the new convent.

"God promised to provide," cried Teresa, weeping for joy, "and He did."

It was Monday, August 24, 1562, when we ventured out past midnight. The blacksmith's forge was silent and no glow was visible in the brazier's workshop. The mercer, the miller, the cooper, the tanner, and the arrowsmith had put down their tools for the day. A mauve owl, perched on a deep purple branch, hooted softly, and the dogs of Ávila, midnight marauders, advanced like grey smears against the grey stones of the town arcade. The warm August night was alive with fairies and fireflies. In the sky, a blithe moon danced, her hemispherical skirts spread wide. She was rejoicing. We had just won our first victory. The three of us—Doña Guiomar, Teresa, and I—hurried down the street, sometimes tripping over our skirts in the shadows. On the way, we thanked God for His favor and thanked the moon for her light, for in order to avoid the neighbors' watchful eyes, we carried no lanterns.

The next morning, as the sun rose over the knolls, the bells of all the churches and convents in Ávila clanged in unison to call the faithful to prayer. To the familiar sound of the bells of San Gil, Santo Tomás, Santa Ana, Nuestra Señora de la Gracia, and Encarnación, the tinny-sounding bell of San José added its clink-clink. It was a tiny bell that had come from the foundry with a hole in it. All the better, said Teresa, since its hole made it nice and cheap. The neighbors were astounded. They'd seen workmen come and go for months at Juan de Ovalle's house, never realizing the place was being turned into a convent.

Father Daza, now a vociferous ally, said Mass, and Teresa presented four novices to become the convent's first inhabitants. The women received their habits and took new names. Úrsula de Revilla became Úrsula de los Santos; Antonia de Henao, Antonia del Espíritu Santo; María de Ocampo, María

Bautista; and María de Ávila, María de San José. It was then that Teresa de Ahumada took the name Teresa de Jesús and I became Angélica del Sagrado Corazón instead of just Sister Angélica. The nuns were formally encloistered, and it was done. Teresa had founded her convent, the Carmel of San José de Ávila, the first discalced Carmelite convent in the history of the world.

Afterward, Úrsula, Antonia, and the two Marías scampered around like frisky kittens, setting the sewing room in order, hanging pots from hooks in the kitchen, decorating the dormitory with images and crosses. Teresa and I settled in by the window, watching and purring like two fluffy old cats in the sunlight.

But like I said, this isn't a pretty romance where all the lords and ladies wind up happy and dancing the *paván*. Once the citizens of Ávila realized that Teresa had pulled the wool over their eyes, all hell broke loose. Fray Ángel, enraged, ordered Teresa and me back to Encarnación, so Teresa appointed Úrsula de los Santos to serve as prioress. The mayor, a certain Horacio Suárez, summoned the city council to discuss the terrible problem of the women who had occupied the house in San Roch, and the horrendous burden the new institution (with its enormous population of four sisters!) imposed on this town of wealthy merchants.

Mayor Suárez, accompanied by a throng of curious townspeople, came banging on the door. "I'm sorry," called Sister Úrsula through the crack. "This is a cloistered convent. No one is allowed in, and we don't go out." The mayor commanded the women to pack up and leave. "We only take orders from our superior, Mother Teresa," Úrsula shouted back.

The townspeople cheered him on—some, the same folks who only weeks before had called Teresa a saint and begged her to bless their children. But then, Suárez caught sight of the Blessed Sacrament. Our little chapel was very simple—plain white walls, a stone floor, wooden pews and a wooden altar—but Doña Guiomar had supplied a beautiful gold monstrance. It was shaped like a sunflower, its precious petals reaching outward to the Father, to the faithful, to the earth. In the center was an opening for the host, Jesus's sacred body, white and fragile. A glimpse of that holy vessel must have been enough to move Suárez's heart, because he suddenly turned and left. It was Teresa's first miracle at San José!

It was a Tuesday. Not Tuesday the thirteenth, the traditional bad-luck day, but Tuesday, nevertheless. As everyone knows, when bad things happen, it's usually on a Tuesday. But that week, every day was a bad-luck day. On

Wednesday morning the mayor met with the city council. I wasn't there, of course. Women weren't allowed to attend the meetings. But I can just imagine the town bigwigs strutting about, their black doublets and gold braid, their wide black hats with multicolored plumes, crows masquerading as peacocks, all squawking, all cawing, all deliberating on the very serious matter of the four discalced Carmelite nuns who were determined to live in poverty and eat almost nothing, but were certain to break the city's coffers.

On Sunday, after Mass, representatives of the nobility, the gentry, the merchants and the learned assembled in the town hall to deliberate. Apparently, San José represented a menace to Ávila as portentous as pestilence, fire, flooding, or a second Moorish invasion.

Now the bishop rises. He's a magnificent specimen, a glossy raven in his *zimarra,* the black, cassock-like garment of his rank, with its manly shoulder cape trimmed in amaranth and his violet sash. All beaks turn toward him, all glassy gazes rest on his large, gold, pectoral cross. "Brothers in Christ," he begins. "In general, I agree with you. We cannot just accept innovations willy-nilly, nor can we allow an excessive number of religious houses to be founded in a small area." Chirps of approval. Twitters of delight. "However, I must tell you that permission to found this convent was duly applied for and was given with my consent. His most Holy Father in Rome, Pope Pío IV, has issued this Brief." He then goes on to read the papal document giving permission for the foundation. Teresa had played by the rules.

That should have been the end of it, but the Devil always plays dirty. Now the stonecutter Lázaro Dávila, Inspector of Wells, comes forward. He is worried about certain constructions he has noticed in the convent yard.

"Hermitages, tiny retreats where the nuns can meditate or pray," says someone.

"Let them pray somewhere else," growls the Inspector of Wells. "Those hermitages or outhouses or whatever they are inflict material damage on that sector of the city. One of them shuts off the sunlight from a small vaulted edifice that shelters public springs. Without the sunlight, the water will freeze in the winter, leaving that section of the city almost dry."

The mob grows angrier. Hysteria sets in. People call for the Inquisition, for a royal investigation. They call for God Himself to send a lightning bolt to strike down the nuns of San José. Nearly everyone has turned against us. Where are our friends the Jesuits? Not one of them rises to defend Teresa. The only man to put in a good word for her is the young Dominican,

Domingo Báñez. I can imagine him standing there dressed in the white wool tunic and black cloak of his order. (The followers of Saint Dominic wear wool, even in the summer). He looks like a white-breasted black swan, tall and svelte and graceful. "It may seem foolish to contest the findings of such eminent citizens who have advanced such convincing arguments," he begins, and then goes on to do just that.

Finally, the city council proposed a compromise. Teresa could keep her convent, provided she accept a sponsor. If San José were endowed, said the town fathers, it would be less of a threat to the community, because the citizens of Ávila wouldn't have to support it.

Teresa knelt before the image of Our Lady and prayed for guidance. The shadows of the statue grew longer and darker. The Virgin herself yawned with exhaustion, and still, Teresa prayed, her head bowed, her eyes shut. Finally, she got up and went to her cell.

"What did the Holy Mother tell you?" I asked.

"She didn't tell me anything. Neither did Saint Joseph or Jesus. They must be on holiday." Teresa sighed and stared out the window at the heavy autumn sun.

"What are you going to do?"

"Find a sponsor, I guess. Otherwise they'll close San José."

"Wait a few days. Maybe God will send an answer."

"I can't let them close the convent. So many people have made so many sacrifices, including you, Angélica." She looked exhausted.

The next day, she met with Daza. He advised her to give in. He'd find her a worthy sponsor, he said. She squinted and rubbed her temples as if she had a migraine. "At least, with a sponsor, the nuns won't starve," she sighed.

"It's not what you wanted."

"No, I didn't want to be beholden to anyone. I wanted independence. If you have a sponsor, he'll have something to say about how you run your convent. Well," she said wearily, "I guess a partial victory is better than no victory at all."

That night I fell asleep the instant my head touched the stone I now used for a pillow. I dreamt about the city council, all gathered in the *municipio*, only instead of human heads they had bird heads. All of a sudden I heard a banging at my door. I thought it was part of the dream, that a band of Jesuit chicken hawks was demanding access to the meeting, but then I opened my eyes and saw Sister Radegunda standing over me, a lamp in her hand. "Get dressed," she ordered. "Teresa needs you." I thought she must be sick again, but I found her throwing things into an overnight bag by candlelight. "It's my sister," she said. "Juana has gone into labor."

With all the uproar over the new convent, I'd practically forgotten Juana. By the time we arrived at the house in San Roch, it was almost over. The midwife was lifting the baby from between Juana's legs. I sponged Juana's forehead while the midwife cut the cord, cleaned the infant, and then handed him to his mother to nurse. The child suckled only a moment before releasing the nipple. To me he appeared sickly, but I held my tongue in order not to alarm the family. "His name will be Josepe," whispered Juana before falling into a fitful sleep.

Teresa took the newborn in her arms and looked into his thin little face. Then she turned to me and raised an eyebrow, as if asking my prognosis. I bit my lip and shook my head slightly. She repeated the gesture, this time directing her gaze toward the midwife. The woman looked down and pretended to wash her equipment.

"May it please God to take this little angel," whispered Teresa, "before he offends Him."

Three weeks later Josepe died, and the whole town was once again abuzz with talk of miracles. "Teresa de Ahumada is a seer," people said. "She foresaw the death of her little nephew." Then they remembered about Gonzalo. "This is her second miracle," said others. "Don't forget she brought her other little nephew back from death."

The day Juana gave birth, we returned to Encarnación in the late afternoon. We hadn't eaten since the day before, and Teresa was famished. Mother Josefa ordered that dinner be brought, although the other nuns had eaten hours before. After supper, Teresa fell asleep in her cell and slept all through the night. The next morning, she awoke refreshed.

"Do you know who I saw last night?" she asked. "I saw Fray Pedro de Alcántara."

"Fray Pedro isn't in Ávila," I said, suspecting what was coming. "I think he's in Rome."

"Maybe, but I saw him. He told me not to compromise on the matter of sponsors, not to accept Daza's offer. Today I'm going to send my response to the city council."

The city leaders were furious. They called her capricious and stubborn. The battle wore on for the next three weeks, but Josepito's death had weakened the opposition. By Christmas, Teresa had won the battle. Fray Ángel allowed the two of us to move into San José. Finally, I thought, this is over.

But a few months later, Teresa awakened in the middle of the night and came running to my cell. "Angélica," she cried, "wake up! I just had a wonderful vision! I saw Jesus, and do you know what He said? He said, 'Teresa, my daughter, San José was just the beginning. I want you to found many more convents, all of them in poverty, without endowments.' Isn't that thrilling, Angélica? We've only just begun!"

I rolled over and closed my eyes. "Go away and let me sleep," I grumbled.

Angélica del Sagardo Corazón
Toledo, 12 September 1576

PART III
From Ávila to Heaven

CHAPTER 17

Deliver Us from Evil

SERGE IS AN EVEN-SIDED, TWILL-WEAVE, WORSTED FABRIC SUITABLE FOR BOTH men's and women's clothing. My Tía Cati taught me to make serge when I was just a child. You sew a two-up, two-down diagonal pattern, sometimes with a contrasting color, if what you want is to make something very imaginative and original. Serge is very durable, which is why it has been used since the beginning of history—well, maybe not that long, but for a long time— for nun's habits. The important point here is that serge is highly resistant to fleas.

No sooner had the four novices settled into their new convent than María Bautista (always one to take things to extremes) decided that our serge habits were just too comfortable. "How can we be one with Jesus if we don't suffer as he did?" she complained to Teresa, now installed as prioress of San José. "Instead of soft, serge habits," argued María, "we should be wearing coarse sackcloth." Teresa thought about it. It seemed logical that discalced Carmelites should wear bristly material in honor of Christ's passion, but before giving permission, she decided to try out the idea herself. She cut a tunic of sackcloth and wore it for a few days. It seemed to work. The new attire was serviceable and appropriately prickly. The novices followed suit, and soon we were all wearing sackcloth habits.

I was the first to complain. The new habits were too itchy. "They're supposed to be itchy," said María. "We're suffering for Jesus." Every night when I took off my habit, I examined my arms and calves. They were covered with red welts, not welts caused by the barbed filaments of sackcloth, but by some insect. They were fleabites! The new habits were breeding grounds for fleas. All the women agreed: something had to be done.

As usual, María had the answer. "What's the best insecticide around?" she asked.

"White arsenic," I said. "Or else potash, or sulphur. It depends what you're trying to kill." "No," said María. "The solution to every ill is Jesus. We should have a procession."

It seemed logical to everyone else, so I went along with it. The next morning before dawn, we each lit a candle and filed from our cells to the choir, where Teresa knelt in prayer. María Bautista led the procession carrying a small crucifix high above her head. As we processed we sang psalms: "Come, let us cry out with joy to Yahweh, / acclaim the rock of our salvation. / Let us come into his presence with thanksgiving, / acclaim him with music." And then, against our enemies, the fleas: "He turns back their guilt on themselves, / annihilates them for their wickedness, / he annihilates them, Yahweh our God." When we arrived at the choir, each of us prostrated herself before the large crucifix in the sanctuary. I thought the situation called for *coplas*. Teresa, who composed poetry for every celebration, thought a minute, then improvised.

Hijas, pues tomáis la Cruz,	Daughters, accept your Cross
tened valor,	and be brave,
y a Jesús, que es vuestra luz,	look to Jesus, your light,
pedid favor,	He who gave
Él os será defensor	Everything to defend you from
en trance tal.	Dangers grave.

To which we responded:

Pues nos dais vestido nuevo,	Since you've given us new habits,
Rey celestial,	Heavenly King, please
librad de la mala gente	Free them from evil critters
este sayal.	such as fleas.

Teresa took a large vial of holy water and a cross. The procession wound its way through the convent—around the refectory, the laundry, the pharmacy, the cells, the locutorium, the patio. As we processed, she sang, "*Hijas, pues tomáis la Cruz, / tened valor, / y a Jesús . . .*" and we responded, "*Pues nos dais vestido nuevo . . .*" She flicked drops over everything from chairs to dirty linen, taking special care to douse the habits. She skipped along like a kid in a pasture—and don't forget she was nearly fifty. "*Hijas, pues tomáis la Cruz, / tened valor, / y a Jesús . . .*" She didn't have a great voice, but her singing made us giddy. She grabbed her tambourine, and the rhythmic jingling made her sing all the louder.

What a beautiful morning! The clink and tinkle of bells, the not-quite-seraphic voices of the not-quite-in-tune San José sisters! And the best part is that it worked! I don't know if processions are always such effective insecticides, but the truth is, after that, San José was never again troubled with fleas, and the same is true of other discalced Carmelite convents. No fleas. Ever. Anywhere. Of course, it's also true that we burned the sackcloth habits and started wearing burlap, which is made of jute, not hemp or flax, like sackcloth, and is as resistant to fleas as serge.

Those were wonderful years. San José was such a small convent that each of us had several jobs. I ran the sewing room, the laundry room, and the pharmacy. I also tended the herb garden, where I planted shoots I needed for cures. Before long we started to grow. Juana Isabel and Radegunda joined us, becoming novice mistress and chief cook. Then came Marcela, who was cellaress but whose real talent was writing doggerel for feast days and professions. Teresa put a limit of thirteen on the convent, so we remained a small, happy, active group.

Whenever a new nun professed, we gathered in the meeting room to celebrate and put on skits. We were poor and sometimes didn't even have a loaf of bread to divide among us, but we turned it into a joke and killed our hunger with laughter. For one profession, Sister Marcela wrote this poem, making fun of herself and the other two cellaresses, Mariana and Escolástica:

POEM DESCRIBING A VERY POOR CONVENT

It had cellaresses so terrible,
their cruelty's verifiable
their personality's just miserable,
thoroughly despicable.
One tyrant was marcelicle,
The other quite marianicle,
Which means a meal's a miracle,
And probably inedible.
And then, there's Escolástica,
As shrewd as she's contemptible,
Her nastiness unforgivable,

in no way justifiable.
But it's really not practical
To complain about Escolástica.
She controls all our victuals,
Which she serves in little particles.
None of them's magnanimous,
Kind or simpáticas,
But they're quite unintelligent
To get on the wrong side of us.
Because we can get fanatical,
Vengeful and implacable,
When we're feeling ravenous,
Angry and cantankerous.
So I'll end my little canticle,
But it really is quite pitiful,
We can't eat just a bitiful
Of something rich or succulent.
I wish they were more lovable
Kind, sweet and adorable,
Instead of just deplorable,
But I won't say any morable.

She left us in stitches, the way she played on her and Mariana's names—
"marcelicle," "mariancle"—I don't know whether my stomach hurt more
from laughing or from hunger. Although on that particular day, we did eat
better than usual. Radegunda made *yemas,* and after the clothing ceremony
we sat around the fire eating bonbons, listening to Marcela's poems, and putting on skits. In one of them, a poor student comes to the door and begs for
food, only to discover the nuns are so poor, even the mice have abandoned
the larder. When the cellaress refuses to give him even a crumb, he curses all
the sisters in the convent in the most awful language.

Sor Bitch, Sor Witch, Sor Miserly!
You, virtue? What hypocrisy!
I curse your greed and perfidy,
Your maleficent inhumanity!

I played the student, and I have to say, I must have a knack for acting, because Juana Isabel and Radegunda laughed so hard they wet their under-skirts. Silence at San José was sacred, but so was laughter. Teresa also wrote a poem, but hers was serious. After all, she was the prioress.

Dichoso el corazón enamorado	Happy is the enamored heart
que en sólo Dios ha puesto el pensamiento,	that puts its thoughts only in God,
por Él renuncia todo lo crïado,	renouncing for Him all created things,
y en Él halla su gloria y su contento.	finding in Him its glory and joy.
Aun de sí mismo vive descuidado,	It lives unconcerned for its own well being
porque en su Dios está todo su intento,	because God alone is its objective,
y así alegre pasa y muy gozoso	and so it weathers cheerfully, joyfully
las ondas de este mar tempestüoso.	the thrashing of the tempestuous sea.

Oh, I admit it was difficult at first. When we lived at Encarnación, we could go out to San Gil, to Doña Guiomar's, or to visit Teresa's sisters. We could gossip at the grille. At San José we lived cloistered and in silence, speaking only when necessary or during the *recreos*.

One thing Teresa was very strict about was what she called "special friendships." There could be no best friends or cliques that excluded this one or that one, no touching or kissing, no walking arm-in-arm in the garden, as close friends sometimes do. Women like Cándida, who had once grabbed Teresa's breast, well, they weren't allowed. The rule about special friends troubled me at first. Teresa and I were like sisters. Did this mean we could no longer be close? Did it mean we could no longer share secrets or give each other a pat of encouragement once in a while? But as it turned out, nothing changed between us. What Teresa wanted to do was provide an environment conducive to a prayerful life, not turn herself into a tyrant. She didn't go around flicking the switch at nuns who gave each other an occasional sisterly hug. It was gossip and cliquishness she worried about. That and women like Cándida.

We had a small locutorium with a grille, where we could receive family members and friends. María Bautista thought there should be no visitors at all, but Teresa said that was too severe. "Women need conversation," she insisted. "Otherwise, they'll go crazy." But with visitors we were supposed to talk only about God, never about the affairs of the world. The extern was to monitor conversations and report inappropriate chatter to the prioress. The penalty for breaking the rule was nine days in the convent prison, with a public scourging in the refectory on the third. "Discipline is essential to the order," insisted Teresa. "Obedience is the most sacred of our vows. Submission to the prioress is a way of restraining the will, of keeping one's sense of one's own importance in check. Obedience makes us holy." She said these things, and yet, as I said, she wasn't a tyrant. "Rules don't exist for their own sake," she insisted. "What's the point of being a slave to rules if your rigor makes you cruel, rather than sensitive to the needs of your sisters?"

Teresa refused to check up on the lineage of her nuns. After all, how could she, the daughter and granddaughter of Jews, insist on "purity of blood"? At San José, there was no distinction between Old and New Christians, between ladies and commoners. True to her word, she abolished titles. There were no *doñas* or *señoras*, only sisters. Even so, she kept the traditional two-tiered system of black-veiled and white-veiled nuns. Once there were enough sisters, black-veiled nuns performed the more intellectual duties—administration, accounting, chronicling—while white-veiled nuns performed manual tasks, like scrubbing pots and chopping wood. Later, when Teresa wrote the constitution of the order, she stipulated that all nuns had to learn to read. Only black-veiled nuns had to learn to write, though. Usually the white-veiled nuns were poor girls used to doing heavy lifting and content to sign their names with an *X*. But when Teresa saw that one of them had talent and potential, she made her learn to write and take the black veil.

The habits themselves were black, although later we adopted brown. We were allowed no ornamentation, no color at all. Choir mantels were of the same rough material as the habits, but white. On our feet we wore hemp sandals, with stockings of tow, not for warmth, but out of modesty. The cells were small. Mirrors were forbidden. The beds had no mattresses, only bags of straw covered in cloth, except in the case of sick nuns, who were allowed sturdy beds with mattresses and whatever else they needed to recuperate. For pillows we used stones. We ate no meat, except on Thursdays, when we were allowed some sort of poultry—chicken, plover, partridge, dove, or goose. During Lent we had a piece of salted cod. In our ovens we baked coarse bread, and in our garden we grew vegetables and fruits, which we dried for the winter. Sometimes there was so little to eat that Radegunda had to cut a turnip into a dozen pieces to make it go around. Once in a while the mother of a novice sent some jam or cheese.

Does this sound austere? Yes, I think I've made our lives sound a bit ascetic, but the truth is, it was wonderful. No gossip. No politics. No kissing Sister So-and-So's ass because she was the niece of Bishop Something-or-Other. Convent life isn't that different from life at court—well, I've never been to court, it's true, but I can imagine the shifting alliances and power plays. At San José, you could just pray and work and think about God without distractions.

I think it was during those days at the new convent that I felt closest to the Lord. In the spring, I rejoiced in the morning sun, in the purple saffron flowers pushing their heads through the still hard soil, in the novices saying their prayers. In the summer, I saw God in every marigold, every shoot of mint, every cooing dove in the dovecote. I delighted in the hectic goings-on of honey-gathering bees, in the frantic flirtations of sparrows and jays. I heard God in the singing of Radegunda as she boiled fruits for the preserves we would use when the ground slept. Fall brought the cooling relief of God's fresh breath on my cheek, the consoling beauty of red, orange, and gold leaves wafting unhurriedly toward the fading flowerbeds. In the winter, I could feel God's love in the steady, soundless fall of snowflakes and in the relaxed movements of sisters stitching silently by the crackling fire. I sensed God's graciousness in Apolo, the convent cat, who began his day with a prayer of thanks, stretching and bowing his head. We named him for a pagan god because he wasn't baptized, and yet, he clearly had a sense of the divine. What holiness there is in a cat who curls up on your lap and eases your anxiety by allowing you to run your fingers through its fluffy fur. Most of all, I felt God's love in our community of sisters, in the affection we had for one another, in the new kind of spiritual life we were forging.

Fray Julián de Ávila, brother of María de San José, was our chaplain. He was a jovial, self-effacing man, kind and patient. "Quick confessions, easy penances," was his motto. He was a native of our town, about twelve years younger than Teresa, and had studied philosophy with the Dominicans at Santo Tomás. As he told the story, one day, on his way back from school, he began to worry that his father would be angry at his tardiness, so instead of going home, he took off for Toledo. After wandering around Spain for several years, he settled in Córdoba, but eventually got homesick and decided to return home. On the way, his mule flinched at a jackrabbit and threw him. He fell on his sword and was so badly wounded that he almost died. While he was recuperating, he began to meditate on the fragility of life and decided to become a priest. When he finally made his way back to Ávila, he confessed to Father Daza, who facilitated reconciliation with his father. Fray Julián was ordained about four years before Teresa founded San José. Rumor had it that he had wanted to be a Jesuit, but, being of *converso* background, couldn't stand the sight of pork. Ever since the Jesuits of San Gil had expelled twenty-five *converso* priests, they'd become touchy about lineage. They manifested their *pureza de sangre* by serving Serrano ham at least twice a week. It was too much for Julián, so he became a Carmelite instead.

It was Daza who introduced him to Teresa, and Julián adored her with the kind of devotion one sees in dogs. He wasn't an original thinker or a brilliant administrator, but whatever Teresa wanted, he'd do. He'd get up in the middle of the night to hear the confession of an ailing nun or, later, when Teresa started to travel, drop everything to accompany her to some ramshackle inn in the middle of a godforsaken village. He never said no.

San José was like a peaceful island. Year followed year. Spring came on time, exuberant butterflies played tag in the garden, and blossoms splashed color over the earth. In the summer frisky rabbits stole our marigolds and performed their love rites, oblivious to the titters of consecrated virgins. Then came fall, with its cool evenings and smells of newly baled hay. In winter, dancing angels filled the night sky, only to be chased away, in springtime, by almond trees bulging with dainty white flowers. Every day the sun rose in the East and set in the West just the way it's supposed to. Vigils, Matins, Lauds, Prime, Terce, Sext, None, Vespers, Compline. Everything orderly, regular, methodical. God in His heaven and the sisters in their cells.

Although Teresa seemed happy enough, she had little time to enjoy the marigolds. She was busy revising her *Life,* since Father García de Toledo had commanded her to make certain corrections and to include a chapter on the founding of the new convent. As prioress, she had to oversee finances, secure supplies, attend to the upkeep of the building, interview prospective novices, and deal with her superiors. During the *recreo* she wrote, seated on a cushion by the window, paper and inkwell on the ledge. Even when the wind howled and rain battered the burlap window cover, making the candle flicker, she wrote. And then, after the rest of us went to bed, she wrote still more, often working hours past midnight. Not only did she have to finish her memoir, but she also had to make a copy of it to send to the censors. It was Christmas, 1565, when she handed the final manuscript to García de Toledo, who in turn sent it to Domingo Báñez, who in turn submitted it to the Inquisition in Toledo for its imprimatur.

García de Toledo had had Teresa write the book to prove her orthodoxy, but we all knew the project could backfire. The Council of Trent had inflamed the king's zeal for purity of faith. Don Felipe had been harsh before, but now he was ruthless. With his blessing, the Inquisition came down harder than ever on people claiming to be seers or mystics. Luther had accused Catholics of superstitiousness, and the council was determined to crack down on popular belief and unsubstantiated claims to holiness. Teresa's *Life,* full of descriptions of visions and ecstasies, was bound to be suspect. García decided to take preemptive action. He contacted Don Francisco de Soto, the inquisitor in charge of the case. Soto suggested Teresa send her *Life* to Juan de Ávila, a theologian of impeccable credentials, whose verdict he, Soto, promised to accept. Teresa sat down to begin the tedious job of making a second copy. When it was finished, she sent it to Doña Luisa de la Cerda, who was leaving soon for an estate near Fray Juan's monastery, and promised to deliver it to him. Five years later, the book was still in Doña Luisa's hands.

For the moment, these tempests passed right over me. For me, San José was like a little corner of paradise tucked away in San Roch. My life was perfect. I never wanted it to change. Of course, when the Devil sees souls at peace, he has to stir things up. Although I can't really blame the Devil, because this time God Himself was the culprit. He kept nudging Teresa to found another convent. He sent her visions, sometimes of angels, sometimes of Jesus, always telling her the same thing: Carry on with the reform. He must have been poking around at the Council of Trent too, because when it closed in 1563, the fathers announced that from then on, all nuns had to be cloistered. Our most gracious king had never been in favor of enclosure, but he was a stickler for rules, and now that the council had taken a stand, he begged the pope to send supervisors to make sure the Spanish orders were complying. Word soon came that Father Juan Bautista Rubeo, the Carmelite general, would be visiting Spain to enforce the council's reforms.

Teresa didn't expect problems from Rubeo. We already followed rules far stricter than those imposed by the Council. Our troubles came from elsewhere. News had spread all over Spain that a nun from Ávila had started a new convent that followed the primitive system of the desert fathers: poverty, silence, and mental prayer. Carmelites everywhere balked. In particular, the Andalusian brothers were enraged. Who was this arrogant woman? How dare she change the rules? They were a wild crew, those Andalusian

Carmelites, known more for whoring, gambling, and drinking than for piety. They adorned their habits with fancy buttons or else paraded around town in elegant street clothes. They got into brawls and carried daggers. Oh, I don't doubt they prayed. They prayed for luck at cards, for a good kill when they hunted, brave bulls at the bullfights, and buxom wenches at the taverns. The pope, spurred by the council's demand for reform, ordered an investigation of their conduct. It was Rubeo's job to force the unruly brothers into submission. "Make them behave!" His Holiness instructed. "Fat chance!" the friars responded when they heard Rubeo was coming.

Rubeo went first to Seville, where he was received with pitchforks and knives. He hightailed it out of there so fast his horses kicked up a dust storm on the way to Madrid, where he was supposed to meet with the king. However, that mission failed, too, since Don Felipe was reluctant to tangle with the powerful and politically connected Andalusian Carmelites, and refused to see him. There was nothing left for Rubeo to do but go back to Rome. However, before he left Spain, he wanted to confer with this reformist nun, Teresa de Jesús, about whom he'd heard so much and with whom he shared certain ideas about the value of austerity and discipline. He arranged for a meeting at the church of Nuestra Señora de la Anunciación, the Masonic-looking structure where we had once met Fray Pedro de Alcántara.

Teresa asked me to go along. She'd been trying to charm me into becoming her secretary for a while now, but I resisted. Teresa had a huge amount of correspondence, and she required two or three copies of every letter, since thieves—some of them working for the Inquisition—often waylaid couriers. She also needed someone to take notes at meetings and write up reports. These were tasks that had to be entrusted to someone absolutely dependable, someone capable of keeping secrets. I understood the situation, but still, I told her no. I liked my humdrum routine, and I didn't want any extra work. San José was supposed to offer repose and recollection. Why should I let Teresa lure me into a position that would expose me to politics and intrigue?

She could have ordered me to be her secretary. After all, she was the prioress. But that wasn't her way. "Forcing nuns into submission makes for unhappy nuns," she said, "and unhappy nuns do sloppy work." So instead, she begged. She wore me down. "Who else can I depend on? I can't manage without you, Angélica. Just this once." I'd been cloistered for five years. I was used to mixing compounds in the morning, sewing in the afternoon, and stroking Apolo after supper. The truth is, I was afraid to go out. But Teresa always got what she wanted.

The instant we left the convent, the afternoon assaulted me. The roar of the street—clattering hooves, cartwheels on cobblestones—gave me a headache. We made our way across the once familiar Plaza de San Jerónimo, and I stared at the houses and shops as though I'd never seen them before. We continued toward the city walls. Everything looked familiar, yet I had to say the names of places out loud in order to fix them in my mind. We entered intramural Ávila through the Puerta del Peso de la Harina. It was a cold, clear April morning. The blinding brightness of sunlight against stone made me squint. Our mules walked lazily, unperturbed by the iridescence of the red tile roofs. We crossed the Plaza de la Catedral. The sky was a fathomless, inverted, mother-of-pearl bowl. The majestic building—part temple, part fort—reached toward heaven, its towers and spires piercing the sheen. We headed toward the Plaza del Mercado Chico, then veered right toward the church. It wasn't such a long way, but by the time we arrived, I was panting and disoriented.

I don't know what I expected Rubeo to look like, but I didn't expect him to look like Christmas dinner. He had the head of a suckling pig, with feathery hairs sticking out of his ears like tender, young celery leaves. His torso reminded me of a partridge breast, broad and meaty. His hands were small and his fingers short like baby carrots. His legs, the outlines of which were visible under his habit, were fat at the thigh and narrow at the ankle, like parsnips. He burped unceremoniously when he saw us.

Teresa greeted him with deference. "Oh, Father Rubeo," she oozed, "what an honor for this poor, insignificant, little nun. I admit I don't know a thing about running convents. Fortunately, it's His Majesty Himself who guides my hand."

"Yes . . . well . . . I hear you're doing a magnificent job," stumbled Rubeo clumsily.

"If I am, it's because I have help." I looked up to see if she was going to give me some credit. "God Himself helps me," she went on. "He talks to me. He encourages me."

He nodded. "You are right to acknowledge your limitations, daughter."

I took notes while they talked. She explained the importance of mental prayer, through which the nuns maintained an active, dynamic relationship with God. She talked about recollection and interiority. She explained the need for absolute poverty, which enabled the nuns to avoid the temptations of the material world. She praised silence, essential to a nun's spiritual health. He lapped it up. When she was sure she had him in the palm of her hand, she squeezed. God wanted her to found other convents, she explained. He had told her so. He also wanted her to found friaries. In order for the reform to be successful, she said, she had to have a male branch, not only because the sisters needed confessors who understood their brand of spirituality, but also because an order consisting entirely of women would never be taken seriously.

Rubeo shrugged. He'd have to inspect San José, he said. If he liked what he saw, then he'd see. "Of course, Father," she said. "You're right, Father. I put myself entirely in your hands, Father. I submit to your authority."

"What the hell were you doing back there?" I hissed on our way back to San José. "Why are you kissing Rubeo's hindquarters like that?" She got that pious look on her face, the one that made her look like a constipated cherub. "No wonder he couldn't get anywhere with the Andalusian friars," I added. "He learned his manners at the King Herod School of Charm."

She turned and looked me right in the eye. "We need him, Angélica. In order to found more convents, I need patents. Only Rubeo can issue them. And he *will* issue them."

The minute we got back to San José I went to my cell and flung myself down on my sack of straw. I was exhausted, and my limbs ached. I skipped Vespers and Vigils, pretending to be sick, and I didn't respond to the supper bell, either. But I couldn't fall asleep. I heard Apolo creep out from under my bed and felt him nestle against my body. Before long, he was purring softly, and the steady "Rrr rrr" calmed my nerves.

When I was certain the others had retired for the night, I snuck my copy of my favorite pastoral novel, *The Seven Books of Diana,* out from its hiding place under my dirty laundry. I lit a candle, opened the volume to Book II, and began to read, "Love is such, beautiful Nymphs, that the lover is not subject to reason . . ." Who knows how long I read. The intricate love affairs of shepherds and shepherdesses lulled me. Reading brought me the kind of relief I got long ago, as a young woman, from touching certain sensitive parts of my body. I dozed off just before dawn and awoke with the terrible sensation that my routine was about to be shattered.

Teresa turned out to be right about Rubeo. On April 27 he issued a patent authorizing her to acquire "houses, churches, sites, and other property in any part of Castile subject to my jurisdiction, on behalf of the Order." He stipulated that both friars and nuns were to wear brown serge, and in no convent would they number more than twenty-five. Serge, not burlap. Teresa knelt before the statue of Our Lady and gave thanks.

Almost immediately, Teresa started making plans to found in Medina del Campo, about twenty-five leagues from Ávila. I had no intention of going with her. I'd found God at San José. I loved to listen to the monotonous drip-drip of raindrops on the eaves. Raindrops had been falling since the beginning of time, even as God set Adam in the Garden of Eden, and they would be falling at the time of the Apocalypse. My life would come and go, but raindrops were timeless. In the monotony of raindrops, I discovered Eternity. "No," I told Teresa, "I won't go."

"I need you, Angélica," she said sadly. I was sad, too. We hadn't been apart since we were children. "Jesus wants this new convent. It's our duty to go to Medina del Campo."

"No, Teresa. Every time you want someone to do something, you say it's Jesus's will."

"But it is!" Teresa de Ahumada had gotten her own way since she was a child. She tensed her jaw and pursed her lips. "This is God's will," she said firmly.

"Jesus told *you* to found convents, Teresa, but he never said a word about it to me."

"As your superior, I command you go with me to Medina, Sister Angélica."

I knew she didn't mean it. I looked at her calmly. "You're a hypocrite, Teresa," I said, without raising my voice. "You gave us the cloister so we could retreat from the world. Now you're in a snit because I won't leave San José to trudge over dusty roads with you."

Anger flashed in her eyes. Then she smiled faintly. I'd called her bluff.

"Pray for me while I'm away," she whispered, kissing my cheek.

"No kissing in the convent!" I laughed.

"Between sisters, it's okay," she said. "I mean, between real sisters. Anyhow, the spirit of the rule is more important than the rule itself."

I felt as though the nail were being yanked from my finger. But I couldn't go with her. I was happy at San José. I just couldn't give that up. "I'll pray for you," I said.

"I know." Her eyes were filled with tears.

Sister Angélica del Sagrado Corazón
Toledo, 20 September 1576

CHAPTER 18

Correspondences

TO BE HONEST, I'VE NEVER HAD A MYSTICAL EXPERIENCE. I'VE NEVER LOST myself in prayer to the point I became unaware of the boundaries of my being and merged completely with God. Sometimes I wonder what it would be like to see—or sense—Jesus standing by me. Sometimes I think, what if I was defecating into my chamber pot and suddenly Jesus was there? I mean, he doesn't tell you when he's coming. He's come to Teresa at the most outlandish times. Once she was in the kitchen slicing eggplants when she suddenly felt Jesus by her side. She almost cut off her finger, and I had to make her a plaster!

Jesus will never come to me because I'm not a good person. I broke my vow of chastity and besides, I read forbidden books. Teresa says that Jesus loves a sinner, and that we shouldn't try to figure out why He seems to favor some people and not others. I hope if Jesus ever does come to me, it won't be while I'm engaged in some embarrassing activity. But I suppose it wouldn't matter. No human activity is alien to Jesus, so I guess if He caught me peeing, I'd just have to say excuse me, Jesus, I need a minute to clean up, and then get on with the interview. I used to think about it sometimes, and it made me nervous. When I bathed or, when I was younger, I washed bloody menstrual rags, I tried to hurry so that Jesus wouldn't catch me doing something dirty. And now, when I read those delicious romances, which I admit I'm still addicted to, I worry even more because, at least bodily functions are beyond our control, but novels, well, I can't imagine they're part of God's divine plan.

Some of the other women at San José have mystical experiences all the time. Once, when Úrsula was meditating in her tiny hermitage in the garden, she saw three figures at the other end of the yard. They looked like workmen, and she thought they were gardeners come to prune the hedges. She was surprised because no one is allowed on the convent grounds, not even laborers. As she approached them, she saw they were translucent. Then, suddenly, they disappeared. "I understood they were angels," she said, "come to watch over us." I admit I felt jealous. No angels ever visited me. Teresa always said we should attend to our own souls and not pay attention to what graces God granted other people, but still, it didn't seem fair.

Sometimes I think about what it would be like to see Jesus. I imagine I'm in the pharmacy making lozenges from slippery elm bark (very good for coughs) or brewing celery seeds for Úrsula's rheumatism. Suddenly, (in my fantasy) I'm aware of a strange odor, slightly briny. Without looking up, I know it's Jesus, just back from fishing with the Apostles. I feel His breath on my skin, I sense his Sacred Humanity by my body. I want to cry, mixing the saltiness of my tears with the saltiness of His sweat, but I'm transfixed, unable even to blink. He doesn't speak. Everything is silence. The way I imagine Jesus, He doesn't have a booming voice that topples you with its intensity. Jesus speaks softly, almost inaudibly. What I think is this: that love sneaks up on you, it catches you unawares. Love whispers like a breeze, the drone of bees, the dullness of dripping water. Jesus doesn't tell me to found convents. He's just there. He just *is*. I've never had a vision, but I think that's what it would be like. Very hushed. Very gentle.

I missed Teresa. Every day I thought about her, but I was convinced I'd done the right thing by staying in Ávila. Úrsula was a competent, even-handed prioress. Things went on the way they always had, and I was happy in my routine. What broke the tedium was the letters.

I received four in 1567 and 1568. The first came from Medina, in the dead of winter. The courier could hardly make his way over the snow-laden roads. I recognized Teresa's handwriting right away, that distinctive scrawl that looked like it was produced by a horseman galloping full speed ahead, full of crossing out and half-written words that you were expected to reconstitute as you read. I imagined her writing in a moving cart on her way to a foundation, although I knew she always wrote crouched on the floor by a window. Her *v*'s were like a child's sloppy cartwheels, one leg flung out to the side, the other flopping in the opposite direction; her *t*'s, like broken crosses, with transverse bars drooping to one side; her *y*'s, like the rear end of a mouse traveling sideways and dragging its long tail. Her margins were sometimes jagged or slanted, but her lines were straight and easy to follow. Around that

time my eyes were beginning to weaken and I needed a reading stone to deci-
pher letters—probably God's punishment for my bad habit of reading
romances at night by candlelight.

It was a long, newsy letter. She talked about the Medina fair, probably
because she remembered how much I'd enjoyed looking at the stalls full of
wares in Toledo. The Medina fair was spectacular, she wrote. Tapestries from
Flanders. Silk from Valencia and Granada. Spices from India. The rest of the
letter was about the foundation. The money. The haggling. The patents. Fray
Julián had rented a house near the Augustian monastery, and the
Augustinians were up in arms because they thought the sisters would com-
pete with them for alms. Finally they'd found another house, but it was
falling apart. Renovations. Angry neighbors. I'd been through it all before,
when we founded San José. I did the right thing by staying here, I thought.

The next letter came about six months later, from Malagón, and brought
the sad news that Teresa's brother Fernando had died in Colombia. The rest
of the missive was less gloomy. Doña Luisa de la Cerda had given money for
a new convent on her property, about a day's journey to the south of Toledo,
where she had an ancestral castle. The only thing was, Teresa would have to
accept an endowment. "I know what you're thinking," she wrote. "I promised
I would found all my convents in poverty, but I have to be practical. I can't
afford to anger Doña Luisa." I shrugged. She was modifying her original plan,
just like a general who recalculates his maneuvers as circumstances change.
What of it? Another interesting piece of news had to do with a recently
ordained priest, a certain Fray Juan de la Cruz, who had turned up at a propitious moment offering help with the friaries. His timing couldn't have been
better. Teresa needed a male collaborator, and she was clearly quite taken with
this young man. "When I looked through the grille," she wrote, "do you know
what I saw? A boy, not more than twenty-five, so tiny he looked like a child
or a dwarf! I call him my 'half-friar' because he's so small. He was so composed
and articulate, so learned and perceptive, you would have thought he was
some elderly, erudite teacher from the Court of Rome. The soul has no sex or
age, Angélica. I'm twice as old as Fray Juan and a woman, and yet, I feel we're
kindred spirits." I yawned and threw down the page.

Teresa's reputation was growing. Or maybe that's an understatement.
Maybe I should say: Teresa was famous. Fray Julián brought news not only
of her activities, but also of what people were saying about her. They called
her a saint, he said, especially the common people. They liked her patched

habit and her earthy conversation. She put them at ease, and they flocked to her, women—and men, too—hungry for the kind of raw spirituality she taught, a simpler kind of spirituality that led people to seek the Lord in their own hearts. She showed them God's love in the ordinary and humdrum—a baby's crying, a simmering stew, a winter storm. She made them see that life's tragedies—illness, suffering, loss—are blessings because they remind us of Jesus's suffering. Well, good for her, I thought. Let her be a celebrity. I'm not going to let her drag me into her projects. I'm a simple woman with simple tastes. I want to be left alone.

Fray Julián wrung his hands. The authorities were gnashing their teeth, he said. The provincial, Fray Ángel, was incensed because Teresa had over-stepped her bounds. She'd already founded three convents and now there were rumors of a fourth, in Valladolid. *Mujer inquieta y andariega,* her detrac-tors called her, "a restless vagabond." What kind of woman behaved as she did, traipsing around Spain like a gypsy? Not only that, Teresa was assuming the role of a priest, they complained, offering spiritual direction to both men and women.

I shared their irritation, I admit it. I'd thought the reform was about rejecting the world and getting close to God. Instead, Teresa was playing pol-itics, raising money, and cozying up to the powerful. "No," I said to myself. "That's not how I want to live my life."

July turned Ávila into a giant cauldron. I know what a kid feels like as it cooks in a stewpot. It feels like we feel in our heavy, brown habits in mid-summer. Toward the end of the month Fray Julián brought news that Teresa had indeed obtained a deed to a property in Valladolid. He also slipped me a small package, which I took into my cell to unwrap. It contained a brief let-ter and a length of ribbon of the type that might be used to trim the garment of a plaster saint. The letter wasn't from Teresa. I didn't recognize the hand-writing, but I guessed it was a woman's. The characters were clear and well formed, aristocratic in their boldness.

For Sister Angélica del Sagrado Corazón:

Christ be with you, Sister. I beg you to pardon my audaciousness. Trusting in your kindness and mercy, I direct this missive to you. I dare not speak directly to Mother Teresa, who is here with us now in Toledo.

I am María de Salazar, the unworthy girl you met at the court of Doña Luisa de la Cerda. I have delved into my heart and I am sure God has called me to serve Him as a discalced Carmelite sister. When I mentioned to the holy Mother the first time she came to Toledo that I was thinking about taking the habit, she discouraged me, telling me that I should wait and pray. I believe she thinks I am still the frivolous child given to pretty gowns that she saw four years ago. However, I want to assure you that I have spent many hours examining my soul. I have struggled with my vanity, and I have put worldly desires behind me. I know I was a spoiled, giddy girl, but redemption is possible, even for fools such as I was, through Our Lord Jesus Christ. Since I dare not approach the most holy Mother Teresa myself, I beseech you to intervene on my behalf and explain to her that I am now certain I want to profess. I know she will soon leave for Ávila.

From Toledo, the 27th day of July, 1568,
Your unworthy servant,
María de Salazar

Of course I remembered María de Salazar. She'd always reminded me of an overwrought lapdog, scampering around, doing tricks, jumping up and down with her tongue lolling out and begging, "Look at me! Look at me!" I recalled her as a bright child, an avid reader and proficient at languages. She had a lovely face, resplendent hair, and a cheerful disposition, but her animal vitality left everyone exhausted. Still, Teresa couldn't be everywhere at once. She needed skilled women to carry forward the reform, and she knew how to harness others' energy and put it to work for her. María de Salazar might be very useful. I made a mental note to mention her to Teresa when she returned to Ávila. María would be, I thought, a better traveling companion for her than I. But then another letter came, and I forgot all about María de Salazar.

The low-quality paper was folded neatly and sealed with red wax. The hand was scratchy and masculine and familiar. The man who brought the missive wasn't a regular courier but a Benedictine monk who handed it to me, then left without a word. I tucked the letter into my sleeve, went into my cell, and closed the door. I trembled as I broke the seal and glanced at the signature to confirm what I already knew: the letter was from Braulio.

My Angélica:
I know I have no right to call you mine, but in the terrible turmoil in which I find myself, it is only by holding on to what is still dear to me that I can find the strength to go on. The messenger with whom I send this letter is a trusted

friend and so innocuous-looking that I doubt he will be stopped and questioned. I pray for his safety, for were this letter to be intercepted, both you and I would be in danger. I beg you to destroy it the moment you have finished reading.

Perhaps you have heard of the Count of Egmont, Angélica. He was an exemplary man, a Flemish noble about your age, a statesman, a general, and son of one of the finest families in the Low Countries. I had the honor to meet him when he came to the Carmelite monastery in Brussels for spiritual direction, and I daresay he was one of the most worthy cavaliers in all Christendom. He was a handsome, good man whose purity of soul was reflected in his clear, cerulean eyes. I hope I'm not committing the sin of pride when I say I considered him a friend.

I'm not sure how much news you receive from the Low Countries in your isolated cloister. You must know that King Felipe has put the Duke of Alba in charge of this region. The duke has allowed his henchmen to establish the Inquisition here, a grave error, since it has enraged the people. I know this is complicated for a woman to understand, Angélica, but you are very bright, and I think these elementary political concepts will not tax your female brain too much. The fact is that instead of trying to win over the local populace with Christ's love, the duke has incurred the wrath of all Dutch and Flemish patriots, Catholics as well as Calvinists, by stationing Spanish troops throughout the Netherlands. The people are infuriated, and rightly so. No population appreciates an occupying force. You can't imagine how ghastly this is, Angélica. The duke has unleashed a reign of terror here, presided over by Javier Sánchez Colón, to our shame, a native of Ávila. I've mentioned this man to you before, Angélica. He's an inquisitor in Valladolid, but the duke brought him here especially for his sham trials. The duke holds daily public executions. Blood flows in the streets like rainwater after a storm. Thousands and thousands of people have died. I fear thousands will lose their lives before this madness ends. He is a tyrant and a fanatic who does not understand the true meaning of Christ's sacrifice, but only uses religion as an excuse to persecute his opponents. And to think a native Avilés is his henchman!

Dearest Angélica, a massive uprising against the Spanish is going to occur, I'm sure of it. William of Orange has retired to Germany, where he is organizing a rebellion. This man was raised a Catholic, Angélica, but the abuses of Alba have made him turn to Calvinism out of patriotic duty. As a priest and a lover of Jesus, I burn with shame. Instead of winning souls for Christ, this brutish duke is driving good Catholics away from the church. But, dear friend, I have not told you the worst of it. Several months ago Alba arrested the Count of Egmont and con-

fiscated all his property. The count was not a follower of William of Orange, but even so, the duke saw him as an enemy and had him executed.

I was present at his beheading, which was performed in public. It was dreadful. I have not stopped sobbing since that horrid, fateful day. The Duke of Alba and his entourage sat on plush chairs on a nearby balcony so they would have an unencumbered view. The inquisitor, blond and pale, sat beside him. The executioner, regally dressed in black velvet and gold braid, appeared on a platform before a huge crowd that had come to witness the event. He wore a heavy gold belt, a gift from the pope to the duke, and fine black kid gloves. His boots were of the best quality, high and elaborately worked. Had it not been for the wool hood he wore over his head, you would have thought he was going to a ball at court. Before he committed the horrible deed, he lifted his sword for all to see. It was of sturdy metal, with a gorgeously decorated hilt. The gold and silver glittered in the sunlight, for it was a bright day that would have brought joy to my heart under different circumstances. The spectators oohed and aaahed in admiration.

They led the poor count, dressed in a vulgar penitent's robe, to the platform, as though he were a lamb being led to slaughter, with a rope tied around his neck. They had cut off his beautiful bronze-colored hair in order to leave his neck free. They didn't even have the decency to blindfold him until he was on the platform. He had to look at his executioner, elegant sword in hand. He had to see the wooden boards where his head would roll and the stake upon which they would raise it before placing it at the top of the town hall, so that passers-by could look up and glimpse what awaited them if they defied the duke. There it is and will stay until it starts to rot, just like the other scores of skewered heads placed daily on display.

The duke called out to Egmont jovially, like one friend to another. With cruel satisfaction he laughed and saluted him, winking and waving. Finally, the executioner's assistant placed a blindfold over the count's eyes. I had to look away. I couldn't bear it. But then, out of respect for my beloved friend, to whose death I was to bear witness, I turned back. The black-hooded assassin lifted his sword high, then brought it down on the count's neck. But horror of horrors, he missed his target and only cut a vein. Blood spurted out over the count's coarse robe, and he let out a chilling scream. The executioner lifted his sword again, and this time he succeeded. That lovely head bounced to the ground. The blindfold fell off, and the face lay facing upward, its azure eyes wide open as if to accuse the onlookers of complicity.

Dearest Angélica, what is to become of me? I cannot bear to stay here. I have petitioned the provincial to send me to England, where I know I will die, for there the Protestants treat the Catholics with the same cruelty that our Catholic brethren use here against the followers of Calvin. What pains me most is to see how the Duke of Alba, who thinks himself a great defender of the faith, shames us with his conduct. He has had a statue of himself erected in the city of Antwerp. It is vile. My having to witness these things must be God's punishment for the terrible way I treated you. Please find it in your heart to forgive me, dear Angélica, and please pray for me to the heavenly Father, His Divine Son, and Our Holy Mother Mary. Please also pray for the soul of my cherished friend, the count.

From Brussels, this day of Our Lord, 12 June, 1568.
Yours in Christ,
Braulio Estévez y Pontenegro, Carmelite

I dropped Braulio's letter and rushed to the chamber pot to vomit. I could imagine what state Braulio was in. For better or worse, he was a passionate man, and I could sense his fervor intensifying as he wrote this letter. And Don Juan, Teresa's cousin! How could he be a party to such atrocities? I picked up the letter and read it again. Then, instead of destroying it as Braulio had asked, I hid it with my books. Where was Braulio now? It was mid-July. He had written the letter over a month ago, on June 12. He might be in England already, I thought. Or else, he might be dead. I shuddered. Every day after that, I waited for a new message from Braulio. None came.

Teresa passed through Ávila on her way to Valladolid, but we had little time to talk. She was upset with Doña Luisa because that selfish, lazy woman still hadn't sent her *Life* to Fray Juan de Ávila, as she'd promised. "I'm sorry to hear that," I said curtly, making it clear I didn't want to hear complaining. I stayed away from her. I tended my herb garden and stitched by the window. I was angry because she was pressuring me again to go on the road with her. No, I thought. I won't go. I don't want to leave San José. Not now. Not ever.

Angélica del Sagrado Corazón
Toledo, 25 September 1576

CHAPTER 19

The One-Eyed Devil

A GENTLE APRIL RAIN HAD LEFT THE BRANCHES OF THE TREES IN HER ladyship's park glistening in the sunlight. Hidden among the leaves sparrows, or maybe robins, I don't know much about birds, chirped gaily, in utter distain for our human quandaries. Easy for the birds. When hostilities break out in one tree, they can just fly away to another. They can build their nests and lay their eggs and not give a royal damn about spoiled princesses who wear patches over one eye and spit orders at you as though you were a slave. The bitch.

Well, Teresa wore me down. I wound up going back to Toledo with her, not because she forced me to, but because she made me feel so guilty, as though I'd forsaken her. I folded my few possessions—two clean shifts, an assortment of herbs and pastilles, a few forbidden books, a package of letters—and stuck them into a burlap sack. With a lump in my throat I looked around my cell as though to fix it in my mind. The bare, wood-frame window that overlooked a red pantile roof. The heavy wooden beams that crossed the ceiling. The plain wooden crucifix that hung over my bed. The blue and white ceramic wash basin. I walked out and closed the door, knowing some other nun would sleep in my cell that night. Mother Úrsula accompanied me to the gate, and I climbed into the covered cart. The driver snapped the reins, and the wobbly contraption began to lurch unsteadily down the road. Fray Julián mounted his dapple and trotted beside it. I wanted to cry.

I wasn't surprised to see Doña Luisa and Teresa waiting for me in the great hall. Her ladyship looked the same, except that her hair was sparser and greyer than the last time I'd seen her, and she had a few more lines by her eyes and over her lip. What mesmerized me was the exquisitely stunning creature that stood beside her. She was like those portraits of goddesses you see in grand houses, goddesses with unnatural features such as branches for arms—beautiful, yet grotesque. She had a complexion like moonlight and thick black hair coiled high on her head to form a cone into which gold ribbon was woven. A billowy ruff of the finest lace encircled her alabaster neck and a heavy gold chain lay on her bosom, rising and falling with her breathing. Her lips were like a rose, just as poets describe the lips of beautiful ladies in books. Her nose was aquiline and aristocratic, and her cheeks high and sculpted. But her eyes were what held my attention. One, edged with sweeping, silken lashes and surmounted by a perfectly arched brow, glistened with the richness of polished mahogany. The other was invisible, hidden by a patch.

Doña Luisa nodded slightly in acknowledgment of my presence. "Doña Ana de Mendoza y de la Cerda, Princess of Éboli," she said, by way of introduction. The breathtaking cyclops with the pointed head looked down her perfect nose and nodded without smiling. Doña Luisa's fluffy, brown and white dog scampered into the room. I don't know whether it was Brutus or a younger replacement. "Lift your leg and pee on the princess," I whispered under my breath, but the animal ran up to Teresa, yipping and wagging its tail. Doña Luisa laughed indulgently. Doña Ana looked on with indifference. "Go on," I whispered inaudibly, "pee on her."

Of Doña Luisa's ladies-in-waiting, only María de Salazar was present. She had changed. Instead of a frilly gown and gaily colored hair ribbons, she was wearing a plain, gray dress. Her hair was tied back in a knot. She greeted me with imploring eyes. I suddenly remembered this girl had begged to me to intervene with Teresa to help her become a nun, but Braulio's letter from the Low Countries had made me forget all about her. I'd never answered.

I was waiting for Doña Luisa to ask me if I was hungry after my long journey, but since she had already had her dinner, it didn't occur to her.

"Perhaps Sister Angélica and Fray Julián would like to eat something," said Teresa, reading my mind. "There was so much left over from the midday meal."

Doña Luisa raised an eyebrow, as if surprised by this novel idea. "The servants have already cleared the tables," shot back Doña Ana.

"No matter," said Teresa with defiant cheeriness. "I'll serve them and clean up afterward." She took my arm and led me out of the room. I sensed tension. What was going on? Teresa had always navigated deftly through the shark-infested waters of Doña Luisa's moat.

"I can attend to it," said Doña Luisa, a smile like a porcelain doll's painted on her face. "I'll ring for a kitchen maid."

"Never mind," chirped Teresa. "Your Ladyship hasn't been so good at attending to things lately."

Doña Luisa looked at Teresa as if she hadn't quite grasped her meaning. Doña Ana shot her poisoned darts out of her one gorgeous eye. She must have been asking herself who this cheeky nun took herself for. Still, she didn't dare reprimand her. Teresa might not be a high-ranking noble, but she was a celebrated holy woman with a huge following. Even a powerful woman like the Princess of Éboli thought twice about tangling with her.

Teresa guided me into the servants' quarters and brought me what for Doña Luisa were leftovers, but was for me, used to the sparse pickings at San José, a luxurious meal. She directed a manservant to bring a slice of partridge and some vegetables to Fray Julián in the room where he would spend the night before heading back to Ávila.

"What was that all about?" I asked, as soon as we were alone. "Has she still not sent your memoir to Juan de Ávila?"

"She sent it, *finally*, and Fray Juan sees nothing objectionable in it, praise God." She was picking at a poultry wing. "It certainly took her long enough," she added.

"I thought you'd already eaten. Where do you come off, telling the duchess she's incompetent?"

"Oh Lord, when there's food in front of me, I just can't leave it alone. Lead me not into temptation," she intoned, pushing away the wing. "No, this isn't about my book. It's about the new foundation in Toledo. Doña Luisa keeps saying she'll help, God love her, but like so many other rich ladies, she's so consumed with her jewelry and parties, she never gets around to keeping her word. I've been trying for weeks, but I haven't been able to find a suitable house for a convent." She picked up the wing and began to nibble. "You'd think with all Doña Luisa's connections in this city, she'd be able to find us a place. She promised to make inquiries, but the days go by and she does nothing. What's worse, I haven't even been able to get the consent of the archbishop to found a convent." She cut a large piece of cheese and put it in front of me. "Eat this, Angélica, and try these grapes." She started eating them herself.

"Because Doña Luisa hasn't helped set up a meeting with him?"

"No, because he's been arrested by the Inquisition for advancing Lutheran ideas. He's in Rome now awaiting judgment by a papal court. It's a tragedy, really, because he would have been sympathetic to our cause . . . I think. Now the government of the diocese of Toledo is being run by a pack of fools headed by a certain Gómez Tello Girón. Doña Luisa has made a few half-hearted attempts to petition him on our behalf, but she could try harder."

"Even if Doña Luisa is dragging her feet, you can't go around insulting a benefactress."

"I hate the whole idea of benefactresses. And now, since Doña Luisa has a convent on her property in Malagón, that one-eyed devil Doña Ana wants one on her own estate in Pastrana."

"That's not a very Christian attitude, Teresa. The poor woman is half-blind."

"Don't pretend to sympathize with that monster. I saw the way you looked at her. You were hoping Brutus would pee on her skirts, weren't you!"

"Damn! You're a mind reader, Teresa de Ahumada." We both burst out laughing. "But you're right. There's something so haughty about the woman." Teresa had polished off the grapes and was now cutting slivers of cheese—tiny slivers, so minuscule I guess she thought I wouldn't notice.

"She's the wife of Ruy Gómez de Silva, the king's best friend and confidant, so you can see why she's full of herself. He and the princess have nine children."

"Heavens, she's as slim as a girl. Teresa, if you want a piece of cheese, just take it."

"*Vade retro, Satanás,*" she growled, pushing the cheese under my nose. "If I eat one more piece, I'll have to go to confession and own up to the sin of gluttony. Do me a favor, Angélica. Eat the damn thing." She paused for me to slice off a portion, place it on a piece of bread, and pop it into my mouth. "Yes," she went on, "she's as slim as a girl. Of course, if you had unlimited money and an army of servants to boss around, you'd be in good shape too. Although I'm sure our way of life is much healthier for the soul. Anyway, that spoiled brat of a woman is so puffed up with her husband's importance that she dared to order me to accompany her back to Pastrana. On second thought, give me one teensy slice more of that cheese. No, no . . . that's too big. An itsy bitsy piece."

"What did you tell her?"

"That I was busy in Toledo. That I had to finish my business here before I could even think of another project. I'm stalling, of course. Eventually, I'll have to tell her no outright."

"Listen, I forgot to tell you. That girl, María de Salazar, wants to become a nun."

"I've been here for weeks. Why didn't she tell me?"

"She's afraid of you, so she wrote to me, instead."

Teresa chuckled. "I wondered why she'd given up all her pretty dresses. Well, I'll talk to her. If she's serious, I'll find a place for her. She's very smart. She'd make a good prioress."

As I entered the sumptuous room the duchess had assigned to me, I caught my breath at the reflection that flickered back at me from the mirror over the mantel. I hadn't seen my own image in a mirror for seven years. I was forty-nine years old. I'd never been pretty, but the face I remembered at least held the ripeness of youth. The one in the glass—drawn and sallow, with creases by the eyes and mouth—had lost its juice. I thought suddenly of Braulio. "I'm glad he's gone," I whispered. "I'm glad he never saw me like this."

The next day Teresa sent for Isabel de Santo Domingo, an old friend from Ávila, a tough, practical woman known as "the advocate" because she could argue any detractor of the reform into the ground. She was more than twenty years Teresa's junior, but already known as a master of rhetoric. Her first oratorical victory was over her uncle, Antonio de Vera, a member of the town council that had tried to shut down San José. When Isabel told him she wanted to join precisely that convent, he had a fit. Isabel entered anyway, and Don Antonio threatened to appeal to the bishop and have her removed by force. But when he went to give her his ultimatum, she argued her case so eloquently through the grille that she reduced him to tears. Now, whenever there was a battle to be won through language, Teresa called on Isabel.

Sister Isabel was a fighter, but she was happiest doing the dishes. At San José, I often saw her scrubbing pots, lost in prayer. It was as though the act of scraping food off a pan calmed her, allowing her soul to soar. It was a form of recollection. Sometimes when a sister was feeling down, Teresa would send her to the kitchen to scrub with Isabel because she believed that hard work was the best cure for melancholy. "You can be just as holy in the kitchen as in the chapel," she'd say. "Just look at Sister Isabel. God also roams among the pots and pans."

Isabel arrived in Toledo the next day. After she'd rested from her journey, she and Teresa set out for a little church near the house of Don Gómez Tello Girón. I stayed behind to make some medicines. A flu was going around, and several of Doña Luisa's servants were ill. I imagined Teresa and Isabel hurrying along the narrow, winding streets, sometimes making a wrong turn and having to retrace their steps. (Toledo is a labyrinth, full of alleys and dead ends, identical side streets, and mews that open onto tiny plazas.) I imagined people turning to look at them, two nuns in a hurry, each shabbier than the other. Then I forgot about them and got to work.

Hours later, they returned, exhausted but satisfied. They'd managed to get permission for a new Carmel, provided it had no endowment or sponsor. That was fine with Teresa. She hadn't wanted a patron to begin with. During the next few days she was so busy with the negotiations with Gómez, she hardly noticed that the Princess of Éboli had left Toledo, practically without saying good-bye. Doña Ana had been escorted, according to Amalia, the parlor maid, not by her husband, but by a handsome young courtier named Antonio Pérez.

Within the next few weeks, Teresa managed to find a house on the Calle de San Juan de Dios, in the old Jewish quarter, near the building that had once been the Sinagoga del Tránsito. Doña Luisa made no move to open her purse, so Teresa had to borrow money from the wife of the duchess's valet for the down payment. The official founding date of the Toledo Carmel is May 14, 1569. It was the poorest foundation Teresa had made so far. Doña Luisa left town without giving us so much as a candlestick for the chapel. "We don't have enough wood even to roast a sardine," grumbled Teresa.

"Don't complain," I said. "At least she took María de Salazar with her to Malagón, and she's going to pay the child's dowry. The only thing is, the girl is going to profess as María de San José. I wish she'd take another name. We already have a María de San José in Ávila."

"You can't do too much honor to Saint Joseph," shot back Teresa. "Listen, are you going to eat that bit of bread?"

In spite of its destitution, the Toledo Carmel thrived. "I wasn't worried," Teresa told me nonchalantly. "God told me everything would work out."

One morning, just after we'd settled in, an Italian-style coach of the kind they call a *carroza* arrived at the gate of the new convent. It was a magnificent vehicle drawn by six black horses, with a black roof and exterior walls decorated with flower motifs of gold inlay. A sole passenger descended. I happened to be at the turn. "Doña Teresa de Ahumada," he said curtly.

"Do you mean Mother Teresa de Jesús?" I answered, just as curtly.

"I have orders to bring her back with me in the coach," he said, ignoring my question.

I considered what to do. He was obviously an emissary from a noble house. His rudeness made me want to send him to the Devil, but I consid-

ered the possible consequences to the reform of insulting an influential aristocrat, and thought better of it. "One moment," I said. "I'll get her."

Actually, it would have been pointless to send him to the Devil because
he came from the Devil herself. I was in the kitchen with Isabel plucking
chickens—a gift from some kind neighbors—when Teresa rushed in and
ordered us to drop everything and get cleaned up. "We have to leave for
Pastrana," she said.

"Just like that?"

She sighed. "The princess has sent for us, and she's not used to being dis-
obeyed."

"To Hell with her," growled Isabel.

Teresa shook her head. "I'm sorry," she said, "but her husband is one of
the most powerful men in Spain. If we make her angry, she could cause terrible problems for the reform."

We traveled all night, and by the next morning the *carroza* was rolling into
Pastrana, a beautiful old town that had once belonged to the powerful Knights
of Calatrava. Doña Ana de Mendoza, mother of the one-eyed princess, acquired
it long after the knights were gone from the town. She had had a magnificent
ducal palace built on the grounds, which the Princess of Eboli now possessed.
Still, the princess wasn't satisfied. Her cousin Doña Luisa had a convent on her
property, and the princess wanted one too. But she was determined to do Doña
Luisa one better. She'd have not only a nunnery, but a friary as well.

Breakfast at the Eboli palace was usually around ten o'clock. By then,
Teresa, Isabel and I had been up for hours. As in the convent, we rose at five
o'clock, prayed Lauds, and began our daily tasks. Mine were to attend to
Teresa's health needs, brewing chamomile tea and preparing charcoal pastilles
to calm her stomach. Isabel was in charge of laundry. While we worked,
Teresa wrote. Her Dominican friend, Father Báñez, had asked her to compose a book on prayer suitable for nuns. She'd completed a first version of
The Way of Perfection, but the censors demanded corrections, and now she
was finishing the revision. By the time we joined the princess for breakfast,
she'd put in hours of writing. Her head was clear, and her stomach was calm.

Doña Ana's first order of business was the closestool, a lidded, box-like
chair with a plush seat, open in the center, which stood by her bed.
Underneath was a gilt chamber pot designed to catch Doña Ana's patrician
shit. Next to the closestool was a jug of salt water and a sponge on a stick to
wash the aristocratic bottom, along with a porcelain container filled with

moss and lavender to deodorize and perfume it. After the servants had emptied the pot, the princess, still in her nightshift, received her entourage. Together with her ladies she knelt in prayer in her private oratory. Then she returned to bed, where, propped up on enormous feather pillows, her long, black hair scattered wildly on her shoulders, she breakfasted with her *doncellas,* who sat on cushions around her bed. Servants brought in silver trays laden with ham, cheese, sardines with olives, sweet red peppers, and beer imported from the Low Countries.

For me, the early morning hours were glorious, filled with quiet activity or cheerful chatter. But the moment we entered Doña Ana's *inner sanctum,* I felt morose. The imperial boudoir stank of excrement, sweat, and sardines. Even rosewater couldn't disguise the stench. Teresa, Isabel, and I squatted on cushions and waited for the headaches we'd soon be nursing.

"I've begun to furnish your new convent," the princess gurgled one morning. She popped a fig into her mouth and waited for Teresa to protest. "I've bought paintings, a solid gold monstrance, a silver incense boat, a Dutch lace altar cloth, and a crucifix inlaid with mother-of-pearl. Only the very best for my nuns. Have a slice of Serrano ham, Mother. It's very good."

Teresa bit her lip. "Thank you," she said finally.

"We have the permits," said the princess, looking out over the room as though she were King Don Felipe addressing an assembly. "I think you'll be able to move in by the end of June."

Teresa chewed her ham without looking up. "As much as I appreciate Your Highness's generosity," she said, "I must ask you to consult me before buying anything more." She smiled grimly. "Poverty is an essential element of the discalced Carmelite rule."

Doña Ana turned to chat with one of her ladies-in-waiting about a Chinese vase she'd seen at court. She was going to ask the king to give it to her. Don Felipe was very fond of her, she said pointedly.

"By the way," she said to Teresa without looking at her, "there's a nun I want you to take. Catalina Machuca. She's been in an Augustinian convent in Segovia, but she's a friend of mine, and I want her here. I've already sent for her."

"I don't know if I'll go ahead with this foundation," Teresa shot back, clearly at the end of her tether. "Discalced Carmelite convents are supposed to be founded without benefactors."

Doña Ana popped another fig into her mouth, then licked her fingers slowly. "You'll go ahead with it," she said. "You gave my husband your word." She turned to face Teresa. "My husband, advisor and lifelong companion to the King. And don't tell me you don't accept benefactors. Doña Luisa is sponsoring one of your convents in Malagón."

"Well, actually," began Teresa thoughtfully, "perhaps I will accept an endowment."

"Yes," said the princess, "of course you will." She pretended to adjust her eye patch.

"I'll accept it," said Teresa, "but I want a guaranteed monthly income, to be fixed in advance. I'll have Fray Domingo Báñez draw up an agreement. He's one of the best legal scholars in Spain." She paused. "By the way, tell your friend Catalina Machuca not to burn her bridges with the Augustinians."

The blood drained from Doña Ana's cheeks, and for an instant she forgot the half-eaten fig in her hand. "A guaranteed monthly income! What are you talking about?"

"If I'm going to install eight or ten nuns on Your Highness's property, I have to make sure they'll be provided for. What if Your Highness loses interest in this project in a month or two? A convent is not like a pretty bauble, Your Highness. You can't just walk away and forget about it when you get bored." Teresa gave her a smile that oozed warm molasses. "And about Catalina Machuca, I'll have to interview her. No postulant can enter a Carmel without my permission."

Doña Ana's chin quivered. Suddenly, a long, high-pitched squeak like air escaping a valve filled the room, followed by a fetid odor. The ladies ate their breakfasts, pretending not to notice. I covered my mouth to stifle a laugh. It's the figs, I thought. They've upset her stomach.

"I want to be alone," snapped the princess. Her ladies quickly abandoned their plates and disappeared.

"She needs to use the closestool," I whispered to Teresa, when we were out of earshot.

Catalina Machuca arrived in a simple mule-drawn coach the next day. I expected a haughty aristocrat like Doña Ana, but she turned out to be a small, mousy girl bedeviled by nervous ticks. Whenever she felt pressured, she rested her right hand on the crown of her head and rubbed her left eyebrow with her middle finger. She jerked her head incessantly when she answered questions and tapped her foot when she prayed. It was clear she wasn't cut out for the life of deprivation and discipline a Carmel would expect of her. Even so, Teresa treated her kindly, interviewing her at length and explaining the difficulty in changing religious orders.

"You know I want the best for this convent," Doña Ana told Teresa. She was standing with her arms crossed, in a pose that said she meant business. "Doña Catalina is the youngest daughter of a distant cousin of my husband. My husband, the king's most intimate friend. She's an extraordinarily devout young woman. You simply must admit her."

"I have written to Fray Domingo Báñez for his opinion on the matter," said Teresa calmly. "I should have an answer in a few days. I will abide by his decision."

I didn't see her letter to Báñez, but I'm sure Teresa explained she meant to reject the girl. Within a fortnight, Báñez wrote admonishing her not to allow Doña Ana to dictate who would enter the convent. Catalina burst into tears when Teresa gave her the news. She whimpered and hiccoughed all afternoon until Vespers, then retired to Doña Ana's suite.

"She's disconsolate," I said to Isabel as the two of us sat sewing.

"She'll get over it."

"I have the feeling Doña Ana will do something to get even. Women like her are not used to being crossed."

I was right. That evening, after the post-supper entertainments, the princess asked Teresa for a copy of her *Life*.

"I'm sorry, Your Highness," Teresa said resolutely. "I wrote that book for my spiritual directors. It's very personal."

"Doña Luisa read it," snapped the princess. "I know you brought along a copy written in your own hand. Why shouldn't I be allowed to read it? Am I less trustworthy than my cousin? I promise no one will see it except me. I'll guard it with my life!"

Teresa held firm until the princess's husband intervened. Don Ruy was such a decorous man, so elegant and honorable, how could Teresa say no? Especially since he, as the king's confidant, had considerable power over the reform. Finally, against her better judgment, she handed a copy of her memoir over to the Princess of Éboli. It was a terrible mistake.

Angélica del Sagrado Corazón
Toledo, 30 September 1576

CHAPTER 20

Traitors and Spies

THE PASTRANA CONVENT, NAMED SAN JOSÉ JUST LIKE THE ONE IN ÁVILA, was launched at the end of June. Teresa stayed only until mid-July, when the Pastrana friary opened. She was anxious to be on her way. She was bored with the princess's gilt chamber pots and dictatorial ways. Besides, she was planning to found another Carmel in Salamanca, and there was work to be done. She left Isabel and me in Pastrana. Isabel was to be prioress. My task was to visit the princess daily to give her an account of the convent's needs and the spiritual progress of its inhabitants. At least, that was my supposed assignment. In reality, I was a spy. It was up to me to observe the one-eyed Devil and report any dangerous machinations.

I can't say I disliked visiting the princess. The July heat was oppressive, and in my heavy brown habit, I sweated like a pig. I know that's not a very elegant thing to put down on paper, but I'm not a fancy lady like Teresa or her aristocratic friends. They "perspire." Me, I'm just a simple woman, and I write how I speak. Doña Ana's palace had thick walls, as wide as two men lying on the ground feet to head, and they kept the rooms cool. Besides, she had her own ice deposit and always served tasty, chilled drinks and flavored ices. Well, I know we're supposed to be suffering for Christ, but Jesus doesn't want me to collapse from the heat, does He? What good would I be to the reform then? I'm sure He'd rather I enjoyed some ice-cold pomegranate juice.

Spying was fun. I'd spied once before for Sister Josefa, and I had a knack for it. I had the keen eye of a seamstress raised in an orderly workroom. Everything in its place. Embroidery thread here. Sewing thread there. Pins in the pin box sorted by size. I noticed things that a less observant person might overlook. For example, one morning, visiting the princess in her boudoir, I noticed a pillow had fallen to the floor. It wasn't one of the princess's pillows, which were all tucked neatly behind her. The princess used five pillows for her morning receptions, and those five pillows were all in place. No, this was a superfluous pillow that didn't match the others. It was lying on the opposite side of the bed from the *estrado,* away from the princess's mid-morning guests. It was as if someone had leapt out of bed in a hurry, knocking it aside.

Don Ruy wasn't in Pastrana. He was busy with affairs of state because at that moment, the *morisco* problem was intensifying. Everyone said the *moriscos* were just like the *conversos,* pretending to be Catholic while practicing their old religion in secret. The king decided it was time to clamp down. First, he levied a tax on silk, their main source of income. Then he forbade them to own slaves, wear their dress, practice their customs, carry arms, or speak their language. The *moriscos* rebelled. In March, 1569, only months before Teresa founded the convents in Pastrana, the Christian army recaptured several of their villages, then expelled all *moriscos* from Granada. Between the *morisco* mess and the mess in the Low Countries, the king's advisers had their hands full. Don Ruy had to stay away from Pastrana for months at a time.

The next day after I'd seen the fallen pillow, I noticed something else. Her highness's nightshift was normally wrinkled and damp from the summer heat, but that morning it was perfectly fresh, as though she'd just put it on. After breakfast, when she got up for her maid to dress her, an unusual odor emanated from her bed, one that was familiar yet odd. It reminded me of . . . what? . . . I had to think before it came to me. It reminded me of Braulio, of those forbidden moments I'd spent with Braulio in his family's house in Ávila. I'd heard rumors about Doña Ana, but I'd always doubted them. After all, she had given birth nine times. When would she have time for an affair? Or maybe, I thought, it was precisely at this moment when she was ripe for an affair. She'd been married at twelve and had completed her childbearing duties. Now thirty, she was still stunning and loved the attention of men. Her husband was gone most of the time, so what was to prevent her from doing what I'd heard most noblewomen did: take a lover.

That day I invented things to talk to her highness about. The convent needed more cooking utensils. There wasn't enough flour for bread. Would she object if I kept a kitten? I'd had one at San José, and I missed him. What did she think about the plan to tighten the screws on the *moriscos?* Yes, it was wonderful that the king was going to repatriate two hundred *morisco* families to Pastrana. Granada's loss was Pastrana's gain, since the *moriscos* were wonderful artisans. Would Don Ruy be away for long? I asked slyly. It helped that she liked me. I was just a common woman with no pretensions, one who never talked back to her. She chatted more willingly than I expected and then, she did exactly what I wanted her to do. She invited me to dinner.

If Doña Ana was sleeping with someone, I had to find out who with. First of all, I was curious. But also, if she tried to pull anything at the convent—put in her own postulants, for example, or redecorate the place—it would be good to have something on her. It's called coercion.

As I recall, the midday meal at Doña Ana's was around three, right after the liturgical hour of None. Even daily meals at the palace were sumptuous, but this time I was interested in the guests, not the food. Bishop So-and-So was there, also Count Such-and-Such, but the man I had my eye on was Antonio Pérez, the king's personal secretary. I'd seen him before, and he'd always struck me as a slippery sort, ambitious and ingratiating. He was elegantly dressed, not in black as was the custom for servants of the king, but in gold, white, and burgundy. He was a small man, but his clothes were contrived to add bulk. The outfit accentuated the slimness of his waist and the breadth of his shoulders. His heavily padded doublet consisted of white and gold panels. It buttoned down the front and fitted over a *jubón* with fashionable slashed sleeves of which long cuts down the deep red arms revealed contrasting white fabric. His upper stocks, worn over white stockings, were puffed and slashed in white and gold to match his doublet. The codpiece, of the same gold cloth as the panels of the doublet, doubtlessly exaggerated his endowments. Pérez hovered over Doña Ana like a hummingbird over a honeysuckle, and the princess made no effort to disguise her pleasure.

When we retired for the *siesta*, Pérez and Doña Ana left discreetly in opposite directions, but I saw them give each other a look that meant . . . what? Meet me in my suite in half an hour? I wondered if the princess would go back to her bedroom and slip off her gown, her underskirts, her farthingale, her hose. I wondered if she'd slip off her underbritches, or whether her husband forbade her to wear any because he thought, as so many men did, that fabric rubbing against a woman's bare thigh excited her unduly. (This was something I'd heard noblewomen talking about in the great houses I once sewed for.) Would she perfume her body, powder her breasts, apply *solimán* to her face? Would she await her lover in a freshly ironed shift of gossamer and lace or bare under the sheets?

I imagined Pérez knocking lightly at her boudoir door and the maid, privy to all her highness's secrets, showing him in. I imagined him sitting on Doña Ana's high, four-poster bed with eight mattresses, each stuffed with high-quality, carded wool. I imagined him pulling back the coverlets and the sheets, revealing the nude body of the princess, smooth and white as ivory, still exquisite after nine children. I imagined him unbuttoning his doublet, removing his *jubón,* undoing his codpiece, dropping his stocks, slipping out of his embroidered kid slippers, unrolling his hose. It's so much easier with a priest, I thought. All he has to do is pull up his cassock.

All that thinking about Antonio Pérez taking his clothes off made be feel all damp and jittery. I needed some air. Instead of taking my *siesta* at the palace, I walked back to the convent. The sisters had napped hours before and were busy at their tasks, some sewing, some washing, some ironing, some cooking, some sweeping. Instead of going to the sewing room, I went back to my cell and lay down to think. It was clear to me what was going on between the princess and Pérez, but I needed proof. And when I had it, what then?

The next time I returned to the palace, Pérez was nowhere in sight. Doña Ana's personal maid, Lis, pointed me toward a shady spot in the garden, where the princess and her ladies often gathered to gossip and sip cool drinks in the late afternoon. Even before I saw them, I heard their squeals. First a high-pitched giggle, then a screech, then a yelp—like piglets at the trough. As I drew closer I could see them gathered around Doña Ana, who had a book in her hand and was reading aloud, "*The great blessings possessed by those who practice prayer—and by this I mean mental prayer—have been described by many saintly and good men.*" She stopped and looked around at her entourage, a smirk on her lips. "*I can say what I know from experience, namely that however sinful a man may be, he should not abandon prayer once he has begun it.*"

I recognized the text immediately. It was from Teresa's *Life.* The princess had promised not to show it to anyone.

"She thinks she's a theologian," snorted the princess.

"Women aren't allowed to preach," murmured Catalina Machuca, who was sitting on a stool by her protectress.

The other women were settled on stone benches and chairs the servants had brought outside, their silk dresses spread around them like petals around a flower. One groused, "I don't like the way she's always talking about her experience. 'I know from experience,' as if she were saying, 'You can't argue with me because I've *experienced* this.'" The speaker was seated on a wide chair called a "maid of honor," built to accommodate a farthingale.

I approached the group. Doña Ana and her ladies were so engrossed in their reading, they didn't see me. I hid behind a clump of rose bushes and listened.

"How about this!" giggled the Princess. "'*Mental prayer is, as I see it, simply a friendly intercourse and frequent solitary conversation with Him who, as we know, loves us.*'"

"A conversation with God!" sniggered the woman on the "maid of honor" chair. "She has conversations with God! She's a regular Magdalena de la Cruz!"

"Wait! It gets better!" said the princess, wiping tears of laughter from her cheeks. "'*Oh my God, how infinitely good You are! Oh joy of the angels, when I think of it, I long to dissolve in love for You!*'"

"Dissolve in love! Dissolve in love!" squealed the women.

"Read about the visions," begged a girl in yellow. "Read about how God sneaks up and tweaks her on the elbow!"

The princess leafed through the pages. "Here's a good one," she said finally. "'*I saw a huge crowd of devils around me, but I seemed to be completely enveloped in a great light, which prevented their coming near me. I realized that God was guarding me so that they should not approach me and make me sin against Him.*' The Calvinists are attacking in the Netherlands and the *moriscos* are rebelling in the South, but God has nothing better to do than to guard Teresa de Ahumada so the devils won't get her!" snickered Doña Ana. "Either she's mad or she's a fraud."

I'd heard enough. I turned and made my way back through the palace to the street. I felt nauseous, as though a stone were lodged in my gut. I wanted to cry. Back in the convent, I sat down to write Teresa a letter. I had to let her know how the princess was mocking her, how she had abused her trust. But where would I send it? Teresa was probably already on the road to Salamanca, and I had no idea where she'd be staying in that city. I hid the paper with my books.

Summer drew to a close. The shadow of the chapel spire grew longer and darker. The princess left Pastrana for long periods of time, but whenever she was back, she called for me. Were our needs being met? she wanted to know. Who were the new postulants? Were the confessors adequate? She was going to make some changes in the chapel, she said. She despised the simple wooden crucifix in the sanctuary. People would think the convent's benefactress was stingy. She had purchased a new one of solid gold. Also, she had a friend with two daughters who wanted to take the veil. The prioress—what was her name again?—had to interview them. Nuns were a joy, she said, but the friars were a handful. Fray Baltasar de Jesús, the prior of the discalced monastery, was a rigorous disciplinarian, using the whip excessively. Now some of his charges were threatening to revolt. But, oh well, she said, they were men, they'd work it out.

Our first Christmas at San José de Pastrana was a joyous affair. Fray Julián said Mass, and it was wonderful to hear his familiar voice in this strange and bewildering place. He brought news of Teresa. She'd been ill, but was forging ahead with plans for the foundation in Salamanca. I pulled out the letter I'd written about Doña Ana's treachery and added a few lines on the problems in the friary, but softened it with some good news: The convent was running fairly smoothly in spite of the princess's constant intervention; we had new postulants, some of them very promising; we had enough to eat; no one was seriously ill. Besides, a new friar, Jerónimo Gracián, had joined the male convent and had become a popular spiritual director. I didn't mention that the man rubbed me the wrong way. I gave the note to Fray Julián to deliver to Teresa.

Snow was on the ground, but I still trudged dutifully to the palace two or three times a week. I was the only sister allowed to leave the convent. Although I loved the cloister, I admit I was glad for the change of scenery. One afternoon, it must have been in February, I stood shivering by the door for what seemed like an eternity waiting for the manservant to open. He knew me, of course, and showed me in without hesitation. Lis took me from the vestibule to Doña Ana's quarters. She seemed to be in a hurry. She was carrying a pile of linen, apparently to ready a room for a guest. It seemed strange that Doña Ana's personal maid would be assigned such a task, but I didn't give it much thought. I scurried along impatiently, not because I was looking forward to the princess's company, but because I knew that whatever room Doña Ana was in would boast a roaring fire to thaw my numb fingers.

"Her highness is there," said the maid, signaling the princess's suite.

I thought she meant for me to go in alone, so I knocked lightly, and when no answer came, I pushed on the door. It wasn't bolted. I rushed in, anxious to get to the warmth of the chimney, then froze in my tracks. The scene before my eyes caused the blood to curdle in my veins. "Oh, God," I prayed silently. "Oh, Holy Virgin Mother, I know I'm a sinner, but please help me!" The curtains that separated Doña Ana's boudoir from the sitting area were completely open, and in her bed, she and Antonio Pérez were fornicating like two demons in Hell.

Suddenly, Doña Ana pulled away from her lover and sat up. She was completely naked. Her shoulders were as white as snow and her waist, slim. Her legs were long and shapely, and although the sponginess of her belly evinced frequent pregnancies, she was by no means fleshy. Her pubic hair lay in damp, black curls between her legs. Her breasts, firm and creamy as those of a young girl, stood looking at me like two cyclopses, while the eye of the principal cyclops, Doña Ana herself, blinked furiously. It had been years since I'd seen a naked body. In the convent, we kept ourselves covered at all times, even when we bathed. When I examined a sick nun, I kept my touching to a minimum and never exposed any part below the neck. I was mesmerized.

Pérez rolled over and sat up next to her. He took one look at me and burst out laughing. He had a loud, thunderous laugh that seemed to come from a much larger man. He was naked too. His torso, much slighter than I had expected, was sculpted and strong. His chest and legs were hairy and his feet, rather small. I averted my eyes to avoid seeing his sex.

"Good afternoon, Sister," thundered Pérez. "Care to join us?"

I wanted to run, but my feet seemed embedded in the floorboards. "I'm sorry," I stammered. "I . . . I didn't realize . . ." Finally, I forced myself to turn and flee.

By the time I got back to the convent, I was sweating icicles. I went to bed and woke up hours later with a raging fever.

After that, I stayed away from the palace. When the cellaress told me her highness's secretary hadn't come with the month's allotment of flour, I pretended to be ill. Even when the princess sent for me, I invented reasons not to go. I was certain she was planning to have her men ambush and murder me as I walked from San José to the palace. But one day when I came down from my *siesta*, a novice told me I had a guest waiting to see me in the chapter room. As the benefactress of San José de Pastrana, Doña Ana could, of course, enter the cloister. But why would she want to see me? I wondered. Any decent woman would hide in shame.

Doña Ana greeted me just as brazenly as if I hadn't caught her buck naked fucking the king's secretary while her husband was away. I expected her to hiss and bare her claws. Instead, she chattered chirpily about a new statue of Saint Joseph she'd purchased for the convent vestibule. She inquired about the novices. Too bad Mother Teresa had sent away Catalina Machuca, such a lovely girl, she said. It had been so long since my last visit, she went on. Did we need anything? She was sorry about the delay in the monthly payment, but her secretary would be over in a day or two with the money. I listened, tight-lipped, until she got up to go.

"By the way," she said as she rose, "I finished Mother Teresa's *Life*. Fascinating, really. I'm so honored she allowed me to read it."

"I'll probably be seeing Mother Teresa soon," I lied. "I'd like to have it back so I can return it to her."

"Oh, don't worry," said the princess. "I'll make sure it gets into the right hands." There was something sinister about the way she smiled, her one good eye glimmering in the candlelight. I felt as though I were suffocating.

I wrote Teresa that very evening and dispatched the letter to the address in Salamanca Fray Julián had given me. I begged her to allow me to leave Pastrana and join her. But it was too late. By the time my letter reached the university city, Teresa had left. A fortnight later, a letter came from Ávila with this disturbing piece of news: the provincial had commanded Teresa to return to Encarnación to serve as prioress. She begged me to join her. I frowned. Why would Fray Ángel make her prioress of a place where resentment against her was still intense? It didn't make sense.

Of course, I would join her. Not only was I anxious to get out of Pastrana, but I missed her. Besides, she'd become a larger-than-life holy woman, a great mystic and reformer. Nobles, ecclesiastics, and even royalty held her in esteem. She was now the most important religious woman in Spain, and, somehow, being her friend made me important, too. But before I could go to Ávila, I had an urgent task to perform: I had to get her *Life* back from Doña Ana.

I knew the princess would never simply hand over the book. I'd asked her for it several times, but she always put me off. I would have to resort to subterfuge. The person best equipped to help me was Lis, Doña Ana's maid, who certainly knew where the book was hidden and could easily filch it. However, in order to buy her services, I'd have to offer her something. I had no money, but perhaps I could sew her a gown. I thought about how to broach the subject. I sensed Lis resented the rough treatment she sometimes got from the princess, but that was no proof she'd help me. It was possible the maid, seeking ways to ingratiate herself to her mistress, would become a double agent, betraying me in hopes of receiving a reward. And then what would happen to me? I'd already caught her highness *in flagrante delicto* and now I was bribing her maid in order to steal a book. A familiar queasiness came over me, a feeling I remembered from long ago, when Don Alonso caught me eavesdropping on him and his brother. I'd thought he'd throw me down a well to keep me quiet. I had no doubt the princess would devise a worse punishment.

I was absorbed in these thoughts when Isabel de Santo Domingo knocked at my door—three raps, distinct and sharp. The instant I saw her, I knew something was wrong. Her jaw was set, her large blue eyes blazed. "Do you know where Mother Teresa is?"

"She's on her way to Encarnación," I said. "Maybe she's there already."

"Do you know why?" She began to pace back and forth. "I found out from my confessor. It seems Mother Teresa is getting too independent. She's been too successful and has too many friends in high places. Fray Ángel wants to manacle her, so he made her prioress of Encarnación, where nearly everybody hates her. It's an impossible job, and it'll keep her busy and out of his hair for years. It's a death knell for the reform, Angélica. That bastard! That *canalla!*"

"Sister Isabel," I said sternly. "What kind of language is that!"

"Spanish," she growled.

"She wants me to leave Pastrana and go with her."

"You should. That way, you can keep and eye on things and keep me informed."

Another spying job. I left for Ávila without talking to Lis and without getting back Teresa's *Life*. Teresa and I met at San José, where we could talk about what awaited her at the convent she had abandoned nine years earlier. She expected the worst. The sisters were accustomed to choosing their own prioress and were furious that an outsider—and a traitor at that—was being imposed on them.

We moved in on October 6, 1571. I wouldn't remember the date except for the fact that the Battle of Lepanto took place the next day. We didn't know it then, but at the very moment we were packing our bags for Encarnación, King Felipe's bastard brother, Don Juan de Austria, was preparing to lead a Christian fleet to victory against the Turks. Perhaps if we'd known about that felicitous event at the time we were leaving for Encarnación, we'd have been more optimistic.

On the day of our move, Fray Ángel met us at the gates of San José, where we climbed into a mule-drawn carriage that took us across town. Along the streets people hissed at Teresa. Many had relatives in the convent, and naturally took the nuns' side. Some cursed and threw eggs or stones. Once we arrived, Fray Ángel sliced through the crowd, a cross heaved above his head. Men in intricately embroidered doublets and women in graceful gowns blocked the door, hurling insults. "Bitch!" "Imposter!" "False *santa*!" With his one free arm Fray Ángel elbowed his way into the vestibule, where a cluster of nuns waited, their sour faces scrunched up like fists. A sister stuck out her foot to trip Teresa. A few others stood silent, among them Cándida the turtle, more hunched than ever and much older looking. Teresa entered carrying an image of Saint Joseph in her arms, which rubbed almost everyone the wrong way.

At last the nuns gathered in the choir. "Go back to San José!" someone hissed. "Take your Unmitigated Rule and go!"

The racket was deafening. Fray Ángel took advantage of the commotion to call out, "Will you have Mother Teresa de Jesús as your prioress?" Hardly anyone heard, except Catalina de Castro, one of the few nuns who supported Teresa. She responded, "We will have her! *Te Deum Laudamus!*" Cándida croaked in her amphibian voice, "We'll have her. *Te Deum Laudamus!*" One or two others repeated, "*Te Deum Laudamus!*" Before the opposition realized what was happening, Teresa's supporters grabbed her and dragged her over to the prioress's chair. It was done.

Afterward, we gathered in the refectory for a reception. Catalina de Castro and her tiny contingent placed plates with apples and little cakes on a table in the center of the room. The nuns milled around. Most of them were furious at having been duped, but nevertheless partook willingly of the treats. Sister Caridad lumbered over to where Teresa was standing, her hand on a firm, red apple. "Don't take more than one, *Madre*," she jeered. "Remember, God is watching."

Teresa turned to her with a smile as sweet as syrup. "Take as many of those little cakes as you want," she said with a conspiratorial wink, "since God has His eye on the apples!"

She made changes slowly, one at a time. First, she banned servants from living in the cells. Then she forbade visits outside the convent. She cut down on time spent at the grille, simplified meals, introduced mental prayer into the daily routine. Finally, she brought in Fray Juan, the "half-friar," as confessor. The sisters scowled. They were afraid of him. They thought he'd be overly rigorous, dishing out cruel penances for snitching a turnip or snooz-ing during Lauds. But he fooled them. He was an angel—patient, kind, knowledgeable, and attentive. Little by little, so gently and gradually that the nuns hardly noticed, she introduced the discalced rule and got rid of the calced confessors. Before long even the most hostile nuns began to support her. Like Don Juan de Austria, she'd faced a fearsome enemy and triumphed. She, no less than he, was a formidable strategist.

One night I said to her, "Teresa, I know you don't like gossip . . ."

"I never repeat gossip. That's why you have to listen carefully the first time!"

I chuckled. At least she hadn't lost her sense of humor. "Do you remem-ber Antonio Pérez?" I said. "You met him in Pastrana."

"The personal secretary of Don Felipe? The one who's sleeping with Doña Ana?"

"You know about it?" I was floored. I'd thought I was going to reveal a secret. I'd put off telling her for months because I hadn't wanted to upset her. I thought she had enough on her hands with the transformation of Encarnación.

"Everyone knows about it. The princess is so brazen. Poor Don Ruy."

I debated about whether or not to tell her what I had witnessed. "You know," I began haltingly, "I actually saw them . . ."

"Pray for the poor sinners," interrupted Teresa. "God is merciful. Even so, they'll probably go to a Hell of their own making. Sooner or later, Pérez will shit in his own soup. As for Don Ruy, no man wants to be a cuckold. He's bound to find a way to take care of Don Antonio."

Teresa was reputed to be a seer, so I wouldn't have been surprised if all her predictions came true. As it turned out, though, before a year had gone by, a letter came from Pastrana announcing that Don Ruy was dead, and the princess had decided to enter San José de Pastrana as a discalced Carmelite nun!

I made cold compresses for Teresa's head and a sedative for myself.

"I'm sorry, Angélica, but you'll have to go back," murmured Teresa. "I need . . ."

"I know, you need someone to keep an eye on things. You need a spy."

"Yes," said Teresa, holding a compress to her brow, "I need a spy."

Sister Angélica del Sagrado Corazón
Toledo, 5 October 1576

CHAPTER 21

On Eagle's Wings

"You have seen what I did to the Egyptians,
and how I bore you on eagle's wings and brought you to myself."
—Exodus 19:4

THE NIGHT WAS BLACK AS SIN AND JUST AS RISKY. I LAY IN BED, FULLY clothed, waiting for Mother Isabel's signal. A soft April sprinkle had fallen in the afternoon, and I wondered if it was still drizzling. The lazy drone of an invisible fly unsettled my gut. I swallowed hard and tried to ignore it. Fear, of course, but excitement, too. I thought of Fray Julián reconnoitering, moving noiselessly up and down streets and alleys on his mule, circling the Éboli palace, peering in windows. When he was sure it was safe, he would whistle softly three times.

Isabel heard his signal before I did. "Okay," she called softly, "*vámonos,* let's go." I grabbed the burlap bag that was lying by the bed. In the pitch-black hall women were lining up in the pre-established order. Each one knew how many steps she had to take in the darkness to get to her proper place in line. I could hear Isabel's tight, uneven breathing. We lit no candles. We couldn't risk a passerby noticing a flicker in the convent window. Once we got outside, it would be easier. We could rely on the midnight moonlight— unless it was raining.

We'd been practicing for weeks, counting the number of steps from the dormitory to the vestibule, from the vestibule to the locutorium, from the locutorium to the path that would lead us to freedom. We rehearsed first in the daylight, then in the dark, giggling and tripping over our feet, the laundry baskets, the cobble stones. We went through the routine again and again. Each time it went more smoothly. Isabel decided what each one would carry. She'd bring the cooking utensils, wrapped carefully in flannel so they wouldn't clang. I'd lug jars of herbs and medicinal compounds in a burlap sack. Sister Inmaculada was in charge of the Blessed Sacrament. Sister Perfecta would handle the chapel linen. We practiced moving like galley slaves chained together at the ankles. We got used to the smell of each other's bodies, the pace of each other's steps. It was fun. We were like schoolgirls preparing for an adventure. Only now we weren't rehearsing. We were fleeing in earnest. "Heavenly Father," I prayed, "deliver us from danger. Carry us to safety on eagle's wings, as You did your people so long ago."

How did the sixteen sisters of San José come to pack up their belongings and steal out of Pastrana in the dead of night? It would never have happened if Doña Ana de Mendoza, Princess of Éboli, hadn't decided to become a discalced Carmelite nun.

The princess's husband, Don Ruy, died on July 29, 1573, a date I wrote down on a scrap of paper I hid in my copy of *Los amores de Clareo y Florisea*, a really exciting novel about two lovers who run away from home—but this isn't the time to tell the story. Anyhow, I put the date in that book so I wouldn't forget it. No sooner had Don Ruy Gómez closed his eyes and gone to live with the Lord forever, than the princess started carrying on and wailing that nothing was left for her but to become a discalced nun. She didn't even have the courtesy to send a messenger to Mother Teresa to ask permission. Ambrosio, a ruddy little friar who witnessed the scene, rode to Ávila to deliver a message from Isabel to Teresa with the news.

"She was so anxious to take the habit that she demanded I take off mine and give it to her!" he said. "I stood there in my undergarments, right in front of Don Ruy's remains! She threw my robe over her shoulders, fell to her knees, and went into a paroxysm of religious fervor. But then," he added slyly, "she's seen plenty of men in the buff, so I'm sure she wasn't shocked. She's still got my habit, the witch! The one I'm wearing now is an extra!"

I didn't think Doña Ana would actually go through with it. The idea of this spoiled princess submitting to a life of austerity was laughable. Even so, I rode back to Pastrana with Fray Ambrosio, as Teresa requested. Not long afterward, the black and gold *carroza* appeared in front of San José de Pastrana. Doña Ana climbed down, Fray Ambrosio's habit still thrown around her shoulders, and bowed before Isabel. She was followed by an entourage consisting of her mother, her maid Lis, a personal cook named Andrea, and eight or ten menservants who carried her valises and trunks into the locutorium. What was Isabel to do? The convent belonged to the princess. The property was in her name, and she'd paid for everything in the house.

"I want to live just like you, in perfect austerity," she declared. She walked majestically into the chapel followed by her mother, Lis and Andrea, and knelt before the crucifix. When the bell sounded for Sext, she was still kneeling, tears of religious fervor streaming down her cheeks. "Dear Jesus," she whispered, her face flush with passion, "bless me and make me worthy."

At mealtime, the princess strode to the prioral chair and smoothed her skirt as though she were wearing a farthingale. Then she moved to sit down. With a flick of the wrist Isabel pulled out the chair and sat down herself. After all, she was the prioress. She looked up at Doña Ana.

"Come, Your Highness," she said, signaling the princess to sit by her side. Normally, I sat to the right of the prioress, but I understood we'd all be expected to make concessions.

Doña Ana stared at her in disbelief, fury darkening her face. "What?"

Isabel nodded to her. "Sit here, next to me," she said quietly.

Doña Ana's lips trembled. Then suddenly, she turned grandiosely on her heel, strode to the other end of the refectory, and sat between two white-veiled kitchen nuns. "I am the lowest of the low," she said solemnly. Since she couldn't occupy the prioral chair, she was going to turn the occasion into a theatrical display of humility.

The next day, she refused to eat in the refectory at all. Her cook would prepare dinner for her, she said, and serve her meals in the cell. Furthermore, Lis and Andrea would be entering the convent along with her, so Mother Isabel should provide them with habits immediately. Isabel de Santo Domingo bit her lip and held her tongue. By the end of the day, I had stitched two extra habits. The princess had had a fine-fitting garment of soft brown serge made for herself. Who knows what she did with Fray Ambrosio's habit. She, her cook and her maid were clothed in a makeshift ceremony by the end of the week.

The princess attracted a procession of visitors. It was the custom for the extern to supervise the grille to make sure conversations revolved around holy things, and Isabel assigned me to the job. At first, Doña Ana's friends came to offer their condolences for her husband's death. "Oh, you poor thing!" "God rest his soul!" The princess received guests with her face uncovered, flitting her fan flirtatiously. Before long, the conversation veered away from Don Ruy toward news from abroad. Henry of Navarra had married Marguerite de Valois, whose magnificent dress was so laden with gems that her ladies-in-waiting had to carry the train during the entire ceremony. On Saint

Bartholomew's Day, the Queen of France had ordered the massacre of two thousand Huguenots who, of course, had it coming. The bad news was that the Duke of Alba was returning from Brussels and would want to reclaim his position as the king's advisor. And, since Don Ruy was dead, who was to prevent him from poisoning his highness's mind against the poor Princess of Éboli, widow of the duke's longtime rival?

I took note of everything to report back to Isabel and then to Teresa. The princess was indignant. Why did the extern have to be there? she wanted to know. She didn't need a chaperone. And why did she have to speak to her friends through bars? Why couldn't they come into the cloister? And what was this business about covering her face before strangers?

Isabel pulled out the constitution of the order, written by Teresa herself. "Look," she said, "Article 15 reads as follows: *No nun should be seen with her face unveiled unless she is with her father, mother, brothers, or sisters. Her dealings should be with persons who are an edification and help for the life of prayer and who provide spiritual consolation rather than recreation. Another nun should always be present unless one is dealing with conscience matters.* Article 18: *The sisters should pay no attention to the affairs of the world, nor should they speak about them.* Article 19: *As much as they can, the sisters should avoid a great deal of conversation with relatives. Aside from the fact that they will become preoccupied with their relatives' affairs, they will find it difficult to avoid talking to them about worldly things.* Article 20: *Let them be very careful in speaking with outsiders, even though these may be close relatives. If these persons are not the kind who find their satisfaction in speaking about things of God, they should be seen seldom, and the visit kept short.*"

The princess, infuriated, raised her hand and knocked the pages to the floor. "I don't care about your stupid rules!" she screamed. "I'm going to see my friends in the parlor!"

Fray Ambrosio was the first to notice that the princess was putting on weight. "She looks . . ." he began cautiously.

"Yes," said Isabel. "She looks pregnant. This cannot go on."

"No wonder she wanted to enter the convent," laughed Fray Ambrosio. "She has to disappear for a while. And who is the father?" he asked with a wink. "It could be Don Ruy, of course, or it could be Antonio . . ."

"Never mind," interrupted Isabel. "The point is, we have to get her out of here."

She called for the princess and suggested that since the rules of the order were not to her liking, perhaps she should retire to one of the hermitages on the edge of the convent grounds, where she would be free to receive friends in her accustomed style. With a swoosh of her graceful habit, the princess, her mother, and her servants withdrew to the fringes of San José. The princess held court every afternoon until she grew bored with the routine, then abandoned the convent altogether and returned to her palace. But out of sight was not out of mind. She sent directives almost daily about the running of *her* convent. The penalty for disobedience was starvation. Without the princess's monthly contribution, we couldn't buy food or fuel. Forbidden to accept alms, we were her prisoners. I sat down to write a detailed report to Teresa.

Dire situations call for radical moves. Teresa ordered us to wait for a propitious moment, then flee. That's right. She told us to abandon San José de Pastrana. The first step was to return any treasures the princess had donated to the convent. But how to do it without arousing suspicion? Mother Isabel sent for a notary and *corregidor* and made them our accomplices. In the presence of the notary, she turned everything Doña Ana had given us over to the *corregidor*. The plan was, we would sneak out in the dead of night, making sure no one saw us. Then the two men would accompany us to where Fray Julián was waiting with carts to whisk us out of town. It would be tricky. Doña Ana's village was a fiefdom. Not only did she have friends among the royalty and Inquisition, but her husband's guards were at her beck and call. Furthermore, Antonio Pérez was known to be ruthless. That's why we had to plan carefully, rehearsing every step.

At Isabel's order, sixteen nuns queued up in the corridor. No one spoke. All you could hear was the strained breathing of anxious sisters carrying cumbersome packages. When Isabel gave the signal, we processed slowly down the stairs. We couldn't hurry. Someone might trip and let out a cry or, worse yet, cause us all to tumble like dominoes. One step. Then another. Then another. We made it to the vestibule, but the most dangerous part lay ahead. We would have to move swiftly and noiselessly through the convent grounds to the street, where the notary and *corregidor* would lead us through Pastrana to the alley where the carts were waiting. The noise of a foot against a stone could set a dog to barking and alert the princess's guards. Or a drunk returning from a late-night bout at the tavern might call out to us. Or an insomniac might look through his window, see a shadowy line of escaping nuns, and run to the palace. Or the princess herself, lazily gazing over her property after making love to Antonio Pérez, might spy a white veil moving jaggedly down the street in the moonlight. I held my breath.

Holding a cross above her head with one hand and her sack full of pots in the other, Isabel marched before us. We made it down the footpath without drawing the attention of any dogs. With the help of our partners in crime, the notary and the *corregidor,* we scurried down the street taking care not to stumble, then dashed through the alley until we came to the carts. The men helped us lift our bundles into the vehicles and climb in. Now there was no way to avoid making noise. The drivers snapped their reins and the mules took off at a trot. The cartwheels bumped and banged against pebbles and stones. I prayed the townspeople were fast asleep or, if they awakened, would be too groggy to investigate the racket outside their windows. The carts rumbled into the countryside and took the road to Saragossa in order to throw any would-be pursuers off track. Then we cut back through the mountains toward Ávila. At last, we were free, snatched from the claws of the She-Devil and borne away on eagle's wings.

People called our escape a miracle. News of it even reached the court, where, we heard, His Majesty Don Felipe could hardly believe that the supercilious Princess of Éboli had been outsmarted by a little old nun in a patched brown habit!

But Doña Ana wasn't a woman to settle for defeat. A few days later we learned the awful news: She'd accused Teresa of heresy before the Inquisition of Valladolid, and turned over her *Life* as evidence. It was a dangerous situation, made more dangerous still by the presence in Valladolid of the brutal Inquisitor, Don Javier Sánchez Colón.

Angélica del Sagrado Corazón
Toledo, 7 October 1576

CHAPTER 22

The Gates of Hell

TERESA DIDN'T ESCAPE FROM ENCARNACIÓN ON EAGLE'S WINGS. INSTEAD, Fray Ángel released her. Her detention there served no further purpose since she'd become popular with the nuns and they no longer tortured her. The other good news we received that spring was that the Valladolid Inquisition had cleared Teresa's *Life*. I have to admit, I was astonished. I'd feared that the Princess of Eboli's accusation would result in an arrest or worse, especially since I'd heard that the ferocious Don Javier was now back in Valladolid. It was especially bewildering that the absolution had come so quickly. The Inquisition is a lumbering beast, an unwieldy bureaucratic behemoth. An accusation can take years to investigate. The Toledo tribunal still hadn't reached a decision on Teresa's book. So far, we'd been lucky. We'd manage to avoid the beast's claws. But that summer, after she'd returned from founding a convent in Segovia, Teresa got it into her head to push the reform south to Beas. It was the move that brought her to the gates of Hell.

Beas is a sunny, southern town near the Andalusian border. We rolled up to the entrance of the cottage that was to house the new convent to find two people waiting for us. Teresa knew one of them: María de San José, Doña Luisa's former handmaiden, had served for a couple of years as prioress of Malagón and developed into a shrewd administrator. Teresa had sent for her to help with the new foundation and had even begun to speak of her as a possible heir to her title of foundress. Teresa was getting older, and someone would have to carry on the reform when she was no longer around. The other person was someone Teresa had never seen before, although I remembered him from Pastrana: Fray Jerónimo Gracián, the handsome young friar with sculpted cheeks who'd won the nuns' hearts with his elegant sermons and easygoing spiritual direction. He was glib and smart and seductive, and he'd already wheedled himself into the powerful position of Apostolic Visitator. His job was to observe the southern monasteries and make sure they were operating according to the rules. That's what had brought him to Beas.

I hadn't liked Jerónimo Gracián when I'd met him in Pastrana. I could tell from the beginning that the man was an operator. The worst thing was that Teresa fell under his spell almost immediately. While María and I swept and scrubbed to get the new house ready, she basked in Gracián's honeyed words. The grille hadn't been constructed yet, so they spent hours in the garden, engrossed in conversation. It made me uncomfortable. What was going on? Was he just a young man overwhelmed by the attention of a celebrity, or was he worming his way into her heart to advance his career? He was thirty. She was sixty. I didn't think they were about to hop into the hay together— although stranger things have happened.

One day I got up the nerve to broach the subject with María de San José. "Don't you think Gracián spends a bit too much time here?" I ventured. "It's unseemly."

I don't know what I expected her to say, but I didn't expect what came. She turned the color of a *pomo amoris* and snapped, "Stay out of it! Just stay out of it!" She glared at me, eyes bulging, then stomped out of the room. "Oh, God," I said to myself. "She's in love with him."

A few days later I was hauling out garbage to be burned when I ran into María in the yard, painting a fence. Tears were rolling down her cheeks. I put down my load and approached her. "Are you all right?" I asked. It was as though I'd opened a spigot.

"Oh, Sister Angélica," she sobbed. "I suppose you haven't heard." My heart leapt with hope. Maybe she was going to tell me that Jerónimo Gracián was leaving. Instead she said, "Mother has taken a vow of obedience to Fray Jerónimo." She fell into my arms, disregarding the rule about nuns not touching each other. "I'm sorry I was cross to you the other day."

A vow of obedience! I left María to weep into the paint and went to look for Teresa. I found her standing on a chair, sandpapering a doorframe. "What's this about a vow to Gracián?" I blurted out. "Are you mad? You hardly know the man!"

"Oh," she said calmly. "I see news travels fast. It's true. As a sign of submission to God, I made a vow of obedience to Father Gracián."

"Isn't that a little rash, Teresa? A woman like you can't afford to be bossed around by a two-bit friar."

"He's not a two-bit friar, he's the Apostolic Visitator, and he doesn't boss me around." An edge had crept into her voice. "He guides me spiritually. This is God's will, Angélica." She stepped down from the chair and sat on it. "I had a vision," she said, regaining her calm. "Jesus told me Fray Jerónimo was to be my spiritual husband. I have to obey him."

I thought old age was making her dotty. It wasn't the first time she'd fallen under the influence of a spiritual director, but I'd never seen her like this before.

It was Gracián's idea that Teresa leave Beas to found a convent in Seville. I thought from the start that the project was doomed. In the first place, Rubeo, who had issued the original patents that enabled Teresa to launch the reform in Castile, had forbidden her from founding in Andalusia—and with good reason. The Andalusian friars were still fiercely opposed to the reform and had threatened violence. Besides, Teresa hated the South—the blinding sun that caused your head to ache, the bright colors, the gaudy baubles that made even decent women look like harlots. (Just because she was a *santa* doesn't mean she loved everybody.) Furthermore, the Seville Inquisition was reputedly the most brutal in Spain. Andalusia was saturated with heretical sects and Lutheran propaganda, not to mention suspect *conversos* and *moriscos*. As a result, the inquisitors were always vigilant, and the penalties for unorthodoxy were unusually vicious.

A vow of obedience binds you in spiritual matters, but not in administrative matters such as founding convents. Besides, the order of a superior always takes precedence. Since Rubeo had banned new houses in Andalusia, Teresa could have told Gracián to go jump in the river.

But Gracián badgered her. "It's a paradise, Mother, with old Moorish palaces like jewels in the sun, gardens of oleander and hibiscus, orchards of oranges and lemons. The ladies are like walking ornaments in their gowns of silk and taffeta." He shot Teresa a smile like spiced wine. "Seville is such a rich port that gold literally drips from men's pockets."

He's carving out a niche for himself in the reform, I thought. Teresa's the foundress, and he wants to be the Founder. "We embrace poverty," I snapped. "We're not interested in gold."

"But Sister," he said sweetly, "we could channel that wealth toward the glory of God."

Fray Julián readied the carts, covering them so we consecrated virgins could travel undetected across lands haunted by gypsies and bandits. Teresa handed him the treasures she always took with her: her hourglass, reminder of the ephemerality of life; her bell, which she rang, even in transit, to announce the Divine Office; and her tambourine, with which she accompanied our singing. Four sisters from Malagón joined Teresa, María, and me. Gracián had to go to Madrid on business, but promised to come to Seville as soon as he was free.

It was only May, but the sun was already ferocious. It beat down on the caravan, causing Teresa to grow dizzy and nauseous. Within days our provisions were ruined. The vegetables rotted, the cheese melted, the water went bad, and the bread grew moldy. It's a bad omen, I thought, throwing everything out. Sometimes in the country we found a farmer willing to sell us vegetables, but in town, we had to stay in flea-ridden inns, eat nothing but salty sardines, and go to bed thirsty. Gracián had praised the Andalusians as good-natured and friendly, but they bargained hard for food, and more than once we were forced to raid an orchard for oranges.

When we reached the Guadalquivir River, the muleteers drove us to the ferry crossing, and Fray Julián hired three boats. The mules boarded skittishly, pulling the carts behind them. Teresa and I settled into a corner of the largest ferry, clutching each other in anticipation of the rocking and pitching that was sure to come. No sooner did the ferryman cut us loose from the dock, than our boat began to lurch from side to side, and the sky spun above our heads like an upside down whirlpool. Teresa, her lips a sickly green, groped her way to the railing and leaned over. I'd seen her vomit almost daily since we were both children, but this was uncanny. Surges of malodorous liquid shot from her mouth—olive-colored muck full of slime and putrefaction. It left the side of the boat reeking, although most of it fell to the roiling waters below. Suddenly, one of the ferries began to pitch and reel violently and then tore loose from the others.

"Oh, God, no!" I screamed. That boat carried two carts and four sisters. The current caught the vessel and carried it off. Teresa and I watched in horror.

"Grab the lines!" she shouted. "Grab the lines!"

Her words were lost in the thrashing of the water, but these were quick-thinking women. They grabbed the haulage ropes and, with the precision and teamwork they had learned from years of convent life, yanked and heaved. God was watching out for us, because rather than capsize and drown its passengers, the boat eventually floated onto a sandbank. The next morning Fray Julián said a Mass of thanksgiving, and we climbed back into the carts.

We intended to replenish our supplies in Córdoba. Teresa and I left the others to scout for food, while Fray Julián went to look for lodgings. A gypsy woman holding a baby approached us. "I'm sorry, daughter," said Teresa. "All I can offer you is my blessing."

Suddenly, the woman made a motion as if to fling the infant at her. Mortified, Teresa raised her arms to catch the child. In a split second the beggar thrust her hand into Teresa's pocket and nabbed her purse. With no money for provisions or an inn, all we could do was fill our water skins, then climb back into the carts and begin the long trek to Seville.

The jewel of Andalusia was as horrific as I'd feared. The blinding sunlight against the white stucco made our heads reel. Our soggy habits lay heavy on our bodies. After much inquiring and many false turns, we finally found the house that Gracián had arranged for us to buy. By then, Teresa was feeling queasy, so I went to the apothecary's shop to beg a bit of elder, peppermint, and yarrow to make a tea, promising to pay as soon as I had money.

Gracián had spread the word that we were coming, and neighbors had left us furnishings in the patio: a bed, three straw mats, a beat-up chair, a broom, a cooking pot, a basin, some tin plates and cups. Teresa had named María de San José prioress, and the younger woman set about furnishing the rooms as best she could. She designated spaces for the chapel, the locutorium, the infirmary, the sewing room, and the chapter room. She assigned cells. She'd brought with her three Italian *albarellos,* long-necked apothecary jars, which Doña Luisa de la Cerda had given her, and she put them in the infirmary. Then she ordered provisions, begging the grocer to send over some vegetables on credit. María's knowledge of Latin didn't prevent her from scrubbing floors and washing windows. Three Andalusian nuns joined us, and María organized everyone into teams, one to clean up the yard, one to set up the kitchen, one to dig a hole for the outhouse. The *Sevillanas* weren't much disposed toward work, but, by the end of the day, somehow we'd managed to make the place look decent.

The next morning, each of the neighbors who had brought a utensil or piece of furniture came to reclaim it. The bed disappeared, then the mats, the broom, the pots. María didn't panic. She sent a messenger to the other convents in the area—the Clarisas, the Dominicans, the Benedictines—asking for help. Once again, the house filled with crude but serviceable furnishings.

"You've done a wonderful job," I told María.

"Fray Jerónimo will be pleased, don't you think?" She said, then reddened suddenly.

"Of course he will," said Teresa, who had pulled herself out of bed and was standing by an empty doorframe. Her tone made it clear she'd understood everything.

At twenty-seven, María was breathtakingly beautiful, even in a habit and veil. Her skin was as smooth and her eyes as luminous as when, at fourteen, she'd curtseyed before Teresa and asked, "Am I pretty, Mother?"

Teresa recognized María's talents. The younger woman was sharp and poised, and her education was far superior to Teresa's. Furthermore, as Doña Luisa's protégée, she had the contacts and pull to keep the movement afloat. Teresa said she loved her like a daughter. But sometimes mothers and daughters become rivals.

The apothecary jars stood proudly on the counter of the infirmary, the only objects of beauty in an otherwise drab room. Such vessels were very much in demand, since they were not only attractive, but also sturdy. Specially designed to contain viscous substances, they were cylinder-shaped, with wide mouths, and tapered in the center to make them easier to hold. The three María had given me were exceptionally graceful, each with a distinct design of interlacing yellow and blue flowers on a gleaming white background.

The minute Teresa felt better, she inspected the new prioress's work. Nothing pleased her. The sanctuary was unduly ornate, the kitchen hearth badly constructed, the pantry smelly, and the straw beds moldy. "I'm sorry, Mother," said María de San José. She pursed her lips and set about rectifying her errors. She'd borrowed the chapel furnishings from a Benedictine convent in the neighborhood, but now she sent them back. She redecorated the sanctuary, climbed up on tables to repair ceiling beams, aired the pantry and changed the bedding. Teresa wasn't satisfied. The cell assignments were all wrong. Friends' quarters were too close to each other, which led the women to gossip, disrespecting the rule of silence. Again, María apologized.

"You're too lax with them," Teresa complained. "This familiarity among nuns is unhealthy. I don't like the way these women hold hands or walk around with their arms around each other's waists."

"It's the custom here," countered María de San José respectfully, but firmly. "Andalusians are more demonstrative than we are. You have to make allowances."

"Are you disobeying me?" snapped Teresa. "Who's the foundress, you or I?" María bowed her head in submission, but I could see the rage in her eyes.

One day, Teresa came into the infirmary and her gaze fell upon the three *albarellos.* "Those should be in the pantry," she declared.

"They're apothecary jars," I said calmly. "They belong here."

"They're lidded. They're for olive oil."

"I use them for arnica."

"Empty them out. I want them in the pantry, out of sight. We don't need such fancy jars decorating the infirmary."

"What's gotten into to you?" I snapped. "Is it the heat or your lack of money?" We owed a fortune on the house, and even though Teresa had taken in some postulants with large dowries, she was worried about finances.

María stuck her head in the door. "I gave those jars to Sister Angélica," she said calmly. "They were mine to give, a gift from Doña Luisa."

"This is a convent, Mother María de San José," hissed Teresa. "The words *mine* and *yours* don't exist. For you these worthless objects have become a source of pride!"

Suddenly, Teresa reached for the three jars, swept them off the counter, and hurled them against the wall. They exploded like towers hit by cannon fire. María and I stared in disbelief.

Teresa looked from one to the other, then at the mess she'd made. Shards of pottery and sticky oils were oozing to the floor. She staggered toward a bench and collapsed in tears.

"Oh, God," she murmured. "Oh, God, forgive me." She looked up at María de San José. "Forgive me, daughters," she whispered. "I don't know what came over me." I put my arm around her. "I'm such a miserable human being," she sobbed. "Your lovely *albarellos.* Material goods are worthless, but my anger, my cruelty . . . how can you forgive me?"

María stood looking down at her, her eyes smoldering. This was her first dynastic battle, and she'd won. She'd made the supreme ruler lose control. She'd reduced her to tears. But Teresa was a formidable opponent, and the hostilities weren't over.

One afternoon a messenger came with a note for Teresa. She took the paper and turned it over in her hands. "It's from Fray Jerónimo Gracián," she said, without betraying any emotion at all. She opened it in front of María and me. "He'll be joining us soon in Seville," she added. The messenger looked at her blankly, sweat dripping from his temples. He was waiting for someone to pay the postage. Teresa went to find her purse, and María ordered that food and ale be brought to him. After he'd taken it outside to eat, the three of us stood there a moment without speaking. Finally, María, flushed and tense, shrugged and went to attend to her chores. Teresa looked at me without saying a word, then went to her cell.

María made subtle enhancements of the premises. Flowers were planted. Rugs were beaten. Candlesticks were polished. The vestibule tiles were regrouted. Teresa had given permission for Fray Jerónimo to take his first meal in the convent parlor, and little by little María filled the pantry with flour, sugar, and spices. Teresa, who usually opposed such luxuries, said nothing. She spent most of her time in a tiny hermitage in the garden, reading and praying.

At last, Gracián walked in the door, his radiant smile as seductive as ever.

"*Gloria In Exelsis Deo*," María greeted him, struggling to contain her excitement.

"*Deus Vobiscum*," he answered, beaming like a ray of sun.

Teresa made an unceremonious entrance. She had a cold, and her nose was red and runny. She looked tired. She was showing her age. The creases around her eyes were deeper than usual. Her voice was raspy. "Good morning, Your Reverence," she croaked.

The two women faced Gracián like the naked babes presented to Solomon by their mothers. One of them would live, and one of them would die. Gracián looked from one to the other as if weighing his options.

"Mother!" he greeted Teresa, oozing warmth.

That's all he said, but that's all he needed to say. His already sunny smile grew sunnier still, and his luminous gaze held Teresa's rheumy one. In a moment of excruciating silence, María de San José looked from Gracián to Teresa and back again. Then it was over. María bowed her head in a sign of submission. "I'll give the order to prepare Father's dinner," she said, excusing herself. Teresa raised her chin almost imperceptibly, and a look crossed her face I hadn't seen in years, the look of haughty defiance. She had won.

She had won because she had to win. Teresa was *la Fundadora*, the foundress. Everyone called her that. Since the beginning of the reform, she'd seen herself as a general in God's army. Someday María might be her successor, but for now, she was only an aide-de-camp. Teresa needed Gracián, not only because he would be able to help her with the male branch of the order, but because he made her feel like the heroine she'd always wanted to be.

With his veneration and deference, he validated her notion of who she was. Teresa couldn't allow María to threaten her position by wresting Gracián's love away from her. There could only be one foundress, and both she and María knew it.

Before long, Gracián was the darling of the neighborhood. His fine looks, brilliant oratorical skills, and good-natured spiritual direction won over the society ladies of Seville. Teresa rejoiced. Contributions rolled in for the convent.

Later that year, a new postulant appeared at our doorstep. Miguela del Corro was already a famous *beata,* and she swept into our house like a princess entering a ballroom. She was in her forties, old for a novice, and claimed to be a noblewoman, although she had no dowry. Neither Teresa nor María wanted her, but Gracián's vote counted for three. He argued that since she was famous for her holiness, she'd bring prestige to the convent. "Maybe Father's right," sighed María. "The whole town has already canonized her. If we don't take her, it will be a scandal."

Miguela immediately took to walking the corridors reciting the *Pater Noster.*

"Your devotion is admirable," María de San José said to her, "but we have a rule of silence. You're welcome to pray aloud outside, but here, you're disturbing the other sisters."

Miguela was a tall, portly woman. She took a few more steps, then turned to face the diminutive prioress. She shoved out her bosom and huffed, "I'm talking to God, not to you."

María de San José had been raised in aristocratic circles, and she wasn't intimidated. "You are welcome to talk to God," she said firmly. "However, right now we're practicing silent prayer. I command you to stop, and your vow of obedience obligates you to comply."

Miguela del Corro turned on her heel and walked in the other direction, reciting her prayers even louder than before. "*Pater noster, qui es in caelis, sanctificetur Nomen Tuum . . .*" The prioress ran to position herself directly in front of the postulant. "Find a quiet place where you can meditate on each line of the *Pater Noster,*" she said. "This is a most beneficial activity."

Again the Del Corro woman turned on her heel and started walking in the other direction, but this time, it was I who placed myself in front of her, while María de San José remained behind her. She was trapped. "I'm going to my cell," she announced dramatically.

That afternoon, in the refectory, Miguela del Corro suddenly began to wail. "I can't eat this food, Mother," she cried. "My fingers are swollen from the heat, and this salty mishmash will make them worse. Can't I have some poultry in my room?"

"In this convent we all eat the same food," snapped María de San José.

Finally, Teresa stepped in. "Let them find something for her in the kitchen," she said. She was anxious to get the insurgent out of the refectory before she contaminated the whole convent.

A few days later, Miguela del Corro packed her bags and left, leaving her habit crumpled on the floor of the vestibule. "Good riddance!" I said to myself.

But she wasn't through with us. Hours later, officers of the Holy Tribunal were banging at our door. I caught my breath and trembled violently. A former inhabitant of the convent had accused us of engaging in certain heretical practices, they said. Naturally, they didn't name the complainant, but we all knew it was Miguela del Corro. Teresa greeted them courteously, diffidently even, but this time, her charm didn't work. She'd avoided the beast for years, but now, her luck had run out. The Seville Inquisition was swift and efficient. Before I knew it, two brawny guards with hands like clamps grabbed me from either side and dragged me out the door. I tried to coil around to see what was happening to Teresa, but the holy policemen yanked me forward with such force that I felt my neck snap. Then everything went black, as they slid a suffocating hood over my head.

Angélica del Sagrado Corazón
Toledo, April 15 1577

CHAPTER 23

Hell

THE FIRST THING I BECAME AWARE OF WAS MY OWN BODY—A TERRIBLE throbbing in my head. I remembered the guards jerking me forward like a rope doll, the crack of my neck reverberating through my skull, which suddenly assumed the proportions of a cavern. Where had they taken me? Where was I now? It occurred to me that if I sat perfectly straight, I could relieve some of the pressure on my spine. I moved my right hand to the ground in order to push myself into an upright position. Suddenly, I felt a swish across my fingers like a lash with a duster. Instinctively, I shifted my weight in order to brush off whatever creature had scurried across my knuckles, only to realize my left hand was pinned to the ground with some sort of metal clamp.

I heard a rustle and a whisper. Someone else was there. I squinted in the darkness and intuited rather than saw two bodies—whether they were men or women, I couldn't tell. I felt heaviness in my kidneys and realized I needed to use the chamber pot.

"It's right next to you," said a hushed female voice, as though she'd read my mind.

I walked the fingers of my right hand—the hand that was free—along the dank ground until they made contact with a hard, cold, basin-like object. I maneuvered it under me and relieved myself, then pushed it away.

"It's always the first thing they need when they come to," said the same voice.

"Thank you," I whispered.

My eyes were growing accustomed to the dark. I could tell I was in a dungeon, in a space about the size of a convent cell. The walls were clammy and malodorous, with metal bands positioned at strategic locations—some up high, to hang you from your wrists, some near the ground, to pin you on the floor. For a while I drifted in and out of wakefulness. My cellmates eyed me suspiciously and remained silent, except when they thought I was asleep. Then they whispered feverishly, so low that I could hardly make out a word. With time I began to realize they were repeating the same lines over and over. First one would ask a question and the other would reply, like schoolgirls at a lesson. If the respondent made a mistake, her partner would correct her and make her repeat the answer. Then they switched roles. I don't know how long I sat there, waking, dozing, straining to hear.

After a while, one of the women ventured a cautious question: "What are you here for?"

"Unorthodoxy, I guess. I don't know the details," I said truthfully.

They peered at me a long time. Then one of them whispered almost inaudibly, "*Chemá.*"

"*Yisroel,*" I responded automatically. Suddenly, I panicked. Why had I said that word? What if these women were spies sent to ensnare me? I'd fallen right into their trap. Now they could testify against me. They could confirm I was a Judaizer, that I prayed like a Jew. I'd just condemned myself to the stakes without even appearing before an inquisitor.

"Us, too," whispered the woman, smiling slightly. "We can help you."

I didn't trust them. I didn't believe they were really prisoners. I thought they were informers. Soon someone would take them away to debrief them. I forced myself to stay awake so I could watch them. I counted the cockroaches scurrying into the walls, gigantic roaches the size of mice. I picked the silverfish out of my soggy stockings. I scratched my flea bites. I stared at my cellmates through the murk.

"My name is Vida," volunteered one of the women. "This is my sister Sara."

I didn't answer her. After a while they went back to their exercises, one asking questions, the other answering them, even though they knew I could hear them. "Name?" "Vida Santana y Córdoba de Montes." "Occupation?" "Midwife." "Do you know how to read?" "Only a little." They practiced a long time. No guards came. Maybe they weren't spies, I thought. Maybe they really were Jews. People surnamed for saints or cities usually are. In the old days they exchanged their Jewish family names—Benlevi, Benabú—for others that sounded more Christian, or at least more neutral. Many took the names of the cities where they lived: Jaén, Toledo, Córdoba.

Eventually, the guard did return, but he didn't call for either Vida or Sara.

Instead, he shoved a new prisoner into our cell and flung a metal bowl down next to her. Just as I had, she fell into a stupor, then awakened in a daze and asked for the chamber pot. The stench was asphyxiating. No one had emptied the pots since I'd gotten there. Vida and Sara observed the newcomer a while, and then, almost inaudibly, Vida pronounced the word, "*Chemá*."

The new detainee rubbed her ear as though she felt a gnat. "Did you say something?"

"Say something? Oh, no. I was just humming to myself."

The woman instantly forgot about the sisters. She lifted her skirt to rub her leg, revealing calves crossed with whip marks. In a while the guard came and took her away.

When she was sure no one was in earshot, Vida whispered, "Listen, we can help you. We have to stick together."

Finally I put two and two together. They're clandestine Jews, I thought, and they think I'm Jewish, too. They really do want to help me. I looked at Vida in askance.

"We have friends who've been interrogated and released," Vida went on. "They've told us about the kinds of questions the inquisitors ask. They've taught us how to fool them." I doubted anyone could fool them, but I listened.

"You have to rehearse," piped in Sara. "You have to practice so you'll always say the same thing, even under torture. It's hard to remember the right answer when you've got a wrench squeezing your tit. You have to practice until your responses become automatic."

I must have flinched because Vida stretched out her hand, as if to comfort me. She couldn't reach me because she was shackled, but I found the gesture moving. I peered across the dimness at the women. Vida looked to be the older. I guessed she was about thirty-five, but it was hard to tell. She wore a shabby grey dress, very plain, and a smudged white apron. Her hair was pulled back into a knot and covered decorously with a tattered lace coif. Her sister, about two years younger, was dressed the same, except her dress was blue. They might have been servants or fishmongers or shoemakers' wives— but Vida had said she was a midwife.

"They'll ask you what your mother did when someone died," said Sara. "Don't say she tore her sleeve because they know that's a Jewish custom. Say she prayed the rosary."

"She did pray the rosary."

"Go ahead and tell them that, but they won't believe you. They'll try to make you say she tore her sleeve. They might slap you a few times to see if you change your story. If you don't, they'll put a clamp on your fingers and squeeze. And if that doesn't work, they'll pull off your dress and whip you until you bleed. What they want is to make you scream. People admit all kinds of things while they're in pain."

"The best thing to do is envision the scene in your mind," interrupted Vida. "Try to feel the smart. Imagine yourself crying out. Can you hear yourself screaming? What words come out of your mouth?"

I shook my head. "I don't know . . . I just . . . I just scream." I closed my eyes and heard myself let out a bloodcurdling shriek.

"You have to scream, 'Holy Jesus!'" said Vida. "Otherwise, they'll know you're a Jew."

"If you just say, 'Oh God, help me!' or something like that," explained Sara, "they'll say you don't call on Our Lord Jesus Christ in times of travail. Do you see what I mean? But because you're a Jew, those words won't come to you automatically. That's why you have to practice. At home we practiced all the time because you have to live, as we say, *a la defensiva,* defensively. You never know when some neighbor will turn you in and you'll wind up in jail, just like now. You have to be ready. I have three children, and Vida has two. We can't afford to die."

"How did you . . . What I mean is, did someone denounce you?" I asked cautiously.

"Brother Malquiel, who runs the orphanage by the cathedral," said Vida. "I gave him a ham three years in a row at Christmas."

"What's suspicious about that?"

"Well, we don't buy much meat, of course, except once in a while to throw them off the track. Whatever we buy from the Christian butcher, we feed to the dogs, we don't bring it in the house. It's a small price to pay for peace of mind. Once a year, at Christmas, I order a ham, just like the neighbors, in order to avoid suspicion. Then I donate it to the orphanage. Well, this year Brother Malquiel was talking with the butcher, and the butcher told him I always ordered just one ham. Well, if the Montes family orders just one ham and gives it to us, he must have thought, then what do they eat themselves? They and their kids must eat something else. You can see how he figured it out." A large rat darted across the floor, right by her foot. Vida stopped talking and stared at it. I would have squealed, but she didn't. Her composure was astounding.

"Such treachery!" I exclaimed. "I suppose you thought you could trust him."

Vida shrugged. "You can't trust anyone. That's just the way things are."

What amazing women, I thought. It's true they were Jews, but I couldn't help but admire them. No feeling sorry for themselves. No wailing and whining. "That's just the way things are," and carry on with your life. The Christians called secret Jews *marranos*, pigs, but there was nothing swinish about Vida and Sara. They were tough, smart women struggling to keep themselves and their kin alive. They're of the same race as Teresa, I thought. No wonder she's a fighter. My back ached from being pinned in one position for so long. I tried to shift my weight, but that only made it worse. I felt as though the pieces of my spine were fused into one solid rod that pressed into my waist like a huge nail.

We began our rehearsals. Name? Pancracia Soto y Fuentes. Domicile? Ávila. Father's occupation? Tailor. "Say needleworker," said Vida. "Tailor is a Jewish profession. Not all tailors are Jews, of course, but just to be on the safe side."

"Above all, avoid all-out lies," said Sara. "If you start to lie, then under torture you'll get your stories crossed for sure. People who lie always slip up eventually. And if they prove you've lied, things will go worse for you. It's better to tell half truths. For example, don't say you don't have a menorah, when it's very possible they've searched your house and found one. What they'll probably do is show you one and order you to explain what it's for. Then you say, 'We have a little candelabrum that looks like that. My husband bought it at a fair. I had no idea it was used for a Jewish ritual!'"

I was beginning to feel nauseous.

"You're a nun," said Vida, "but that won't protect you. Lots of *judaizantes* are nuns. Still, if you're looking for a cover, nun is a good profession. Better than lapidary. Now, the first thing they'll want to know is if you're a virgin. Are you?"

I bit my lip.

"No matter. I'm menstruating right now. I have a piece of sponge I can douse in menstrual blood for you to insert at the mouth of your womb. Most of the time it fools them. Unless they call in a midwife. If they call in a midwife, you're dead, but probably one of the inquisitors will conduct the examination. Now, this is important, Pancracia, because if you're a nun with a broken hymen, they'll say you've been fucking the Devil and call you a witch, which is as bad as being a Jew. What I mean is, it's a death sentence for sure. So it's essential you convince them you really are a virgin. This will be awful, Pancracia, but it's important for you to prepare yourself mentally. They'll stretch you out on a table and hike up your habit. Two of them will hold you down, and the rest will get a nice eyeful of pussy while the examiner pokes around inside of you. You have to hold yourself tight, as if you were trying to prevent yourself from peeing. That and his bloody finger will convince the examiner that you really are a virgin. But the important thing is this: When you scream, scream for Jesus. Scream, 'Holy Jesus, help me!' Can you remember that? Now let's practice, Pancracia. They've got you on the table. They've hoisted up your skirts. You're completely exposed. You're humiliated, mortified. Can you feel it? An obese inquisitor with stinking breath is leaning over you? Can you smell him? Do you feel his sweaty hands on your sex? You scream in agony. What do you say, Pancracia? What do you say?"

I saw what it was like for these people. Fear was a way of life. It penetrated every aspect of their daily routine. They had to live self-consciously, attentive to every move, every thought. They had to be able to justify every detail of their existence. They had to invent stories and revise them incessantly. They had to rehearse them mentally, so that they could tell them at a moment's notice under pressure, under torture.

Whenever the guard brought in a new prisoner, one of the sisters would put her to the test. "*Chemá*," she would whisper, almost inaudibly. None of the two or three flea-infested wretches who staggered into our cell gave the response that would earn her Vida's and Sara's assistance. Since we couldn't practice out loud before outsiders, I rehearsed mentally or else let my mind wander. Where was Teresa? Was she in a dungeon like this one, or had they given the foundress more comfortable quarters? Had they already interrogated her, or was she still languishing, as I was? Would they torture her? If they did, I was sure she would call out for Jesus, but they might accuse her of *judaizante* even so. Would they drag in Alonso Sánchez's forced conversion, his march through Toledo in a Sambenito, his purchased (and therefore bogus) patent of nobility? Would they show her a spice tower with foreign letters on it, like the one I'd once seen in Martín de Guzmán's house? Would she tell them what the letters meant? How would she have responded to Vida's hushed "*Chemá*"?

Finally a guard came for me. "The nun who came in with Mother Teresa de Jesús," was how he identified me. "Empty your bladder. We'll be back for you in fifteen minutes."

I tried to do as I was told, but my legs were so stiff I could hardly move them. My knees and ankles were swollen and jolts of pain shot though my right hip. The hours and days of immobility had produced a temporary paralysis.

"Rub them, Pancracia," said Vida. "And here, take the sponge." She worked it up under her skirts to fill it with blood, then threw it to me. Somehow I managed to insert it. Then I spat on my hands and rubbed them on the floor and my skirt to get rid of the stains. Every muscle in my body ached.

"What about you two?" I whispered. "When will they call for you? You were already here when I came!"

"Who knows," shrugged Vida. "Maybe God is protecting us. Better to be in here than out there on the rack. Anyhow, remember what we practiced. May the God of Abraham, Isaac, and Jacob be with you."

"And also with you." I dug a tiny rosary out of my pocket, not the big, wooden beads that all nuns carry, but a much smaller one that Teresa had once given me. "Here," I said. "Take this. It'll help you convince them you're good Catholics. Do you know how to say the rosary?"

"Of course. We know all their prayers."

"God bless you. Thank you for your help."

"Dear Jesus, Holy Virgin Mary, Saint Joseph," I prayed as the guards pushed me down the corridor on my rigid legs, "watch over those women. It's not their fault their parents never taught them the one true faith." It occurred to me that in their own way, they were heroes, just like Teresa. They'd reached out to me and shown compassion. They took risks to save their own people. I couldn't find it in my heart to condemn them, even though they were heretics.

The guards jostled me into a room furnished only with one long table behind which three chairs were placed. Three blacked-robed men came in and sat down. I expected them to be hooded, as in the Holy Week and Corpus Christi processions, but instead their faces were bare, veiled only by the flickering shadows produced by the tapers on the table. The guard signaled me to another chair in the middle of the room, facing the men. At first, I was so nervous I couldn't focus on their faces, which seemed to stretch and condense in the darkness like reflections in an unstill pool. The inquisitor in charge explained to me that this was not a trial, just an interrogation, although it could lead to a trial if answers were not forthcoming.

I felt as though a rock were caught in my stomach. My limbs still ached, and even though I'd tried to use the fetid chamber pot before leaving the cell, a sudden need to urinate made me shift my weight in the chair. I struggled to remember the answers I'd rehearsed with Vida and Sara. "I was born Pancracia Soto y Fuentes." "My father worked with the needle. He died when I was little." "No, your Reverence, we had no books in my home, none at all." "My mother wanted to marry me to a local boy named Basilio, a cartwright's son, but I heard the call of God and entered the convent instead. That's where I became Sister Angélica." "Yes, your Reverence, I learned all my prayers when I was little: *Salve María, madre de Dios . . .*" I was calming down a bit. I could feel my breathing grow steadier. The urge to urinate disappeared.

I began to focus on my interrogators. The inquisitor asking the questions was a portly man with multiple chins. "My mother and I lived with my aunt Catalina, your Reverence. She and my mother were seamstresses." My eyes moved from him to the notary, a skeleton of a man so emaciated he looked as though he should be dead. "I met Teresa de Ahumada when I was a child, your Reverence. My mother sewed for her household." Suddenly, a bloodcurdling shriek pierced the drone of the interrogation. It must have come from a torture chamber in some other part of the building. It sounded far away, yet near enough to cause my arm to jerk like a stick on a coil. "No, your Reverence, I never saw anything unusual in their home." My breathing had become jerky again, and the pressure on my kidneys returned with a vengeance. Beads of sweat formed on my brow. This must be what Hell is like, I thought. But Hell was yet to come.

My eyes darted fretfully from the interrogator to the notary to the secretary. I hadn't noticed the secretary before. He was hunched over the table, quill in hand, face rendered almost invisible by the angle of his body and the quavering light. I caught my breath. Something about him was familiar. Something about the graceful way he moved his hand. Something about the turn of his jaw. His tonsure left only a perimeter of graying hair. Deep furrows ran from the corner of his eye to the bottom of his ear. Still, there was no doubt in my mind. I hadn't seen him in about forty years, but the man was Javier Sánchez Colón, Teresa's cousin. I was sure of it. "Yes, your Reverence, Mother Teresa does eat pork. She's very fond of Serrano ham." Don Javier wrote without raising his eyes. He looked determined and tense. For him this apparently wasn't just a run-of-the mill interrogation.

It was clear where the questioning was going. They weren't really interested in me at all. They didn't care whether my father was a needleworker or a swineherd. They weren't going to check to see whether or not I was a virgin. The one they were out to get was Teresa.

A horrifying thought flared up like a boil: He's come to exact reprisals. She dumped him forty years ago, and the sore has been festering ever since. He joined the Dominicans because they run the Inquisition. All he had to do was bide his time and wait until they trapped her. He'd been in Valladolid and Brussels, but he'd been watching Teresa's career from afar. When she agreed to found in Andalusia, Fray Javier found his way here. Miguela del Corro had given him the opportunity he'd been waiting for. The Seville tribunal, with its reputation for ferocity, offered him the chance to settle the score. A perfect vengeance. An institutional execution. The Holy Office would be serving the faith, and his hands would be clean. My head was reeling. "No, your Reverence, Mother Teresa doesn't rest on Saturday." I was trembling like a child on the verge of tears. The pressure on my bladder was unbearable. "Forgive me, your Reverence," I whispered. "I need to urinate." The interrogator looked at me as though I'd stabbed him. "You should have attended to your bodily needs earlier," he said gruffly. "You'll have to wait."

"I can't your Reverence."

"Then you'll have to wet your habit."

I crossed my legs and tightened my muscles. I'd envisioned chains and clamps and prongs, but I hadn't foreseen this particular form of torture. My shoulders started to tremble, and my eyes became teary. The interrogator pretended not to notice. A former resident of San José de Sevilla had made an accusation, he said. This was not a formal trial, he reminded me, but he had to clarify certain things. Did we practice mental prayer? "Yes, your Reverence." Had I ever witnessed one of Teresa's raptures? "Yes, your Reverence." Had I ever seen any strange artifacts in her possession? Objects with foreign symbols on them? "No, your Reverence."

He signaled to a guard, who brought in a wooden box about the size of a traveling case. The guard took out an object—it reminded me of the spice tower I'd seen in Don Martín's drawer—and handed it to the interrogator. "What is this?" ("It looks like a spice tower, your Reverence.") "Does Mother Teresa own one of these?" ("Not to my knowledge, your Reverence.") "This object is used in what the Jews call the Havdala, the ceremony closing their Sabbath." I looked at him blankly. Why don't you ask your secretary? I thought. He's the one who knows about such things. He pulled out a large plate with what looked like separate cavities for different types of food. At the center of each were characters with little feet. "What about this?" ("I don't know, your Reverence.") "Jews use it for their Passover." I offered him the same vacant stare as before. A trickle of urine flowed out of my body, but I concentrated on not altering my expression. A flinch, a wince, a gulp—anything could make them think I'd lied. Was Teresa in contact with foreigners, the interrogator wanted to know? Germans? Dutch? French? "No, your Reverence." Did she hear confessions? "Oh, no, your Reverence!" Did she sometimes override the decisions of priests? "Oh, no, your Reverence!" Don Juan looked right at me, but I saw no flicker of recognition in his eyes.

Another guard came in with something the inquisitor called a "memory device." It's a kind of vise that clamps over your hand and bends your fingers backward. They show it to you first and tell you what they're going to do. They start slowly, one finger at a time, the pinky . . . bend, bend, bend . . . the ring finger . . . bend, bend, bend . . . until finally, crack! Your knuckles are flat against your wrist. "Did Mother Teresa preach to the nuns?" "No, your Reverence! Holy Mary, Mother of God!" The screw turns. The clamp tightens. The fingers bend farther. "Did she ever defend Lutherans?" "No, your Reverence! Jesus, Mary, and Joseph!" "Did she ever pray for Lutherans?" "Only for their return to our Holy Mother Church!" "Swear it on the Torah!" "What's the Torah, your Reverence?" They let me go.

The guards led me back to the cell, but Vida and Sara weren't there. "Oh God," I sobbed into my sleeve. "Oh, Jesus. Oh, Holy Mother of God. If that's what they did to me, who knows what they did to Teresa? And what about the poor Jewish sisters?" My underskirt and habit were drenched. I didn't care. I sank down into the piss and muck and fell asleep.

The next thing I remember is a guard shaking me and dragging me to my feet. Oh, God, I thought. They're not done with me. They want more. They're going to kill me. Don Javier wants revenge on Teresa, and, to get it, he'll destroy me. They'll trap me into denouncing her, and by doing it, I'll implicate myself. I'm as good as dead. Again, the guard shoved me down the corridor, only instead of to the interrogation room, he led me to the vestibule of a very old building with splintering window frames and crumbling interior walls. Teresa was chatting amicably with a man whose eyes were locked on hers. It was Javier, a look of uncanny tenderness on his face.

How could this be? Javier Sánchez, the cruel inquisitor of Valladolid and Brussels, deep in conversation with his childhood sweetheart? It took me a moment to take in the scene. Don Javier was smiling and nodding, as if he were inquiring about old friends or catching up on family gossip, as if nothing ghastly were going on in the inquisitorial chambers next door. He was engrossed in her, hanging onto her every word, his eyes fixed on hers. He raised his hand to make a point, and his fingers brushed lightly against her habit. She didn't move away. She stood there looking up at him, animated, excited. He stopped talking, as if to catch his breath. His lips quivered slightly, and he leaned toward her. He was very close, but still she didn't move. They stared at each other, their eyes speaking, their mouths silent. Slowly I began to grasp what was happening. He still cares for her, I thought. He didn't come here to punish her, but to keep her from harm. That's why they're letting us go. Don Javier has intervened on Teresa's behalf. He protected her in Valladolid, and he has protected her here.

"What did you tell them?" I asked her when we were back at the convent.

"Oh," she said. "I just explained to them that the whole thing was a big misunderstanding." She was lying of course, but there was no way to pry the story out of her. About Javier, she said not a word.

"Teresa . . ." I said gently. She refused to look at me. Something had changed. Something inside her was broken. She looked old. This was, I knew instinctively, the beginning of the end.

Jerónimo Gracián had gotten us into this mess, and in a strange way, he got us out. The calced friars of Andalusia were enraged. It was bad enough that Gracián, as Apostolic Visitator, had forbidden them to wear street clothes and attend bullfights, but he'd also helped that gadabout Teresa de Ahumada found a discalced convent where she had no right to be. The infuriated friars went to Rubeo and lodged a complaint.

Rubeo had his own bone to pick with Gracián. He was trying to get the Andalusian Carmelites to behave like priests instead of hoodlums, but his idea was to coax them into compliance. Gracián, on the other hand, was a bully. He threatened to excommunicate them. In response, they threatened to poison him. Everything was chaos. And now, to make matters worse, rumors were spreading that Teresa planned to make additional foundations in the South. Rubeo was beside himself. He had to clip her wings in order to prevent a mutiny. In consultation with Ángel de Salazar, the Carmelite provincial, he not only forbade Teresa to found any more convents ever again, but declared her "apostate and excommunicated." Then he ordered her to choose one convent in Castile and stay there. This was, he notified her, the end of the reform.

Teresa buried herself in her cell. She had no choice but to comply. After a few days' thought, she decided to retire to Toledo. She tried to make it sound like a holiday. Father Rubeo and Fray Ángel had actually done her a favor, she insisted. She was exhausted. She needed a rest. She bade María de San José good-bye with tears in her eyes.

"Teresa," I said, once we were in the cart that would take us north. "I hope you see now that you were wrong to put so much faith in Fray Jerónimo."

She closed her eyes and pretended not to hear.

Sister Angélica del Sagrado Corazón
Toledo, April 25 1577

CHAPTER 24

One Dark Night

THE INSTANT WE WERE OUT OF SEVILLE, THE GOSSIP STARTED.

"Have you heard? The Ahumada woman has a lover!"

"I don't believe it. She must be over sixty!"

"That doesn't mean she can't open her honey pot for a young cub who wants some of the sweet stuff."

"But she's a holy woman. Of course, they're all holy until some cub knocks the lid off the tub. And there's no hungrier bear than a priest."

"If you're talking about Fray Jerónimo Gracián, I hear he's hot for the young one, the little prioress who knows Latin."

"You know what they say about women who know Latin. *Mujer que sabe latín.* Too smart for their own good. I heard from my friend Abelardo that when Fray Jerónimo is supposed to be hearing confession, he's actually got his hand up their skirts."

"I should've been a priest instead of a carpenter. Those guys really have fun!"

Well, I didn't really hear this conversation, I only imagined it. María de San José wrote hair-raising letters from Seville. The calced friars were spreading horrible rumors about her and Gracián, about Teresa and Gracián, about everybody and Gracián. From the notary to the kitchen maid, people were saying Fray Jerónimo Gracián had betrayed his vow of chastity. It was all part of the calced scheme to discredit the reform, wrote María de San José. The worst of it was that they were dragging Mother Teresa's name through the mud. *"From my window I hear carpenters and pavers jabbering about it while they work,"* she wrote. *"You don't know how it mortifies me!"* I read María de San José's letter over and over, and I imagined those conversations. Was there any truth to those stories about Gracián and

María? I couldn't know for sure, but it seared Teresa to the quick even to think about it.

It's been ages since I last put pen to paper. Over a year. My last entry was April 1577, and now it's nearly November 1578. I can say with certainty that these past two years have been the worst in my life. Seville was the turning point. I'd say that after Seville, everything went to Hell, except that Seville was Hell. After Seville, we just seemed to fall deeper and deeper into the inferno. The thing is, though, when you're in the middle of a battle with comrades falling all around you, you can't really know what direction the war is taking.

"What an awful piece of luck that Del Corro woman landed on our doorstep in Seville," I told Teresa.

"There's no such thing as luck," she said. "It's all part of God's plan."

"You mean practically getting my fingers broken by Inquisition torturers is God's plan?"

"Oh, dear God," she said, clearly shaken. "I had no idea. They treated me so gently." I waited for her to explain, to say something about her cousin Don Javier, but she just pursed her lips and shook her head. "Even your suffering could be part of God's plan," she said finally. "At any rate, I don't think Miguela del Corro's appearance was just a piece of bad luck. We're imperfect beings, Angélica, and we can't understand the workings of God. Let me tell you a story.

"There was a farmer whose well went dry," she began. "Everyone said, 'What terrible luck!' 'Good luck? Bad luck?' said the farmer. 'Who knows what God's plan is?' He picked up his shovel and went to dig a new well. After a few hours' work, his shovel hit something hard. It turned out to be a coffer full of gold coins! 'What wonderful luck!' his neighbors said. The farmer shrugged. 'Good luck? Bad luck?' he said. 'Who knows what God's plan is?' With the money he bought more land, and he and his son started working it. But one day, while his son was plowing, his foot got caught in the blade and was badly cut. 'What terrible luck!' said the farmer's friends, when they saw the boy confined to the porch, his foot tied up in bandages. 'Good luck? Bad luck?' answered the farmer. 'Who knows what God's plan is?' Not long after that, the king's army passed through the village, conscripting every young man over the age of fourteen. But when they saw the farmer's son was injured, they let him alone. Now, Angélica, do you think that was good luck or bad luck? What I'm saying is, we can't know God's plan. Perhaps our being interrogated by the Inquisition serves some higher purpose."

I shrugged. As far as I could see, the only thing to come out of Seville was our exile to Toledo. That and some very sore fingers. Teresa's excommunication was short-lived, but our confinement seemed to drag on forever. For some reason, Teresa still didn't see that Gracián was the source of our headaches. She didn't see that if she hadn't founded in Seville and riled the calced friars, none of this would have happened. Or maybe she did, and just refused to admit it.

Every time a letter came from María, I felt myself die a little. I walked around with a dull ache in my stomach, as though sobbing deep inside. María wrote that the situation was intolerable. Gracián had been replaced by Father Tostado, an angry little man hell-bent on undoing Teresa's entire reform. His plan was to bring all the discalced houses under the jurisdiction of the calced. The result would be to suppress the Seville Carmel and crush María.

On top of that, the Inquisition had continued to sharpen its incisors. There had been a spate of autos-da-fe: *"Last week they burned a slew of Judaizers,"* wrote María, *including two women, Vida and Sara Santana, who showed the judge a rosary they claimed was given to them by a certain Sister Pancracia of this convent. During the interrogation, several sisters swore there had never been a Sister Pancracia here. Besides, the butcher and Brother Malquiel, director of the orphanage, presented evidence that these women ate no pork."* I hid in my cell and cried all day. I'd never told them my Carmelite name, only my baptismal name. Even the guard hadn't called me Angélica, only "the nun who came in with Mother Teresa." Oh, Jesus, forgive me, I prayed, and take Vida and Sara to your bosom, even though they're not Christians. How was I going to live with such sorrow and guilt?

I got through the days by writing. Writing was like an opiate. When I wasn't writing, my mind wandered, and, like Penelope in the old legend, I wove and rewove mental images of carpenters and pavers, priests and paramours—and autos-da-fe. Teresa wrote, too. A Jesuit friend of hers named Ripalda had ordered her to describe how she founded her convents, so she began *The Book of the Foundations.* Then, last year in June, she began a book on prayer, *The Interior Castle,* at the behest of Gracián. I think it's the best thing she's ever written. In it she describes the soul as a "castle made out of a diamond or of very clear crystal," in the center of which lives the King, who is God. Prayer is, she explains, the journey inward in search of that King. When I read the manuscript, I wept at the exquisiteness of her words.

Mostly, though, Teresa wrote letters. For her, it was a form of doing battle. Still the general, she wrote to her captains—María, Gracián, other prioresses and friars—to whip them into line. The situation was so dangerous she started using code names to protect her collaborators. You could never tell when mail would be intercepted and fall into the wrong hands. Gracián was "Elías" or "Paul," the discalced nuns were "butterflies," the calced friars were "eagles," Tostado was "Peralta," and she herself was "Ángela." I wasn't important enough to have a code name, but still, in an army even petty officers have a role. Mine was to make two or three copies of each letter in case the original got lost or stolen.

Teresa is like those magicians you see at carnivals. Someone ties the guy up with ropes, and then he miraculously manages to work himself loose. The difference is, Teresa works her magic with words. She can talk herself out of anything, and somehow, last July, she finally convinced Rubeo to let her leave Toledo. I don't know exactly what she told him, but a few days after they met at the grille, Fray Julián came to take us back to Ávila, this time in a fancy carriage supplied by Teresa's brother Lorenzo, who had rented a house in town. Teresa's plan was to bring San José de Ávila under Gracián's authority in order to protect it from Tostado.

We entered Ávila after midnight, like prowlers or marauding rats. A dead moon hung in a black sky. A feeling of gloom crept around my shoulders, and the morning light did nothing to dispel my uneasiness. I'd held memories of an idyllic San José de Ávila close to my heart during my trek through southern Spain, but everything had changed. Mother Úrsula had died two years before, and Fray Julián, the convent confessor, was so unassertive that both the nuns and the vegetation were out of control. Paint peeled from the interior walls. The stones in the patio were loose and uneven. The garden where I'd spent quiet days in meditation was overrun with weeds. Instead of maintaining silence, the sisters gossiped incessantly. Sister Juana Isabel was so feeble and disoriented she hardly recognized us. Fray Julián's sister, the other María de San José, had become a recluse. Apolo had disappeared. Perhaps he'd passed on to that special part of Heaven tended by San Francisco de Asís, lover of animals, or perhaps he'd simply wandered off to some alley where he could scavenge for food.

Tostado, now Commissary General, appeared unexpectedly in the locutorium one fall afternoon, looking like a gnome, his small, round skull with its bulging eyes bobbing crazily on the dowel that was his neck. Under each eye shone a clump of golden freckles. His hair shot out in shaggy plumes around his tonsure. "Who is *she*?" he hissed, jerking his head at me.

"This is Sister Angélica. She's here to take notes for me," said Teresa dutifully. Tostado didn't say hello.

"We have to get rid of Gracián," he blurted out. No preamble. No *I'm sorry to have to tell you this, Mother.* "He's an embarrassment," he went on. "They say he's having an affair with . . . What I mean is, they say he's guilty of culpable intimacy."

"Excuse me, Your Paternity," said Teresa. "I'm just a sick old woman, and not very bright at that. What exactly does culpable intimacy mean?"

Tostado turned so red he looked, in fact, *tostado,* "toasted." "It means he's having sexual relations with women." He wheezed and looked at the ground.

"What women?"

"Nuns and . . . the women he confesses."

"Oh," said Teresa, her eyes wide with feigned astonishment. "That seems impossible to me. But you know how addlebrained those of my sex are. Perhaps I just don't understand."

"They say he's sleeping with the sisters!" screeched Tostado. "And not only the sisters, with other women, too! Influential noblewomen!"

"They also say he's sleeping with me!" snapped Teresa, suddenly aggressive. "And I can assure you I hardly have enough energy to shove the chamber pot under my . . . uh, nether parts . . . let alone cavort under the blankets with a frisky, young friar."

She paused, bowed her head, and stood in silence a long time. Then she rubbed her hands together, in a slow, wringing motion, as though asking God for guidance. "I'm sorry, Father," she said with exaggerated submissiveness. "I beg Your Paternity to forgive me. I only mean . . . I just don't know why you would believe these terrible lies. And they *are* lies. Fray Jerónimo is as pure as spring water. These are fabrications spread by the friars of the cloth." "Friars of the cloth" is what we called the calced. I bit my lip when she said "pure as spring water."

"I know they're lies," said Tostado.

Teresa jerked in astonishment. "You know? Well then . . . of course, I'm not telling you how to do your job . . . but it seems to me you should punish those guilty of spreading rumors."

"Rumors, I might add, that have reached the king himself, greatly discrediting the order." He stared at Teresa through the grille, his Adam's apple rising and falling inelegantly.

"Then please discipline those slanderous calced friars."

"It's not the calced friars who are behind them."

Tostado paused for a moment, taking pleasure in Teresa's confusion.

"I don't understand," she whispered finally.

"Oh, I admit your calced adversaries are busy defiling your dear Gracián's good name in Seville. In fact, there are those who would even like to do away with him. But Gracián has other enemies, too. The man who denounced him to the king isn't a friar of the cloth, but Fray Baltasar de Jesús Nieto, prior of the Pastrana friary."

"Nieto! I sewed Baltasar de Nieto's habit with my very own hands when he became a discalced Carmelite!"

"Your beloved protégé has risen too fast in the ranks of the order. Nieto is jealous. He'll do anything possible to prevent you from putting San José de Ávila under Gracián's authority."

Teresa was speechless. "How did Your Paternity find out about my plan?" she asked quietly. "It was a secret."

"Oh, you were quite explicit about it in your letter to Gracián."

"And you intercepted it?"

"Not at all. He showed it around."

Teresa wobbled an instant, as though she were going to faint. Instinctively, I moved behind her and placed my hand under her elbow.

"The boy is cocky and not too bright," added Tostado, delighted to have caught Teresa off guard. His golden freckles sparkled teasingly. Teresa was pallid. Not only had Gracián been betrayed by his discalced brothers, but she had been betrayed by Gracián.

The convent air seemed suddenly rancid. Beads of sweat formed along Teresa's wimple. Mechanically, I lifted my hand to wipe my own brow. By the time Tostado left, I had a splitting headache. I helped Teresa back to her cell and sat down on a footstool near her bed.

"Don't you dare say I told you so," she grumbled. She was holding back tears.

"Lie down awhile," I advised. "I'm going to get you some juice."

"I have to write a letter." She took the quill and put it to paper:

To Don Felipe II, King of Spain.

    Jesus. The grace of the Holy Spirit be always with Your Majesty. Amen.

    I have been informed of a memorandum which has been sent to Your Majesty against our Father, Master Gracián, of such a nature that I am horrified at the ruses of the Devil and of these calced fathers. In order to defame this servant of God—which Gracián truly is—they have made use of a discalced friar by urging him to make certain absurd accusations. If I did not fear the harm the Devil can do, I would laugh at the claims they are making, but from the point of view of the order, this is monstrous.

For the love of God I beseech Your Majesty not to allow these infamous accusations to be brought before the courts. The world is such that even if they were disproved, a suspicion of evil might remain. Let Your Majesty consider this matter as touching on your own honor and glory.

May it please God to hear the prayers of the discalced friars and nuns that He preserve Your Majesty for many years, for we have no other support on earth.

Written in the convent of San José de Ávila on 13 September 1577.
Your Majesty's unworthy servant and subject,
Teresa de Jesús

Writing to the king was an audacious thing to do, but she was desperate. Her life's work seemed to be falling apart, and her beloved Gracián's life was in danger. She took another sheet of paper and put the quill to it.

Mother María de San José in Seville:
Jesus. The grace of the Holy Spirit be in your Reverence's soul, my daughter.
I will write quickly, as I am feeling very tired and still have a lot to accomplish before Vespers. Our dear friend Paul is in terrible danger. The eagles have spread calumnies here that are as outrageous as those circulating in Seville. I suspect they are going to try to do Paul great harm, perhaps even poison him. I want you to insist he take all his meals in the Seville Carmel, in the convent parlor. Make sure your own cook prepares the food, and taste it yourself before giving it to him. He is exhausted and his health is not what it should be, so make sure he gets enough, even if you have to do without yourself. No one must see him eating in the parlor, since it would certainly give rise to gossip. If you need money to buy food, by all means borrow it. You can always pay it back later. May God bless you and make you holy.

Your Reverence's,
Teresa de Jesús

"Teresa," I said to her, "are you mad? Jerónimo has ruined everything. Why are you asking María to risk her life to protect him?" But she turned away and refused to discuss it.

That afternoon, while I was boiling water to do laundry, a novice handed me a crumpled paper. "It looks like this has been around," she said. "Apparently, it went to Beas and then to Seville before coming here." She stood there a moment, as if waiting for me to read it out loud. When I made

no move to open it, she left the room. A shiver crept up my arm the instant
I saw the handwriting. It was from Braulio.

To my Sister in Christ, Angélica del Sagrado Corazón.

*Peace be with you, Sister. I beg you, please destroy this letter the moment you
read it. I fear it could put you in danger. My dear sister, after witnessing the horrible violence your king's emissary, the Duke of Alba, wrought in the Netherlands,
I decided I had to find a way to leave the country. The duke ruled with such bru-
tality that the people hated him. After he established the Inquisition, any
Dutchman suspected of being a Protestant was put to death. More than six thousand died. I couldn't bear to see such terror perpetrated in the name of Christ.
Naturally, the Protestants reacted in kind. They attacked monasteries, dragging
friars out into the streets and slitting their throats. I am not trying to justify such
behavior, but the duke's cruelty certainly provoked much of this violence.*

*One dark night I snuck out of the monastery. Just when I thought I was safe,
a Protestant soldier saw me and pursued me to the city limits. After barely escaping with my life, I made my way to Germany. I am now living in Wittenberg,
where Luther taught at the university and came to question Rome's notions of
faith and grace. This will shock you, Angélica, but I have followed his example
and renounced the church.*

*My dear Angélica, Luther understood what I've long known: that the desire
of man for woman is so strong that it cannot be denied. Luther himself married
in order to provide an outlet for his bodily yearnings, and I, too, have taken a wife.
Although I am over sixty, I have found a lovely young girl of nineteen, an orphan
with no means to support herself, who has promised me her undying devotion. At
least she will care for me in my old age, although I think I'm still young enough to
have a family. If I have a son, I will name him Martin, after the man who dared
to challenge Rome, and if I have a daughter, I will name her Pancracia, after you.*

*Dearest Sister, forgive me for all the grief I've caused you and the grief I'm caus-
ing you now. I know they've taught you that by embracing a purer faith, I've condemned myself to eternal suffering. They're mistaken. They are the ones who God,
in His unspeakable wrath, will punish. My poor Sister, to think you are still in their
clutches! You can't know how it saddens me.*

*This is the last letter you will receive from me. Oh, how I wish we could
meet in Heaven!*

Yours in Christ,
Braulio

Teresa found me sobbing over the laundry basket. "It's Braulio," I whispered.

"Is he dead?"

"He's as good as dead. He's Lutheran."

Teresa took my wrist in her hand. "We'll pray for him," she said softly. "It always saddens me when a soul turns away from the Sacraments. But let's pray for him."

She was so exhausted she could hardly drag herself around, and yet, there she was, comforting me. Puffy bags had formed under her eyes, and her once beautiful hands were now spotted and gnarled. But worse, much worse, than the degeneration of the body is the weakening of the spirit. I don't mean to say she lacked will or faith. She still had the fortitude of a soldier. But the constant warring between the calced and discalced, the political maneuvering, the slippery ways of prelates like Tostado—it was beginning to take a toll.

I didn't throw away Braulio's letter. I had so many dangerous things—books of chivalry, pastoral novels, this memoir—what difference did one more make? I folded it and placed it carefully in my copy of Jorge de Montemayor's *Seven Books of Diana*.

Early one December morning we were awakened by fearsome banging on the door accompanied by hysterical screams. Radegunda opened the turn and words like "kidnap," "prison," "torture," "Fray Juan" came hurdling through. Teresa came tearing down the stairs, pushing her sixty-two year old body faster than it wanted to go. "What's happened to Juan?" she panted. "What's happened to my *frailecito*!" A crowd of women from Encarnación was waiting for her at the door. Armed men spitting obscenities had barged into the little hut on convent grounds where Fray Juan slept and dragged him off to prison.

Teresa's knees buckled. I slipped my arm around her waist to keep her from falling. "Where . . . where did they take him?" she stammered.

"To Toledo," said one of the women. "To the calced monastery. Father Hernando de Maldonado, the prior, had the constable arrest him." The Carmelite leadership under Rubeo had ruled that the calced could use secular law enforcement to bring the discalced under control. Rubeo, once Teresa's great ally, had turned into her worst enemy.

Within minutes, the news had shot through San José. A great cacophony of wailing and moaning filled the halls. Teresa didn't waste

time crying. She ran back to her cell, got out her quill, and again wrote
to the king.

To the King Don Phillip II.

 *The grace of the Holy Spirit be with Your Majesty, amen. I strongly believe
that Our Lady has chosen you to protect us, and so I cannot fail to have recourse
to you now. For the love of Our Lord, I beg you to pardon me for so much boldness.*

 *When I first went to Encarnación as prioress, the calced confessors there
treated the nuns very harshly, giving them cruel and unjustified penances.
Because the nuns were so unhappy, I replaced the calced confessors with a discalced friar, Fray Juan de la Cruz. Fray Juan is such a great servant of Our Lord
that everyone considers him a saint, and in my opinion, he is one and has been
one all his life.*

 *When the Papal Nuncio learned of the harm the friars of the cloth were doing,
he gave orders that Fray Juan remain at Encarnación. He also ordered that no friar
of the cloth under pain of excommunication go to Encarnación for any reason. As a
result, the house was in a good state and the nuns were happy. However, Fray
Hernando de Maldonado has now forcibly taken from the nuns their confessor. He
is holding him captive in his monastery in Toledo and is going to make him a martyr. The whole city is scandalized. I would consider the confessors better off if they
were held by the Moors, who perhaps would show more compassion. Fray Juan is so
weak from all he has suffered that I fear for his life. I beg Your Majesty for the love
of Our Lord to issue orders for the calced friars to set him free at once.*

 *May it please Our Lord that for our sake you live many years. I pray to Him
for your health continually. Dated in San José de Avila, 4 December 1577.*

 Your Majesty's unworthy servant and subject,

Teresa de Jesús, Carmelite

After that, Teresa's dizzy spells came back. She refused to eat. She couldn't
sleep. She prayed, and she cried. Sometimes at night I'd hear her pacing back
and forth in her cell, and the sound of her sandals shuffling over the cold tiles
made me feel as though someone had died.

It was Christmas Eve. The king had still not responded to Teresa's letter,
and there was no intelligence from Toledo. The only news was from Madrid,
and it was bad: The recently appointed Nuncio, Felipe Sega, was entirely

opposed to the reform and was doing everything possible to keep the discalced friars harnessed and under the control of the calced. I coaxed Teresa to eat a bit of broth and sat her in front of the fire. A bitter wind was blowing and drafts came under the doors and through the windows.

"I'm going to the chapel to light a candle for Juan," she said, easing herself off the chair. "Alright," I said. "I'll light a lamp for you."

She took it and started down the stairs. "Wait," I said. "I'll go with you. Just let me get a shawl." But she'd already started down.

Suddenly, a blast of air whipped through a window, sending a chill through the corridor and slamming shut the stairwell door. I heard a moan or a whine, like the bleating of a frightened lamb. I ran to the stairs and peered downward, into the darkness. Someone was whimpering.

"Teresa," I called. "Is that you?"

"I'm hurt," she hiccoughed. "I've hurt my arm."

The blast of air had put out her lamp and caused her to trip. It was a miracle she hadn't hit her head. I had to muster all my strength to carry her upstairs and lay her on the infirmary bed. I touched her arm gently, and she winced. I knew it was broken.

"It's Satan," she moaned. "He sent a gust from Hell."

"The bastard," I said, trying to make her comfortable. "He just can't leave us alone." I called for a messenger and told him to go for a doctor.

"But actually, he's done me a favor," she countered, "because now I can offer up this pain for the safety of my *frailecito*. Dear God, please let him escape!" Just like her, I thought, trying to turn bitter herbs into relish.

Reports began to arrive from Toledo. Maldonado had thrown Fray Juan into the monastery dungeon, forcing him to sleep on the hard, cold ground in a tiny cell populated by vermin and insects. Calced guards beat him daily—I imagined the zap of the cowhide on his frail back—and deprived him not only of food and sleep, but also of communion. But God did answer Teresa's prayer. Fray Juan found a way to escape his tormentors, not by running away but by composing— in his head, since they wouldn't give him any paper—the most exquisite verses I've ever read. His poetry tells how the soul, captive in its "house," the body, waits for the inhabitants (the senses and intelligence) to fall asleep, then flees to its lover, God, with whom it's united in an act of total surrender.

It's late now, and I want to go to bed. But before I close this entry, I'm going to copy Fray Juan's poem, which he wrote down much later.

En una noche oscura,	One dark night,
con ansias, en amores inflamada,	afire with love's yearning,
¡oh dichosa ventura!	oh, wondrous fortune!
salí sin ser notada	I went out unseen,
estando ya mi casa sosegada.	my house now still.
A oscuras y segura,	In darkness, and secure,
por la secreta escala disfrazada,	by the secret ladder, disguised,
¡oh dichosa ventura!	oh, wondrous fortune!
a oscuras y en celada,	in the darkness and concealed,
estando ya mi casa sosegada.	my house now still.
En la noche dichosa,	On that blessed night,
en secreto, que nadie me veía,	in secret, for no one saw me,
ni yo miraba cosa,	nor did I observe anything,
sin otra luz y guía	with no other light and guide
sino la que en el corazón ardía.	but the one that burned in my heart.
Aquésta me guiaba	This light guided me
más cierto que la luz del mediodía,	more surely than the light of noon,
adónde me esperaba	to where He was waiting for me,
quien yo bien me sabía,	Him I knew so well,
en parte donde nadie parecía.	in a secluded, solitary place.
¡Oh noche que guiaste!	Oh guiding night!
¡Oh noche amable más que el alborada!	Oh night more exquisite than the dawn!
¡Oh noche que juntaste	Oh night that brought together
Amado con amada,	Lover and beloved,
amada en el Amado transformada!	Beloved in Lover transformed!
En mi pecho florido,	Upon my flowering breast,
que entero para él solo se guardaba,	that I kept for Him alone,
allí quedó dormido,	there He fell asleep,
y yo le regalaba,	and I caressed Him,
y el ventalle de cedros aire daba.	in the breeze from the fluttering cedars.
El aire de la almena,	The breeze from the turret,
cuando yo sus cabellos esparcía,	as I played with His hair,
con su mano serena	with its gentle hand
en mi cuello hería	wounded my neck
y todos mis sentidos suspendía.	and suspended all my senses.

Quedéme y olvidéme,
el rostro recliné sobre el Amado,
cesó todo y dejéme,
dejando mi cuidado
entre las azucenas olvidado.

I succumbed to Him and forgot myself,
laying my face on my Beloved,
everything stopped, and I lost myself,
leaving my cares
forgotten among the lilies.

Angélica del Sagrado Corazón
San José de Ávila, 28 October 1579

CHAPTER 25

A Quiet Victory

PEOPLE SAID THAT THE VIRGIN HERSELF MANEUVERED FRAY JUAN'S ESCAPE. His jailers had transferred him to an isolated and inaccessible tower guarded by sinister friars armed with harquebuses and daggers. One night, as Fray Juan knelt in prayer, Our Lady appeared at his window, dressed all in blue with a crown of gold. She called to him. He'd languished in prison nearly a year, and he was flea-bitten and scarred from whipping. But at the sight of Our Lady, his pain vanished and he prostrated himself before her.

"Follow me," she said softly.

Fray Juan rose, staggered toward the window, and gave the Holy Mother his hand. With superhuman strength, she heaved him up to the casement and told him to hang on. Then, Hercules in an azure gown, she spread the iron bars. Fray Juan crawled out, and the two of them floated down to the ground as gently as robin's feathers. Our Lady led Fray Juan to the street, across the town, out the gates, and finally through the mountains to Ávila, where she left him at the great *portón* of Encarnación Convent.

There was also another version of the story, however. A few skeptics insisted that Teresa herself had arranged Fray Juan's rescue, ordering two discalced friars to breach the monastery grounds, shinny up the tower, and pass the *frailecito* a rope to slide down. Whichever account you believe, the fact is that one night Fray Juan de la Cruz showed up at the door of Encarnación, where he'd served as chaplain and confessor. Mother Anastasia de Toledo, the prioress, awakened to the sound of the rattling chains of the convent gate. When she saw Fray Juan, she fainted. She thought he was a ghost. Teresa had always called him her "half-friar," but now he was a fraction of his normal size—a quarter-friar, I guess. Once she was able to think clearly, Mother Anastasia opened the lock, hugged the bedraggled Fray Juan, and led him inside. She brought him a scrap of goat meat, a straggly carrot, an onion, some garlic, and some dry bread. It was all she could find in the pantry. Then she lit a fire in the parlor and served him there. "Let the tongues wag," she reputedly said. "If evil people want to make a scandal about my feeding this poor man in here, let them. I'm sure even Mother Teresa would agree that I did the right thing." Teresa did agree. She had her sister Juana send Mother Anastasia six large hens to show her appreciation.

Teresa was beside herself with joy to see her *frailecito* free, but his imprisonment had taken its toll on her health. She'd been frantic for months, writing letters, petitioning authorities, contacting allies, praying to the Virgin. Her headaches and dizzy spells were worse than ever, and now palsy invaded her limbs. All of a sudden, her hands would start to shake uncontrollably. I made potions and compresses. Nothing helped.

The truth is, I was growing tired myself. I no longer had the strength to stay up at night tending to Teresa.

That's why I agreed to take Ana de San Bartolomé as my assistant. A brawny peasant woman with the stamina of a mule, La Bartolomé showed up one day at the convent door and begged to be taken in. She's an odd type, a giantess with hands like pressing irons. She doesn't like men, although I never had the impression she liked women the way Cándida did. She's never met a man as beautiful as Jesus, she says, and why settle for second best?

Her brothers, all farmers, wanted her to take a husband who would help with the sowing and tilling, but she fought them tooth and nail. One night La Bartolomé dreamed she was entering the front door of a convent, where all the smiling sisters greeted her with open arms. When her brothers arranged a marriage for her, she ran away and, with the help of a cooperative priest, made her way to San José de Ávila. The moment she entered the convent, she recognized it as the same one she'd seen in her dream. She's been my apprentice ever since. La Bartolomé is a marvel. She can lift an ailing sister with one arm and carry her to the infirmary. She can go for nights without sleeping. She has the patience of the Virgin with cranky, finicky old nuns who refuse to take their medicine. She has no book learning, but she's a visionary who can always count on Jesus to appear at the foot of her patient's bed and guide her through the cure. It was she who massaged Teresa's palsied extremities and coaxed my concoctions down her throat. Wherever Teresa went, there was La Bartolomé, sitting by her feet, her muscular legs sprawled out on either side of her, looking like a meaty, brown bullfrog.

For Teresa, Fray Juan's incarceration was the reform's darkest hour. The calced were not only tormenting her *frailecito,* they were swallowing up our convents one after the other, abolishing the discalced rule and imposing their own. "The reform will triumph," Teresa kept saying, "because God wills it." To me that sounded like wishful thinking. I was ready to retire to Ávila and submit to the inevitable—chaos and calced bullying. That's why, when late in November a messenger banged on the convent gate, I instinctively readied myself for bad news.

"If you have a letter, put it through the turn," I growled.

"I have to see Mother Teresa," the courier declared importantly. "I come from the Office of the Nuncio, Don Felipe Sega." I peered through the opening. The man wore the costume of a papal servant. I showed him to the locutorium and went to find Teresa.

I approached gingerly. I didn't want to upset her. Lately, messengers always brought bad news, and it was no secret that Sega was furious with Rubeo for releasing Teresa from Toledo.

"Sega's messenger is here," I said gently. "He wants to see you."

Teresa paled, but dutifully pulled herself up and made ready to go downstairs. I could tell she was in pain, but she didn't ask me to accompany her, so I didn't.

The next time I saw her, she was kneeling in the chapel, head bowed, cheeks glistening. Oh no, I thought. Who did they kidnap this time? Then I noticed her hands. They weren't shaking. Her face was serene, her body relaxed. For a moment, at least, the palsy had left her. Her lips were moving. She was talking to God, but she didn't appear to be in a trance. Finally, she rose and moved toward the door. "Teresa," I whispered, "what happened?"

She turned to me. "It's a miracle."

"What are you talking about?"

"The Nuncio Felipe Sega. He's given us back our independence! The calced no longer have any power over us. The nuncio has taken away their authority!" She looked up at the statue of Jesus that stood by the entrance. "Thank you, my Lord and my Savior. You've freed us from our oppressors!" She bowed to kiss Jesus's holy feet, and then looked up at the light streaming through the stained glass window. That's the way I want to remember her, I thought, her eyes as lustrous as topaz, her face radiant with joy.

"What made the nuncio change his mind? He was dead set against dividing the order. "

"Yes, but the pope has been trying to discipline those unruly calced friars for years. When he received the report explaining what they were doing to us, he decided to take action."

"What report?"

"Oh," she demurred, "the Holy Father knows what's going on. We have ways . . ."

But of course. She'd worked behind the scenes. All those letters. All those couriers dispatched at ungodly hours. I'd thought they all were aimed at achieving Fray Juan's release, but she'd been fighting battles on different fronts at the same time. And now, the victory we'd all yearned for, prayed for! I expected bells to toll. I expected the town council to set off fireworks, the way it had decades before when Francisco Borja visited Ávila. I expected the town crier to scream all through the night, "Teresa de Jesús has won! Viva Teresa!" I expected cheering and parades and jugglers in the plaza. But there was no triumphal march into the city. The Virgin didn't applaud in her niche in the chapel. No angels danced wildly in the sanctuary. Instead, there was . . . silence, serenity, hushed rejoicing. There was no need for grandiloquent proclamations or shrill victory cries. I knew God exulted with us. I felt His delight in the stillness, in the quivering breeze, as gentle as a child's whisper.

"You see?" said Teresa. "Good luck? Bad luck? You never know. It's because we went into Seville that the calced attacked the reform, and it's because they were so awful to us that the papal nuncio finally granted us independence." A few weeks later an official communiqué arrived from the King Don Felipe, formally approving the separation of the Carmelites into two orders. We would write "discalced" with a capital *D*—Discalced Carmelites—as a sign of our sovereignty. We would follow our own rule and pray in our own way.

But Teresa's health continued to worsen. One afternoon I entered her cell to find her lying in bed, a warm compress pressed to her stomach. A putrid odor filled the room.

"What's going on? What have you been doing?" I asked.

"I've been praying."

"It smells to me like you've been sitting on the chamber pot."

"I've been sitting on the chamber pot and praying."

I took the pot and covered it, then called for a white-veiled nun to remove and wash it. "Shitting and praying at the same time sounds sacrilegious, Teresa," I said.

"The prayers are for God," she retorted, "and the shit is for the Devil."

I shouldn't have snickered because not only did God receive Teresa's prayers wherever they were offered, but the Devil got her due as well. The Princess of Eboli—the she-demon—had been arrested and imprisoned in the tower of Santorcaz, on the outskirts of Madrid. She'd been charged as an accomplice to Antonio Pérez, who had orchestrated the murder of a high government official to further his own career. "You see," Teresa said without a hint of smugness. "God knows what He's doing." And in fact, He seemed to be taking care of everything.

Things were peaceful for a while. I was looking forward to a good rest. Finally, I thought, we can stay put and enjoy our successes. But then, early in 1580, Teresa got it into her head to found another convent. "Let someone else do it," I told her. "Send María de San José. She's young and strong."

"And I suppose I'm old and feeble."

"Yes, as a matter of fact, you are. Much too old and feeble to traipse through the snow in the middle of winter."

A priest from Villanueva de la Jara had written to her that nine devout women had come to him begging to take vows. They wanted to be Discalced Carmelites, with a capital D, he said. They wanted to cultivate their inner spirits, to withdraw from the world and devote their lives to prayer. Teresa gave the order to load the carts. I couldn't let her go alone, so I packed my bags and charged La Bartolomé with preparing Teresa's medicines. I needed the giantess to come with us. I could no longer manage alone.

Villanueva de la Jara is a pretty town in the area of Cuenca known for its mushrooms. As we headed through the mountains, whole villages came out to meet our caravan. At inns people swarmed through the doors and even windows. "Mother Teresa," they called. "Pray for me! Pray for my children." Anything to catch a glimpse of her. We arrived in Villanueva de la Jara toward the end of February, and the entire population, with a robust young priest at its head, processed into the house where she was to make her foundation.

It was a dreadful winter that produced nearly famine conditions. Even so, the families of the novices gathered enough bread, cheese, onions, and mushrooms to make a celebration. There was a bit of meat, but mostly, there were mushrooms—lamb and mushroom stew, mushrooms stuffed with garlic, white rice with mushrooms and leeks. We ate with as much pleasure as if we had capons. Afterward, Teresa got out her tambourine and, in spite of her bad heart and weak limbs, found the energy to dance and sing.

Caminemos para el cielo	Onward toward Heaven
monjas de Carmelo.	sisters of Carmel.
Abracemos bien la Cruz	Let us embrace the Cross
y sigamos a Jesús	and follow Jesus
que es nuestro camino y luz	our path and our light
lleno de todo Consuelo	source of all consolation
monjas de Carmelo.	sisters of Carmel.

The next day we went out to supervise the digging of a well. Why? Well, Teresa liked machines, and she was a stickler for detail. She knew exactly how wide the well had to be, how many times the crank should turn to bring up the bucket, what kind of stone she wanted to line the sides. She had an idea how far down they'd have to dig to reach the water table. She squatted down to feel the earth to see its consistency, and the workmen gathered around her, shovels and picks in hand. A tall, burly man held a windlass, the horizontal cylinder to be turned by a crank in order to hoist up buckets of water. It was a heavy, cumbersome affair, and the man held it awkwardly. He was shifting his weight to heave it up on his shoulder when suddenly the instrument flew out of his hand. It took a split second to hit its mark.

I didn't see it strike her—it happened too fast—but the next thing I knew, Teresa was sprawled flat on the ground, blood oozing from her forehead. Her eyes were closed and her face looked as though it had suddenly been enveloped in hoarfrost and frozen stiff. I crouched down beside her. "Teresa," I whispered. I touched her hand. It didn't move. I was sure she was dead. I started to sob. But then, slowly, she blinked and opened her eyes. Struggling for breath, she raised herself up on her elbows.

"Thank God you're alive," I whispered. "Don't try to move. Rest a moment."

She grabbed my arm and struggled to get up. "You're lucky Saint Joseph is watching over me, *joven*," she said to the worker.

The young man was mortified. Tears streamed down his cheeks. "I'm sorry, Mother," he hiccoughed. He wanted to set Teresa on her feet, but hesitated as though he thought it might be improper to touch a *santa*.

"Oh, it'll take more than the likes of you hurling a windlass at my head to kill me off," she spluttered. "When the good Lord wants me, He'll take me without any help from you."

I examined the wound. It was superficial, but within days an abscess formed. Teresa's dizziness was almost constant. "You're too weak to travel," I told her. "Wait awhile." But she was anxious to be off. Gracián was to meet us near Toledo, and she was eager to see him.

Gracián was full of news. The Princess of Eboli had returned home and been put under house arrest. Antonio Pérez was sure to be executed. King Felipe II had just inherited the throne of Portugal, uniting the Peninsula under one monarch. Since Portugal was a major naval power, the merge greatly strengthened the Spanish crown. Teresa listened, but frequently her eyes closed, her head lurched forward, her hands trembled. By the time we reached the Toledo Carmel, she was so ill she was unable to get down from the coach by herself. La Bartolomé lifted her to the ground. I put her to bed, and we managed to keep her still until almost the end of April.

Teresa's *Life* had been in the hands of the Toledo Inquisition for over ten years, and Gracián thought it was time to press the issue. As soon as Teresa was well enough to travel, he insisted on taking her to see Archbishop Quiroga, the Inquisitor General of the city. "She's not up to it," I kept saying. "Please let me take her home to Ávila. All this traveling is killing her."

But who was she going to listen to, Gracián or me? I wasn't surprised to find her preparing to visit the archbishop in his palatial offices early in May. She returned from the meeting all smiles. The Holy Office was still examining the book, she said, but the archbishop had assured her she had nothing to worry about. True to his word, before the end of the year—it was 1580— he sent a messenger to Ávila with the final decision: the censors had found nothing to condemn and much to praise in Teresa's *Life*. It all really is working out, I thought. God gets the praise, and the Devil gets the shit. Now, finally, she can calm down, relax, and attend to her health.

But as they say, "Man proposes, and God disposes." Shortly afterward another messenger came with more news: Teresa's brother Lorenzo had died, and he had named Teresa his executrix. She had to take care of matters. Once again, she was caught up in a flurry of letters, deeds, and promissory notes.

One morning I went to her cell to help with the correspondence. She was sitting at her writing table filling the inkwell. She could no longer squat by the window. Her back was too twisted. I watched her pour black fluid into the container. Her fingers were stiff, and her shoulders drooped. "Teresa," I murmured, but she didn't hear me. Her mouth was opening and closing like a fish's. I shuddered. This wasn't the Teresa I'd once known. This was an old woman. But I was an old woman, too. I looked down at my hands. They were wrinkled and crisscrossed with bulging veins. It had been years since I'd seen my face in a mirror, but I imagined it skeletal and saggy. Maybe I'll die before she does, I thought. But I knew I wouldn't. Teresa was very ill.

"Rest, Teresa," I kept telling her. "You have to take care of yourself." A flu they called *el catarro universal* was going around, and several old friends had died from it.

"I'll rest when I get to Heaven," she snapped. "*If* I get to Heaven."

"Right," I said. "*If* you get to Heaven. Because God doesn't like it when you put Him to the test. What I mean is, when you dare Him to take you by playing with your health."

Money was pouring in, and Teresa wanted to found convents in Granada and then Burgos. It was time for me to go into battle on my own. I gathered the sisters together and said, "Let's elect her prioress. That way, she'll be forced to stay in one place. Anyhow, she deserves to be prioress of San José. It was her first foundation!" She was too old, they said. She had other responsibilities. I've never been much of an orator, but I argued my case as best I could. In the end, they agreed. They elected her prioress. They did it to protect her from her own ambition.

But Teresa was not so easily yoked. In the fall she wrote to Fray Juan de la Cruz about founding in Granada. He knew Andalusia. He'd been in Baeza, far to the south, where he'd started a *colegio* and was serving as its rector. She felt uncomfortable around southerners—she'd never forget the nightmare of Seville—but she'd go to Granada if he'd go with her.

Early in November her *frailecito* packed his mules and set off on the arduous journey to Castile through the rugged mountains of the Meseta Meridional. The weather is always bad that close to Christmas, but last year, 1581, it was especially ferocious. Messengers told of bitter winds and freezing nighttime temperatures. In the mountains the snow never stopped falling. The roads were treacherous—icy and slick. Enormous trees, toppled by the winds, lay in the mud like the corpses of giants. Still, Fray Juan and two companions trudged on. They arrived in Ávila on a blustery day early in December. They intended to pick up Teresa, then head back south. Fray Juan slept in his old quarters, the little hut on the grounds of Encarnación. The next morning before dawn, he appeared at the gates of San José with mules packed and ready to go. But Teresa was ill. She had a terrible sore throat. She could hardly swallow.

"I can't . . ." she stammered, blinking at Fray Juan through the grille. Her eyes were teary, whether from congestion or frustration or sadness, I couldn't be sure.

"We can wait for you, Mother," said Fray Juan. "At least, for a couple of days. The snows are already bad, and they're going to get worse, but we can wait a day or two."

"No," whispered Teresa. She paused, struggling for words. "God doesn't want me to go to Granada. Last night He told me, 'Teresa, your next foundation is to be in Burgos.'"

A flash of irritation flickered in Fray Juan's eyes. He'd traveled for days over brutal terrain to reach Ávila, and now Teresa was refusing to return with him. He bowed his head and said nothing, but there was something about the way he tightened his jaw that disturbed me.

He doesn't believe her, I thought. Fray Juan was a scholar. He'd once been a student at Salamanca. Most learned men didn't believe in the apparitions and locutions experienced by women. Even a deeply spiritual friar like Juan must have had his doubts.

"I'm sorry," she whispered. She looked drained.

"Good-bye, Mother," he said sadly.

"God be with you, Father." He turned and left. Teresa never saw him again.

I put her to bed and sat by her side the rest of the day. She hardly moved. She refused even broth. She was ill most of January and February, but by March she'd made up her mind to push on to Burgos. "No," I told her. "You're not well enough. Rest, Teresa. You have to rest."

"God told me to go," she snapped. "Who should I listen to, you or God?"

Once again, Fray Julián hitched the mule and packed the carts, even though it was sleeting. By the time we reached Burgos, Teresa was vomiting blood. La Bartolomé thought she was going to die then and there, but it must be true that God wanted her to make that foundation, because within a few weeks she was on her feet again and up to her old tricks—ordering around workmen, sweeping out cellars, hanging crucifixes. "Slow down, Teresa," I told her. "Rest, rest."

"You rest, you lazy girl," she'd bark at me, and I'd laugh because, after all, I was no girl. By then I was already sixty-two years old.

Burgos is a majestic city, a monarch of cities. It looks down from a mountainous plateau high in Castile-León onto lesser towns and villages, like an emperor on a throne surveying his serfs. Like all monarchs, Burgos can be harsh. Its winters are the coldest in Spain, so cold your breath freezes in your throat. Ice coats your nose and makes your eyes tear, and when they do, drops freeze on your cheeks and lashes. But like a good ruler, Burgos can also be kind. If the winter is brutal, the warmer months are delightful. In the summer, the city regales its inhabitants with beautiful vistas—the serpentine Arlazón River that sparkles in the sunlight, the gorgeous cathedral of white limestone that reaches up to the turquoise sky with its lofty, filigree spires. The Cid, a great hero of old, was born in Burgos and is buried in the cathedral along with his wife, Doña Ximena. On a summer's day you can walk through the plaza full of flower vendors and children and hear his voice: "Ximena," he says. "Ximena, I love you."

I'd have been happy to spend the rest of my life in Burgos. But as I wrote before, man proposes and God disposes. When the messenger came with news that the sisters in Alba de Tormes were feuding, I knew we'd soon be on the road again. By then, it was late September, and the storms had started. It was no time to travel. Drops pelted the ground like stones dropping from the sky, but Teresa insisted she had to make peace among her daughters. There was no doubt in my mind that she was approaching the end of her journey.

Angélica del Sagrado Corazón
Alba de Tormes, 3 October 1582

CHAPTER 26

Muero porque no muero

THE ROOM WAS SO STILL THAT BREATHING SEEMED A SACRILEGE. PARTICLES of dust hung in the air as though trapped in glass. A delicate luminosity swathed every object—sheets, basin, crucifix—and a sweet floral fragrance emanated from somewhere, although there were no flowers. Peace permeated the room. Teresa lay silent, her eyes closed, her eyelids as silky as rose petals. The deep furrows that crisscrossed her cheeks had almost vanished, and her alabaster skin had recovered its youthful glow. Her hands lay on the coverlet—two doves at rest. Yes, once again, two doves. La Bartolomé stood at the foot of the bed, eyes fixed on a scene invisible to the rest of us. "The Lord is here," she whispered, "accompanied by ten thousand angels and ten thousand martyrs, just as our holy Mother Teresa once saw in a vision."

Gracián took Teresa's hand gently in his own. He seemed to be struggling to contain his tears. He gazed at it lovingly, as though he were going to kiss it. Then, he bent down and took something out of a brown leather satchel. It was a hunting knife. He slipped it out of its case. The blade glimmered like a jewel. He lifted the knife in his right hand, and then, with the expertise of a butcher, lopped off Teresa's index finger. A tiny puff of air escaped from my lungs. I shuddered and blinked back tears. Gracián took out a handkerchief to staunch the blood, then bound Teresa's hand so artfully that it looked whole. He wrapped the finger in a coif. It was a reasonable thing to do, of course. Teresa would someday be canonized, and her body would be cut up in pieces for relics. Fray Jerónimo Gracián was simply claiming his memento in advance. Who would get her heart? Her foot? Her ear? What lucky monastery or cathedral would get the rest of her hand?

The evening before, La Bartolomé came to get me.

"Has Mother Teresa taken a turn for the worse?" I asked.

"She's still the same, but I want to show you something," she said. "Come with me." She walked to the window and pointed. A dazzling star, more brilliant than any other, hung in the heavens over the convent. Its nimbus formed a translucent cross in the sky. It was breathtaking.

"It's like the Star of Bethlehem," I whispered.

"For the last few nights it has appeared in that very place, always between eight and nine o'clock. What do you think it means?"

"You know what it means," I whispered. "It won't be long now."

It was pouring when we left Burgos. Torrents swelled waterways and turned roads into roiling rivers of mud. Roofs, gutters, chairs, dishes, spinning wheels, shirts, sandals, shepherd's crooks, and the carcasses of animals —the entire lives of inhabitants of the tiny villages along the River Arlanzón floated downstream in the muck. It would have been an exhausting trip for anyone, but Teresa was weak from fever, chest pains and an intestinal ailment. She coughed and wheezed, spitting bloody mucus into a handkerchief.

"This is crazy," I told her, "Wait till the storm passes. There's still work to do in Burgos."

But she refused to delay or to stop and rest. We spent the night in the Carmel of Valladolid, where her niece María Bautista—the former María de Ocampo—was prioress. Teresa was irritable. She scolded María constantly. She hated the decoration of the chapel, the crudeness of the stove, the new postulants, the color of the refectory. Finally, she dropped into a fitful sleep.

The next morning the skies, stuffed with heavy black clouds, were still as dark as a tomb. Nevertheless, we piled back into the cart. The driver steered us onto the road to Alba de Tormes, and we inched along, spewing cascades of mud. We didn't see the carriage approaching from the opposite direction until it was practically on top of us.

A man pulled aside the curtain and shouted something. It was hard to see him in the rain, especially since he had a cape pulled up over his head. All that was visible was a face—it looked ancient—as wrinkled as a wadded up paper. "It's Fray Antonio de San José," said Teresa, peering into the darkness. I knew him. He was a friar from Alba de Tormes.

"I was headed for Burgos to find you," he shouted at us, dragging out the syllables. "Heeeaaaded . . . Buuuurgos . . . youuuuu." He muttered something else, but his words disintegrated amongst the splattering drops. Fray Julián road up to his carriage, stuck his head in, then carried back the old friar's message.

"The Duchess of Alba needs you right away, Mother," he told Teresa. "Her daughter-in-law is going into labor. She wants you there to bless the birth. She sent her carriage for you."

Teresa crossed her arms. "I'll go in this cart," she growled hoarsely.

"Your Reverence must climb into the carriage, Mother," commanded Fray Julián. "That way your Reverence will stay drier and safer. I'll keep my mule and Fray Antonio will go in the cart." I think it was the only time I ever heard the gentle Julián give Teresa an order.

She didn't have the energy to argue. La Bartolomé climbed down, lifted her, and carried her to the carriage. When we finally arrived in Alba de Tormes, Teresa was drifting in and out of consciousness. We took her straight to the convent infirmary.

La Bartolomé and I stood staring at the radiant heavenly lantern that dazzled like the Star of Bethlehem. "Yes," said La Bartolomé. "It won't be long now."

When we returned to the infirmary, Father Antonio was standing by Teresa's side. The Duchess of Alba was sitting on a stool near the head of the bed, dressed in an elaborate black brocade dress. She'd come to the convent to take the *santa* back with her to bless her newborn grandson, but after being apprised of the situation, she insisted instead on attending to Mother Teresa in her illness. La Bartolomé didn't think it was a good idea, and neither did I. Neither did Teresa, who had implored us not to let her in. "The stench in here will kill her. Tell her to go away." But the duchess took a seat and refused to budge. Eyes filmed with tears, she peered down at Teresa's face. With her manicured, aristocratic hands she fed Teresa from the cheap pottery bowl in which La Bartolomé brought broth.

My stomach knotted. Teresa's skin was as transparent as onion skin. "Teresa," I whispered. "After sixty years . . . how can you leave me?"

She opened her eyes. "Angélica!" she whispered back, and I'm sure I saw her smile.

She asked for *Viaticum*. La Bartolomé and I wrapped a white choir mantle around her shoulders. The Alba de Tormes nuns filed in carrying lighted candles and formed a semicircle around her bed. Gathering all her strength, Teresa set her gaze on the sisters. "*Señoras y hermanas,*" she said in a voice that was weak, but clear. "I beseech you to get along with one another, for the love

of the Spouse you serve, and to always respect the constitution of our order."
Father Antonio arrived with the Blessed Sacrament, and Teresa sat up without any help to take the host in her mouth. After she'd taken communion, La Bartolomé and I eased her back down into the bed. A little later, she asked to be anointed, and Father Antonio brought the oils.

The sisters still stood around her with their tapers. "A psalm," uttered Teresa. "I thank you with all my heart, Lord my God." We took up the melody: *I thank you with all my heart, Lord my God, / I will glorify your name forever, / for your faithful love for me is so great / that you have rescued me from the depths of Sheol.* Teresa mouthed the words. "My tambourine," she whispered. I laid it on the bed, but she was too weak to pick it up. Finally, the nuns placed the tapers around the infirmary and filed out.

The next morning—it was October 4—Teresa could hardly lift her head. La Bartolomé and I sat with her the entire day. Towards evening, Fray Antonio came in. For a moment, Teresa seemed more alert. Then she closed her eyes, and her hands went limp. I held my breath. I took her wrist between my thumb and index finger. She still had a pulse, weak but discernable. I held my hand above her mouth. Her breathing was like a breeze passing through fallen leaves. Suddenly, she opened her eyes.

"Where is María de San José?" she whispered.

"In Seville, Teresa."

"Are we in Seville?"

"No, Teresa. We're in Alba de Tormes. Remember? We came here from Burgos."

"That girl has no respect for the Rule. She's far too lax, and she spends too much money on decorations for the convent!" said Teresa, with unexpected energy. "Is Father Gracián with her? He should be here with me!"

"Try to rest, Teresa." I said.

"I can't rest. I have to go to Seville. Tell Julián to harness the mule. I'm going to give that girl a piece of my mind. She thinks that just because she knows Latin . . ." She closed her eyes again, dozed a few minutes, then awoke with a start. "Is Fray Jerónimo here?" she gasped.

"No, Teresa," I whispered. "I think he's in Madrid."

Again she closed her eyes and dozed a few minutes. Suddenly, she opened them again. She started to tremble, flinging her arms wildly, as if trying to shoo away bats. Her eyes were filled with tears. Had she seen a vision of Hell? "Angélica," she said. Her voice vibrated like the whirr of ladybug wings. "Tell María de San José something for me, will you? Tell her I love her like a daughter. And tell her I'm sorry I broke the apothecary jars in the infirmary."

Why would she remember a thing like that? I wondered. "That's long past, Teresa," I said. "Don't think about it any more."

"But it was an awful thing to do. After all, what's more important than the happiness of the people you love?" A salty drop trickled from the corner of her eye to the pillow. "My Lord and my God," she intoned, "forgive me for my pettiness, my temper, my . . ." Her voice trailed off. She was silent a moment or two. Her face grew serene, her body, still.

Father Antonio bent over her. "Where do you want to lie, Mother?" he asked delicately. "Here in Alba de Tormes or in Ávila?"

"I have nothing of my own. Can't they give me a bit of earth here?"

Again, she turned to me. "Angélica, I've lived in poverty, and I want to die as I've lived. A simple slab on my tomb will do. In exchange, I promise to keep a nice, comfortable room for you up in Heaven, if that's where God in His divine mercy sends me." Her voice was barely audible. "A room with a kitten," she added. And this time I'm sure she smiled.

Calm enveloped the room. Teresa was breathing evenly. After a few minutes she once opened her mouth to speak. "Bear witness," she whispered into the night, "that I die a daughter of the church." At about nine o'clock she closed her eyes forever.

The star over the church burned with such intensity that the sky shone diaphanous. Light flooded the infirmary with a calming luminosity, more subtle than daylight, yet exquisitely bright. I remembered something Teresa had said years ago, when she awakened from a sleep so deep we had dressed her for burial: "You'll know I'm dead when you see my body covered with a cloth of gold." In the starlight, she did indeed appear to be swathed in gold.

Sweet harmonies charged the air. The tinkling of bells. The plink of lutes. The deep resonations of oboes d'amore. I closed my eyes and felt my soul drenched with love. I'd thought I would sob when the Lord came for Teresa, but instead of melancholy, I felt joyous—joyous and completely serene. I knelt by her bed. God's presence permeated my spirit and freed my mind. "Holy Mother, Saint Teresa," I murmured, "pray for me."

Starlight bathed the infirmary until dawn, when the sun crept over the horizon and stroked the morning with its autumnal glow. Teresa lay as still as a sleeping child. Gracián arrived before midday. He secured and wrapped

his relic, then bound the packet with a bit of yarn and stuffed it into the pocket of his habit. The surgical procedure disturbed the atmosphere. It was as
though someone had raped the air. La Bartolomé became fidgety, and I began
to hiccough inexplicably. Gracián stood perfectly silent. After a while, he
began to drone softly, "*Vivo sin vivir en mí.*" It was a poem Teresa had written
long ago about her desire to die in order to be with God. "*Muero porque no
muero*" was the refrain. She was "dying to die," yearning to leave this valley of
shadows and enjoy the "real life" beyond. We all knew it by heart, and so we
all joined in, reciting together as though we were saying the rosary.

Vivo sin vivir en mí	I live without really living,
y de tal manera espero	and yet I hope so intensely,
que muero porque no muero.	that I'm dying because I don't die.
Vivo ya fuera de mí,	I've lived outside myself,
después que muero de amor	ever since I began to die of love
porque vivo en el Señor,	and live in the Lord,
que me quiso para sí.	who chose me for Himself.
Cuando el corazón le di	When I gave Him my heart,
puso en él este lucero:	He put this sign on it:
que muero porque no muero.	I'm dying because I don't die.
¡Ay, qué larga es esta vida!	Oh, how long this life is!
¡Qué duros estos destierros,	How hard to live in exile,
esta cárcel y estos hierros	enchained in this prison
en que el alma está metida!	in which my soul is held captive!
Sólo esperar la salida	Just to be yearning for release
me causa un dolor tan fiero,	causes such terrible pain,
que muero porque no muero.	that I'm dying because I don't die.

La Bartolomé sobbed silently, her large, manly body stooping like a
wind-battered tree. After Gracián had left, La Bartolomé and I bathed her
and dressed her in a habit she herself had made. It was patched and frayed,
but impeccably clean, just as she had wanted.

"We should bury Mother Teresa's tambourine along with her," com-
mented La Bartolomé, as she adjusted the wimple.

"So she can play and sing for the angels?"

"I'd say she's earned herself a bit of revelry." La Bartolomé began to
tap a spoon against a bedpan, keeping rhythm as she chanted, "*Caminemos*

para el cielo / monjas del Carmelo." I chanted with her, quietly at first. After all, we were in the presence of a body from which the soul had recently departed. But as we worked, we began to sing louder. We were both singing at the top of our lungs when Sister Susana, one of the Alba nuns, burst in.

"What's going on?" she barked. "This isn't a party."

"Yes, it is," La Bartolomé barked back. "We're having a going-away party for Mother Teresa." She was standing there with the bedpan and spoon in her hand, leaning slightly forward, in the ready position of a dog about to attack. She towered over Sister Susana. "She's going straight up to Heaven on a shooting star, and we're seeing her off in style."

Sister Susana turned on her heel. "This is an outrage," she spat over her shoulder. Shortly she returned with Fray Antonio, that sweet, old creature with ears like dried apricots.

Father Antonio tried to screw his face into a scowl. He looked from La Bartolomé to me, then back to her again. His lips were stern, but I caught the twinkle in his eye. "Having a party, are we?" he said. Sister Susana's eyes grew large and round. "Father . . ." she began. "I should have brought my *zampoña*!" he interrupted her. "What's missing here is a flute!"

Sister Susana looked ready to grab the chamber pot out of La Bartolomé's hands and hurl it at the old priest, but instead, she turned and stomped out.

"It's time to move Mother Teresa to her room," I said.

La Bartolomé bent down and picked up Teresa gently, then carried her to her cell and placed her on the bed. We lit candles, filling the room with light. Teresa's face glowed like the Virgin's in the painting on the chapel wall. "*Descansa, Teresa,*" I told her. "Rest."

We buried her there, in Alba de Tormes, not in her beloved Ávila. As she'd requested, it was a simple ceremony. We didn't embalm her body, but simply shrouded her and placed her on a bier. Carrying lighted candles, we lined up behind Father Antonio and processed to the wall of the lower choir of the convent singing the traditional "*Dies Irae: Dies irae, dies illa / solvet saeclum in favilla, / teste David cum Sibylla.*" We lifted the plain, wooden casket into the grave. I'd dressed her myself and helped them put her in the coffin, and yet I couldn't believe that Teresa, my Teresa, was there, alone, without me. We had always been together.

The sisters entombed her under an arch attached to a wall of the lower choir of the convent, then piled rocks, lime, and bricks over the grave so that no relic-seekers would disturb it. She was gone. I stared at the grave and tried to fix it in my mind.

But that's not what I'll remember. Years from now, when I close my eyes and recall Teresa, what I'll see in my mind is a woman of dazzling beauty, a woman in a brown habit and a black veil dancing, twirling, leaping joyously in the air while she bangs a tambourine and sings (slightly off key), "*Caminemos para el cielo / monjas del Carmelo.*"

Angélica del Sagrado Corazón, Discalced Carmelite

Alba de Tormes, 15 October 1582

Epilogue

MORE THAN TWENTY YEARS HAVE PASSED SINCE I'VE LOOKED AT THESE pages. After Teresa went to God, I buried her story in straw, sewed it into my bedding, and forgot about it. Now I'm an old woman of nearly eighty-six. I'm going to die soon. Oh, I'm in reasonably good health, although my shoulders are stiff and my fingers are knotted. The point is, I don't expect to die of old age.

I've received intelligence that the inquisitors are coming for me. What would they want with an old lady like me? I don't know. They never tell you what they're after. They arrest you and make you talk. When you say something incriminating, they say you've confessed. You don't even know what the question is, when they tell you you've answered it, and you've answered it in such a way that you've shown yourself guilty of some crime.

Fray Julián died a few months ago. He was my best source of information. Fray Teodoro, the new chaplain, isn't such a good mole. He doesn't lose himself in the crowd and perk up his ears, the way Fray Julián used to. I have to depend on Sister Ágreda. She has a brother who's a counselor to the new king, Felipe III, so she hears quite a bit. She's the one who told me the Inquisition was after me. She was trembling because when they investigate one person in a convent, they also investigate everyone else.

It's hard for me to write. My fingers are stiff and my wrists ache. Still, I want to finish this before they come for me. Afterward, they'll never let me put quill to paper again, except to write my confession. Or maybe not even then. Sometimes they make you say your confession out loud, and the inquisitional secretary writes it down—which means he can change things, put words in your mouth that you didn't say. Who knows what they'll make me confess to. Reading novels, maybe. That's definitely a crime worthy of the flames.

They'll beatify Teresa soon, but I won't be able to testify because I'll be dead. That's why I want to give this testimony to someone for safekeeping. It has to be someone who'll speak on Teresa's behalf at the beatification hearing. Besides me, the people Teresa was closest to were Juan de la Cruz, Gracián, María de San José, and Ana de San Bartolomé. But I can't give these pages to any of them because they're all dead or far away.

After Teresa's burial I stayed on a while at Alba de Tormes. Torrential rains had obliterated the roads, making a journey to Ávila impossible. Anyhow, I was exhausted. I needed some time to get my bearings and decide what to do next. Sometimes I'd pray at Teresa's grave. Whenever I dozed off, strange sounds jolted me awake. A flittering flapping of wings. A puff of air, like a gasp. It was as though Teresa were thrashing around in her grave. At first, it frightened me. Later, I thought it was funny. "So, you're holding the whip to me from the other side," I laughed. "You won't let me sluff off even now!" And I noticed something else: the air was redolent of roses, especially on the feast days of her favorite saints, like Saint Joseph's, March 19.

Nine months after Teresa died, Gracián passed through Alba de Tormes and stopped by the convent to visit her grave. The nuns, curious about the sounds and smells coming from the burial site, begged him to exhume her body. In the presence of four prelates, he broke the seal and gently opened the casket. It was cracked throughout, and moist earth had worked its way though the fissures. The wood splintered and disintegrated in his hands. Teresa's body was covered with soil. Gracián brushed it away and unwrapped the corps. The aroma of roses grew stronger. When at last Teresa lay exposed, we were astonished to see that although her habit had decomposed, her body was perfectly incorrupt. I forced myself to look at my sister's bloodless face. It was serene and somehow reassuring. The other nuns were staring at her, their eyes wide and bright. Then, one by one, they fell to their knees, bowed their heads, and prayed. After the prelates verified the unspoiled state of her body, we dressed her in a fresh habit and laid her in a new coffin.

La Bartolomé and I wanted to take her back to Ávila. The San José nuns were enraged that she'd been buried in Alba de Tormes. They wrote to me constantly, complaining of the audacity of the Alba sisters, who had assumed that because Teresa had died on their property, they had a right to her for all eternity. At first, I argued with them. I told them Teresa had said she'd be content to leave her mortal remains in the place where she'd taken her last breath. But then, after the disinterment, it seemed easy enough to transport her back to the city of her birth. I planned to return to Ávila to spend the rest of my days there, and I wanted to take her with me. It would be our final journey together.

But the Alba nuns wouldn't give in. "You will not take this body out of our convent!" they cried. "It's a holy relic! You can't move it!" In the end, we left it, but two years later, in 1585, I returned to Alba de Tormes and watched a surgeon remove Teresa's arm—as indifferent as if he were removing the wing of a roasted squab—and give it to the prioress. I wanted to scream, "That's my friend you're mutilating!" But I just stood there watching and sobbing quietly. The rest of Teresa's body was sent secretly to Ávila. That was supposed to settle the dispute, but the Alba nuns still weren't satisfied. They demanded Teresa be exhumed again and buried in her original resting place. And she was. At least, most of her. Bits have already been sent here and there for relics, and more will be dispersed with time—one finger to Paris, another to Brussels, another all the way to Mexico. Her heart, which they cut out and placed in a reliquary, has a little hole in it where the angel of the Lord once pierced it. Some day, when she's been canonized, people will kneel before those relics and pray.

Where can I leave these pages? I'd have liked to send them to María de San José. Beautiful María, so smart and full of life! She's dead now, victim not of the Calced friars who tormented us for so long, but of her very own Discalced brothers.

They thought she'd become too feisty and independent. They wanted to rewrite the constitution of the order, the constitution Teresa herself had created. María wouldn't let them. She went above their heads, directly to the pope. I can imagine her scouring her repertory of Latin phrases for just the right way to tell them to go to Hell: *Graviora manent,* "the worse is yet to come," you ass! *Mali principii malus finis,* "from a bad beginning a bad ending!" *Irritabis cabrones,* "you'll stir up the hornets!" I don't know Latin, but I heard her fling these expressions around enough times for me to hold onto a few of them. I especially like the last one because it sounds in Spanish something like, *me irritas, cabrón,* "you're getting on my nerves, shithead." What a girl, that María de San José. I wish I could insult people in Latin. But where did it get her? They tortured her and sent her away to die.

Fray Juan de la Cruz almost fell victim to the same pack of vermin, but God took him before they could kill him. Gracián rotted in prison for a while, and then headed for Rome to argue his case. The last I heard he was captured by Turks on the Mediterranean and forced into slavery. La Bartolomé crossed the Pyrenees to found a convent in a city called Dijon, somewhere in France, and I haven't heard from her since.

So what should I do with this testimony? Everyone is gone. I can't leave it here. There are too many incriminating pages. It's not myself I worry about. It's my sister Teresa. I have to give this to someone who will know how to use it, someone able to pick out which things can be told at her beatification proceedings and which must be concealed.

I'll have to burn my books tonight. I have eleven of them, a treasure trove of romances. It shreds my heart to part with them. They've been my companions for decades. Besides, a book is a precious object. There's no help for it, though. I can't give them away without implicating myself or putting someone else in jeopardy. Maybe I'll bury them in the garden and hope some sister, some secret reader, will find and enjoy them.

This testimony is a death sentence. What shall I do with it? Who shall I give it to? It's nearly dawn. They'll be here soon. I have to decide.

Angélica del Sagrado Corazón
Ávila, 30 October 1606

Author's Note

TERESA DE AVILA CAME INTO MY WORLD DURING A TIME OF PERSONAL trauma. I found in her not only a spiritual guide, but also a role model—a tough, energetic woman who confronted myriad obstacles without ever losing her faith, warmth, and sense of humor. Although I was not a religious person, Teresa's *Interior Castle* gave me a new way to think about prayer. By describing God as a King lodged deep within a castle that is the soul, Teresa makes it possible for people of different religious backgrounds to find faith by turning inward. Teresa helped me to muster the inner strength to face the challenges in my life, and *Sister Teresa* is my thanksgiving offering. It is also my way of sharing Teresa's spirituality with readers of all religions and backgrounds.

From Teresa's writing emerges the image of a complex and sometimes contradictory woman. Teresa was a mystic and spiritual teacher, but also a shrewd administrator, politician, and fundraiser. She challenged authority, yet seemingly conformed to the rules. She could be manipulative, but also naïve; her trust in her allies was so complete that she sometimes fell victim to the manipulation of others. A woman of *converso* background living in a Spain obsessed with "purity of blood," Teresa never mentions her Jewish ancestry. Yet, scholars such as Catherine Swietlicki and David Gitlitz, have demonstrated how her Semitic roots influenced her thinking. The peculiarities of Teresa's personality made me wonder what it would be like to be close to such a person. What would it be like to live with a woman who talked to God, saw visions, and slipped into trances, yet played the tambourine and told jokes? Sister Angélica is the narrative device I invented in order to observe Teresa from an essentially secular perspective. Although Angélica follows Teresa into the convent, she remains attached to the material world. For her, Teresa's ecstasies are both wonderful and frightening.

Is Teresa saintly, she wonders, or just crazy? Teresa's own descriptions of others' reactions to her experiences make Angélica's confusion perfectly credible.

Sister Teresa required an immense amount of research. In addition to all of Teresa's writing, I immersed myself in many areas of history: Carmelite, conventual, Spanish-Jewish, and women's. I read Inquisition documents, nun's letters, and countless scholarly analyses of Teresa's work. By writing a novel, I aspired to conjure up Teresa's world. To do so, I had to learn about daily life in early modern Spain—everything from farthingales to chamber pots, from marriage rituals to eating customs. I am indebted to the work of many researchers, in particular, Efrén de la Madre de Dios and Otger Steggink, Teófanes Egido López, Américo Castro, Alison Weber, Jodi Bilinkoff, Gillian Ahlgren, Carole Slade, Joan Cammarata, María Carrión, James Casey, Víctor García de la Concha, David Gitlitz, Henry Kamen, Cathleen Medwick, Ildefonso Morriones, Edgar A. Peers, and John Welsh.

Although my portrayal of Teresa's career in the Reform is historically accurate, because this is a novel, I took certain artistic liberties. Most of the characters that appear in the book are historical (Juan de la Cruz, Gracián, María de San José, Ana de San Bartoloméo, Rubeo, Sega, and Tostado). However, two main characters, Angélica and Braulio, are fictional. Don Javier is also fictional, although he emerged from Teresa's intriguing admission, at the end of Chapter 2 of *Life,* that she originally entered the convent because of a "friendship with one of my cousins [which] was in view of a possible marriage." She does not elaborate on this friendship except to note that her confessor told her that she was "doing nothing against God." Some investigators, notably Victoria Lincoln, have interpreted this comment as an acknowledgment of sinful behavior on Teresa's part. However, in the absence of any concrete evidence on this relationship, I have spun the mysterious cousin into Don Javier. In some cases I changed the name of historical characters in order to avoid a superabundance of Marías, Juans, and Pedros. For example, Don Alejo, the seductive priest of Becedas, has been identified by researchers as Pedro Hernández. Miguela, the woman who turns Teresa over to the Inquisition in Seville, was actually María del Corro.

I would like to express my gratitude to the novelist Janice Eidus, my agent Anna Ghosh, and my editor Alex Young for their very helpful suggestions. I also wish to thank my husband, Mauro E. Mujica, for his patience and support during the writing process, and two special friends, Janet O'Brien and Jeffrey von Arx, S.J., for their unflagging encouragement. Finally, I thank the two Carmelite monasteries of Washington D.C.— Calced and Discalced at last united in a common purpose—for carrying on Teresa's legacy.

Cast of Characters

TERESA DE JESÚS (1515–1582), born Teresa Sánchez de Cepeda y Ahumada and known in the English-speaking world as Teresa of Ávila. The daughter of a *converso* merchant, Teresa first entered the convent to avoid a scandal that arose over her relationship with a cousin. After a profound spiritual conversion before a statue of the wounded Christ, she experienced repeated visions and locutions. Distraught over conventual laxity, she strove to reform her order, the Carmelites, by creating convents that promoted an intimate, authentic relationship with God. However, her ecstasies and emphasis on mental prayer aroused the suspicions of church officials, who associated her with the *alumbrados,* a sect considered heretical because it stressed personal enlightenment rather than the sacraments. Over the course of her career Teresa founded seventeen convents and a new order, the Discalced Carmelites. She is considered one of the most important figures of the Counter Reformation. She was canonized in 1622 and declared a Doctor of the Church in 1970.

ANGÉLICA DEL SAGRADO CORAZÓN (Pancracia Soto y Fuentes). Teresa's best friend. The daughter and niece of seamstresses, she entered the convent when an arranged marriage failed to materialize. An expert herbalist, she became Teresa's nurse as well as her confidante. She assisted Teresa in many of her foundations and wrote a personal testimony describing her experiences.

Historical Characters

ÁGUILA, FRANCISCA DEL. Prioress at the Carmelite convent of the Encarnación.

AHUMADA, BEATRIZ DE (1494–1528). Teresa's mother. Alonso de Cepeda's second wife.

AHUMADA, JUANA DE (1528–1591). Teresa's younger sister and wife of Juan de Ovalle, who purchased the house in Ávila that Teresa turned into the first Discalced Carmelite convent, San José.

ALBA, DUCHESS OF (María Enríquez de Toledo, ?–1583). A contributor to many religious institutions, the duchess supported the Reform and Teresa's foundation in Alba de Tormes. She called for Teresa to bless the birth of her grandchild, but when it became clear that the foundress was too ill to travel to the duchess's palace, Doña María went to the convent to attend to her sick friend.

ALBA, DUKE OF (Fernando Álvarez de Toledo, 1508–1582). Governor of Flanders (1567–1573), where his brutal policies toward Protestants led to insurrection.

ALEJO (Historical name: Pedro Hernández). Priest at the church of Becedas. He was having an affair with a woman he claimed held him her in power with an amulet.

ÁLVAREZ, BALTASAR (1533–1580). Álvarez, a Jesuit at San Gil, was twenty-six and had been ordained only the year before when he became Teresa's spiritual director. He was uneasy about directing her and fearful of displeasing his superiors. As a result, he did not offer much support when she was harassed by priests who thought her visions came from the Devil or when townspeople opposed her foundation at San José.

ANA DE SAN BARTOLOMÉ (1549–1626). The mystic Ana de San Bartolomé was the first white-veiled nun to enter San José in Ávila (1570). She became Teresa's nurse, secretary, and companion. Ana says in her autobiography that she learned how to write miraculously by imitating Teresa's hand. After Teresa's death Ana took the Reform into France and the Low Countries.

ÁVILA, MARÍA DE (María de San José). Julián de Ávila's sister. One of the first four novices at San José in Ávila. [Not to be confused with María de San José Salazar.]

BÁÑEZ, DOMINGO (1528–1604). Dominican friar and professor at Santo Tomás in Ávila from 1561 until 1567. He defended Teresa before the city council of Ávila, which opposed her starting a new convent without a sponsor. He was briefly confessor to Teresa and the nuns at San José. Báñez was one of the most highly regarded preachers and theologians of his time.

BARRÓN, VICENTE. Don Alonso's Dominican confessor who counseled Teresa after her father's death and reassured her during periods of doubt.

BORJA, FRANCISCO DE (1510–1572). Great-grandson of Pope Alexander VI on the paternal side and of the Catholic King Fernando of Aragon on the maternal side, Borja, the Grand Duke of Gandía, was from one of the most powerful families in Spain. He accompanied the Emperor Carlos V on many campaigns. In 1539 he escorted the body of the Empress Isabella, reputedly the most beautiful woman in Europe, to Granada to be buried. Upon seeing her corrupted corpse, Borja vowed never again to serve a mortal human being. After his wife died and he had placed his eight children in suitable positions, he became a Jesuit. His support of Teresa became very important to the success of the Reform. He eventually became Father General of the Society of Jesus. He was canonized in 1670.

BRACAMONTE, RUBÉN DE. Rich converso who financed the construction of the Church of Nuestra Señora de la Anunciación in Ávila.

BRICEÑO Y CONTRERAS, MARÍA DE. Novice mistress at Nuestra Señora de la Gracia, Augustinian convent Teresa entered as a boarder in 1531.

CANINIUS, PETER (1521–1597). Dutch Jesuit who devoted his life to strengthening the faith of wavering Roman Catholics. He preached vigorously in West and South Germany, trying to reconvert those areas to Catholicism. He was canonized in 1869.

CANO, MELCHOR (1509–1560). Renowned theologian from the University of Salamanca.

CARLOS I, CARLOS V (Charles I of Spain, also known as Charles V, of the Holy Roman Empire, 1500–1558). Grandson of the Catholic monarchs, Fernando and Isabella, he assumed the Spanish crown when his mother, Juana la Loca, was deemed incompetent to rule. Born in the Flemish city of Ghent, he inherited the lands of the German Habsburgs as well as Spain and her holdings in the New World. His empire was so vast, it was said that the sun never set on it.

CASTRO, CATALINA DE. Sister at Encarnación. One of the few nuns who supported Teresa when she returned to be prioress.

CAZALLA, AGUSTÍN (?–1559). Professor of theology at the University of Salamanca and Chaplain to Carlos V. During the reign of Felipe II, he was accused of holding secret meetings with Lutherans in his home, and although he confessed his "sin" and begged for mercy, he was burned at the stake by the Inquisition.

CEPEDA, AGUSTÍN DE (1527–1591). Teresa's youngest male sibling followed his elder brothers to the New World. The wildest of the Cepeda men, he fought in Chile and was made governor of Peru before returning to Spain with Lorenzo and Pedro.

CEPEDA, ALONSO DE (Sánchez) (1480–1543). Teresa's father. A *converso* merchant, he, like his father, purchased a patent of nobility in order to prove his Old Christian lineage. He eventually gave up his silk and woolens business in order to disassociate himself from his Jewish origins. As a result, Don Alonso incurred many debts, which complicated Teresa's task when she became executrix of his will.

CEPEDA, ANA DE. One of Teresa's cousins.

CEPEDA, ANTONIO DE (1520–1546). Teresa's younger brother, who died at Iñaquito.

CEPEDA, FERNANDO DE (1510–1565). Teresa's older brother, who died in Colombia.

CEPEDA, INÉS DE. One of Teresa's cousins.

CEPEDA, JERÓNIMO DE (1522–1575). Teresa's younger brother, who fought in the Americas with Lorenzo and Agustín and died in Panama.

CEPEDA, LORENZO DE (1519–1580). Teresa's younger brother, who often sent her money for her foundations from Quito. After he returned to Spain, he continued to help her. Of all Teresa's siblings, Lorenzo was the closest to her.

CEPEDA, MARÍA DE. Teresa's older half-sister, who married Martín de Guzmán. Daughter of Teresa's father, Don Alonso de Cepeda, and his first wife, Catalina del Peso y Henao.

CEPEDA, PEDRO DE (1521–?). Teresa's younger brother, who returned from Quito with her brother Lorenzo.

CEPEDA, PEDRO DE. Don Alonso's brother and Teresa's uncle. He gave her a copy of *The Third Spiriitual Alphabet,* by Francisco de Osuna, which changed her idea of prayer.

CEPEDA, RODRIGO DE (1511–1537). Teresa's older brother, who died in Chile.

CERDA, LUISA DE LA (?–1596). Daughter of the second duke of Medinaceli, Doña Luisa was widowed in 1561. Seeing her disconsolate, her children asked Ángel de Salazar, the Carmelite provincial, to allow Teresa to come to Toledo to comfort her. Teresa's six-month sojourn with Doña Luisa gave her time to work on her *Life.* Doña Luisa sponsored a foundation in Malagón, where her protégée, María de San José (Salazar) professed. When Teresa founded in Toledo, however, Doña Luisa did little to help her.

CETINA, DIEGO DE (1530–?). Teresa's first Jesuit confessor and spiritual director.

CORRO, MIGUELA DEL (historical name: María del Corro). Celebrated *beata* who entered the Seville Carmel and left disgruntled. She denounced Teresa and the other nuns to the Seville Inquisition, one of the harshest in Europe.

DÁVILA, LÁZARO. Stonecutter and inspector of wells in Ávila.

DAZA, GASPAR (?–1592). A learned priest to whom Teresa confided her mystical experiences. Convinced her visions came from the Devil, he publicized them throughout Ávila and insisted she be exorcized, causing her much psychological harm. Eventually, he became Teresa's defender. It was he who said the first Mass at San José de Ávila and gave the habit to the four first Discalced Carmelite nuns.

ÉBOLI, PRINCESS OF. See Ana Mendoza de la Cerda.

EGMONT, COUNT OF (1522–1568). A member of one of the most influential families in the Netherlands, Egmont, along with William of Orange, opposed the introduction of the Inquisition in Flanders. He even traveled to Spain to plead with Felipe II for a change of policy. When the rebellion against the Spanish began, Egmont, a devout Catholic, remained loyal to Felipe. Nevertheless, The Duke of Alba had him arrested and condemned to death.

FELIPE II (Philip II of Spain, 1527–1598). Son of Carlos I of Spain (Carlos V of the Holy Roman Empire). His reign (1556–1598) suffered from economic instability and constant wars. He appointed the Duke of Alba to halt the advance of Calvinism in the Netherlands, but the duke's violent tactics provoked the Dutch Revolt and the secession of the Netherlands. Other crises were the Morisco Revolt of 1568, the Antonio Pérez (q.v.) affair, and the defeat of the Spanish Armada in 1588. A religious zealot, the king mercilessly persecuted the *conversos*.

FELIPE III (Philip III of Spain, 1578–1621). Successor to Philip II. A weak ruler, Felipe III allowed himself to be unduly influenced by his advisor, the Duke of Lerma.

GARCÍA DE TOLEDO. Dominican friar who was Subprior at Santo Tomás, the Dominican monastery in Ávila. Teresa met him in Toledo in 1562, and he became one of her confessors. He is one of the persons who commanded her to write her *Life,* and it was he who asked for the expanded version of the book, which includes a short treatise on prayer and an account of the foundation of San José.

GÓMEZ DE SILVA, RUY (1516–1573). Prince of Éboli, Secretary to King Felipe II, and husband of Doña Ana de Mendoza de la Cerda.

GÓMEZ TELLO GIRÓN. Ecclesiastical governor of the diocese of Toledo who opposed Teresa's founding in that city.

GRACIÁN, JERÓNIMO (Fray Jerónimo de la Madre de Dios, 1545–1614). One of Teresa's best friends, although he caused her much aggravation. Ordained in 1571, Gracián joined the Carmelite Order and entered the novitiate in Pastrana, where he preached and gave spiritual direction to the nuns while still a novice. He became visitator and then vicar general of the Carmelites in Andalusia, but questions arose regarding the legality of his appointment. As a result, Nicolás Ormaneto, the papal nuncio to Spain, named Gracián and Francisco Vargas visitators *in solidium.* Gracián met Teresa in Beas in 1575. She was immediately taken with his profound spirituality and compassionate approach toward convent governance. She made a vow of obedience to him in spiritual matters, while he promised to consult her in all matters pertaining to the Order. At Gracián's urging, Teresa founded in Seville, which put her in violation of Rubeo's directive that she start no Discalced convents in Andalusia. The Calced Carmelites responded by persecuting the Discalced and even making threats on Gracián's life, tactics that continued until the pope allowed the two groups to form separate provinces. In 1581 Gracián became the first provincial of the reformed Carmel, but he was not a shrewd politician and made many enemies. In the conflict between Nicolás Doria and María de San José (Salazar, q.v.), he sided with María. Doria and his allies maneuvered to send Gracián to Mexico. Although that plan never materialized, Gracián was imprisoned in Madrid and forbidden to write any letters without permission from Doria. In 1592 he was pronounced incorrigible and expelled from the Order. Gracián traveled to Rome to appeal his case. He was captured by Turks who left him in Tunis, where he was held captive for two years. In 1596 a pontifical brief absolved him of any misdeeds, and he was allowed back into the Order. In 1607 he left for Flanders, where he promoted Teresa's writings and, with Ana de Jesús, published those of Teresa's works still unavailable to the public. It was not until December, 1999, that the Discalced Carmelite Order, in an effort to restore Gracián's good name, officially revoked the sentence of expulsion against him.

GUZMÁN Y BARRIENTO. Martín de. Teresa's brother-in-law. María's husband.

GUZMÁN, ALDONZA. Doña Guiomar's mother.

GUZMÁN, FERNANDO DE. Influential priest and son of Rubén de Bracamonte (q.v).

HENAO, ANTONIA DE (Antonia del Espíritu Santo). One of the first four novices at San José, in Ávila.

IGNACIO DE LOYOLA (1491–1556). Founder of the Society of Jesus (Jesuits), canonized in 1622.

ISABEL DE SANTO DOMINGO (1537–1623). A pious but supremely practical woman, Isabel served as Teresa's confidante and assistant on many occasions. As Prioress of the Pastrana Carmel, she helped her nuns escape from the domination of the Princess of Éboli, then became prioress in Segovia. She founded a convent in Zaragoza in 1588 and became the first prioress in Ocaña in 1598.

JUAN DE AUSTRIA (1545–1578). Illegitimate son of Carlos I and Barbara de Blomberg. In 1571, as Captain General of Granada, he put down the Morisco uprising and then went on to lead the flotilla of the Holy League in the successful battle against the Turks at Lepanto. He was governor of Flanders from 1576 to 1578, in the middle of the Protestant uprising.

JUAN DE ÁVILA (1500–1569). Called "the Apostle of Andalusia," Juan de Ávila devoted himself to an impassioned ministry in southern Spain. Respected as a theologian, a teacher, and a mystic, he is best known for his work *Audi filia* (*Listen, Daughter*), which was placed on the 1559 Index. Teresa was anxious for him to approve her *Life*, which he did in 1568, although it remained in the hands of inquisitors. Juan de Ávila was canonized in 1970.

JUAN DE LA CRUZ (1542–1591). After studying at the University of Salamanca, Juan de la Cruz met Teresa at Medina del Campo. Greatly impressed with his spirituality and intelligence, she recruited him for the Discalced Carmelites. He was one of two founders of the first Discalced Carmelite monastery in Durueolos. In 1571 he was named rector of the new Discalced college in Alcalá, but left at Teresa's request to serve as confessor to the nuns at Encarnación. In 1577 he was seized and imprisoned by Calced friars. He escaped on August 15, 1578. While in prison he composed some of his most beautiful verses. After Teresa's death, Nicolás Doria tried to have Juan sent to Mexico as punishment for encouraging María de San José to defy him. However, Juan died before Doria could implement the plan. Juan de la Cruz is considered Spain's greatest mystic poet and treatise-writer. He was canonized in 1726 and declared a Doctor of the Church in 1926.

JULIÁN DE ÁVILA (1527–1605). Teresa's traveling companion and chaplain of San José de Ávila.

LÓPEZ, MENCÍA. Widow of Jorge de Nájera and founder of Nuestra Señora de la Gracia.

LUIS DE GRANADA (1504–1588). Dominican friar who was highly respected for his preaching and writing. His most famous book, *Guía de pecadores (Guide for Sinners)*, was one of Teresa's favorites. It appeared on the 1559 Index along with his treatise on prayer.

MACHUCA, CATALINA. Augustinian nun, friend of the Princess of Eboli. The princess tried unsuccessfully to force Teresa to admit Catalina to the Pastrana Carmel.

MAGDALENA DE LA CRUZ (1487–1560). An influential holy woman and visionary widely held to be a saint, Magdalena was abbess of a Franciscan monastery in Córdoba. After falling seriously ill, she scandalized Spain by admitting to being a fraud. She was tried by the Inquisition and condemned to perpetual imprisonment in an abbey.

MALDONADO, HERNANDO DE. Prior of the Calced Carmelites in Toledo who had Fray Juan de la Cruz arrested.

MARÍA BAUTISTA. *See* Ocampo, María de.

MARÍA DE SAN JOSÉ. *See* Salazar, María de.

MARIDÍAZ (María Díaz, 1495–1572). A holy woman highly regarded in Ávila, she lived in absolute poverty. People flocked to her with their problems and highly valued her counsel. Juan de Prádanos, who became Teresa's confessor, placed her as a servant in the house of Guiomar de Ulloa so she would not have to beg. On the advice of her spiritual directors, she left Doña Guiomar and went to live in a gallery in the convent of San Millán. Teresa met her in 1557 while staying with Doña Guiomar.

MENDOZA DE LA CERDA, ANA (Princess of Éboli, 1540–1592). Wife of Ruy Gómez de Silva, a close friend and advisor to King Felipe II, and cousin of Doña Luisa de la Cerda. She insisted that Teresa found a convent on her property in Pastrana, and, due to Don Ruy's position, Teresa consented. However, she refused to let Doña Ana impose her will on the convent, thereby provoking the princess's resentment. When she was widowed in 1573, Doña Ana decided to become a Carmelite nun, but instead of following the rules of the Order, she insisted on special treatment. Teresa instructed her nuns to abandon the convent, and they snuck out in the middle of the night in April 1574. Furious, the princess took vengeance by turning Teresa's *Life,* over to the Valladolid Inquisition, which kept it only a short time. She was rumored to have had an affair with Antonio Pérez (q.v.). When Pérez was accused of murdering Juan Escobedo, secretary to Don Juan of Austria, Doña Ana was arrested as an accomplice and confined to the castle of Santocraz. Eventually, she was placed under house arrest at her palace in Pastrana.

MONARDES, NICOLÁS. A celebrated doctor who believed that tobacco was good for migraines and other illnesses.

MONTEMAYOR, JORGE DE (1520–1561). Popular Portuguese-Spanish writer, author of *The Seven Books of Diana,* one of Sister Angélica's favorite pastoral novels.

NIETO, BALTASAR DE JESÚS. Prior of the Discalced monastery in Pastrana, who denounced Fray Jerónimo Gracián to the king.

OCAMPO, MARÍA DE (María Bautista, 1543–1603). Teresa's niece and great friend. Teresa brought her to Encarnación to be educated, and when Teresa founded San José, María gave her one thousand ducats from her inheritance. María entered San José in 1563 and professed in 1564. She became prioress of the Valladolid Carmel in 1571.

OSUNA, FRANCISCO (1497–1540?). Franciscan mystic whose book, *The Third Spiritual Alphabet,* was influential in Teresa's concept of prayer.

OVALLE, BEATRIZ DE. Daughter of Juan de Ovalle and Juana de Ahumada (Teresa's sister).

OVALLE, GONZALO DE. Son of Juan de Ovalle and Juana de Ahumada. When a wall fell on him during the construction of San José, Teresa predicted he would live and recover.

OVALLE, JOSEPE DE. Son of Juan de Ovalle and Juana de Ahumada. He lived only a short time.

OVALLE, JUAN DE. Teresa's brother-in-law, husband of Juana de Ahumada. It was he who purchased the house Teresa transformed into San José, the first Discalced Carmelite convent.

PEDRO DE ALCÁNTARA (1499–1562). One of Spain's greatest mystics, Pedro de Alcántara was a Franciscan of the Stricter Observance known for his austere life and pious works. He founded a new province, called the Alcantarines, whose friars practiced rigorous asceticism. He encouraged Teresa to found San José in Ávila.

PÉREZ, ANTONIO (1540–1611). As Secretary of State for Italian Affairs, Pérez enjoyed the confidence of King Felipe II. However, he became embroiled in a plot to assassinate Juan Escobedo (1578), secretary to Juan de Austria, the king's half brother. Rumor had it that Escobedo discovered an affair between Pérez and the Princess of Éboli, but most historians reject this hypothesis. Imprisoned by the King, Pérez escaped to Aragón, and then to France, where he died.

PESO Y HENAO CATALINA DEL. Alonso de Cepeda's first wife.

PONCE DE LA FUENTE, CONSTANTINO (1502–1560). Court preacher imprisoned in an Augustinian monastery after it was discovered that he was a secret Lutheran. He committed suicide.

PRÁDANOS, JUAN DE (1528–1597). Jesuit priest who, in 1555, replaced Diego de Cetina as Teresa's confessor and spiritual director.

QUIROGA, GASPAR DE (1507–1594). Archbishop of Toledo and Primate of Spain, Quiroga met Teresa in 1580, when she and Gracián visited him to request permission to make a foundation in Madrid. He told her he had read her *Life* and found it sound and beneficial.

REVILLA, ÚRSULA DE (Úrsula de los Santos). One of the first four novices at San José in Ávila, she served as prioress of the new convent while Teresa was at Encarnación.

RIPALDA, JERÓNIMO DE. Jesuit friend who ordered Teresa to write *The Book of Foundations.*

RUBEO, JUAN BAUTISTA (Giovanni Battista Rossi, 1507–1578). As Carmelite General, Rubeo tried to reform the houses of the Order, restoring poverty, solitude, and affective prayer. However, Rubeo was not a charismatic character, and the Andalusian Calced Carmelite friars resisted his efforts. By appealing to the king, they managed to undermine Felipe's confidence in the general. Unaware of the king's opposition, Rubeo began his visitation of the Castilian convents in 1567. He authorized Teresa to found houses for nuns, and later, for friars as well. However, due to the antagonism of the Calced friars, the permission did not extend to Andalusia. When, at Gracián urging, Teresa founded in Seville, Rubeo became angry. At a chapter in Piacenza he led the Order to resolve that Teresa should choose a convent in Castile and remain there, making no more foundations. Teresa was deeply hurt by Rubeo's hostility, which she believed was due to a misunderstanding.

SALAZAR, ÁNGEL DE (1519–1600?). Carmelite provincial who opposed Teresa's plan to form a new community of nuns. His opposition to her project caused her many difficulties.

SALAZAR, MARÍA DE (María de San José, 1548–1603). One of Teresa's closest friends. As a little girl she entered into the service of Luisa de la Cerda, where she received an excellent education. Teresa met her during her stay at Doña Luisa's. María professed in Malagón in 1570, taking the name María de San José. As prioress of the Seville Carmel, she suffered persecution by the Calced Carmelite friars. Teresa thought María de San José would succeed her as foundress. However, after Teresa's death Nicolás Doria, a Discalced Carmelite who had been Teresa's financial advisor, attempted to change the Order's constitution, and when María appealed to the pope to stop him, Doria—and later, his successors—persecuted her mercilessly. Francisco de la Madre de Dios, the Carmelite General, exiled her to a convent in the remote town of Cuerva, where she died shortly afterward.

SALCEDO, FRANCISCO DE (?–1580). Teresa called him "the holy cavalier" and praised him for his charity and goodness in her *Life.* Married to Mencía del Águila, a cousin of one of Teresa's aunts, Salcedo studied theology with the Dominicans for twenty years, becoming a priest after his wife's death. Teresa confided her mystical experiences to him, but Salcedo took a skeptical stance. Convinced her visions came from the Devil, he only changed his mind after Pedro de Alcántara took Teresa's side.

SÁNCHEZ DE TOLEDO, JUAN. Teresa's grandfather. A *converso* merchant, he was prosecuted by the Inquisition for Judaizing in 1585.

SEGA, FELIPE (Filippo, 1537?–1596). Appointed papal nuncio in Spain in 1577, Sega at first supported Tostado's efforts to suppress the Reform. It was he who called Teresa a "restless vagabond." However, under pressure from Rome he eventually acquiesced to the Discalced Carmelites' request to form a separate province.

SOTO, FRANCISCO DE. Inquisitor in charge of the investigation of Teresa's book.

SUÁREZ, HORACIO. Mayor of Ávila who opposed the foundation of the new convent of San José.

SUÁREZ, JUANA ISABEL (historical name: Juana Suárez). Teresa's cousin and a nun at Encarnación, it was she who convinced Teresa to join the Carmelites.

TOLEDO, ANASTASIA DE. Prioress at Encarnación when Fray Juan de la Cruz returned from prison.

TORRES, MIGUEL. Jesuit priest whose talents as a negotiator were highly regarded in Ávila. Before he met Teresa, he had arbitrated a conflict at Encarnación.

TOSTADO, JERÓNIMO (1523–1582). As apostolic visitator, reformer, and commissary general of the Spanish provinces, Tostado tried to suppress the Reform.

ULLOA, GUIOMAR DE (1529–?). One of Teresa's best friends. Left a widow at twenty-five, Doña Guiomar devoted the rest of her life to charity. She had at least one daughter at Encarnación, which is where Teresa probably met her. She surrounded herself with some of the most influential and progressive spiritual thinkers of her day. It was she who introduced Teresa to the Jesuits and to Pedro de Alcántara.

VÁZQUEZ, DIONISIO. Rector of the Jesuit school of San Gil. Baltasar Álvarez's superior.

XAVIER, FRANCISCO (1506–1552). Jesuit who founded missions in India and Japan, canonized in 1622.

Fictional Characters

ÁGREDA. Sister at the convent of San José in Ávila upon whom Angélica relied for information.

AMBROSIO. Friar in Pastrana.

ANDREA. Princess of Éboli's personal cook, who entered the Pastrana Carmel with her.

ANSELMO. Father of Basilio, to whom Pancracia (Angélica) was engaged.

ANTONIO DE SAN JOSÉ. Friar in Alba de Tormes.

BASILIO. Cartwright to whom Pancracia Soto (Sister Angélica) was engaged before entering the convent.

BEATRIZ. Pancracia's (Angélica's) great-aunt, sister of her grandmother Catalina.

BELISARDA. Angélica's maid at Don Pedro de Cepeda's house.

BERNARDA. Pancracia's (Angélica's) cousin. Daughter of Tío Celso and Tía Cati.

BRÍGIDA. Sister at Encarnación.

CÁNDIDA. Hunchbacked sister at Encarnación. Niece of the Grand Inquisitor of Toledo.

CARIDAD. Tough Andalusian nun at Encarnación. Teresa's nemesis.

CATALINA. Pancracia's (Angélica's) cousin. Daughter of Tío Celso and Tía Cati.

CATALINA. Pancracia's (Angélica's) grandmother.

CELSO. Pancracia's (Angélica's) cousin. Son of Tío Celso and Tía Cati.

CELSO. Pancracia's (Angélica's) uncle and Tía Cati's deceased husband.

CORDOBA, RAQUEL. Medicine woman in Becedas in charge of curing Teresa. Her excessive bleedings almost killed her patient. (Based on an historical character.)

CRISTINA. Nursemaid of Teresa's nephew, Gonzalo de Ovalle.

ELENA. Sister at Encarnación.

Escolástica. Sister at Encarnación who claimed to see Teresa levitate. Later she entered San José in Ávila and became the convent cellaress.

Estévez y Pontenegro, Fray Braulio. Angélica's confessor with whom she had an affair.

Felipe. Pancracia's (Angélica's) cousin. Son of Tío Celso and Tía Cati.

Félix. Don Lope's father.

Fuentes de Rojas, Catalina (Tía Cati). The aunt that Pancracia (Angélica) lived with when she was growing up.

Fuentes de Soto, Inés. Pancracia's (Angélica's) mother.

Gisela de San Agustín. Prioress at Nuestra Señora de la Gracia.

Ignacia. Nurse at Nuestra Señora de la Gracia.

Inmaculada. Sister at San José in Pastrana.

Irene. Pancracia's (Angélica's) cousin. Daughter of Tío Celso and Tía Cati.

Josefa. Sister, nurse, and pharmacist at Encarnación who eventually became prioress.

Lis. The Princess of Éboli's personal maid.

Lope. Rosa's suitor who visited the grille at Encarnación regularly.

Lucía. Sister at Encarnación.

Malquiel. Brother who denounced Vida and Sara Santana y Córdoba to the Inquisition.

Marcela. Cellaress at San José in Ávila.

Mariana. Cellaress at San José in Ávila.

Martínez, Ana. Sister at Encarnación.

Paula. Prioress of San Miguel de Pinares whom Teresa knew from her days with the Agustinian sisters.

Paulina. Sister at Encarnación.

Perfecta. Sister at San José in Pastrana.

Porcia. Father Alejo's lover.

Radegunda. Sister at Encarnación and later at San José de Ávila.

Raimundo. Priest at Encarnación.

Ramona. Sister at Encarnación who became intimate with Fray Braulio after Angélica.

Remedios. Sister at Encarnación.

Rogelio. Rosa's father.

Rosa. Novice at Encarnación who fell in love with Don Lope, a young man who visited her at the grille.

Sánchez Colón, Javier. Teresa's cousin and suitor who became a Dominican priest after Teresa entered the convent.

Santana y Córdoba, Vida and Sara. Clandestine Jews who were Sister Angélica's cellmates in Seville.

Sergio. Teresa's confessor at Encarnación. Angélica's confessor after Bráulio.

Silvia. Teresa's childhood maid, who accompanied her in the convent.

Susana. Nun at the Carmel in Alba de Tormes.

Tello. Don Lope's father.

Teodoro. Chaplain at San José after Fray Julián de Ávila died.

Tomé. Angélica's first confessor at Encarnación.